BROKEN TOYS

A NOVEL

NEEL LATCHMAN

Second Edition September 2023

Front cover design, format and interior design
by Neel Latchman.
Editing/ Proofreading by Kaylee Labban.
Special Thank You to these amazing readers
Amber Goodrich, Crystal Howell, Audrey Lee, and
Nicolette "Moons" Joseph.
Very special thanks to the ARC Reader team!

ISBN 979-8-3545-1468-7 (paperback)

Contents

GALAN RAIN

AGE: 25
SIGN: LIBRA
FUN FACT: "I LIKE TO LISTEN TO 80'S ROCK."

Chapter One

Who are you? I mean, I know exactly who you are, Aria Scarlet. Who doesn't? You're everywhere, posing for pictures in every major hotel around the world, thanks to your dad owning all of them. But why are you here in Salt Pine Acres? It makes sense. This is somewhat of a secret society where rich douchebags relocate to escape the downsides of fame. It's quiet and free of fans and media trying to invade their personal lives every ten minutes. But people who come here aren't like you...

Everyone here is as fake as they come, but they all have one nauseating thing in common—they are always smiling. So, why aren't you? I see you. Why are you walking down the street with your head hung low, faking a smile when passing someone? I *know your real smile; those dimples shine bright when you do. When you really smile, I mean.*

Galan contemplated deeply as he stood in his spacious office, mesmerized by the enchanting view stretching beyond the windowpane.

You're in pain; I can see it. Your walk is without purpose, and your hair is messy. Don't get me wrong; I like the messy look. You're not here to hide, are you? I mean, look at you. A pair of diamond earrings, a black laced choker around your caramel-kissed neck, a hoodie, and sweats? That look makes no sense, but why do you look so good in it?

You want someone to notice you... Don't you? You are in pain but don't know how to cry out for help. Galan placed his palm on the glass. *I'm not that person anymore. If this was eight years ago, I would be your knight in shining armor. I would make sure your smile never left those cherry lips. So, why am I doing this now? This isn't me; it hasn't been me, not since her. I know what love can do to me, and I will not put myself in that line of fire again. I have been burned one too many times.*

A sudden knock on the door disrupted Galan's train of thought, jolting him back to the present moment. As he turned his attention towards the source of the sound, a young woman gently pushed open the door, her presence subtly intruding upon the room. Leaning in slightly, "Mr. Rain, we have word from the buyers. Grounded Coffee House has been sold!"

"That's excellent news, Alliyah. Schedule our final meeting to sign over the café tonight at seven," Galan responded with nonchalance, his expression betraying no hint of interruption. Acknowledging Alliyah's presence with a brief nod, he watched as she silently retreated from the room, quietly closing the door behind her. The faint sound of the latch clicking echoed in the now-quiet office, leaving Galan alone once more with his ruminations.

Finally! I was almost beginning to think they would back out. After so many years of living amongst these people, it's ironic I decided to leave the moment I became their equal.

I guess this is goodbye to Salt Pine Acres. Goodbye to the fake-ass people who walked into my coffee house every day and pretended to care about how my day was going. Galan's gaze returned to the window, where he caught a fleeting glimpse of Aria gracefully sliding into the plush comfort of the backseat of her awaiting car. *Goodbye, Aria. Maybe in another life, I would have tried to fix your smile, but you showed up just a bit too late.*

Galan sank into his office chair, his eyes intermittently darting back to the window, unable to shake off the thoughts that lingered there. The room filled with an uneasy silence, only to be interrupted by the restless tapping of his feet against the floor. His mind teetered on the precipice of anticipation, awaiting the resolution of the unknown scenario that lay beyond the glass. *Why can't I stop thinking about you? Is it because I saw you in person? Is it because I like how laced chokers look? No... No! I know how this goes. I'll get too involved, and if I get attached, I'll just repeat the same mistakes I made with her... Get it together, Galan! You set out to achieve something when you founded the café, and today, you'll accomplish that.*

Sign those papers and leave. Aria doesn't even know who you are. She's never even been in the coffee house; what well-adjusted person isn't

3

dependent on coffee? Come to think of it, she has a driver; maybe he gets her coffee? Why not come in yourself? Do you like people doing things for you? I would do things for you. No, no, let's not go there. Just drop it. Galan got up in a hurry and stormed out of his office. "Alliyah, I will be back tonight for the meeting. I'm just stepping out for a bit to clear my head," he mumbled as he hurried down the corridor, passing Alliyah sitting at her desk.

The streets of Salt Pine Acres were perpetually deserted, creating a desolate atmosphere where encountering pedestrians became a rare occurrence. Galan, well aware of this peculiar characteristic, inserted his earbuds and triggered a playlist, allowing the melodies to wash over him and momentarily drown out his own ruminations. The music served as a shield against the stillness of the town, creating a personal sanctuary where Galan could find solace amidst the void.

Galan strolled through the streets, his eyes scanning his surroundings. Every passing figure carried the potential to be Aria, a glimmer of hope he couldn't help but cling to. Yet, as each person he encountered proved not to be her, a peculiar sense of relief washed over him. Galan reached a breathtaking lookout point atop the mountain, cradling Salt Pine Acres. The town seemed to nestle against the rugged terrain, overlooking a mesmerizing waterfall cascading gracefully into the depths below. From this vantage point, Galan beheld a panoramic view that extended far beyond the town's borders, revealing a tapestry of cities and their twinkling lights in the distance. Perched thousands of feet above the ground, Galan leaned against the sturdy railing, his gaze fixed upon the enthralling sight of the sun's descent. The crimson orb painted the sky with hues of fiery red and gold, gradually dipping below the horizon. Clad in a sleek black suit, his silhouette starkly contrasted against the vibrant backdrop. As the radiant light bathed his features, an orange glow caressed his skin.

The internal chatter gradually gave way to a tranquil silence. After what seemed like an eternity, Galan delicately slid up the sleeve of his jacket, revealing his watch. With a purposeful gaze, he checked the time, realizing that his meeting was swiftly approaching. Six thirty-one, the crimson skies gradually transitioned into a serene, darker blue; Galan realized the fleeting moments he had to return to the office for his meeting. The coffee house, a twenty-minute walk from the lookout, beckoned him.

In his rush, Galan swiftly pivoted to head back towards the office; preoccupied with the upcoming meeting, he bumped into someone, spilling their coffee all over him.

"Oh, fuck, I'm so sorry," the stranger apologized.

"Hey, it's fine, see?" Galan held up his jacket where she had spilled her drink and said, "It's hydrophobic."

"So, you just happen to walk around in a suit that is water resistant?" the stranger questioned.

I'm sorry, I didn't realize I was supposed to allow you to fuck up a ten-thousand-dollar suit! "Actually, I work around coffee all day. After a few spills, I figured this was a necessary investment," Galan chuckled.

"You own Grounded?" the stranger inquired.

"I do," Galan replied.

BROKEN TOYS

"How the fuck do you run a business when you don't even know how to watch where you're going, dipshit?" the stranger scowled, tossing her empty cup in a bin next to them.

The fuck? "Excuse me? How old are you, like 12?" Galan retorted.

"None of your business, but you owe me a coffee!" the stranger argued.

Who raised you? What I should do is toss your rude ass off this lookout. Nobody is around; who would know? Spoiled little brat. "Ok, how about this. I'm headed over there now to get to a meeting. Come by before we close at eight, and I'll personally make your coffee," Galan said with a smile. *Hopefully, you choke on it, you little shit.*

"See, was that so hard?" the stranger responded with a dismissive roll of her eyes before swiftly walking away.

Galan couldn't help but chuckle in sheer disbelief. *This is why I hate it here.*

Chapter Two

Galan hurriedly returned to the office just minutes before his scheduled meeting. Standing around the reception desk were the representatives of the prospective buyers, all adorned with smiles on their faces and holding bottles of champagne and glasses in their hands.

"Ahhh, Galan, my boy. Come, come, and let's celebrate new beginnings!" the buyer's rep cheered.

Galan led the buyers' representatives into his office, where a sense of significance permeated the air. The paperwork for the handover, symbolizing the sale of Grounded Coffee House, awaited their signatures on the desk. Each pen stroke solidified the ownership transition, marking a new chapter for the beloved establishment. Upon signing the dotted line, the buyers popped champagne and shared it with the entire staff. Galan politely refused to drink but took a glass to toast the success of the deal with his team and the buyers.

"What's the matter, Galan, my boy? Not a fan of champagne?" the buyer asked.

I can smell the booze on you from over here. Clearly, you've had a lot already. "No, that's not it. I just don't drink alcohol. I prefer to stay sober and enjoy the moments," Galan replied.

"If my company sold for two-hundred-million dollars too, I would drink to that!" the buyer remarked.

Please stop talking. I'm beginning to taste the alcohol on your breath. I think I'm gonna throw up. Galan shook hands with the buyers, congratulated them on being the new owners of the coffee house, and left the room in a hurry. Descending the spiral steps that led to the main floor, Galan's attention was unexpectedly drawn to the familiar figure seated at the bar. There sat the same girl who had spilled coffee on him earlier. Galan removed his jacket, walked behind the bar, and rolled his sleeves to make her a new coffee.

"Bumped into anyone else on the way here?" he asked her, chuckling. The stranger rolled her eyes and said nothing back to him. Galan approached her at the bar and asked her what she would like.

"I'm sorry, I'm just having a bad day. You happened to be the unfortunate idiot that gave me a chance to rant," the stranger apologized.

"You are? I didn't notice; you're such a ray of sunshine," Galan smirked.

The stranger raised her middle finger at him and rolled her eyes.

"Hey! What is your problem?" Aria shouted upon entering the door.

Oh no... What is she doing here?

"Apologize! Now!!!" Aria grabbed the stranger forcefully by her arm.

"Okay, okay. I'm sorry, geez," the stranger apologized.

"It's fine. When people don't have their coffee, life seems just a bit more unbearable; I'm used to it. Now, what would you like?" Galan repeated with a smile. *Fuck, why do I feel like I suddenly do not know how to make anything here?*

"I'll have the caramel macchiato," the stranger ordered.

"Ok, coming right up," Galan said as he grabbed a cup.

"Hey, I would also like to order something, too," Aria announced.

Fuck, I didn't ask her. I was too busy trying to not stare at her and look like a creep. "I'm sorry, yes. What would you like to have tonight?" Galan beamed. *Ideally, the response I would like is for you to say you would like to have me tonight... No, no, don't do this now. Focus!*

"What can you recommend for a non-coffee drinker? Something so good that it would change the fact that they have never had coffee in their life," Aria inquired.

So, that's why you never came into the café. You don't drink coffee. Judging from the way you spoke to this little ball of sunshine, I can only assume family. But it's your first time drinking coffee? Why are you so interested in it now? Is this an attempt to break the ice? Is this your attempt at flirting? You want a reason to talk to me? Well, I'm willing to give you what you want! Galan proceeded to make the stranger's drink while explaining what Aria might enjoy. "Well, for a non-coffee person, I would usually go with something that's more familiar; chocolate seems to be something most people like. We have a great mocha blend: a dark roast hazelnut with a splash of almond milk," Galan advised while he finished off the stranger's order and slid it over to her.

"What else would you recommend?" Aria asked.

You do just want to talk to me. You could have said what you didn't like about the drink I recommended, but instead, you are just trying to get me to talk to you. Message received. "Well, tell me about the things that you like. I can recommend something based on your tastes," Galan remarked, smiling. Galan leaned on the bar, his gaze locked with Aria's eyes; a moment of connection unfolded between them.

"I don't know," Aria claimed.

Mysterious, you don't want to give any details away. You want me to work for it. "I think I know just the thing. No bells and whistles, I'll just keep it simple," Galan responded. As Galan expertly prepared Aria's drink, he couldn't help but feel a sense of enchantment as her unwavering gaze remained fixed on him. "Here you go, Colombian blend, fresh ground, no cream." Galan slid the cup over to her gently.

"That's so lame. You're pushing a basic drink that's easy to add anything to it. You're not catering to the customer. No offers of a menu or any specials. It's a good thing this place is in new hands," the stranger grunted.

How does she know that? "I'm sorry?" Galan said, confused.

"Ignore her. Little Miss Marketing over here has spent her entire life selling her brand; she's quite the business mind. She also has a boyfriend with a liking for coffee, so she bought this place to impress him," Aria explained.

I miss the days when teenagers bought flowers and trinkets to impress someone they liked. How did it go from that to shoveling out two hundred million for a company? "You're the buyer?" Galan questioned.

"My dad is; he bought this for me because I can turn this into something even bigger than you ever imagined it would be. And ignore my sister; I am not buying this because of my boyfriend. He just happens to be one of the most influential content creators on any social media platform to date. Having him endorse this place and expanding outside of this isolated town can turn this into a multi-billion dollar company," the stranger boasted.

I guess our goals were different. To me, millions could change my life; to her, it's pocket change. As rotten as she is, the little punk is really driven. Respect. "Well, I can't wait to see what else you bring to the table," Galan praised.

"Anyway, this was fun, but we should be going. Thanks for showing me what not to do, except for the hydrophobic suit; that one I'll steal. See you," the stranger announced after finishing her drink. Aria got up and followed her to the door.

"I never got your name?" Galan shouted as they approached the door.

"That's not an accident," the stranger teased as she walked out the doors.

Aria stopped and turned around. "That's Dana, my little sister. I'm Aria, by the way," she said with a wicked smirk and a glimmer in her eyes as she walked out the door and disappeared into the night.

What was that? She didn't need to say anything. She wants me to know who she is. She wants me to chase her. My God, that smile... I could feel a chill down my spine and my stomach in knots. Who is this girl, really? I don't think I can leave just yet; I need to know. No, I need to be the reason she smiles again!

Galan's curiosity led him to retrieve his phone, unlocking it with a swift motion. As he tapped on his browser, a cascade of tabs revealed a digital collage solely focused on Aria Scarlet, capturing his undivided attention. Galan's gaze momentarily shifted to the window, where he caught a glimpse of Aria stepping into her car. As she prepared to leave, their eyes met one final time before getting into the car. Galan's focus shifted to his other hand, which clandestinely concealed a second phone. With a touch of secrecy, he unveiled the hidden device. *I guess I have a good reason to see you again now.* Galan tapped the side button, and the screen lit up, displaying a picture of Dana and her boyfriend plastered on the lock screen. *How old is this guy? He looks like he is in his mid-twenties; you barely look like a teenager. Wait, it's not fair to assume you are that young; the miracle of social media is that basic information is at your fingertips. Here we go. Dana Scarlet. Private? You would actively flaunt your dad has hundreds of millions to buy you a café but not display your profile?*

Well, thankfully, your dad isn't that shy, as seen on the cover of endless magazines. Just need to filter the articles where he is with you and... Bingo. 'Billionaire charity event, next to his two kids, Aria (Left), 25, founder of LVTCH cosmetics, and Dana (Right), 16. Just because Dana's insanely rich doesn't mean it's not rape, you sick bastard. I can't imagine you've been together a short while, either. I mean, you don't go buying businesses to impress someone you just met.

Anyway, this isn't my concern, but it does say a lot about you as a sister allowing these predators around your baby sister. Is that who you are? I don't think so, but I need to be sure. What if you allow men like that around our kids? Someone needs to protect them from the monsters in this world. I will do that for you. You wouldn't need to worry. I will keep you safe and set a better example for your sister.

Maybe the reason you don't smile as brightly anymore has something to do with this? Of course, you wouldn't choose this for your sister, but you are too busy fighting your demons to help her identify hers. Here I come, Aria. I can help as long as you let me. You just don't know you need me yet, but you will. Galan smiled and rushed out the door and into his car.

He opened an app on his phone for the Coffee House's security system. Flipping through the camera feeds to find the storefront camera, he rewound the footage to view the car Aria got into. *There we go, luxurious German engineering, plate number Z8175. Fast forward a bit; let's see where you went. Left... That's where the Salt Pine Acres lookout is. Only three houses are on that stretch. Seems simple enough.*

Galan started his car and headed in that direction. Coming up on the turn, he saw the car that the girls left in turning out just before he reached the street. Because it was heavily tinted, he was unsure if they were still in the vehicle when it drove off, headed in the other direction. *Fuck, what do I do here? Should I follow the car or see if I can catch a glimpse of them at the house? No, don't follow the car; it would be too much of a creepy move. Go to the house; it's on the way to the lookout where Dana saw you earlier, better deniability.* Galan flicked the turn signal and turned left onto their street. Slowly driving along the street, there were no other vehicles, apart from a few parked at the side of the road.

Thankfully, the houses here all have this huge glass window wall aesthetic; it wouldn't be hard to see who lives there. The first house is a bust, and the second is a lovely Asian family who frequents the Coffee House often, so I know it's not there. Are you the last house on the street before the lookout? Makes sense; it has the most gorgeous view here. Your castle towers above the other houses in this town. Have you been waiting for someone like me to come rescue you?

Galan slowed down and stopped behind a car parked on the road just outside their house. Looking over subtly, he tried to catch a glimpse inside while the car idled in park. *I don't see anyone; I guess it would be creepy to sit out here until I did. I should go. I could keep tabs on the café's security until you come in tomorrow. And, of course, you would. You would do it for your sister because you are a good sister when given a chance.*

A knock on the glass made Galan flinch. *FUCK!* Galan rolled down his window. A figure wearing a hoodie and hat leaned over from the neighboring car, their face partially concealed. "Can I help you, Sir?" the stranger commanded.

Play it cool; you did nothing wrong. "No, I'm good. I just stopped to take a call," Galan replied calmly.

"Right... Is that why you were slowly cruising down the street and looking into all these houses?" the man replied firmly.

Fuck... Wait, how did he know I was doing that? Has he been watching me since I got onto the street? Why? This town isn't open to any and everyone. We don't even have the police here, yet you're suddenly suspicious of a car on the street? Galan smiled awkwardly and replied, "Look, I'm a very busy person. I need to attend to clients' and business queries all of the time. Plus, I am in the middle of moving to a new city soon. So, excuse me if I was driving too slowly while tending to my personal life and felt the need to stop and deal with it rather than to keep driving."

Abruptly, the man slammed his hand forcefully on the roof of Galan's car, jolting the vehicle and filling the air with a sudden tension, "That's bullshit! I saw you looking into the houses."

Did this son of a bitch hit my car? Filled with a surge of anger, Galan swiftly exited his car, his emotions boiling over as he snapped, succumbing to the intense wave of frustration, "Hey, who the fuck do you think you are?"

With measured steps, the man approached Galan, his face concealed in shadows, his expression stoic and unreadable. He opened his mouth to speak, his voice laced with an enigmatic tone that hung in the air, "Get back in your car and be on your way if you know what's good for you!"

Please, oh please, hit me. Let me show you what the sidewalk tastes like, douchebag. Wait… What is that smell? Smells like… Coffee? Galan peered behind the man and noticed the bin behind him. *It's coming from there, the Columbian blend; this is her house. I guess this waste of semen served a purpose after all.*

Galan looked at him and snarled, "Touch my car again, and someone will have to wheel your ass around this town for the rest of your life. And why were you spying on people outside the Scarlets' house?" The man's eyebrow twitched. *I knew it; he was not supposed to be here. Who the hell are you? It's a good thing I found you, Aria; you needed me more than I realized. You're not safe.* "Do me a favor and leave me out of it next time." Galan stared daggers as he walked back to his car and drove off to the lookout.

Peering into his review mirror, Galan witnessed the strange man entering a car and driving off, turning right at the end of the street. *Where are you going?* Galan opened the camera feed on his phone and saw the car coming down the street. He took a snapshot once the vehicle was close enough to the Coffee House to see the license plate on the car and a clear enough image of the person inside. "Let's save this for later," Galan mumbled while getting out of his vehicle and proceeding to the lookout's platform.

I'm going to miss this when I leave: this view, the quiet. This alone is almost enough to make anyone stay here, no matter how miserable they are. You, on the other hand, Aria, I would stay for you if you wanted me to, and I think you do want me to; you just… Don't know that yet. I mean, a stranger followed you home, and another sketchy character was camped just outside your house in the dead of night, and your driver didn't notice anything. Well, I would ensure you get home safely; I would make sure there aren't any monsters under the bed or lurking around outside. You would be safe. I will keep you safe, always.

Chapter Three

As the soft glow of dawn seeped through the room, penetrating the veil of darkness, Galan found himself in bed, his weary eyes reflecting the toll of sleepless nights. Yet, despite the weariness, a smile graced his lips, an echo of newfound hope. With his arms tucked comfortably behind his head, he gazed up at the ceiling, a canvas for his dreams and aspirations, embracing the possibilities ahead. *I'm not one to lose sleep over someone. Usually, I'm in bed at nine and fully asleep by ten. Those lucky bastards who can slip into deep sleep seconds after touching their pillows, how I envy you. But today, I didn't get a wink of sleep. I spent all night turning in my bed, trying to clear the noise in my head, but I couldn't. All I could think about was you, Aria. Your thick, curly, dark hair, those soft, plump lips, the way*

you smile, and all I can see is the dark in your eyes.
Today is a good day; today, I will give you a reason
to smile again.

Galan leaped out of bed and stumbled slightly, feeling lightheaded. He took a moment to gather himself and inhaled deeply. Entering his gym, Galan sparred with wooden dummies, boxing bags, and upper torso replicas to get his blood pumping. Galan dedicated a full hour to an intense workout, pushing his body to its limits. Afterward, he slipped into his running shoes and fastened a weighted backpack, embarking on a cool-down jog. His path meandered through the quaint town, its streets alive with the hum of daily life, before leading him toward the majestic mountains adorned with a dense blanket of pine trees. As his feet rhythmically hit the ground, he immersed himself in the serenity of nature, finding solace in the harmonious interplay between his pounding heartbeat and the tranquil surroundings.

At the summit of the mountain, Galan encountered a frigid body of water, its icy temperature nearly taking his breath away. A small pond, intricately connected to the main stream, formed a cascading waterfall that adorned the picturesque lookout. After completing his morning training, Galan indulged in a few precious minutes immersing himself in the chilling embrace of the water. The crisp sensation on his skin awakened his senses, rejuvenating his body and mind leaving him invigorated and ready to embrace the challenges ahead.

No one else ever came this far up the mountain since there was a specific route for joggers made into the trail. Craving a greater physical challenge, Galan had deviated from the familiar fla terrain, venturing off the designated path in search of a steeper incline. It was during this exploration that he stumbled upon the hidden pond, a serene oasis nestled within the mountain's embrace. The unexpected discovery rewarded his curiosity, offering both a refreshing respite and an opportunity to test his mettle against the demands of a more arduous ascent. Galan's morning routine, coupled with the absence of a local coffee shop amidst the chilly and misty mornings of Salt Pine Acres, ignited the spark of inspiration that led to the creation of Grounded Coffee House.

Galan's commitment to crafting an exclusive coffee brand resonated deeply with the people of Salt Pine Acres. He spared no effort in sourcing only the finest, highest-quality ingredients, ensuring that each cup of coffee served at Grounded Coffee House was a testament to excellence. With an extraordinary lineup of options carefully curated from various corners of the globe, Galan's establishment stood as a beacon of distinction, offering a sensory experience unparalleled anywhere else in the world. Each sip became an exploration of flavors, a journey into the realm of coffee mastery, captivating the palates and hearts of coffee connoisseurs far and wide.

Although Galan's prices at Grounded Coffee House were significantly higher than those of other coffee shops, his unwavering commitment to quality justified the premium. With years of hard work, dedication, and an unyielding pursuit of perfection, Galan brought his long-cherished dream of owning a coffee house to fruition.

Refreshed from the rejuvenating soak, Galan traded his damp attire for a cozy, long-sleeved black sweater and comfortable jeans. As he descended the mountain, the rhythmic sound of crunching leaves and pebbles beneath his feet accompanied his leisurely stroll through the serene woods. The tranquility of nature embraced him, casting a peaceful aura as he made his way back to town. Unlocking his phone, Galan eagerly opened the app that granted him access to the cameras installed at Grounded Coffee House. A heartfelt smile adorned his lips as he beheld the scene before him. Aria, Dana, and the dedicated employees were diligently preparing to open the doors and welcome the day's first customers.

Galan's stride carried an extra bounce of excitement as he briskly made his way back to town. Arriving at Grounded Coffee House, he couldn't resist peering through the frosted windows, their gentle haze offering a glimpse into the bustling interior. His eyes settled on Aria, her warm smile illuminating her face as she conversed with three individuals, a cup of coffee cradled in her hands. *What have we here? Those aren't customers. I know every face in this town that frequents the coffee house. Two girls and a guy. Elegantly dressed. Sure as hell fits into the aesthetic of this town, but they have visitor bands. I see. These are your friends. They wouldn't open this place to customers outside of the town; that would defeat the purpose of the town itself. Those visitor passes aren't cheap, either. No customer will pay a cool fifteen thousand to buy a sixty-dollar cup of coffee. Friends mean they got in here free: they came to support even though this isn't yours but your sister's. Aw.*

I like them already; any excuse to see you is exactly what I would do. I should introduce myself.

Galan entered the café, making his way toward the bar where Aria stood. A genuine smile graced her lips as she turned towards him, accompanied by a subtle wave. However, Galan walked past her, seemingly oblivious to her presence, his focus fixated elsewhere. Aria's smile faltered briefly, a flicker of confusion crossing her expression. As Aria's hand fell back to her side, a hint of disappointment tinged her diminished smile. Her three friends, observing the situation unfold, followed Galan's every move with curious eyes. Galan approached the bar and lightly knocked on the counter, seeking Dana's attention.

"Ari… Who is that?" Eyla's gasp echoed through the air, eliciting murmurs among the group as they exchanged surprised whispers.

Galan stood confidently at the bar, a slight smile playing at the corners of his lips. His demeanor exuded a sense of composure and self-assurance, as if he held a secret that only time would reveal. *Step one: ignore her in favor of someone else in the room. Subconsciously, she will feel insecure and develop a need for the attention she was not given. Now she's in her head wondering, 'Why didn't he look at me, answer me, or wave back, even though I was wearing this gorgeous low-cut top, hair done, and pants that hug all the right places?' She thinks she knows me because we spoke, and her last interaction was flirty. She's wondering if it wasn't effective; maybe I wasn't interested.*

But why wouldn't I be? She's beautiful, bold, and one of the most powerful women in the world. She'll think, 'So, why did this guy ignore my very presence in front of my friends?' And while her friends contemplate the situation and what they would have done, you would drown it all out and focus on me. Thinking to yourself, 'Let's try this again, just to be sure what happened really happened.' It's a challenge for you now. You want basic acknowledgment from a stranger, and that weird feeling you have now is what is going to keep you coming back. Because I can say without a doubt that no guy has ever made you feel like that before; you demand respect and attention when you enter a room, and you are going to show me just who you are.

The approaching sound of footsteps caught Galan's attention, causing his smirk to grow wider. As the steps drew nearer, Aria leaned gracefully against the bar, positioning herself next to Galan. Her smile matched his, and their eyes locked in an intense gaze. Slightly tilting her head, she said, "Excuse me, when someone smiles at you, the polite thing to do is smile back." Aria's friends huddled closely together; their eyes fixated on Aria and Galan.

Step one: check. Galan turned towards Aria, a gentle gesture of brushing his hair backward to reveal his face. His grey eyes met hers; he prepared to reply to her, "Hello gorgeous, I'm sorry. I didn't mean to be rude or anything. I'm just not in a talking mood until I've had my morning coffee. I figured you deserved a better version of me than that first thing in the morning." He scooted over slightly and continued, "But I will make an exception this one time."

"Hey! Loser!" Dana's voice rang out, drawing Galan's attention as she approached the bar, clad in the café's uniform. Her attire consisted of a sleek black shirt and pants adorned with a coffee-brown apron and a matching tie. As Aria shifted her attention to her sister, Dana, Galan found himself captivated by the sight of her. In awe of her presence, he couldn't help but hold his gaze on her for a few precious moments longer. Unbeknownst to Galan, the intensity of his gaze did not go unnoticed by Aria's friends. Their perceptive eyes followed his every glance, picking up on the way he looked at Aria, their curiosity piqued by the unspoken dynamics between them. It was a subtle exchange that spoke volumes, leaving the friends intrigued and eager to unravel the mystery that seemed to surround Galan and his connection with Aria.

"Hey there, I have something for you," Galan responded. Retrieving her phone, he slid it across the smooth surface of the bar,

"My phone!" Dana exclaimed.

"So, let me ask you this. How do you intend to run a business if you can't even watch your personal items?" Galan teased. Dana used the cloth behind the bar to hide her hand as she flipped off Galan and rolled her eyes.

Ok, that's enough chit-chat. Time for step two: create urgency. "Dana, do you mind if I come behind the bar one last time since I'm leaving today?" Galan asked politely.

Aria's gaze shifted quickly towards Galan. *I saw that. You don't want me to leave just yet. It's ok, gorgeous; by the end of today, I will stay back for you, but only if you ask me to do so. Just be patient.*

With a nod of acknowledgment, Dana broke her gaze from Galan and gracefully moved toward the other end of the bar to attend to customers. As she shifted her focus, Galan rolled up his sleeves; standing behind the bar, he directed his gaze towards Aria.

"Welcome to Grounded. Have your friends join us. I'll be your barista this morning," Galan exclaimed.

Aria's smile brightened as she turned towards her friends, a genuine expression of joy illuminating her features. The four of them took their seats at the bar, their excitement palpable as they settled in. "Well, let me introduce everyone. This is Eyla; she owns a bookstore called S.A.Q. Bodhi runs the best hair salons in the city; it's how we all met. And last but not least, Maeve is a surgeon in training."

"Pleasure meeting you all. I'm Galan," Galan smiled. "Walk me through your perfect day."

"Our perfect day?" Eyla queried.

"Yes, everyone has an idea of what a perfect day would look like. For some, it's events that could happen; for others, it's stuff they don't want to happen. And most people have it all laid out, from the company to the weather to the zip code. What I have found in my own pursuit of the perfect day is that it needs to start with the right cup of coffee to get you to that place," Galan explained slowly, never taking his eye off Aria as he recited the last sentence.

"You're the expert; why don't you suggest something, or are you going to give them plain coffee and tell them they can add whatever they like again?" Dana's playful taunting reached Galan's ears, originating from across the bar. However, Galan remained steadfast in his focus on Aria, his gaze unwavering. With a warm smile gracing his lips, he leaned slightly off the bar, seemingly unaffected by Dana's teasing.

"Come over here for a minute, Dana," Galan called out. Dana, wearing a smug expression, and arms folded, made her way over to him. "People can tell you a lot if you know how to listen to them. Sometimes, customers will not know what they want, but they will show you who they are, and it's up to you to match their energy. Let's start with Eyla. You own a bookstore. Based on your attire, I can see you accessorize with novelty items subtly. Your style is unique and signature to the literary world. You love what you do, and you love books. Your ideal day is curling up with a great book and reading for pleasure. You don't need energy for that, so you want something delicious and calming: light roast, spicy, and cream. A spiced Irish coffee with a dollop of whipped cream and a sprinkle of cinnamon would be ideal." Eyla looked shocked and turned to her friends.

"Bodhi, great name, by the way. They said you ran several salons. You must interact with customers often. Based on first impressions, you have a non-threatening presence, very kind and polite. Dealing with people does take a toll on your energy levels throughout the day, so you would go a bit stronger on the coffee. Espresso, maybe a Frappuccino, iced, blended—caffeine hits that would keep you going throughout the day," Galan analyzed. Bodhi nodded his head slightly and smiled.

"Finally, Maeve. Quiet, less forward, new surgeon, you love helping people... Dressed in a pantsuit on your day off, you like to treat yourself and feel amazing, right? You would opt for a treat rather than the energy: a scoop of ice cream, caramel shot, ice blended, something sweet and dessert-like," Galan suggested. Maeve looked over at Aria and smiled.

"I'm impressed, but one mistake. She's allergic to cinnamon," Bodhi commented.

"Yes, you killed me," Eyla teased.

"Aww, now I need a new friend; thanks, Galan," Aria remarked. Dana's gaze settled on Galan, a mixture of surprise and admiration reflected in her eyes. His ability to dissect their complex relationship and translate it into something as seemingly simple as a drink captivated her. Her expression showed a sense of awe and appreciation, as if she recognized the depth of thought and understanding that Galan had poured into his creation. It was a testament to his insight and creativity, weaving together the intricacies of their connection and transforming it into a tangible representation.

"I guess you're not as useless as I thought," Dana's whispered words lingered in the air as she walked away, her steps carrying a sense of contemplation and introspection. She gracefully made her way toward the customers seated at the other end of the bar, shifting her focus to attend to their needs.

"How about we try something different? This is the opening of the new Grounded Coffee house. How about a celebratory drink?" Galan asked.

"Yesss!" they replied in sync.

"Alright, coming up," Galan replied as he prepped four glasses on the bar and opened a display behind him, showcasing the lineup of exquisite liquor. Galan made the cocktails with flair, smooth pours, and well-executed bottle tricks without spilling a drop. "This is called a Long Island iced coffee: Irish cream, coffee liqueur, and a light splash of tequila, still creamy but strong, so tread lightly."

Aria and her friends took their first sip; the little dance they did was a good sign that they liked it.

"What about you? Not having one with us?" Bodh[i] asked.

"No, I don't partake in alcohol, but I do love a good cup of coffee," Galan answered before making himself a salted caramel cream mocha, cold brew. "[I] save this for special occasions. I think me leaving counts as one!" *And now the sense of urgency i[s] burdening your friends. Now, you are going to have some external pressure to savor the time we have before I disappear from your lives. Bodhi is the mos[t] engaging; he seems to be the closest to you. Forge[t] about the others; he is my golden goose. Time for my next step, letting you know where to find me.*

"Bodhi, speaking of special occasions, I thin[k] moving away is a pretty big step. New life, new city[.] And I think a new me would be a good move. I don'[t] trust anyone with my hair, but how about we schedul[e] an appointment? Are you free anytime today?" Gala[n] asked, sipping his drink.

Bodhi looked at Galan from head to toe befor[e] saying, "Actually, I am not. Today is my day off t[o] be there for Aria and D."

This would have been a problem, Aria, bu[t] here is the thing. I get the things I want because I pu[t] in the work for them. While I couldn't sleep last nigh[t] I did my research, and I found your friends. Unlik[e] your sister, they are as open as it gets because of wha[t] they do and how many people they interact with on [a] daily basis. Bodhi set out to be the best stylist in th[e] world, and the first step in getting that was moving t[o] the city where dreams come true. But even thoug[h] he's made it, something doesn't feel right. He feel[s] like he is missing something. So he's expanded hi[s] horizons, changed his style, and started a ne[w] chapter to find himself because he feels lost among these people.

"I wish I knew people like you. I came out here years ago to make it. I came from nothing. I was running from my problems, and nothing changed even after I made this place, and it turned out the way it did. I felt alone even though I was surrounded by people who were part of the things I was passionate about. Even now, I still feel out of place. I feel like I lost myself chasing this, and I just want to find that part of me again," Galan stated.

"And you think a new hairstyle is going to change that?" Bodhi responded.

"No, but it's a start. That's the thing about being lost... It doesn't matter what step you take because no matter what direction you move in, you will still be lost." Galan looked over at Aria before continuing, "That is until you find what you are looking for."

Bodhi looked over to Aria and back at Galan, "Maybe I can give you some tips. I'm sure I can find a few minutes in my day to do a mini-consult."

Best friend on board... Check.

"I really appreciate that. I'll be packed by tonight at ten. You can drop by any time before that," Galan's words hung in the air as he swiftly took a piece of paper, penning down his address and phone number, and handed the slip of paper to Bodhi.

Chapter Four

The door swung open, revealing the figure of a man adorned in a hoodie. "Maeve, I'm going into the city for an errand. Can you catch a ride back?"

"Sure, I can find my way back home," Maeve waved at him.

The man's steps grew nearer as he closed the distance, his gaze focused on Aria. With a deliberate motion, he reached up and removed the hood that concealed his features, revealing his face. "Hi," he said, making Aria instantly uncomfortable.

Who the fuck is this guy? Wait, that guy from their street. Is that him? Fuck, he is going to tell her I was lurking around outside; if he does, I lose all credibility with your friends, Aria.

"Get out of here, Garrick, not today," Bodhi said sternly. Aria's discomfort was palpable, evident in her body language and the subtle shift in her demeanor.

"Nobody is here for you, Bodhi!" Garrick responded hastily. He placed his hand on Aria's shoulder, expecting a connection; she instinctively leaned away, an unmistakable gesture of repulsion. Her body language spoke volumes, expressing her discomfort and desire to create distance between herself and Garrick.

Sensing the tension in the room, Bodhi rose from his chair with a determined look as he approached Garrick, ready to intervene or address the situation, "Leave, now!"

Despite Bodhi's approach, Garrick seemed undeterred, choosing to persist in his attempt to engage Aria in conversation. Ignoring the presence of others and the growing commotion, he focused solely on trying to reach out to her. However, as the situation intensified, Dana swiftly left her post, recognizing the need to intervene and offer support to her sister, "Garrick, get the fuck out of my café. And leave my sister alone!"

"Easy, D. I'm just here to talk. I don't want any trouble," Garrick replied.

"Garrick, she doesn't want to see you. Get out of here and take your shit with you," Eyla blurted.

Bodhi acted swiftly, reaching out to grab Garrick by the shoulder in an attempt to physically separate him from Aria. However, Garrick reacted forcefully, swinging his hand in a circular motion to break free from Bodhi's hold. In the process, he struck Bodhi's hand, bending it behind his back.

"Eder!" Dana shouted.

Responding swiftly to the distress, Eder Barlow, her boyfriend, emerged from the back office his presence commanding attention. With determination, Eder rushed in to intervene, forcefully shoving Garrick away from Bodhi. The two men now stood face-to-face, their eyes locked in a confrontation. "That's enough. Leave now, Garrick," Eder calmly said.

"Or what?" Garrick snarled, leaning in slightly.

"Garrick!" Maeve called out.

"Shut the fuck up, Maevy," Garrick yelled.

Reacting instinctively to the escalating situation, Galan swiftly vaulted over the bar, landing beside Eder. "Out! Now!" he ordered.

As Bodhi positioned himself on the other side of Eder, the confrontation took on a new dynamic. As the intensity of the skirmish reached its peak, Garrick's emotions seemed to spiral out of control. His veins bulged on his neck, and his breathing became heavy, reflecting his heightened state of agitation. However, as his eyes met the steady gazes of Galan, Eder, and Bodhi, a flicker of realization passed through him. With a slow, deliberate nod, Garrick took a step back, distancing himself from the charged atmosphere within the coffee shop. The weight of the situation settled upon him, prompting a decision to disengage. Without saying a word, he turned on his heel and made his way toward his truck fueled by a mixture of anger and frustration. The sound of his tires screeching against the pavement echoed through the air as he drove off.

"You ok, Bodhi?" Eder asked.

"I'm fine. One day that asshole will get what's coming to him," Bodhi mumbled. Galan's eyes met

Dana's, and he subtly gestured for her to join him at the other end of the bar. Recognizing the urgency in his expression, Dana swiftly made her way through the gathered group of friends, leaving behind a sense of curiosity among them, with a determined stride.

Dana approached Galan. "Dana, who was that guy?" Galan queried.

"Garrick Wilder, Aria's ex," Dana exclaimed.

"I didn't want to say anything because I didn't know who he was, but last night, I was on my way back to the lookout when I saw your vehicle pass me. I had planned to drop off your phone if I saw you outside. But that Garrick guy was sitting in a car outside a house, watching everyone who got on the street. He pulled me out of my car, and we had a little altercation," Galan explained.

"That sick fuck. I'll let my sister know he's doing it again," Dana answered.

"Again?" Galan inquired.

"He used to show up everywhere, and it drove her insane. We came out here because no one can get in easily. It's a safe place where we didn't have to worry about that, but he and Maeve are siblings. I'm guessing it's how he found us," Dana informed him.

"Can't your dad do something about it?" Galan suggested.

"Dad loves him. Garrick's a professional fighter. He has a lot of connections, and he can really put on a show. Dad doesn't see him for the asshole he is. All he sees is the money and the accomplishments," Dana replied.

I see. He's dangerous for us. More importantly, he's a danger to you. Is this the reason you don't smile as brightly anymore? Don't you worry about him, Aria! Guys like that will meet their match one day. I won't let him get to you. Now, he has no hold over me. I am free to protect you without him dirtying my image with his secrets of me. Next time, he will not get close enough to make you cringe at his presence. Unprecedented, but this works in my favor. People bond over common enemies. I guess he served more than one purpose, that waste of life.

Galan walked over to Aria, "Are you ok?"

"I'll be fine. I'm just sick of his shit ruining good things," Aria ranted.

"I'm sorry to bring this here, Ari," Maeve apologized.

"No, sweetheart, don't say that. You are not responsible for him, brother or not," Aria appeased her.

Amazing! You are taking the blame for this because you don't want your friends to bear the burden of what happened. Your heart is so pure; people like you and me don't exist anymore. How dare someone hurt you? If you were mine, I'd protect your happiness all the time, the way you do for your friends. I would make sure the bad things don't come near enough that you feel the need to apologize. I promise.

"Maeve, I can drop you off if you need a ride. I'm free until tonight. Maybe tag along with Bodhi when he comes over, and I can take you home after," Galan offered.

"You don't have to do that," Aria insisted.

"I'd be happy to. I may as well use the remainder of my time here doing some good," Galan smiled. "I don't live too far from here. I'm going to get some other stuff sorted out, but I'll be around. Tell Dana if she needs anything from me about the café, Bodhi has my info. She can reach out to me. I'll be happy to help." Galan's gaze met Dana's, and a bittersweet smile formed on his lips as he waved goodbye to her. Galan turned his attention back to the group. "It's been great meeting you all. Bodhi, looking forward to seeing what you can do later. Hope you guys enjoy the rest of your day." Galan left with a wave and a final glance at Aria, subtly smiling before he walked out of view from the window.

Not the first impression I had hoped for, but I am adaptable if nothing else. Now that this asshole may have ruined all the plans I had in motion in the beginning, you may need a little reminder and some more persuasion to get back on track and out of that funk that he put you in. Don't worry, Aria; this is nothing but a minor setback. It might be a little extra work, but I will go above and beyond for you.

Chapter Five

Garrick, concealed within the shadows of his dark green truck, watched intently as Galan emerged from Grounded Coffee House. A surge of emotion coursed through him, causing his knuckles to tighten around the steering wheel, their strain evident through the distinct sound of the leather crumpling beneath his grasp.

Garrick's gaze, unwavering and intense, followed Galan's every step as he swiftly passed by the truck's driver's side window. His eyes continued to track Galan's movements even after he disappeared from his direct line of sight, fixating on the side view mirrors. The reflection in the mirrors became Garrick's lifeline, his focal point, as he maintained a watchful eye on Galan's progress down the street.

ARIA SCARLET

AGE: 25

SIGN: CANCER

FUN FACT: "I ONCE BOUGHT OUT ALL SEATS AT MY EX-BOYFRIEND'S BIGGEST EVENT SO NO ONE COULD ATTEND AFTER WE BROKE UP."

Garrick's expression twisted into a grimace of displeasure, a subtle sound of disgust escaping his lips. He shifted his attention from the mirrors to the window of Grounded Coffee House, straining to catch a fleeting glimpse of Aria amidst the bustling activity inside the café. Though his view was brief, Garrick managed to catch a glimpse of her figure gracefully navigating through the space.

Garrick remained deep in thought, his gaze repeatedly drawn towards the café as he pondered. Time slipped away as minutes turned into moments of reflection. Eventually, with a heavy sigh, he ignited the engine of his truck and set off on his departure. Guiding the vehicle skillfully, Garrick executed a precise U-turn in the street, leaving the café and its surroundings behind and headed to the gates that left Salt Pine Acres. Unbeknownst to Garrick, Galan lurked stealthily in the nearby alley, his phone poised and ready. Galan swiftly captured a clandestine snapshot as Garrick's truck passed by, capturing the vehicle's image in secrecy.

That's not the same vehicle from last night: smart. But nobody spies on me without me knowing about it. I've had eyes in the back of my head since my last heartbreak. I learned a very valuable lesson: you must be completely aware of everything around you. My love blinded me last time; I missed every sign, but not this time. This time, I'm ready for anything. That includes jealous ex-boyfriends, cautious friends, skeptical family members, you name it. Love is a game, and the rules are always changing. You can never be aware of all the variables that will exist in each love interaction. However, to win, you just need to be one step ahead of the known variables.

In this case, your friends, your ex, your sister, and you.

Each one of these variables is playing his or her own game, and their endgame is to either make our love happen or prevent it. That's why first impressions are crucial. If you can sway the other opinions in your favor, it makes the main objective more attainable. Generally speaking, if the average person were to move forward with this in mind, they would have a slightly better chance of making it work than others. There are downsides to this, though. Exes have a history that you will never be able to compete with, and friends will have their claws in your life, preventing you from having a mind of your own. In this case, you spend so much time trying to outrun the baggage that comes with it that you end up burning out before they ever see the real you.

This is something my last heartbreak taught me. But I found a way around the baggage. All games have cheat codes hidden in their designs. Play them long enough, and you find them. You just need to know where to look, and thanks to your trashcan of an ex, I have a walking cheat sheet for your life.

Galan stowed his phone away with a satisfied grin and strolled purposefully towards his house. He knew all too well that Salt Pine Acres was an exclusive community, not easily accessible to outsiders. Merely passing through the gates necessitated having a connection with a resident. Galan had shrewdly discovered a loophole within Salt Pine Acres. Recognizing the layout of the town, he realized that businesses were strategically situated nearest to the gates. Galan had fortuitously secured a position as a groundskeeper for a butcher's shop in Salt Pine Acres, a role he assumed after the previous manager's passing. This employment allowed him a means of access to the community's shuttle service, which ferried employees residing in a housing complex located a few miles down the mountain.

After devoting several months to meticulous cleaning and maintenance, Galan began to perceive the untapped potential within the vacant building he tended to. This three-story structure boasted a dynamic layout: the ground floor served as the primary shop area, while the upper floors offered expansive office space and cold storage facilities. Galan's keen eye recognized the possibilities concealed within the walls of this building, igniting his imagination and entrepreneurial spirit. Seizing the opportunity presented by the building's impending sale, Galan boldly pitched his visionary idea to the deceased owner's family. Recognizing the potential of transforming the space into a bustling café, Galan proposed a mutually beneficial arrangement. In exchange for their financial support to kickstart the business, Galan offered to defer all profits until the building was fully paid off.

Through unwavering dedication and relentless efforts, Galan's vision materialized into reality. Grounded Coffee House flourished and swiftly established itself as an integral part of the Salt Pine Acres community. Galan had not encountered an empty café since its inception, a testament to the café's popularity and success. With astute financial management, he accomplished the remarkable feat of fully paying off the building within the first year of operation.

Benefiting from a unique provision within Salt Pine Acres' rules, which granted property owners the right to own housing within the town, Galan secured a residence in the very community he had worked so hard to be a part of. As the years went by, Galan's unwavering commitment and entrepreneurial spirit solidified his place in Salt Pine Acres, while Grounded Coffee House became an indispensable local gem. After spending six years confined to the upper floor of Grounded Coffee House, Galan decided it was time for a change. He opted to lease a unit on the top floor of a condo complex within the town of Salt Pine Acres. This particular complex, boasting a staggering thirty-two floors, catered to individuals who did not have long-term plans of residence.

Nestled within the sprawling condo complex, Galan's new unit boasted an impressive expanse of four thousand square feet. This spacious abode offered ample room for comfortable living and various amenities. The unit featured two bathrooms and three bedrooms, a living and dining area, a gym, and a significant portion of the unit was designated as free space, intended for a media room.

Sensing the weight of Garrick's watchful eyes upon him after his departure from the café, Galan swiftly altered his course, intentionally moving in the opposite direction to create a diversion and potentially shake off any pursuit. Diligently ensuring that Garrick had genuinely departed Salt Pine Acres, Galan proceeded cautiously, carefully navigating the town's streets, remaining vigilant for any signs of lingering surveillance.

Once he felt confident that he had successfully eluded any potential followers, Galan continued his journey, making his way to his apartment.

BROKEN TOYS

The condo tower in Salt Pine Acres implemented strict access control measures, allowing only residents to utilize the elevators. The tower's ground floor consisted of an expansive open space parking lot adorned with imposing pillars that added to its architectural grandeur. Positioned closest to the street, a glass elevator stood as a prominent feature, offering both functionality and a touch of elegance to the building's entrance.

The condo tower in Salt Pine Acres featured advanced security measures, including a thumbprint scanner at the entrance of the elevator. This biometric technology ensured that only authorized residents could gain access to their designated floor. By placing their thumb on the scanner, residents could unlock the doors and initiate the elevator's ascent or descent, limiting entry to their own floor.

A manual override system was put in place inside the elevator to accommodate visitors. This system allowed residents to manually open the elevator for their guests. In the event that the resident was occupied or unable to physically operate the manual override, a voice recognition feature was available as an alternative. Through voice authentication, authorized individuals could gain access to the desired floor, providing a convenient solution for granting entry to visitors when needed.

These sophisticated security and access control mechanisms ensured that the condo tower maintained a high level of privacy and restricted entry to only those with proper authorization, providing residents with a sense of safety and exclusivity within their living space.

As the glass elevator smoothly ascended, Galan leaned against the walls, his gaze fixed on the café he had recently left. The transparency of the elevator's walls allowed him an uninterrupted view of the surroundings, including the familiar streets of Salt Pine Acres.

What you do with the next twenty-four hours will make or break us. I will stay here for you if this goes well. If it doesn't play out how I hope it does, I'll at least leave this place behind me and get a fresh start. I can finally outrun my past and her.

Chapter Six

Upon reaching his floor, the elevator emitted a gentle ding, and its doors gracefully slid open. Galan stepped out, triggering motion detectors that instantly illuminated the lights and adjusted the window blinds in response to his presence. As Galan navigated through his apartment, the automated systems seamlessly adapted to his movements, creating a convenient and welcoming atmosphere. Galan ascended the stairs, reaching the landing where his bedroom door awaited him, positioned as the first door on the right. However, at the end of the walkway, he turned to another door that stood out from the others within his apartment.

Casting a quick glance at the intriguing door, Galan's attention shifted as he entered his bedroom. Swiftly undressing, he prepared for a refreshing shower to wash away the day's events. Meanwhile, his phone, placed face down on the bed, illuminated and vibrated with multiple incoming messages.

Standing beneath the showerhead, Galan tilted his head downward, letting the cold water cascade through his hair and trickle down his face, momentarily obscuring his vision. With closed eyes, he found himself immersed in vivid recollections of Aria. Images of their initial encounters and the precious moments they had shared played like a reel in his mind, each memory etched deep within his thoughts. Aria's words resonated within Galan's mind, each syllable echoing through his thoughts. The radiant smile she had shared with him had left an indelible mark, captivating him and fueling his unwavering determination to witness that joyous expression once more. Abruptly, Galan's eyes snapped open, his breaths becoming deeper as he attempted to regain control over his racing thoughts.

Stay focused, don't let her take your eyes off the game. She is the summit of this mountain; keep your eyes on the journey ahead for now. No distractions and no interference this time. Don't fall in love until you know she will be there to catch you. You have been through this before, Galan. You know better. You know you were starved for attention all of your life; you know you cling too fast to the slightest sign of affection and acceptance. You need to heal before she can love you; she does not deserve a broken version. She needs the best of you. That starts with acknowledging your flaws first and being willing to work on them. Fight your demons before you decide to drag hers to hell with you.

The obstacles in front of you now are her friends. Earn Bodhi's respect and get Maeve to tell you all she can about Aria. Two out of three isn't bad. Even if you and your other friend don't think we should be together, that still leaves two who would fight for us, and I will be the swinging vote. Of course, I would rather spend my time in the same room as you, breathing your air, receiving your smiles, and hearing the harmony of your voice in my ear. I would love nothing more. But this is for us; I'll sacrifice a little time now so I can spend the rest of my life with you.

Having finished his shower, Galan emerged from the bathroom and dressed himself in his room. As he moved about, he caught the faint vibration of his phone on the bed, indicating a new incoming message. Curiosity piqued, he walked over to his phone, eager to discover the identity of the sender and the content of the message that awaited him. Galan glanced at his phone and discovered that the text message was from Aria. Instantly, a warm smile graced his lips.

What do we have here? 'Hey Galan, Bodhi didn't have his phone, so I just wanted to let you know he and Maeve will be heading over in twenty minutes. Maeve has to get back to the hospital earlier than expected.' *You want me to have your number, and you're being forward about it. I was hoping Bodhi gave it to you, but I didn't expect you to run with it this quickly.*

If this isn't a sign that you are at least interested, I don't know what is. Message received, loud and clear. Galan replied immediately. *What should I say? I don't want to seem desperate, nor do I want to acknowledge that she now has my number. "Thanks, Aria," should be good, and a little smiley face emoji so it seems playful. And send.*

"This message was sent twelve minutes ago; they will be on their way soon," Galan mumbled to himself as he finished getting dressed.

Seated at a table in Grounded Coffee House, Aria and her friends savored the last sips of their drinks. With her phone clutched in her hand, Aria eagerly opened Galan's reply, her eyes scanning the words on the screen. Excitement danced in her expression as she absorbed the message.

"I don't have my phone? Really Ari? Who goes anywhere without their phones?" Bodhi teased.

"I panicked, ok. Let me be," Aria giggled.

"I've seen you make rooms of powerful businessmen quake with your very presence, but you're panicking to ask a nobody for his number?" Eyla blurted.

"That's a little harsh. I mean, he did build the place we are all celebrating today from the ground up," Aria defended.

"But who is he? People take one look at you, and they know you are Aria fucking Scarlet, a self-made billionaire, entrepreneur, and the founder of LVTCH cosmetics. Your face is plastered on the cover of every major magazine in the world. Who the fuck is Galan... What's his name?" Eyla argued.

"Galan Rain, and that nobody did all of this without his daddy's money, Eyla," Dana intervened.

"Dana!" Aria shrieked.

"What! The only reason she is even relevant is that her father is our Godfather. Elya, you can talk shit about everyone all you want, but you know deep down that if our parents hadn't known each other, you and Aria would never be in the same room, let alone be friends," Dana stated.

Eder put his hand on Dana's shoulder. "That's enough, D, please," Eder begged.

"You want to talk to me about Daddy's money? Your sister built her fortune with nothing. But you asked your father for a café, and he wrote the cheques without a second thought. Don't be a hypocrite, Dana. It's not a good look," Eyla said.

"Oh, a hypocrite? That's rich because I remember that Garrick only met my sister because of you. You were being a slut and chasing after Maeve's older brother, and when you got bored of him, you tossed him on my sister," Dana belted.

"Dana!" Aria exclaimed.

"And you messed around in her personal life by venting to Garrick about all the things you didn't like about my sister whenever it suited you just so you could get some pity dick. And when you saw him happy with her, suddenly you wanted him back and played little miss homewrecker. You lied to him about her cheating, so Garrick...." Dana was cut off.

"Dana!" Aria interjected, "Eder, take her in the back to cool off. I'll be there in a minute." Sensing the tension between Dana and Eyla, Eder nodded understandingly and gently took hold of Dana's arm, coaxing her to step away from Eyla's presence. Initially resistant, Dana's gaze remained fixed on Eyla, her expression filled with animosity. Eyla, seated and holding onto her handbag, met Dana's gaze with a composed demeanor. Employing a gentle yet persistent pull, Eder eventually succeeded in guiding Dana toward the back room.

Eyla rolled her eyes in evident frustration, the tension mounting within her. With a sudden burst of emotion, she slammed her hands down on the table, the loud thud reverberating through the air.

"Are you happy?" Bodhi asked, annoyed.

"Don't give me that! She started it," Eyla grumbled.

"I blame you," Aria retorted.

"Are you kidding me? You just can't see past the fact that she is your sister, so in your eyes, she can do no wrong," Eyla defended.

"Really? Please, tell us anything she said that wasn't one thousand percent accurate. We are all here to support our friend, and you just had to bring your shit with you and ruin a good day," Bodhi commented.

"I am just saying what everyone else is thinking. Whoever this Galan guy is, he has no business with a girl like Aria. I will not apologize for looking out for what's best for my friend," Eyla explained.

Observing Eyla's outburst, Aria couldn't help but release a sarcastic chuckle, her amusement tinged with a touch of irony, "And what do you know about what's good for me? I had to leave my life behind and hide here because Garrick was chasing every single man who even looked my way out of my life. Do you know how many relationships have been ruined because of him?"

"Don't blame me because you attract fragile little insecure excuses for men who run whenever the slightest inconvenience comes their way," Eyla argued.

"Inconvenience? Are you going to brush off the fact that Garrick beat someone so badly that he is still in a coma on life support in the hospital?" Maeve added.

"Maeve, I am not responsible for your brother's anger management issues. Aria is a big girl. She can make her own choices, and she chose to date Garrick," Eyla said.

"I see. So, I can make my own choices when it's convenient to remove any responsibility from you. But otherwise, I can't?" Aria retorted.

"Ugh, why is this so hard! All I'm saying is that you shouldn't be chasing a nobody," Eyla explained.

"This isn't about him. This is about you, and I am just about done with your shit, Eyla. I have not been happy for some time, and you are sucking out the little happiness I have left out of my life. We have been friends since the beginning. I grew up in the same crib as you, and despite your nasty flare-ups, I do love you. So, for me, if you cannot be my peace, then this friendship will not work anymore. Are we clear?" Aria calmly stated.

Eyla's complexion grew pale, and her breathing locked up for a moment. "I'm sorry, Ari, please, I didn't—" Eyla stuttered.

"Save it; let me be very honest. I only see you a handful of times a year. If I wasn't dealing with difficult people on a daily basis, I would not have time for your little tantrums. Now that I am settling and trying to enjoy life, I will be more available. But if I have to deal with your shit more often than I already do, I will drop you without a second thought. Don't guilt me into staying in your life. I have way more respect for myself than to be manipulated by someone who thinks they are entitled to my life choices. Oh, and if you talk to my sister like that again, we are going to have bigger problems," Aria exclaimed, glaring at Eyla.

"Easy, Ari. Today is a day of celebration. Put your claws away," Bodhi said, smiling.

While silently observing the unfolding tension between Eyla and Aria, Maeve found herself entertained by their verbal exchange. With a soft chuckle escaping her lips, she savored her drink, enjoying the spectacle before her.

Aria stood up from her seat, resolute in her intention to approach Dana in the back room. Determinedly, she made her way through the café, navigating past tables and customers. *They can't get their own lives in order but are trying to tell me how to live mine! Maybe if you weren't such a shallow bitch, a man would want you for more than just your body, and even then, they can't keep it up. Every time you bitch to us about a guy not finishing, you think we see him in a bad light. But we're all thinking the same thing: you are so insufferable that he can't even keep it together long enough to finish fucking you. You're running around telling everyone about how many guys go limp with you, but people are less focused on that part and more focused on how many guys you have stories about. It says a lot more about you than the guys you try to paint in a bad light.*

If you think I would ever let someone like you tell me what to do with my romantic life, you've got another thing coming, especially after introducing Garrick to me and sharing my private pictures with him. Now, that asshole blackmails me, and the only reason I don't drop your drama-filled ass is that you would do the same with those pictures. My family's name will not be tarnished because you and that asshole, Garrick, feel like you own me. I am not the same person you grew up with!

Upon entering the back room, Aria found it empty, with no sign of Dana or Eder. Determined to locate them, she diligently scanned the room, hoping to catch a glimpse of their presence. Aria even took the initiative to inquire with a few employees, seeking any information on their whereabouts. After a series of inquiries, one staff member informed her that Dana and Eder had headed to the storage unit to retrieve additional products.

In this restricted access environment, Dana had exclusively granted access to herself and Aria for the storage room. As Aria retrieved her phone equipped with the special chip Dana had given her, intended for unlocking secure doors within the café, she became aware of soft moaning sounds nearby. Aria, attuned to the moaning sounds coming from behind the door, leaned in and pressed her ear against it, carefully maintaining a discreet stance. Recognizing the distinct voice as Dana's, she grew increasingly curious about the situation unfolding on the other side. Wanting to make her presence known without causing undue alarm, Aria discreetly kicked the base of the door, aiming to signal that someone was approaching.

Using her phone with the special chip, Aria successfully unlocked the door and stepped into the storage room. As she navigated through the rows of shelves, her eyes landed upon Dana and Eder, holding coffee ingredients boxes. A hint of disheveled hair suggested a momentary distraction, but their focus swiftly shifted to Aria's presence.

Aria looked at Eder and asked, "Eder, could you watch the register for us?"

"Sure, no problem, Aria," Eder replied and left with a smile. Dana returned his smile as he walked away.

"I'm sorry about that, Ari. Eyla just gets under my skin," Dana apologized.

"Are you insane, Dana? To be fucking in the storage room?" Aria sternly chastised.

Taken aback by the unexpected revelation, Dana's expression was forced into one of surprise, and she blurted out, "What?" with a hint of confusion in her voice.

"I could hear your moans from the office area, D. I am not your mother, so I cannot tell what you can and cannot do with your life. But you are sixteen, and Eder is twenty-two. Nobody wants to hear about love, Dana; the age of consent is eighteen. They will label this as rape. What the fuck are you doing?" Aria queried.

"Spare me, Ari. This isn't your concern," Dana replied.

"I was sixteen once, too, and I know, sometimes, love or whatever this is for you, can't wait until you're eighteen. I know I can't stop you, but at least keep your private life private. People are already looking for a reason to flood the news headlines about you and Eder. If Eder wasn't as influential as he is in the online community, there would be numerous rumors about you two. They'd say, 'Life coach and love expert on alleged rape charges,'" Aria ranted quietly.

"You think I don't know that; we weren't having sex, Ari. We were just making out, and things got a little out of hand. But it was nothing," Dana explained, looking away.

"It didn't sound like nothing, Dana. All it takes is one person in here getting wind of anything they can use to blackmail you, and they will sell that to the highest bidder for their story. Trust that I am only looking out for you," Aria said reassuringly.

Dana looked at Aria and rolled her eyes, 'You're so paranoid; not everything is about fame and money, Ari. Not everybody is out to ruin your life."

Aria was mad, but she didn't show it. *I used to think like that, and all it got me was a forced relationship where I was abused and blackmailed by the person I let in. Just like you, I didn't heed the warning Dad gave me when I was coming of age.*

Aria planted a gentle kiss on Dana's cheek before departing from the storage room. Dana, still processing the surprising encounter, released a heavy exhale, a mixture of emotions swirling within her. Gathering herself, she adjusted her apron, proceeded to zip up her jeans, and followed Aria's lead, returning to the main store to continue their journey together.

❧

Sitting on his bed, Galan's attention was fixed on his phone; his gaze focused on the live feed from the café's surveillance cameras. *They definitely had sex, Aria; I don't think they fooled you. So, Dana is sixteen, and Eder is twenty-two, noted. Eyla is bad news, and Garrick is dangerous. I'm learning so much about you. Now, I know exactly what variables I need to take care of and which ones I need to win over. Everything is falling into place.* Galan tapped on an icon displayed on the screen, triggering a message that appeared, indicating that a screen recording had been saved.

Chapter Seven

Maeve and Bodhi prepared themselves to leave for Galan's place. Aria acknowledged their departure, expressing her affection and bidding them farewell. Meanwhile, Eyla remained in a subdued state, quietly moping around the table, refraining from exchanging goodbyes with Maeve and Bodhi as they left. With arms folded, Aria sat across from Eyla. *Wow, not even so much as an apology. You're just sitting there trying to justify what you did so you can keep playing the victim. We are not kids anymore, Eyla. Grow up and start taking a little responsibility!*

"I'm sorry, Ari," Eyla mumbled.

She's apologizing? Wow. Now, wait for it.... 'It's just that—' And then she'll throw the blame on someone else.

"It's just that…," Eyla continued.

Of course. You truly are a piece of work, Eyla. One day, you're going to cry wolf so loud, and nobody will listen.

"I don't want to see you make a mistake chasing after that guy," Eyla finished.

"Eyla, my personal life is none of your business. You can have your own opinion about whoever you want on your own time. But, in case I wasn't clear before, do not bring that here. If I wanted the drama, I would have stayed in L.A. I came here for peace and to get away from that drama you dragged into my life," Aria scolded.

"I also saved your ass countless times, but I guess I don't get credit for that?" Eyla argued.

"Sure, you can take credit for it, as long as you are willing to accept that you put me in every single one of those situations. Or is that fact not convenient enough to make you look like the victim here?" Aria calmly asked.

Tears ran down Eyla's cheeks. Sniffling subtly, she mumbled, "Ok, since you think I'm the problem…."

Here she goes again with her victim mentality. I bet she's going to start whining about people leaving her in three, two, and one.

"I'll leave you alone. I'm used to people walking out on me when I did nothing but show them love," Eyla wept.

Maybe you should get an award for the number of times you've delivered that line. I don't know what to do with you, Eyla. We love you. Aside from your shit, you are a gem to be around. You are loving, and you do care, but you think you own us, and that's the problem. I cannot be around someone who wants to own me. You can share my life with me but not dictate it!

"I'm sorry for being hard on you. You are my oldest friend, for better or worse. But we are not those two kids anymore, running around in pampers. I need your support, not your protection. I appreciate the effort; you're just putting it in the wrong place," Aria reached out to gently wipe away Eyla's tears, planting a soft kiss on Eyla's cheek; Aria demonstrated her care and affection. With a compassionate smile, Aria rose from her chair and made her way towards the bar, her words continuing the conversation, "You owe Dana an apology. Start there."

This is the reason I don't want kids; I've been taking care of a giant baby my entire life, and it's exhausting. Sometimes, I want to knock some sense into you instead of keeping my composure. But I don't think that would do much. You crave my approval, and not getting it hurts more than any physical harm.

Eyla wiped off the rest of her tears and walked over to Dana at the other bar. Aria looked on as she apologized to Dana, whose temper had now simmered down. Eyla walked back to Aria and said, "Sorry. I don't think I was wrong for what I did, but I guess that's part of the problem. I can't make any promises, but I will try and work on it, ok?"

This is a first. Is Eyla Whitlock growing as a person?

"Thanks for coming today. It meant a lot that you were here to be part of this with me today. Have a safe trip back," Aria said as she hugged Eyla tightly.

Lying in bed, Galan focused his attention on the conversation happening at Grounded Coffee

House, attentively listening to the words exchanged by Ari. *Hmmm, I miscalculated. Bodhi isn't the best friend; Eyla is... Well, that became a lot more complicated than I would've preferred. The good news is that it seems like Eyla is in a volatile space in their friendship. If she isn't careful, it could change their entire dynamic. That means there is room for me to creep through to you, Aria.*

So, Eyla thinks I'm a nobody? I am below their social status; I know that. It's the reason I felt like I didn't belong here. Most people here are pleasant in the café, but their energy is different on the streets. Not all of them, though. There are some good apples, and they are quite pleasant to walk past on the street or bump into in the city. The rest of them act as though you owe them for being in their presence. I don't blame them; they grew up differently. Truth is, if I had that upbringing with the values I have now, I would most likely adapt to their way of conduct because it's a different world they live in.

Survival looks different in all walks of life. Why should I judge a different one than what I was born into? I don't dislike you, Eyla. In your eyes, you are just protecting her. I want to do the same thing. We are on the same team here; if only you would see it that way. But I don't like sharing, and you don't strike me as the kind of person who would share, either. That means there is only room for one of us in the long run. Let's see who survives.

The room filled with a melodic tone, signaling Bodhi and Maeve's arrival at the downstairs elevator. "Come in!" Galan shouted. As the voice recognition software recognized his command, the elevator doors gracefully slid open, granting Maeve and Bodhi access. Stepping into the glass elevator, they embarked on their ascent. Meanwhile, Galan, anticipating their arrival, exited his bedroom and made his way to the living room, eager to greet Aria's friends.

As the elevator doors opened on Galan's floor, Maeve and Bodhi stepped out, entering his living space. Galan's face lit up with excitement as he warmly greeted his new friends, extending a welcoming gesture. Eager to ensure their comfort, Galan offered them something to drink, presenting the option of sparkling water. In unison, Maeve and Bodhi responded with a resounding "Yes."

Galan retrieved three bottles of sparkling water from the refrigerator, ensuring everyone had a drink in hand. Leading Maeve and Bodhi toward his room, he invited them into his personal space. Positioned against the wall, facing the foot of his bed, Galan's dresser caught their attention. Adorned with rows of ambient lighting encircling the mirror's frame, it exuded a sense of meticulous organization. On top of the dresser, an array of hair and skin products were meticulously arranged, reflecting Galan's attention to self-care and grooming. The sight offered a glimpse into Galan's personal style and the care he put into his appearance.

Bodhi's eyes widened with surprise and admiration as he took in the sight of Galan's carefully curated dresser, "This is almost as nice as my private studio at the salons. Is this for your girlfriend?"

He's fishing for information, I see. I'm not the only one trying to stay ahead here. "No girlfriend. I just have good self-care practices; I eat right, train, and have proper grooming. It's some of the only things you have full control over, so why wouldn't you do what would be best for you, you know?" Galan replied.

Bodhi's smirk and nod towards Maeve spoke volumes. "I hear that. Alright, well, if you have a pair of scissors, I'll work some magic," said Bodhi.

Galan sat on the stool in front of the dresser and turned on the lighting frame. "Top left drawer has combs, scissors, clippers… Whatever you need should be in there," Galan responded.

Bodhi pushed the drawer inward; it slowly popped out slightly after he released it, allowing him to pull it completely open. "Wow, this is some set-up. You could open a small salon with the things you got here."

"Thank you. I'm one of those people who, once he gets into something, learns to do it to the best of his ability. Grounded Coffee House was a product of that mindset. I got into it and learned everything from how you brew to how it's made, from the beans to the end product. I got obsessed and coupled with the fact that I loved learning more about it, I got to a place where I believed I had something to offer that nobody else could," Galan stated. "Was it like that for the both of you?"

Bodhi grabbed a comb and skillfully ran it through Galan's thick, dark hair, smoothly styling it back. "For me, it was something my mother was amazing at. The way she talked about hair was intoxicating. Listening to her made me fall in love with it. I wanted to experience that passion, too, and when I showed an interest, she gladly mentored me. Fast forward eleven years, and now she and I dominate the industry in Los Angeles," answered Bodhi.

Galan looked at Bodhi from the mirror's reflection and said, "She sounds like quite an amazing woman. It must have been a joy to grow up around someone like her."

Bodhi and Maeve shared a lighthearted chuckle in response to Galan's question, their laughter carrying an air of playful mischief. Galan's smiling face and slightly perplexed tone reflected his curiosity about their amusement, "Am I missing something?"

"Mama B is the scariest woman on this planet. She is the thing nightmares have nightmares of," Maeve commented while giggling.

"I grew up in a mostly male family, Galan. I have six brothers, and most of my cousins are boys. We have three girls out of a family of thirty-one cousins. And there is not one of them today who would dare step out of line when she is anywhere around," Bodhi replied, chuckling.

"Really?" Galan responded.

"All of us have gone on to promising careers. Most of them, like me, run multiple businesses. If you want to get to us, you need to get past several assistants who would likely turn you down because we are always busy. But every third Saturday, once a month, she has a family lunch at her place. Everyone comes over, cooks, and helps prepare everything. Not one of the thirty-one cousins has been brave enough to miss it in the last twenty-seven years of my life," Bodhi explained.

"She sounds even more amazing. Reminds me of my surrogate mother; she passed away a couple of years ago, but she was the most amazing person I have ever known in this life. One look at me walking into her house, and she knew if I was going through something. I have never seen anything like that before," Galan remarked.

"I'm sorry to hear about her passing. That must have been hard on you," Bodhi replied.

"I learned something from her. Her love was unique. She made us all feel like we were her own kids. She had eyes that saw everyone's pain, and she was always the first one through the door when you called for help. The best way I figured to carry on her legacy was to show the same love she showed me because, honestly, I may not have been here right now without it. And I don't mean here in this place; I mean in this life. At a time when I needed someone the most, she heard my silence louder than anyone else, and I am thankful every day for it," Galan responded emotionally.

Bodhi's smile persisted as he maintained his focus on combing and styling Galan's hair, exhibiting both skill and attentiveness. "What about you, Maeve? How did you end up training as a surgeon?" Galan inquired.

"Actually, I went into med school chasing a boy," Maeve blushed.

Bodhi couldn't help but smirk and playfully roll his eyes.

"We had been talking for a few years, and when we finally met in med school, he ignored me and got together with my friend. And Mama B actually gave me the best advice," Maeve said with a smile.

Bodhi's uncontrollable laughter caused his shoulders to shake, and he instinctively covered his face in an attempt to hide his amusement. Galan caught a glimpse of Bodhi's reaction in the mirror and turned his gaze towards Maeve.

"She said if I was a surgeon, I would have access to all sorts of sharp objects, and if I was a great surgeon, I could make it look like an accident," Maeve laughed.

Quiet little Maeve is a fucking psycho, noted.

"I mean, she's not wrong," Galan chuckled.

"So, did you and Maeve grow up together?" Galan inquired.

"Maeve and I dated when we were teens. We ended things because our plans didn't line up. She wanted a big family, and I was focused on being career-oriented. So, we knew we couldn't give each other what we wanted," Bodhi explained while snipping Galan's hair.

"Really? You guys seem so well adjusted for people who dated," Galan observed.

"We were young, sixteen, and sheltered. Bodhi has been my best friend ever since we've known each other, and it's why we gave it a shot in the first place. We didn't break up because we weren't happy. We broke up because we saw that the other could be happier with someone who could give them the things the other couldn't," Maeve replied.

"Speaking of, Galan," Bodhi added.

There it is, the perfect segue to finding out about my romantic life. Your friends are sharp, Aria. I like them.

"What about you? You're a good-looking guy, passionate about what you do, and take care of yourself. Is there anyone in your life?" Bodhi asked.

Time to hit them with a move they wouldn't see coming.

"Honestly, I have been crushing on Aria since I laid eyes on her," Galan replied with a smile.

Bodhi looked up at Galan in the mirror while Maeve looked over at Bodhi quickly and grinned. "I see, so that's why you're doing this? Because you have a crush on Ari?"

"Nope," Galan replied. Bodhi tilted his head in confusion for a moment. "I have the free time, so I offered to give Maeve a ride back. I would have done that for anyone who needed it, and I could have helped. I am starting a new chapter of my life. I wanted something new since I mostly wear dark clothing and refuse to wear lighter colors. My hair seemed like the right choice, and you were praised as the best, so I figured if I could trust my hair with anyone, it was you. As for standing up to that Garrick guy when he was causing trouble, that's because I don't like bullies, and that was not about to go down in my Coffee House.

"The only thing I did because I had a crush on Aria was return Dana's phone myself, so I could have an excuse to see her again, or rather hope I got to see her again. Otherwise, I could have left it on the bar with a note," Galan explained with a smile.

"I appreciate your honesty, Galan. It's refreshing. Most guys that go for Ari are assholes. But you're not special," Bodhi smirked.

What the fuck...

"Excuse me?" Galan replied.

"Ari is special, and what she needs, you cannot give to her. Before you get upset, understand that she likes you. We like you. I honestly think you're a nice person based on first impressions. But we know how this goes. You put on a good show and pitch yourself as the perfect guy, and then you can't meet this standard every single day. Try just being a friend to Ari; you are out of your element with her," Bodhi told Galan.

Oh my God, it's not just Eyla. They all think they fucking own you. No wonder you don't smile as brightly anymore; they are all standing in the way of your happiness.

"I figured as much. It's why I didn't decide to stay. I was out of my element the moment I got to this place; that's why I want a new start. I don't think there is anything else here for me. Any advice?" Galan asked.

"I am not someone to give advice. I am just as lost as the rest; we are all just doing what we can and hoping for the best. But what I can do is fix you a new style. It's a bit thick on the back and sides. If we thin this out, we can keep the length just short of passing the back hairline. You'll keep what you have, but it'll be neater; there's a lot of room to style, and if you really want to mix it up, how about dying it? Silver highlights would take well to this dark hair," Bodhi suggested.

"Sounds good, but I don't have dye," said Galan.

"That's fine; you can come by the salon anytime. I'll see to you personally, and we can meet with my style team and see if you would be interested in what they have to say. And if you really feel lost and want advice, Mama has lunch this Saturday. Join us," Bodhi offered.

"I wouldn't turn down a good home-cooked meal," Galan replied.

After dedicating nearly an hour to Galan's hair, Bodhi finished his work, satisfied with the transformation he had achieved. Galan's face lit up with delight as he admired his new look in the mirror, and he couldn't help but express his gratitude by wrapping Bodhi in a warm, appreciative hug. Bodhi, feeling the embrace, reciprocated the gesture before bidding farewell and making his way back to the café.

Chapter Eight

Galan hurriedly asked Maeve to wait for a few minutes as he needed to wash off the excess hair before they left. Rushing back to his room, Galan swiftly entered the shower, removing his t-shirt in the process. With a sense of urgency, he rinsed off the hair from his body, quickly shampooing his hair while leaning over into the shower, his jeans still on.

While patiently waiting for Galan in the living room, Maeve occupied herself by exchanging text messages with Aria and Bodhi. Engrossed in their conversation, she glanced up and caught sight of Galan stepping out of the shower, his hair damp and in the process of being dried. The sight of Galan, shirtless and focused on selecting an outfit from his wardrobe, briefly captured Maeve's attention.

Maeve's gaze lingered on Galan's figure, captivated by his presence. She momentarily set aside her phone, lost in deep contemplation, as she bit her lips. With a sudden surge of determination, Maeve swiftly rose from the sofa, purposefully ascending the stairs and making her way into Galan's room. As she entered, Galan had just finished donning his t-shirt, unaware of Maeve's presence. The unexpected intrusion caused Galan to turn his attention towards her. "Hey, I'm almost done. I just need to get my jacket, and we can leave," said Galan, still drying his hair with the towel. Maeve placed her palm on his chest and pinned him against the wardrobe, lightly sinking her nails into his pecs and clawing her way down slowly.

"No rush; we could take our time," Maeve purred, leaning in and looking up at him.

What… The… Fuck is happening. First of all, ouch! Are you trying to do a bypass on me? I mean, it feels good, maybe a little harder. No, no! Wait, wait, wait. What the fuck am I doing? Put an end to this now! Take her hand off you; don't let her touch you as she pleases!

Galan swiftly reacted, grasping her hand and gently removing it from his chest, "Maeve, I can't. I'm not that kind of person."

Well, I am, but you don't need to know that. That's for Aria to know.

"You mean the single kind of person?" Maeve asked, biting her lips.

Galan gulped. *Fuck, don't do that. If she calls me 'Sir,' I would lose my shit. Stop this now! Right now, or you can kiss Aria goodbye. It's been too long; I dropped my guard. Before this, I would never have let anyone get close enough to touch me.*

"I'm not the kind of guy that would do something like this with just anyone. I wanted my first kiss to be my last, and someone in my past robbed me of that. But that doesn't mean it changed anything. It's not that you're not attractive or anything; it's just that I would do that to you without any intention of this being something more than a fling," Galan replied, slowly inching away from her.

"It's just harmless fun; who has to know? It could be our secret," Maeve smiled, pulling Galan closer again. Sliding her hands up his chest and around his neck, she got up on her toes to reach Galan's lips.

Fuck. Fuck! Not now.

Galan lifted her off her feet and tossed her onto the bed. Leaning over her, he slowly moved his head closer. She closed her eyes and smiled, their lips reaching for each other. Suddenly, Galan turned away and whispered in her ear, "I think I should try being a friend."

Maeve chuckled and pushed Galan off her, rolling her eyes as she got off the bed and walked out, "Hurry up, I don't want to be late." With a backward glance, she smiled when she saw a flustered Galan breathing heavily on the crimpled bed.

I should have fucking left this place sooner.

Galan grabbed a jacket quickly and ran out of the room. He opened the elevator doors, and they both got on. Maeve turned to him and whispered, "You should know elevators make me horny."

"You should know nutmeg is a hallucinogen," Galan awkwardly replied.

Maeve rolled her eyes as she shook her head at Galan.

That was dangerous. She shouldn't have gotten that close. That whole thing could have turned into a mess really quickly. Get it together, or you'll have a real problem on your hands. Was this a test? Should I tell Aria? Would she tell Aria? What I do now is the crucial part. Your friends are monsters; they all think they own you. This could be a ploy to ensure I don't ever get a chance. And now, I am about to spend a few hours in a car with this girl; I can't fight her off and drive at the same time.

I'm still shaking. I'm surprised I even stopped. I can hear my heartbeat in my head. I can't back out; I would look bad in your eyes, Aria, but going through with it is equally as bad.

The elevator reached the ground floor. Galan stepped off and clicked his car keys, unlocking his car. "Nice car. I wouldn't have guessed you go for muscle cars; you looked more like the import type," said Maeve.

"You know cars?" Galan asked.

"Garrick is into cars; my dad owned a garage, so he has been scrapping down cars and putting them back together since before we were toddlers. Grow up around that long enough, and you learn a few things," Maeve responded.

That's it! Can't touch me if you're driving.

Galan tossed his keys to Maeve. "You would let a stranger you just met drive your car?" Maeve asked, smiling.

"You're one to talk after what happened just now. Besides, I like seeing a girl behind the wheel. Let's see what you got," Galan flirted.

I could replace a car. Well, now I can do it without thinking about it. But I can't replace you, Aria. I'll take my chances. Besides, I heard the engine purring under Garrick's truck; definitely not stock. If Maeve is as close to her brother as she said, then she has been around cars like this more than I have. Logically speaking, it's safer letting her drive than me.

Maeve smirked and got in. The engine roared, and the low growl made the loose, fine pebbles dance on the garage floor. Maeve floored the acceleration; the tires began burning out, and smoke engulfed the car. Galan's face was burdened with a fearful expression. He subtly braced himself in the vehicle as it launched off and out into the street. "Um, Maeve?" Galan panicked.

"You probably shouldn't give strangers your keys," Maeve responded as she looked at him, biting her lips and speeding up as her eyes locked with his.

I'm going to die…

Maeve's eyes suddenly snapped to the road, smoothly following the flow of the road down the mountain, keeping perfectly within the lines of the street. She made sharp bends around the mountain's edges and seamlessly adjusted to the changes in incline on the road. After a swift forty-minute descent down the mountain, which usually took approximately two hours, Maeve stopped at the base of the mountain.

She smugly looked over to Galan, sweating in the passenger seat but sporting a smile. "How was that for seeing a girl behind the wheel?" Maeve asked, leaning in ever so slightly.

"Wow—" Galan said, speechless.

"Your car needs a tune-up. The throttle is falling behind. When you leave Salt Pine Acres, come see me. I'll make sure it will be the best ride you've ever experienced," Maeve advised, driving off when her sentence came to an end.

DANA SCARLET

AGE: 16
SIGN: SCORPIO
FUN FACT: "WHEN I WALK BY PLANTS I
WOULD RANDOMLY BREAK OFF A LEAF
WITHOUT THINKING ABOUT IT."

Chapter Nine

The tension in the car was climbing as Maeve navigated the roads in silence. Galan desperately prayed that she wouldn't break the silence or engage him in any way, fearing the potential unraveling of drama that lay beneath the surface. Maeve remained resolute, her gaze fixed ahead. The silence spoke volumes, carrying the unspoken truth of their unspoken desires. Galan's mind raced as he stewed in the discomfort, silently navigating the uncharted territory so as to not invite unwelcomed attention as the car came to a stop in front of Maeve's house.

Please just get out and say goodbye; this is already so uncomfortable. Why do I volunteer for these kinds of situations?

BROKEN TOYS

"Galan...," Maeve's soft voice broke the suffocating silence as she slowly turned to meet Galan's gaze. His attention shifted to her, his curiosity piqued, as she cautiously continued to speak. "Don't waste your time with Aria. She is not what you fantasize about. Whatever happy fairy tale you are building in your head is far from what it would be like with her. Aria is not like anyone you have ever known before."

I am counting on that. The people I have known before left wounds that still bleed to this day.

Maeve continued, "Even if you don't heed our warnings, you will never make it past Dana. I know you probably thought you would get us to give you information on Aria to help you win her over by being nice to us. But you are not the first and surely will not be the last. You wanted valuable information? Run." Maeve unbuckled her seatbelt and stepped out of the car, leaving Galan to shift from the passenger side to the driver's seat.

Maeve made her way down the long walkway to her house, and Galan patiently waited in the car until she reached the door. Once he saw her safely inside, he drove off, leaving her behind.

Run? Cowards run; if I were to take that advice, I wouldn't be the kind of man you deserve. You need someone who is willing to dance in the rain, not shelter from the storm. Don't worry, Aria, I will be brave for you. I will fight every demon that steps in my way to get to you; after all, I am always one step ahead.

Galan's heart raced as he pulled out his phone, feeling a mix of anticipation and anxiety. With trembling fingers, he tapped the "stop" button on the recording that had been silently capturing every word and sound since he put his jacket on. *You're right, Maeve. I am not the first, but this isn't my first, either. I wouldn't let anything get in my way this time.*

※

Aria received a text from Maeve saying she got home safely. She replied, 'Bodhi seems to like Galan, but you spent more time around him. What is he like?'

Maeve responded, 'He's good-looking and seems nice enough, but something doesn't sit right with me about him. Keep an eye on him around Dana; he seemed a little too friendly with her.'

Aria got upset reading Maeve's message and asked, 'Did he say something?'

Maeve quickly replied, 'Back at the café, he pulled Dana aside and had a pretty shady conversation away from us after Garrick caused a scene. And he was a bit too 'nice' around Bodhi and me. Seems like he is trying hard to overcompensate for something. I don't know anything for sure, but keep an eye on D. I would hate it if he was preying on her.'

Aria looked over at Dana, who was talking and laughing with customers. Her eyebrows creased, and her face tensed as the thought of Galan and Dana crossed her mind. *He was rather cheery with her, and he didn't react to her being rude. He was talking to her alone and met her first at the lookout. Dana might be a child, but she's not stupid. I know that without a doubt. After prying about Eder and her earlier, I shouldn't bring this up now. If it turns out to be false, I might lose her trust. I'll keep an eye on it and judge for myself. Besides, Eder won't let anyone jeopardize what they have.*

"Bodhi," Aria called out quietly, motioning for Bodhi to come with her hand. Her eyes sparkled with excitement and mischief as she beckoned him to her.

Bodhi hurried over to Aria, "Yes, my darling, what's up?"

"Galan. What are your thoughts on him?" Aria inquired.

"Didn't we already discuss this?" Bodhi replied, his confusion evident in his voice.

Let's see if Maeve is up to her manipulative tricks as usual. Let's change the story, she said Dana, so I'll go a different route.

"Maeve told me she had a bad feeling about Galan. She said he was not over his ex and was trying to use me to make her jealous," Aria stated.

Bodhi thought for a moment before responding, "He did mention briefly that he had an ex-girlfriend who broke his heart, but I didn't pay much attention to it. I was more focused on cutting his hair."

Typical Bodhi, playing both sides, with just enough deniability to stand on either side of the truth when it's all said and done.

"So, I have an idea. Do you think I should ask Dana to hang around him and ask about the café so I can get some more info on him?" Aria suggested with a mischievous smirk, her eyes glimmering with excitement and anticipation.

Bodhi smiled, "That sounds like a great plan. D is pretty good at calling out people's bullshit."

Maeve, you little snake. Bodhi wouldn't let Galan near Dana if he thought he was a danger to her; she is Mama B's favorite. He would die before he put her in a position like that. I know the three of you so well; we grew up together and learned this life as a family. Why are you threatened by Galan? Unless you all believe he could replace you... If anything, I am more tempted to get to know him now. He's not exactly my type; to me, he isn't all that good-looking, but I guess he's just enough to not be ugly? He smells good, which moved him from a four to an eight. Well, maybe a seven. He dresses like a gentleman, so I'll bump him back up to an eight.

Normally, I wouldn't bat an eye at someone like him; I probably wouldn't have spoken to him if we didn't need to speak to buy the café. Now that all of you are skeptical of him, it makes me wonder what you all see in him that I don't. I guess it wouldn't hurt to find out. Besides, he would be leaving tonight anyway.

Galan arrived back in Salt Pine Acres exhausted and mentally drained. With heavy steps, he made his way to his apartment and collapsed onto the bed, his body sinking into the soft mattress. The weight of the day's events weighed heavily on his mind. Galan sat up on his bed, holding his phone and using it as a remote control to mirror his screen onto the television. The surveillance footage from the café filled the screen, and he began to scroll through the recordings, his gaze fixed on Aria's every move. His focus intensified as he studied her habits, trying to decipher any clues or patterns that might reveal more about her. Each frame captured her gestures, interactions, and expressions, and Galan analyzed them with keen attention, seeking a deeper understanding of the enigmatic woman who had captured his interest. He scanned the footage until

BROKEN TOYS

Bodhi came back into the café. *Hmm, nothing more than friendly one-liners and uneventful conversations about nothing important.*

Fast-forwarding through the surveillance footage, Galan's gaze remained fixated on the screen as he searched for the moment when Aria's expression shifted. He meticulously reviewed the footage, scrutinizing her face for any signs of change. And there it was, a subtle shift in her demeanor, a flicker of emotion that caught Galan's attention. *What is this, a text? This is around the time I dropped Maeve off. What did that she-bat tell her? Did she tell Aria that she tried to kiss me? No, I don't think Maeve is that dumb.*

Galan adjusted the audio settings, amplifying the sound in the video as Aria engaged in conversation with Bodhi. He leaned closer to the screen, straining to catch every word spoken between them. *I mentioned my ex? I didn't say much about that, though. Is that what Maeve told her? Seems odd, who doesn't have a past? But that alone wouldn't be enough to sink my character. So, you plan to use Dana to get to me? Something seems off about this. Why would someone like you send people to do your dirty work? Unless it's a trick? Is that what this is? Is this all a game to you? I see your friends have already gotten in your head; they have their claws too deep in you, Aria.*

Galan turned off the television, plunging the room into silence. He sat on the edge of his bed, folding his legs and resting his hands on his knees. The weight of introspection settled upon him as he delved into his thoughts, searching for answers and contemplating the path ahead. In the stillness of his room, Galan allowed himself to be consumed by the depth of his reflections. Galan stepped out of his room and turned to the right; the locked door at the end of the hall beckoned him. Taking a deep breath, he slowly made his way to the end of the walkway and placed his palm on the scanner beside the door. As Galan crossed the threshold into the dark room, a hush fell upon him. The familiar click of the door closing resonated in the silence.

Chapter Ten

After several hours, Galan emerged; as he walked toward his bedroom, the ringing of his phone grew louder. Galan paid no attention to the persistent ringing of his phone as he walked past his room. The sound faded into the background as he descended the stairs and entered the kitchen. He reached for a bottle of water from the refrigerator and took a long, refreshing sip, the cool liquid momentarily soothing his restless mind. However, the tranquility was short-lived, and a surge of frustration pushed him to leave the kitchen abruptly and storm into his gym.

Galan's pent-up frustration exploded as he hurled the empty bottle of water at the sturdy boxing bag, its impact echoing through the gym. Without hesitation, he charged forward, throwing a relentless barrage of punches at the bag. Each strike was accompanied by a fierce yell, the culmination of his mounting emotions. The intensity of his punches grew, fueled by a mix of anger, determination, and an insatiable desire to release his inner turmoil. The rhythmic thuds reverberated in the gym.

Despite the storm of rage that had consumed him, Galan found a moment of calm within the chaos. His fists slowly came to a rest, his breathing steadied, and a serene expression settled upon his face. A subtle smile played at the corners of his lips, a sign of newfound tranquility amidst the intense workout. A single bead of sweat traced a path down his cheek.

Galan's rage fueled his movements as he surged forward with greater speed and intensity. With a swift spin, he gathered momentum, his muscles coiling like a tightly wound spring. Then, in an explosive display of power, he unleashed a cross-body kick, striking the boxing bag with incredible force. The impact reverberated through the room, shaking the stabilizer rack and causing it to tremble under the raw strength of his attack. The bag split open, its contents spilling out, while Galan stood there, a mix of fury and satisfaction coursing through his veins.

After the explosive release of his fury, Galan took a few deep breaths, allowing his racing heart to calm. With a newfound sense of composure, he approached the partially dismantled boxing bag hanging from the rack. Gripping it firmly, he carefully removed it from the rack and carried it to one corner of the room. The corner was filled with a collection of other damaged bags and practice dummies, evidence of his intense training sessions. Galan added the defeated bag to the pile. Sliding a door open, he walked into a storage closet lined with boxing bags, took a new one out, and placed it on the rack.

Why do you always fall into the same bad habits, you idiot? That's the last time; keep it together, Galan. You are better than this. You swore you wouldn't do it anymore; this was all part of why you were leaving, so you can leave that behind, too.

Galan's phone rang again, an eighty's rock song as his ringtone. He ran up the stairs and picked up the phone. He saw a number he didn't have saved calling. "Hello?" he answered curiously.

"Hey, Galan, its Dana. Could you swing by before you leave if you've got the time? I saw the way you pushed a new drink even though everyone knew what they wanted. Mind giving me some tips?" Dana asked.

Don't do it. Nope, say no!

"Sure," Galan replied. *FUCK!*

"Hey, I appreciate it. I will compensate for your time; see ya," Dana said before hanging up.

Idiot! Now, you are putting yourself in her presence again.

"Relax, don't get worked up again," Galan mumbled to himself. He hastily put on his jacket, rushed out of his apartment, and headed back to Grounded Coffee House. *Maeve and Bodhi must have gotten to her already. Playing this nice guy routine is a waste now. Just be straight with her and stand your ground. If you try to let this slide, you will only look like a liar.*

Galan came around the corner and found Aria standing outside the store, waving as Bodhi got into a car. *I want you to wave to me like that when I leave. No, I want you to beg me to stay. I feel like I'm giving up too quickly. I can do this. Keep it together. Friends don't mean a thing; they will always leave. Can't even spell the word without 'ends.' The day's almost done. Quality over quantity.*

Galan approached Aria, opening the door for her with a polite gesture. With a gentle smile, he said, "After you."

"What are you doing here?" Aria asked.

"Dana called me about the café; she wanted some advice on some stuff," Galan responded.

Aria's brows knitted in suspicion as she leaned forward. *Oh my God, he really is going after Dana.* "When did Dana get your number?" Aria inquired.

"I thought you gave it to her? Or maybe it was Bodhi?" Galan answered.

Aria: *Why would I give my little sister your number, you creep? Maeve was right.* "I think you should leave, Galan. Stay the fuck away from my sister and me."

Aria whispered angrily to Galan as she approached him, her voice filled with frustration and concern. She closed the front door behind her, not stepping inside.

Galan: *What?*

"Excuse me?" Galan asked, confused.

"Leave. Now," Aria said, her eyes narrowing as she glared at him, her voice filled with anger and suspicion.

Galan's gaze fell upon Aria, his stomach twisted in knots of anticipation. As he turned to peer through the window, a sudden exchange of glances occurred between him and Dana. With an infectious cheerfulness adorning her face, she waved at him, her gesture brimming with warmth. Galan locked eyes with Aria, his resolve evident as he nodded in affirmation. Without a word, he began to retreat, each step deliberate and measured. Once he was out of sight, Aria, with a mix of emotions flickering across her face, turned and made her way back into the building.

As Dana diligently wiped down the bar, her eyes scanned the room in search of Galan. Just then, Aria entered the establishment, catching Dana's attention. "Where is Galan?" she asked.

Aria hurriedly brushed past Dana and disappeared into the back office. Perplexed, Dana's raised an eyebrow, her confusion growing. She instinctively turned her gaze towards the entrance, searching for Galan.

After darting her eyes back and forth between the closed door of the back office and the entrance of the café, a surge of determination washed over Dana. She rushed outside, her pace quickening as she reached the street. As her gaze swept down the road, her heart skipped a beat when she caught a fleeting glimpse of Galan, crossing the street with purposeful strides, his destination set towards the lookout.

Dana swiftly retrieved her phone from her pocket and dialed Galan's number, a flicker of hope in her eyes. However, her heart sank as Galan repeatedly rejected her calls, the notifications of each rejection flashing on her screen. With a mix of disappointment and confusion etched on her face, Dana reluctantly shifted her gaze away from the phone's display and redirected her attention back toward the café.

"What did you do, Aria?" muttering under her breath in frustration, Dana stormed into the café, her footsteps heavy with determination. In passing, she tossed her phone to Eder, a gesture of exasperation. As she entered the back office, her search for Aria intensified, her steps echoing with the weight of her emotions.

Dana stormed into the back office, marching heavily as she looked for Aria. Dana walked up to Aria as soon as she came out of the office's washroom, "Where is Galan?!"

"Why are you so upset?" Aria asked.

"Where the fuck is Galan, Aria!" Dana's voice rose, seething with rage, as she unleashed her pent-up frustration.

"Hey! Watch your tone with me, D. I am your older sister," Aria retorted with an irritated tone, her own annoyance evident in her response.

"I don't care who you are. You have no right to interfere with my personal affairs," Dana responded.

"You don't know what you're talking about. You have no idea who Galan is," Aria fired back.

Upon hearing Dana's heated outburst, Eder entered the room, drawn in by the sound of her raised voice. "D, what's going on?" he asked tentatively.

"Stay out of this, Eder!" Dana fumed.

"Why shouldn't Eder know what you're doing?" Aria belted.

"What I'm doing? What the fuck does that mean?" Dana shouted.

Eder's gaze shifted towards Dana, concern etched on his face. Sensing the tension, Aria moved closer to Dana and muttered under her breath, their exchange filled with an air of heightened emotions, "I will not clean your shit up forever, D. Grow the fuck up; one day, your games will put you in real danger."

Eder's attention shifted from Dana to Aria and then back to Dana, his gaze flickering between the two.

"What is your problem, Aria?" Dana's voice escalated further as she yelled, her frustration pouring out in her words. Sensing the need to diffuse the situation, Eder swiftly moved towards Dana, attempting to gently pull her aside and calm her down, "Don't fucking touch me, Eder,"

Dana's frustration reached its peak as she let out a piercing scream, her emotions overwhelming her. Despite Eder's attempt to intervene, she forcefully pulled away from him.

"D, you need to calm down," Eder said softly.

"I said stay out of this, Eder!" Dana replied furiously.

"Look at you! Look at how you're acting towards Eder when he is only trying to help," Aria pointed out.

"What do I need help with? You came in here treating me like a child, and you have the audacity to tell me I'm the problem? What the hell have I done? Tell me?" Dana's scream intensified, her voice filled with anguish. Tears welled up in her eyes, threatening to spill over. The weight of her emotions became almost too much to bear, pushing her to the brink of breaking down.

"What the hell is going on with Galan?" Aria asked with her arms folded, her voice tinged with a mix of concern and skepticism as she observed the intense emotional state of Dana, seeking clarification or understanding amidst the tumultuous scene.

"What? How would I know what's happening to Galan?" Dana snapped. As Galan's name was mentioned, Eder's gaze forcefully fell upon Dana's face.

"See, this is what I'm talking about. Until you learn to grow up and stop playing these childish games, you will always end up in problems like this," Aria remarked.

Dana fumed and stormed out of the room, Eder quickly following behind her.

Damn it, Dana, why are you so hard-headed? I don't have the time to babysit you all the time. Thank God that Maeve and Bodhi saw this before I did!

Chapter Eleven

Galan finally reached the lookout, his footsteps taking him to the desired destination. As he arrived, he was greeted by overcast skies and a gentle breeze that carried the chill of the cold winds, setting a somber and contemplative atmosphere in the surroundings. *Your mind keeps running blank around her. Saying yes when you mean no, being silent when you have a lot to say. This is worse than before; it was never this bad with 'Her.' As bad as your friends are, Aria, you are my biggest obstacle. You throw me off just by being around me. I can't think straight when you're around. I forget to breathe, and I can't stop shaking. If this feeling isn't true love, I don't know what is. Nothing worth having comes easy. This must be a sign that you are worth every bit of trouble. That being said, I cannot win you over if I am this much of a wreck. I need to remove the obstacles in my way so I can think clearly, starting with the ability to stay composed in your aura.*

☕

Aria stepped out of the office and looked for Dana. Finding her behind the bar, she asked, "Can you ask Eder to help me in the office with the desk?"

Dana looked at her, still angry, but replied, "I don't know where Eder is. Are you sure you trust me to find him, or am I too much of a child to do that?"

"What do you mean you don't know? Didn't he follow you out of the office?" Aria asked.

"He didn't; why? Is he not in the back?" Dana inquired.

"No, I looked in the back for him before coming out here," Aria answered.

"Then where did he go?" Dana asked worriedly.

"Oh, Mr. Barlow left in a hurry not too long ago. He took his car and looked like he was headed into town," Alliyah informed them, overhearing them as she cleared a nearby table.

Dana and Aria exchanged puzzled glances. Dana called out to Alliyah as she walked to the back, "Alliyah, can you take over till we get back? We would only be a few minutes, and you know this place better than anyone."

"Sure, I can do that," Alliyah answered.

With a sense of urgency, Dana and Aria swiftly made their way outside, seeking the privacy of their car. They hopped into the back seat without wasting any time, and their driver, who had been waiting outside the café, promptly took his place in the driver's seat. The engine hummed to life as they prepared to depart. "Where to, Madam?" he asked.

"Drive around town, please, Hans. We need to find Eder," Dana replied.

"Yes, Ma'am," Hans responded, driving off.

"Where do you think he is going? He doesn't have access to the house without us," Aria speculated.

"He wouldn't leave, not without telling me. Plus, he drove the wrong way if he was leaving. What is he looking for in Salt Pine Acres?" Dana wondered.

"You did react badly to him in the office; maybe he needs to cool off?" Aria suggested.

"I know Eder. He wouldn't get upset because someone raised their voice at him. He only storms off when he is angry," Dana explained.

"Did you try his phone?" Aria asked.

"I don't have my phone. I gave it to him. I don't keep it on me when I'm at the bar; I only took it out to call Galan," Dana responded.

Aria raised her eyebrows and said, "Galan! He must have seen your calls to Galan."

Dana glanced at Aria, her confusion evident in her expression as she tried to make sense of the words spoken. A wave of uncertainty washed over her, leaving her perplexed and seeking clarification. "Why would he be upset about Galan?" she couldn't help but ask.

"Really, Dana? Come on, this is serious; if he finds Galan, things could get ugly. Hans, take us to Galan's apartment, the condo tower on Pine Needle Boulevard," Aria ordered.

"Galan isn't there; he went to the lookout," Dana corrected her.

How do you know that? My God, D, and you wonder why Eder is acting out? Did you think you could sneak around with him and nobody would know?

Hearing what Dana said, Hans nodded, grasping the urgency of the situation. He accelerated the car, directing it toward the lookout.

Eder's car pulled up at the lookout, and he swiftly stepped out, closing the door behind him. With purposeful strides, he made his way toward Galan, who was leaning on the balcony, taking in the picturesque view before him. As Eder surveyed the area, his eyes scanning the surroundings, he noticed the absence of any other individuals nearby. With a determined resolve, he rolled up his sleeves. Briskly, he marched towards Galan, his purpose clear and his intent unwavering. Galan's attention was caught by the sound of approaching footsteps, prompting him to turn his gaze behind him. As he did, he caught sight of Eder.

Galan pivoted to face him. With purposeful steps, Eder approached Galan, stopping mere inches away from his face. Before Galan could utter a word, Eder's voice erupted, sharp and commanding, as he barked out his next words, "Stay away from my girl, mate."

Galan, taken aback by Eder's sudden intrusion into his personal space, instinctively pushed him away, "Ease the fuck up off me." As Galan pushed Eder, his hand smoothly slipped the phone back into his jacket pocket, almost seamlessly concealing it from view.

"I'm warning you; you'd better stay away from Dana!" Eder shouted.

"Dana? What the fuck are you talking about?" Galan retorted. *First Aria, now Eder. What the fuck? Why do they all seem to think I'm a danger to Dana?*

"I'm not stupid. I saw the calls to your phone. I also saw you pulling her aside and having a private conversation at the café. I'm putting an end to this now! I won't ask you again; stay away from Dana or—" Eder was cut off.

"Or else what? How old are you, Eder? Twenty-two? Aren't you that social media life coach guy? How would your seven million followers feel when they find out you are sleeping with a minor? I mean, she's sixteen!" Galan, standing his ground, belted out his words.

"You don't know what the fuck you're talking about, mate. And even if you were right, you don't have any proof. Who would believe a nobody?" Eder retorted. Not one to back down, he closed the distance between himself and Galan once again. His face was mere inches away from Galan's as he confronted him with intensity.

Galan smiled and replied, "You're right about one thing. I am a nobody, but who said I didn't have proof?"

Eder's initial anger dissipated swiftly, and his expression softened, his features transitioning from fierce intensity to quiet as he spoke his next words, "What are you going on about?"

"Even if I didn't have any proof, the look on your face right now says it all," Galan said. *Take the bait, you dumbass.*

Eder chuckled, "My face? Do you really think they would buy that? Your only piece of evidence is an expression nobody else but you saw? My followers worship the ground I walk on; no one would buy it!"

"I don't need them to buy it; it's the truth," Galan replied.

"Truth? It's a popularity contest, mate; all I need is the majority on my side. They wouldn't give a fuck about what the truth is," Eder boasted.

Gotcha!

"Look at you, sleeping with sixteen-year-olds. What's wrong? Can't satisfy a girl your age? It must be like throwing a hotdog down a hallway, huh?" Galan taunted.

Eder punched Galan, causing him to stumble back a few steps. Galan looked back at him with blood on the side of his cheek, smiling. *Oh, I'll take pride in fucking up a pedophile.*

Fueled by adrenaline and an intense urge, Galan lunged forward to engage further with Eder. However, Aria, Dana, and Hans swiftly intervened before he could reach him, positioning themselves between the two and forcefully pushing them apart. At that moment, as Galan locked eyes with Aria, he noticed her hand extending towards his chest. In a split-second reaction, Galan swiftly intercepted Aria's outstretched hand, gripping it firmly before it could make contact with his chest. However, as he realized the gravity of the situation and the need for de-escalation, he promptly released her hand, taking a step back to create distance between them.

"Stop it! Both of you!" Dana commanded.

"He ran up on me; I was here minding my damn business!" Galan argued.

"Eder, get in your car and leave now!" Dana shouted.

"Fine, I'll see you at the café," Eder responded.

"No, I meant to get the fuck out of Salt Pine Acres!" Dana fumed.

"What? D…," Eder said.

"What?" Aria added.

"What the hell do you think you are doing, attacking someone? You're risking my business' reputation and my reputation. Are you out of your fucking mind?" Dana belted.

"He is just trying to protect you, D," Aria countered.

"From what exactly?" Galan interrupted. "I feel like someone owes me an explanation for people following me and attacking me for no reason whatsoever. I want answers now!"

"Yeah, I agree with Galan!" Dana chimed in.

"I know you're a predator, and you are fixated on my little sister!" Aria snapped.

What in the actual fuck?! Is this real? Do they not know that Dana is dating a literal predator? How the fuck did I get into that category?

"I'm sorry… What?" a shocked Galan replied.

"Maeve and the others tried to warn me about you. I doubted it for a moment, but I should have known better," Aria stated. Dana's gaze shifted towards Aria; her face showed her shock and disgust.

"Warn you about what?" Galan replied.

"I saw your little 'private conversation' with my baby sister in the café. I know about your calls. I didn't have your number. You gave it to Bodhi, and he gave it to me. So, why does Dana have your contact info? And why does she know you were here?" Aria ranted.

Tears welled up in Dana's eyes, and her trembling lips revealed the depth of her emotions as she struggled to find the right word, "Oh my God. I don't believe this. Is that what you think of me? For your information, I have his contact information because I bought his business. I got it from Alliyah because I needed him to give me some advice before he left. That's why I called him. I wanted to learn to do this better because he is better at it than I am in some respects, and I wanted a little guidance. And after you stormed off and left, I ran outside and saw him heading in this direction. I met him here before. This is the only place he could go because he doesn't live on this street. But thank you for treating me like I'm just a stupid child." Dana stormed off, asking Hans to take her back to Grounded Coffee House.

"D…," Eder tried to talk to Dana as she walked past him.

"Don't touch me right now, and give me back my phone!" Dana fumed.

Overwhelmed by her emotions, Dana snapped in response to Eder's attempt to talk. She briskly walked away, wiping away her tears and taking her phone back from his hand.

Aria observed her sister's shaken strides as she made her way back to the car, her gaze filled with concern and a tinge of sadness. Meanwhile, with his head lowered, Eder directed his attention towards Galan, a sense of remorse or introspection evident in his posture. He approached Galan slowly. "Look, mate, I'm really sorry. I shouldn't have come down here, and I really shouldn't have struck you." Eder reached his hand out to offer a handshake to Galan.

Galan maintained a steady gaze, fixating his eyes on Eder and clenching his jaw. Without uttering a word, Galan pivoted on his heels, leaving Eder behind as he walked away.

"Dana is pulling off; would you like a ride back to the café, Aria?" Eder offered.

"No thanks, I'll find my way back," Aria said, taking off behind Galan. Eder got in his car and left.

"Galan! Galan, please wait," Aria called out, jogging to catch up to him.

"Why? Is there something else they said about me that I don't know?" Galan hissed.

"I'm sorry, Galan," Aria pleaded.

"You know what sucks? I really loved spending time with them; your friends were so nice until I mentioned you, that is," Galan stated.

"Me?" Aria said, stunned.

"Truth is, I had a crush on you the moment you arrived in Salt Pine Acres. Catching a glimpse of you was the highlight of my day whenever it happened, and for the life of me, I cannot get that moment out of my head. When you walked in the night I sold the café, it was the most intoxicating experience of my life. And I used Dana's phone as an excuse to come see you again. I agreed to help out your friends if it meant I could at least let you know how it went after, just so I had another reason to speak to you. And it was great until I mentioned you, then those two bit my head off for it. Maeve tried to make out with me. She had constantly been flirting with me and making advances the moment Bodhi left. Despite that, I followed through because I had a tiny bit of hope that maybe you'd let me see you again if only to say thanks for helping.

"When Dana called me, I wasn't planning on coming back. But a part of me couldn't say 'no' because saying 'yes' meant I might see you again

You have been living in my head rent-free since day one. But after this, I don't know what to do," Galan explained.

"I don't know what to say," Aria responded, her palms sweating.

"I think I've heard enough. Have a good life, Aria Scarlet," Galan whispered to her and walked off.

"Galan!" Aria's voice called out, a plea for Galan's attention, but he remained resolute, refusing to turn back or acknowledge her call. Determined to continue his path, Galan pressed on, his footsteps steady as he walked away.

Galan: *This is exactly what you needed. Her friends caused this drama, but you were in the right. So, now she will be sympathetic to you. The day is almost over; there is still a chance to put something in play today. Just be smart about it. Dana was also wronged, which means she is the best person to be around. Aria wouldn't be able to express how sorry she is without also extending the same sympathy to me. I'll head over to Grounded. I'll call Dana on the way; she probably wouldn't want to be around anyone, but we share the same pain right now. And with Eder leaving the town and her sister basically saying she was a cheating whore, the one person who hasn't judged her might be the best bet.*

Minutes later, Galan reached out, dialing Dana's phone number in a bid to reconnect. However, his attempts to reach her were met with silence, as his call went unanswered. Undeterred, Galan decided to contact Alliyah at the café, hoping for some information. Alliyah, picking up the call, greeted him. Galan wasted no time inquiring about Dana's whereabouts and requested that Alliyah pass the phone to Dana.

Alliyah handed the phone to Dana. "Hello?" she answered, her voice still shaky.

"Hey, I know you probably don't want to be around anyone right now. I'm sorry they treated you that way," Galan sympathized.

"Please, I don't need your pity, Galan," Dana barked.

"Of course, you don't. I'm sorry; I didn't mean for it to come off as pity. It just must suck knowing someone that close thinks so low of you. I can relate to that, and as much of a pain in the ass as you have been since we met, I don't wish that on you," Galan claimed.

Dana's eyes started welling with tears again. She wiped the falling drops into her sleeve quickly, sniffling silently.

"If you still want some advice about the café, I would be happy to help. As fucked up as what just happened was, I worked hard to build Grounded into what it is, and you want to make it better. I don't think you should let something like that get in the way of the potential of the café. But it's completely up to you. Whether it's now or later today, you know how to reach me. I'll be there, ok," Galan continued.

Dana, still visibly affected by her emotions, nodded in acknowledgment as she wiped away her tears. At that moment, Galan ended the call, and Dana took a deep breath, composing herself before returning Alliyah's phone.

As Aria stood on the lookout, awaiting Hans' return after dropping off Dana at the café, her eyes scanned the surroundings. Spotting Galan on the street, walking with determined strides, she couldn't help but observe his presence. The mixture of emotions within her remained palpable, leaving her with a sense of unresolved tension and a longing for clarity in their shared journey. With a deep breath, Aria joined Hans in the car, and they made their way back to the café, their paths converging once again. "Stop here, please," Aria requested. Hans pulled over next to Galan and sent down the rear window.

"Can I at least offer you a ride?" Aria asked.

Galan glimpsed at her for a moment and kept walking. Hans drove past him and then stopped again. Aria got out of the car and walked up to Galan on the sidewalk. "I'm sorry, Galan," she apologized.

"Kindly get out of my way," Galan responded politely, ignoring Aria.

Aria stepped in front of him, reaching out to stop him with her hand. Galan quickly grabbed her hand and stepped back. Aria flinched at his reaction; though his movements were quick, he was still gentle.

"What do you want, Aria?" Galan asked, annoyed, but the way he looked back at her didn't match his tone. He adored the sight of her; the pain came from having to speak to her in that tone. Everything else was pure admiration.

"My friends got into my head. I got a little too overprotective of Dana, and I took it out on you. I am sorry. I was wrong about that. You were just trying to help her out, and I'm sorry I didn't see that. I apologize for letting my own mind get the better of me. You have been nothing but kind to us from the very first moment you met us. I should have at least given you the benefit of the doubt and asked before I hrew around accusations like that. Can I make it up o you?" Aria pleaded.

Galan thought: *And there it is, my golden icket! I now have a chance; it's my job to not blow t.*

Simultaneously, Aria mused, *Please don't say some gross shit like going on a date with you. Ugh, why am I even doing this?*

"Dana wants to learn more about the café. If you can allow me to teach her without the insinuation of me wanting to sleep with her, that would be great. I invested a lot into that place and want to see it do even better. I have a few hours before I need to leave for my flight. If she wants me to help, I will do it for her. Not because you are trying to make up for what happened. You don't owe me anything," Galan answered.

Aria couldn't help but think, *Oh, thank God! Dodged a bullet there.*

"Sounds good. I'll let you know," Aria replied as she backed away from him and got back in the car. "Are you sure we can't drop you off at the apartment? That's a pretty long walk."

"It's fine. I'll manage," Galan remarked. The window rolled up, and Aria waved at him as they drove off.

Galan jogged home. Heading up the elevator, he received a text from Aria. "Could you be here at six?"

Galan replied with a thumbs-up emoji.

This is not going according to plan, but thanks to my face time with Maeve and Bodhi, I've got a free ticket to the show. I guess it's not that bad; all of these obstacles proved to be useful in one way or another. As long as I can be ready for it, I can make this work

Most of the work has been done for me; this last bit is up to me. If I pull this off, not only will she want me to stay a bit longer, she will beg for it.

    With his hands firmly gripping the steering wheel, Eder Barlow descended the mountain road in his vehicle. He tapped the LCD screen on his dashboard, prompting a call to be placed. The screen displayed the words 'Calling Garrick Wilder.'

Chapter Twelve

Six o'clock was rapidly approaching; Galan meticulously adorned himself in a sleek, dark brown shirt, exquisitely rolling up the sleeves to reveal a hint of confidence. His choice of attire continued with the embrace of black jeans, effortlessly combining a sense of style and comfort. Completing the ensemble, he slipped into a pair of sophisticated dark brown Chelsea boots, effortlessly merging fashion and functionality. To accentuate his punctuality, Galan adorned his wrist with a sleek black watch, its face poised to capture every passing second with precision. And on his left hand, a distinguished ring added a touch of individuality, showcasing a glimpse of his personal story. As the hands of the clock inched closer to the desired hour, Galan's appearance reflected a harmonious blend of sophistication and casual elegance. With a swift yet deliberate motion, Galan spritzed a hint of cologne upon himself, elevating his presence with a touch of captivating fragrance. The subtle scent embraced his confident stride as he embarked on his journey.

Navigating the bustling streets, Galan made his way toward Grounded Coffee House. As he approached the café, the enchanting ambiance spilled out onto the sidewalks, beckoning him to step into the midst of the vibrant evening crowd. Conversations intertwined with laughter, blending harmoniously with the gentle clinking of cups and saucers, creating a symphony of bustling energy. Undeterred by the lively atmosphere, Galan confidently stepped through the café doors.

Within the café's lively ambiance, the ceaseless flow of customers had filled every seat, leaving Galan with no option but to settle at the bustling bar. Perched upon a stool, he patiently awaited the appearance of either Dana or Aria. Emerging from the concealed confines of the back office, Dana, a familiar face, finally caught sight of Galan seated at the bar. Her eyes sparkled, and a warm smile graced her lips as she approached him.

"Hey!" Dana's voice resonated across the room, cutting through the lively chatter as she began making her way toward Galan.

Galan addressed her as she neared the bar, "Hey, you seem chipper!"

"People don't come here for my problems; they come for the coffee and great experience," Dana responded with a smile.

Galan reciprocated her smile, his eyes gleaming with warmth, "Are you sure you need me?"

"No, I don't need you, but even a broken clock is right twice a day," Dana teased. Galan erupted in laughter.

"Well, I'm here, whatever you need, alright?" Galan responded.

"I want you to shadow me, stay close, and see how I do things. This is the busiest time, as you know, so keep an eye on me, and if you see places where I need improvement or where I need to focus more attention, I am all ears," Dana exclaimed.

"So, you want me to follow you and watch your every move. Did you miss the part where I was accused of being a predator earlier today?" Galan joked.

In an unexpected burst of playfulness, Dana playfully punched Galan's shoulder. "Shut up," Dana playfully responded.

"Look, you don't need a babysitter watching your every move. Everyone is different. The way you approach people depends on the type of person you are and the type of customer you're receiving. You can learn a lot from the people who work here; we learned this together. Alliyah is a great consultant; you can talk to her if you have any questions. With time, you will learn about everyone in this town: the ones that are chatty, the ones who want you to pretend they aren't there, the ones you don't speak to, the ones you must speak to, and then there are those who don't even speak English. It's all in the experience," Galan explained.

"No shit, Sherlock. God, you are a terrible teacher," Dana replied.

Galan chuckled, "Ok, smart ass, sell me something. I'm a customer. I came in and took a seat by the bar. Go."

"Hi, Galan. How can I serve you today?" With a playful smile on her face, Dana asked Galan a question, her voice filled with curiosity and a hint of mischievousness.

"Right there, you had an opportunity to connect with someone, and you tried to force a sale down their throat," Galan spoke with a serious tone.

Dana's smile disappeared, "What did I do wrong?"

Taking a bold step, Galan moved behind the bar, his voice confident as he addressed Dana from his new vantage point, "Go around and approach me like you're a customer."

Dana complied. Walking around the bar, she approached Galan. "Hi, I'm a customer," she chuckled.

"Hey, still in uniform, I see. Tough day at work?" Galan asked.

"Ha ha, really funny," Dana responded sarcastically.

"I see, so it's not just with work," Galan replied, leaning on the bar. "Something else bothering you?"

"You know what happened; you were part of the trouble," Dana answered, annoyed.

"So, it's not the job, and it's not your personal life. This isn't about today. It's bigger than that. I noticed people came out to support Aria but not you," Galan speculated.

"Eder made the time to come," Dana muttered.

"But then, why do you look so crushed? You're doing great. This is a new journey for you. The person you cared about came to be a part of it, and you've got your sister. You should be full of joy, but you're not. Maybe Eder isn't the person you wanted to come and celebrate with you?" Galan analyzed.

Dana's demeanor shifted slightly, a hint of tension visible in her expression. While she had been teasing moments ago, Galan's perceptiveness allowed him to sense that there was more to her current state.

"I don't know who you are trying to make proud, but I think you should be proud of yourself first. People don't see you until you shine. Your job is to keep shining until it's too bright to ignore," Galan continued.

As Galan analyzed Dana's changing demeanor, unbeknownst to him, Aria silently positioned herself behind him, observing the unfolding dynamic between Galan and Dana with a watchful eye. *He's right. D wanted Dad to be here, but he couldn't make it. She has been trying to win his approval, but he only sees her as his little princess. Dana is more than that, though, and she wants him to see her in that light.*

After a fleeting moment, Dana's smile reappeared, casting aside the weight of earlier events that had troubled her. For that brief respite, her focus shifted, allowing her to embrace the present.

"Is that a smile?" Galan teased.

"Shut up," Dana chuckled.

"Alright, little Miss Attitude, what can I get you?" Galan asked.

"Oh right, we're still doing this," Dana remembered.

"That response right there. There is power in being a people person. If you can connect with your customers and, for a moment, make them forget the world around them, they will always come back and chase that sensation again," Galan explained. As he gracefully maneuvered around the bar, his attention shifted to Aria, whom he spotted during his perambulation. Meeting her gaze, he reciprocated her warm smile, acknowledging her presence. Aria smiled back with her arms folded and a relaxed posture against the wall.

Aria thought, *Maybe you are a little cute, and you're always smiling. You smell good. Ugh! Why is this so familiar? It should be illegal to smell this good.*

Galan stood at the bar, his eyes locking with Aria's in a captivating exchange. For a moment, the world around them seemed to fade away, leaving only their gaze intertwined.

Aria: *How did I not notice he has grey eyes? Damn, those are some pretty eyes. Why am I suddenly noticing things about him?*

"Good evening, Ms. Scarlet. Will you take my order?" Galan smiled at her.

In response to Galan's request, Aria playfully rolled her eyes, a mischievous grin spreading across her face.

"Wait, Galan, do Aria!" Dana suggested.

Galan: *Working on it! Don't rush me.*

"What, now?" Galan retorted.

"Do the customer thing you did to me," With a playful nudge, Dana interjected, gently pushing Galan forward.

"Yeah, Galan, do me," Aria smirked.

Galan: *There you go again. You knew what that sounded like; you were flirting with me, dropping hints. I see you smiling as you look to the floor and pull your hair behind your ear.*

BROKEN TOYS

Galan's apprehension grew evident, his hands quivering with a mix of nervousness and anticipation. The gravity of the situation loomed over him, intensifying the significance of his next move. A sense of pivotal importance hung in the air, underscoring the weight that rested upon his shoulders. "Alright," reluctantly, Galan mustered his courage, taking a deep breath to steady himself before resolutely walking back around the bar.

Aria seamlessly transitioned to the other side of the bar, aligning herself with her sister, Dana, as they shared a playful charade. Assuming the role of a customer, Aria effortlessly blended into the scene, maintaining the facade while keeping a watchful eye on Galan's movements. "Oh, Barista, I would like to order," Aria teased.

Galan leaned in closer to Aria, his gaze locked with hers, a spark of intrigue flickering between them. With a subtle gesture, he adjusted the ambient music in the café, infusing a touch of intimacy into the atmosphere. Behind the bar, he skillfully dimmed the lights, creating a gentle ambiance that enveloped them.

In this private moment, Galan's voice, filled with a mixture of vulnerability and confidence, gently spoke with a deepened voice into Aria's ear. "How can I serve you, Miss?" He drew nearer to her, enabling them to speak in hushed tones.

"I need some coffee at night for some reason," Aria chuckled.

"See, coffee is just the heart of what we do here. People come to Grounded for an experience they can treasure. So, why did you come here? You don't seem like you're looking for what Grounded has to offer you," Galan spoke softly into her ear.

"Actually, I'm here with my family. Starting something new," Aria whispered back.

"Is that why you don't smile anymore?" Galan's question, uttered with a deep resonance emanating from his throat, hung in the air, stirring a sudden wave of nervousness within Aria. The weight and intensity of his words created a momentary pause as anticipation mingled with apprehension, leaving Aria to grapple with her emotions. "I've seen your smile light up a room, but I don't see that light inside you anymore. You are making everyone around you happy, but your light is fading inside. I have a feeling that when you said you're starting something new, you weren't really talking about the café. You're trying to find yourself again because you spent so much time being everyone's light that you burnt out," Galan continued. Overwhelmed by a surge of emotions, Aria found herself struck by the profound accuracy of Galan's words. A realization washed over her—the profound absence of true happiness that had silently plagued her for years, unnoticed by those around her.

Feeling a knot in her stomach, Aria gradually pulled away from Galan's proximity. Her eyes met his intense gaze, reflecting a myriad of emotions swirling within her. The unexpected shift in Aria's demeanor caught Dana off guard, her expression revealing shock and concern. It was a sight that Dana had never witnessed before, as Aria's typically composed and collected demeanor seemed momentarily shattered by the depth of her reaction.

Aria rushed out the door quickly to get some air. Dana tried to go after her, but Galan held her back. "I'll get her. I think I upset her; let her take it out on me," he remarked. Dana, recognizing the unspoken understanding in Galan's eyes, nodded in agreement, giving him permission to go after Aria. Meanwhile, Aria crossed the street and descended a staircase leading her to the lower level of the town, where she hoped to find a momentary refuge from the overwhelming emotions that consumed her.

Maeve Wilder

AGE: 24

SIGN: ARIES

FUN FACT: "GARRICK LOVES HUGS. HUG HIM WHEN YOU INTERVIEW HIM."

Chapter Thirteen

As Galan pursued Aria, he called out to her in a voice filled with concern in an attempt to bridge the growing distance between them. However, Aria remained resolute, steadfastly ignoring him, and continued descending the stairs. Galan, determined to reach her, swiftly ran along the adjacent wall, gathering momentum, and leaped down to the platform in front of her. "Are you insane?" Aria shouted.

"Maybe I am," Galan responded, approaching her.

Aria, unable to meet Galan's gaze, averted her eyes, fixating on the wall beside them. Her steps carried her closer to it, distancing herself from Galan.

"It's ok to be seen, Aria. The only people that see your pain are the ones willing to help you heal," Galan stated as he slowly walked toward her.

"What do you know about me? We only met less than twenty-four hours ago," Aria mumbled. Facing the wall, Aria reached a breaking point, the pent-up emotions within her finally reaching their tipping point. In a moment of vulnerability, she snapped.

"I've known you from before you were Aria Scarlet. You were this beautiful soul who took amazing pictures in hotels around the world, showing off your precious smile. I never cared about the hotels, your dad, or any of it; I just adored that smile. Seeing you next to your little sister was heart-warming when I had a bad day. Fast forward a couple years, and you were walking outside my café. I felt broken seeing you like that. That beautiful smile wasn't the same, and all I could do was hope to see you smile like that again. I'm sorry if I overstepped," Galan expressed, standing just a foot away from Aria.

Aria, overcome with sadness and tears welling up in her eyes, turned around to face Galan. She extended her hand to him in her vulnerability, seeking comfort and connection. However, as Galan instinctively reached out to grasp her hand, Aria flinched. "What the fuck is wrong with you, Galan?" she asked.

Galan's breath grew erratic, his chest rising and falling with an unsteady rhythm as his own emotions mirrored the turbulence of the moment. "I'm sorry, it's just that...." he began.

"Just that what?" Aria, consumed by a mix of emotions, let out a soft growl as she attempted to free her hand from Galan's grasp. However, instead of distancing herself, she took an unexpected step closer to him. Feeling his grip loosen, she cautiously slipped her hand through his, allowing her touch to glide gently along his, almost hovering above it in a delicate manner. As Aria gradually approached Galan, her eyes keenly observed his reaction. Sensing his tension, she gently touched a single fingertip to his chest. Galan visibly tensed to her touch.

Aria: *Oh my God, you don't want me to touch you?*

Galan, with eyes tightly shut, trembled under the weight of Aria's touch; his vulnerability lay bare at that moment. Sensing the intensity of his emotions, Aria placed her palm firmly against his chest, feeling the rapid beat of his racing heart against her hand.

As heat radiated from Galan's skin, his eyes slowly opened, revealing a gaze that held a new intensity. Aria, caught in the piercing stare, felt a chill ripple through her body. She recognized a distinct change in his eyes—a hunger, a raw desire that sent shivers down her spine. The unspoken lust behind his gaze was undeniable.

Aria, drawn to the enigmatic allure of this side of Galan, reveled in the moment. Her hand glided up from his chest, snaking its way to his neck, where her touch traced a gentle path along his jawline, her thumb caressing his skin. Sensing the connection deepen, she lifted her other hand, bringing it to his face, her fingers delicately exploring his features.

In an instant, Galan grabbed both of her hands and lifted her against the wall, holding both arms over her head. Breathing heavily on her neck, he spoke in a tone lower than she'd ever heard him.

"No one is allowed to touch me. Not without my permission. Understood?" Galan said as he held

Aria against the wall, his grip firm yet gentle; he looked up at her.

Aria felt him pressing against her, his body pinning her against the wall as his other hand gripped her leg tightly.

"Tell me you understand," Galan remarked.

Why are you still talking? Aria wondered.

"I understand…," Aria whispered, her lips trembling as she bit them anxiously. She sensed Galan's body shaking, and his grip tightened as soon as she responded. Drawing closer, Aria leaned into Galan, her desire evident. Instinctively, he reciprocated, leaning in towards her, their lips inching closer together.

Galan: *No, no, no. Not like this; you're not this person. You're the good guy. Stop, stop, stop, or else you will lose her.*

Galan gasped, carefully lowering Aria to the ground before slowly stepping back, overcome with a sense of shame. He averted his gaze, his guilt evident. As he continued to retreat, Galan's voice trembled with unease, "I'm sorry," he uttered hastily, hastening his steps as he ascended the stairs.

Dana saw Galan running up the stairs and quickly making a beeline for the town. Aria emerged from the same staircase shortly after that and looked at Galan walking down the street. Turning her attention over to Dana, she signaled that everything was okay and pointed in Galan's direction. Dana understood what her sister meant and gave her a thumbs up.

Galan paced up the street.

Galan: *Fuck, Galan, why? Why did you let her? Now she will think you're like every other asshole who ever wanted her for nothing more than your own pleasure. You had a plan, and you missed your golden chance. Forget it; it's over. Cut your losses and let this be in the past.*

Fury coursed through Galan's veins, his fist clenched tightly as he hastened back to his apartment, consumed by anger.

Marching up the walkway, each step resonating with heavy stomps, Galan reached the wall of the condo tower and pressed the elevator button, his frustration evident. Suddenly, a hand gently touched his shoulder, jolting him from his thoughts. Startled, Galan swiftly turned around to face the unexpected presence.

With a surge of determination, Aria forcefully pushed Galan against the elevator doors, "I didn't say you could leave," Aria said. Smiling, she bit her lips as she wrapped her arms around Galan's neck. She opened her palm at the back of his head and ran his hair through her fingers. Aria then guided his head down, softly kissing his lips.

Aria propelled Galan inside as the elevator doors chimed open, pressing him firmly against the glass walls. Seizing the moment, she leaped into his arms, their bodies intertwining as she kissed him deeply.

With an impulsive desire, Aria swiftly tore open Galan's shirt, causing the buttons to scatter and tap against the elevator floor. Sensing the intoxicating effect of their actions, Galan broke away from her lips and began to trail kisses down her neck, leaving a trail of gentle bites in his wake as they continued to succumb to their escalating passion. Aria moaned; her legs tightened around Galan's waist. The elevator doors opened upon reaching the top floor. Aria got off

Galan and held him by his shirt as she pulled him along behind her.

They stepped off the elevator and into his living room. Galan removed her hand from his shirt, putting both her hands in front of her. Holding her against him, Aria could feel his arousal while he pressed against her back. Galan kissed her neck, sliding his hand down and into her pants. He could feel the warmth of her pussy as his fingers moved down; she felt soft and wet to the touch. Aria grabbed onto his jeans and looked up at him, stifling her moan. Galan's eyes met hers. He slowly leaned down and kissed her lips gently, teasing her, as he slid his fingers inside of her, deepening their kiss when she moaned.

Curling his fingers inside her, he rubbed her G-spot. Letting go of her hands, he slithered his free hand under her top, squeezing her breast. Aria gasped when he quickly removed his fingers from her pussy. Lifting his hand to his face, he licked his dripping-wet fingers while looking at her.

"Don't be selfish," Aria whimpered through labored breaths. She took his hand and put his fingers in her mouth, moaning softly as she tasted herself on him. She unbuckled his belt and slid it out, the metal buckle slamming on the hardwood floors as it fell from her hands. She unbuttoned his jeans and slid the zipper down; Galan took her hand and stopped her.

"Didn't you just say I shouldn't be selfish?" Galan said, smiling. "I can oblige." He took off his shirt and draped it around his neck. Kneeling before her, he pulled down her jeans, lifting her legs one at a time as it slid off. Sliding her underwear off just above her knees, Galan buried his face between her legs and licked her pussy before sliding his tongue inside her. Aria cupped his head in her hands, pushing him into her hips. Looking up at the ceiling, her eyes rolled back into her head as she experienced pleasure.

"Fuck…," Aria moaned.

Galan looked up at her and stopped, slipping her underwear completely off. Aria held onto the ends of the shirt hanging around Galan's neck and pulled him to the sofa, throwing him aggressively onto it. She straddled him while they began kissing. Galan held her tightly to him. She could still feel the warmth of her pussy on his lips with each kiss. Leaning back, she held both ends of the shirt and pulled Galan towards her. Galan smiled and kissed her neck, "That's not what my shirt is for."

"Oh? Then show me," Aria replied curiously.

"Put your arms around me," Galan commanded. Aria let go of the shirt and followed his instructions. "Kiss me," instructed Galan. Whilst her lips met him, she felt Galan's hand moving, and in an instant, she felt him make a sharp movement, and her hands suddenly felt constricted. Galan lifted both of her hands, tied with his shirt sleeves, above her head. "Bend your elbows slightly," Galan commanded. Aria did so hesitantly.

With a slight tug, Galan had her hands tied behind her head and held her with the tail of his shirt. "It's not polite to touch someone without their permission. From this moment, you will not do so unless I allow you to. Understood?" Galan asked. Aria bit her lips and nodded yes. "Tell me you understand," Galan repeated.

"I understand," Aria exhaled.

"Do you want to know what else this is used for?" Galan remarked.

"Yes," Aria answered anxiously.

"Yes… Sir," Galan corrected her.

"Yes, Sir," Aria repeated, biting her lips.

Galan stood up off the sofa, holding the shirt behind Aria's back. "Sometimes, people are not polite, but it isn't their intention to be so," Galan continued, kneeling at her feet. "This ensures they behave," he finished. Galan kissed her inner thigh, slowly trailing gentle kisses as he inched closer to her pussy. He slowly put her leg over his shoulder so that she stood with him and knelt between her legs. He began to slide his tongue between her lower lips. Feeling the tension on the shirt as she tried to move her hands, he gently worked his way up.

Aria yanked at the shirt. Galan stopped and began sucking. Circling his tongue, he listened to her moans and felt her legs tense and tremble as they pressed against him. Only then did he slide two fingers in while he continued sucking. Aria's moans began to turn into screams and obscenities as pressure began to build.

Aria gasped when she felt her feet leave the ground. Galan stood up with her on his shoulders, letting some slack off the shirt. "Hands in front," he ordered. Aria brought her hands in front of her. Galan pressed her against the wall and continued. Aria wrapped her legs around his neck and pulled his face closer as he licked her clit. Galan took her off his shoulders and gently laid her on the kitchen island. He untied his shirt from her wrists and dropped it on the floor beside them. Her essence dripped from his chin as he turned and walked to the fridge, pulling open the freezer drawer. The cluttering of ice could be heard as Galan picked up a piece and put it in his mouth before turning back to her. Walking toward her, Aria had her legs open invitingly atop the mahogany island. Bringing the ice cube between his lips, Galan took her left leg and put it on his shoulder. Pulling the ice cube back into his mouth, he kissed her leg. Aria gasped at the sensation.

As he kissed his way up her leg, Galan placed the ice cube between his lips again and traced his way up her thighs before kissing her clit. Aria moaned, causing Galan to look up at her. Standing up, he leaned towards her, placed his hand on her cheeks, and kissed her, leaving the ice cube in her mouth.

"Save this for me," Galan said as he unbuttoned her shirt and slipped off her bra. Galan pulled her closer, with him between her legs. "Can I have the ice back?" he whispered.

"No, Sir," Aria replied.

"Excuse me?" Galan asked, astounded.

"I tend to swallow, Sir," Aria purred, biting her lip. She reached for Galan's jeans, unbuttoning them.

Suddenly, Aria's phone erupted with a ringing tone, breaking the intensity of the moment. "Oh, fuck!" she muttered. Stepping away from the island countertop, Aria quickly retrieved her phone from her jeans and noticed that Dana was calling. Recognizing the urgency, Aria swiftly answered the call, her voice filled with haste. "Is he there?" she asked anxiously.

Galan could hear Dana screaming over the phone, "Yes, he's here now. Get over here!"

"Shit, I'm on my way," Aria squealed. Hanging up, she hurriedly got dressed.

"Everything ok?" Galan asked, still breathing heavily from the adrenaline.

"I'm sorry, I wasn't supposed to be here this late. I was supposed to be at the café," Aria responded as she scrambled to put on her jeans. Now fully dressed, Aria asked Galan to use a mirror so she could retouch her hair and makeup before heading back to meet Dana. Galan led her upstairs to his room, where Aria swiftly fixed her hair. Considering the dim lighting of the café in the evening, she decided not to put too much effort into her makeup, opting for a more natural look.

"I'll walk you out," Galan offered.

"It's fine, hun. I'll see myself out. Hans is parked right outside the elevator," Aria replied. She leaned in and planted a tender kiss on Galan's cheek as she passed by him.

"Open," Galan uttered, utilizing the voice command to open the elevator for Aria as she hurriedly descended the stairs. Just before reaching the elevator, her phone rang once more, prompting her to answer it. Stepping inside the elevator, she waved a quick farewell to Galan, her expression filled with a mix of urgency and farewell as the glass doors sealed shut.

Your timing could not have been worse, Dana. Fuck! Couldn't you wait just a bit longer? Now my favorite shirt got ripped for no reason! Might as well rub one out while I still have a hard-on. Fuck, this night could have gone just a little differently if it wasn't for that call. Fuck, Dana!

Galan walked over to the window of his room, gazing down at the ground below, anticipating Aria and Hans' departure. As the car pulled out of the parking garage near the elevator, his phone began to ring, breaking the silence of the room. Galan's phone displayed a new text message, and he quickly opened it to find a message from Aria waiting for him. 'Tonight was special, one I will not forget. I'm glad we got to meet Galan *mwah*.'

BROKEN TOYS

She doesn't want me to go; she thinks this is goodbye. I mean, I was supposed to leave tonight. But my flight isn't until midnight, and I can postpone it. The night is young. Don't worry, Aria; nothing will beat the look on your face as I show up tomorrow and you find out I stayed for us, for you.

As Galan closed his apps by swiping up on his phone, he noticed that the device was still recording, likely capturing ongoing audio. *Oh, fuck, I didn't stop this after I tried to get Eder to confess earlier. Damn, no wonder my battery is so low now.*

Next to the app window, Galan noticed the security camera app was still open. Curiosity piqued, he tapped on the app and was greeted with a live feed showing Dana standing outside the café, engaged in laughter with another person. Shortly after, Hans arrived at the scene. Aria swiftly exited the car and energetically leaped into the arms of the guy, showering him with an affectionate kiss.

Who the fuck is this, Aria?

Chapter Fourteen

G alan mirrored the security camera feed on the television in his room, isolating the feed with Aria and this mystery guy. *Who is he? I have never seen him in any of her pictures. I've never heard any mention of him, either. This seems like something her friends would have mentioned, at least.*

As the café doors swung open, Aria, Dana, and the enigmatic stranger sauntered in, drawing the curiosity of onlookers. Their destination? The café's secretive back office. Before parting ways, Dana embraced the mystery man tightly, leaving a lingering sense of intrigue. With a shared glance, Aria and the enigma disappeared into the main office alone, leaving behind a trail of unanswered questions. After bidding farewell to the enigmatic stranger, Dana gracefully navigated back to the café floor.

Meanwhile, Galan's deft fingers danced across the controls, seamlessly flipping through numerous video feeds until he pinpointed the elusive office. With unwavering focus, he meticulously enhanced the audio, capturing every nuance of the whispered conversation between Aria and the mysterious figure, unveiling a potential trove of hidden truths.

In an intriguing twist, their conversation seemed to take a backseat as Aria and the mysterious individual locked lips, their passionate embrace filling the office with an undeniable allure. Observing intently, Galan enhanced the audio in anticipation of any subtle whispers that might explain their connection. However, the magnetic pull of their kisses seemed to drown out any potential dialogue.

What is this? He is barely touching her, and she is kissing him, not the other way around! Her hands are all over him, so why is he keeping his hands on your waist like he is afraid to touch you? You're in a private location now; why is he being shy?

As Galan strained to capture any audible dialogue, his heart sank at the sight before him. Though he couldn't hear her words, Aria's lips formed the profound phrase, "I love you," directed toward the mystery guy. Her smile, luminous and genuine, illuminated the room, leaving Galan shattered within. In that heartbreaking moment, the weight of unrequited love bore down upon him, casting a shadow over his once vibrant spirit.

You what? This can't be true! No, no, no. That's not true, Aria. You don't love him. You don't show him off, and he doesn't treat you the way I would.

You're only saying this to him because you think I'm leaving, is that it? I would stay for you, Aria; you just need to ask. You don't know that I would; that's why you're settling for this guy. I will make sure you never have to settle. I can be everything you need in a guy. I felt you, how wet you were. I tasted how much you wanted me. Those sounds you made and the way you held on to me... That's real. Not whatever this guy is. He can barely touch you. Sure, he's good-looking, but you don't seem to be into the pretty boy type. Jeez, his eyebrows are as perfect as yours. Damn, these middle-eastern mother fuckers are always handsome; they don't even have to try!

A sudden notification lit up the television screen, revealing a text message from Dana, 'Where did you go? What was that about?'

Fuck, she saw me when I ran off. What the hell do I say to her? I can't tell her the truth.

Dana texted again, 'I'm guessing Aria told you about Malek. Sorry, man, but Aria is taken.'

Malek? Who the fuck is Malek? I've never heard of that name before!

Galan began searching for him on social media. After fifteen pages of results, he finally found a profile that matched. *This is the guy? Malek Zakaria, twenty-one, works at a pool supply shop and writes poetry? Who the fuck is this? Why are you with him? What is so special about him?*

Galan texted back, 'Malek?'

Dana replied, 'Crap, forget I said that. Then where did you go?'

Galan replied, 'I made a fool of myself, and I just decided to come back and get ready to leave before I made a bigger fool of myself. You don't need me; you got this. I hope when I visit in a few years, you're still doing great!'

Dana replied with a smiley face emoji.

What's my next play? Damn, this got a bit too complicated. Fuck. Dana, couldn't you have waited a few more minutes before calling? Aria, you could have been with me instead of him now. You would have known this is what you wanted, but now you think this has to end because I'm leaving. I promise it doesn't, Aria. Let me show you I'll make this work.

What are my obstacles right now? It's Malek showing up and me leaving. I can control one of those things. I shouldn't go over there right now. Let them have tonight; this is your last night with him, Aria. Tomorrow, when you see that I stayed for you, you will be back in my arms and won't have to settle.

Throughout the long, restless night, Galan's gaze remained fixated on the array of security feeds, meticulously tracking Aria's every move. As the hours ticked by, Grounded Coffee House, now under new management, experienced a resplendent relaunch. The night unfolded with resounding success as patrons flocked in, filling every seat with lively conversations and the rich aroma of freshly brewed coffee permeating the air. By eight o'clock, the establishment gracefully closed its doors, having left not a single seat unoccupied.

Despite the lingering uncertainty surrounding Aria and Malek, Galan couldn't help but feel a flicker of contentment as he witnessed the triumphant night at Grounded Coffee House. Setting aside his reservations, he found solace in the joy of the occasion. After the final customers bid their farewells, the trio, along with the dedicated staff, raised their glasses in a heartfelt toast, celebrating the success of the day.

At nine o'clock, as the night drew to a close, Aria, Dana, and Malek gathered in Aria's car, ready to return to their shared residence. Hans, their trusted driver, took the wheel, guiding them through the familiar routes that would lead them back home.

No, Aria, no. Why are you taking him to your house? What if he turns out like Garrick? No, you could be in real danger. I'm coming, Aria, I'm coming!

Galan threw on a black hoodie and track pants. *Damn, I can't go in my car; driving there would be too suspicious since I was supposed to be leaving. If my car was seen anywhere near there, it would send off red flags. Damn, I'm going to have to foot it. I still can't leave my face exposed. Hmmm, I could use a mask; there are still people who are cautious of the coronavirus pandemic, so it's not a bad cover.*

Concealing his identity with a mask that shrouded his features from neck to nose and a hoodie drawn tightly over his head, Galan ventured out of his residence. Adopting a brisk jog, he meandered through the town, taking a circuitous route to Aria's street in a bid to evade suspicion. Maintaining a cautious distance, Galan opted to jog on the opposite side of the street, granting him an unobstructed view of Aria's house.

As Galan's observant gaze scanned the surroundings, he noticed Aria's driver preparing to depart, the engine humming to life. Simultaneously, neighbors began trickling back to their homes, some still nestled within the confines of their parked cars. Aware of the potential scrutiny his presence might attract, Galan swiftly adjusted his course, jogging forward without glancing directly toward Aria's house.

Too many people to get a good look. Fuck, waiting it out here isn't a good idea either. With a decisive change of direction, Galan retraced his steps, glancing to his left as he continued his brisk run. As he approached the lookout, perched on the edge of a drop-off, he positioned himself strategically and leaned over, granting him an unobstructed view of the backs of the neighboring houses. As Galan's eyes scanned the surroundings, they landed upon a potential pathway leading to Aria's house. A flicker of boldness sparked within him—an idea forming in his mind. If he could navigate along the precarious ledge, he could stealthily infiltrate the property, gaining a vantage point without arousing any suspicion. However, a daunting challenge lay before him: the looming peril of a fifteen-thousand-foot drop if he were to falter or misstep along the treacherous edge.

It's worth it for you, Aria. Even if I have to risk my life, I will ensure you are safe. Summoning his resolve, Galan steeled himself for the daring venture. Taking measured breaths to steady his nerves, he cautiously maneuvered over the balcony and clung tightly to the wall. The gusty winds proved to be an unexpected obstacle, testing his grip and balance as he inched forward. The arduous climb demanded patience and perseverance, and it took him a painstaking fifteen minutes to progress merely twenty feet. Finally, reaching a temporary respite, Galan pulled himself up to the top of the property's wall, carefully positioning himself to peer over, ensuring he had a discreet glimpse into the inner sanctum of Aria's world. Galan's eyes widened as he surveyed her backyard, revealing a picturesque scene adorned with a pool house, a charming gazebo, and a modest three-foot wall bordering one side. Seizing the opportunity, he swiftly hoisted himself over the barrier. Finding refuge behind the wall he had previously observed, Galan concealed himself from prying eyes, seeking a vantage point that afforded him a closer glimpse into Aria's intimate domain.

"Holy shit, that was crazy, even for me. But I will do crazy things for love, Aria; I would do it for you," Galan muttered.

As Galan's eyes adjusted to the dimly lit ambiance, he marveled at the tranquil atmosphere that enveloped Aria's backyard. Soft, gentle lights cast a soothing glow, fostering an air of calmness and serenity. Aria's house, a testament to modern architecture, boasted vast expanses of open glass windows, blurring the boundaries between indoor and outdoor spaces. Galan's keen observation captured fleeting moments of the trio in various rooms from his concealed vantage point. Dana was in her room, seated at a desk, perhaps engrossed in her own thoughts or engaging in a personal endeavor. Malek stood in the hallway, his presence marked by an air of purpose or anticipation. Meanwhile, Aria was hidden from prying eyes within the confines of her shower.

I can't quite see you, Aria. At that moment, Aria's window changed from opaque to transparent. *I see; it's an electro-chromatic glass. Brilliant, you can change whether the glass is transparent or opaque. I've never seen privacy glass in person; it's quite mesmerizing. Focus, Galan, you're not here for home improvement tips.* Aria gracefully entered the hallway, now clad in a new ensemble that exuded elegance and style. *You needed to wash off from earlier, I see. Did I make you cum too much? What are you saying to him? I need to get closer.* With a keen eye for opportunities, Galan surveyed the sprawling expanse of Aria's property, hoping to discover advantageous positions that would afford him an improved vantage point for both visual and auditory surveillance. Despite the vastness of the backyard, his search yielded limited options for concealing himself. The lack of suitable hiding spots posed a challenge, testing Galan's resourcefulness and adaptability in his quest to unravel the mysteries that unfolded within those walls.

I can't hide outside the walls; it's glass, so they would see me. None of the walls are solid, and none of them stay opaque. Fuck, what's my play here? I could make it to the roof, but what good does that do me?

Chapter Fifteen

*M*aeve, Garrick, and Eder huddled in the car, their eyes fixed on Aria's house just a stone's throw away. Like secret agents on a stakeout, the trio had arrived mere moments ago, quietly parking the car one house over. Maeve and Garrick held their positions in the front seats while Eder took up a post in the back. The atmosphere inside the car crackled with curiosity and intrigue as they anxiously observed every movement at Aria's residence.

"Walk me through the plan again, Maeve. You know I'm not in Aria's good graces right now," Garrick exclaimed.

"You said this Galan guy has stalked her before, right? Now we have Eder telling us about how he is fixated on Dana. This guy is trouble. If you're going to win Aria back, this Galan guy needs to be out of the picture. If we catch him snooping around here again, she will not be able to dismiss all of our claims," Maeve explained.

"We don't need him to do anything. He just needs to be anywhere near this street, and we can make it look like he was stalking her. We could maybe even 'rough' him up a bit," Eder advised.

"Fine, but I hate that her new little boy toy, Malek, is with her right now. I need to see what they're up to. Can we at least drive closer to the house?" Garrick asked.

"If we parked right outside of her house, then we'll risk looking suspicious, too. You know Dana takes random walks. She will recognize us hanging around out here if she does," Eder stated.

"That's the reason we used our dad's car and not Garrick's truck or your car. Besides, Dana and I don't see eye to eye. She doesn't pay much attention to me, so we have the best cover right now," Maeve countered.

"I mean, you fucked her boyfriend before you dumped him on her," Garrick teased.

"Eyla did the same with you and Aria, didn't she, Garrick?" Eder fired back.

"Oh, go get fucked, Barlow," Garrick snarled.

Eder chuckled in response, "Ticked a nerve there, mate?"

"You two need to get along, or else our entire plan will fall apart. We need Garrick with Aria, and Eder needs to stay with Dana. If Galan is in the picture, the risk of you both losing your spots in the Scarlets' fortune increases. You should have seen him at the bar, the way he looked at her. If she gives into temptation and goes there with him, that's going to complicate things. At least while you are with them, we can keep funneling money into our 'Investment' that doesn't exist," Maeve chided.

"Easy, Maevy. We might butt heads, but Garrick and I know what's really important here. We won't risk that just so we can measure dicks," Eder declared.

"It's always about the money with you two," Garrick scoffed.

"What do you think pays for Dad's garage? For your car parts? Our house? My medical school fees?" Maeve retorted.

"Come on, Garrick, it's not like they would miss a couple million here and there, so what's the harm?" Eder asked, putting his hand on Garrick's shoulder.

"I need some air," Garrick hastily announced and exited the car.

"I hope that big oaf doesn't get seen," Eder muttered.

"I'm glad he's gone," Maeve said as she looked back at Eder.

"Why? Do you wanna come in the back and tell me in my ear?" Eder flirted.

"Tempting, but let us at least wait until we are not within earshot of your 'girlfriend' and my best friend," Maeve blushed.

Garrick casually meandered along the row of houses, eventually pausing beside the formidable wall enclosing Aria's residence. With a stealthy finesse, he ventured past the front gate, skillfully treading the fine line between curiosity and caution. Through the gate's alluring design, an enticing panorama of Aria's domain unfolded before him. The gate's strategic placement offered a generous vantage point, granting Garrick an unobstructed view into the heart of the property, free from any obstructing structures that might betray his presence.

The walls surrounding Aria's domain were constructed with imposing concrete pillars. Intriguingly, these sturdy barriers harbored a hidden secret within their structure. Strategically placed between the sizeable gaps of the three-foot wall, large plates of glass presented themselves, teasing the curious onlooker with their enigmatic properties. These glass panels appeared opaque when viewed head-on, shielding the inner sanctum from prying eyes. However, a fascinating transformation occurred with a clever adjustment of perspective and a mere tilt of the head. The glass panels revealed their true nature, becoming transparent at an angle, offering a tantalizing sliver of insight into the mysterious world that lay beyond.

Garrick indulged in the captivating glimpses of Aria's presence inside as he leisurely strolled alongside the alluring wall. Each passing moment was savored as he desired to prolong this tantalizing experience. However, an insatiable curiosity propelled him forward. Turning on his heels, he made his way up the street, heading towards the far end of the wall in a quest for additional time to observe Aria within the confines of her residence.

Finally reaching the end of her property, Garrick pivoted once more, ready to resume his surveillance. It was at that crucial moment that his keen eye caught a flicker of movement at the back of the house.

With heightened determination, Garrick instinctively pressed himself closer to the wall aligning his gaze with the captivating scene unfolding within. And then, as if the universe conspired to grant him a tantalizing revelation, his sharp eyes detected a subtle hint protruding from behind the veil of the pool's gazebo. Garrick's heart skipped a beat, his pulse quickening in anticipation as he beheld the unmistakable presence of a pair of eyes.

Without hesitation, a surge of adrenaline propelled Garrick to make a bold decision. Ignoring any rational thoughts, he defied the imposing eight-foot-high wall with a daring leap, driven solely by his relentless pursuit of the truth. Meanwhile, Eder and Maeve remained blissfully engrossed in their own world of flirtation within the confines of the car, unaware of Garrick's audacious move. Galan, his unwavering focus fixed on Aria, remained oblivious to Garrick's stealthy actions.

Garrick wasted no time, his purposeful steps leading him to the front of the house. Along the way, he seized a sizable rock that lay aligned with the walkway, his grip tightening as he prepared for the unexpected encounter that awaited him.

"Wait. Don't be hasty; you need to get a picture before you do this, so you have proof," Garrick mumbled. With his senses on high alert, Garrick swiftly retrieved his phone, deftly maneuvering the camera to capture a discreet image while carefully peering around the corner of the building. His fingers poised, ready to immortalize the crucial moment in a photograph that held the potential to reveal the truth he sought.

However, fate had other plans. In a momentary lapse of caution, Garrick's flash unexpectedly illuminated the surroundings, slicing through the shadows and betraying his presence to the ever-watchful Galan. The sudden burst of light shattered the veil of secrecy, jolting Galan's attention as his gaze abruptly shifted toward the source of the disturbance.

Galan swiftly sought refuge behind the wall, vanishing from sight in a bid to protect himself from the consequences of the exposed flash. *What the fuck was that? Where did that come from? Shit, shit, shit, shit, I need to get out of here!*

"Fuck! The auto flash was on," Garrick muttered. As adrenaline coursed through his veins, Garrick mumbled under his breath, his mind racing with determination. With agile speed, he sprinted towards the gazebo, his feet gliding across the grass as he fought to bring himself to a sudden halt. Despite not spotting anyone behind the gazebo's wall, his hand remained poised, cocked back, ready to strike, prepared to defend himself against any potential threat that might emerge.

Unbeknownst to Garrick, Galan had swiftly taken evasive action, deftly scaling the pillar while Garrick's attention was consumed by the unintended flash. Now, hidden from view, Galan found refuge on the cone-shaped roof of the gazebo, lying flat and biding his time, eagerly seeking an opportunity to make his escape from the precarious situation.

Meanwhile, Maeve and Eder, momentarily interrupted in their intimate moment by a sense of concern, broke their kiss and cast their eyes toward the surroundings, searching for any sign of Garrick's presence.

"Where the fuck did he go?" Eder inquired, concern evident in his voice as Maeve turned her attention towards searching for her brother, their worry intensifying.

Together, they scanned the streets, their gazes sweeping across the surroundings, yet finding no trace of Garrick's presence. It was then that Eder's eyes were drawn towards Aria's house, where a revelation awaited him. The wall separating her property from the neighboring one stood two feet lower, offering a potential vantage point. With his gaze fixed upon the figure lying on the roof of the gazebo, Eder swiftly made a decision.

Acting with urgency, Eder emerged from the car, his determination propelling him forward. While he focused his attention on the person lying on the gazebo's roof, he recognized Garrick amidst the confusion. Without hesitation, Eder skillfully scaled the nearby pillar, his agile movements enabling him to peer over the wall. Spotting Garrick standing behind the gazebo, a surge of relief coursed through him, prompting Eder to vigorously point upward.

In a synchronous moment, both Garrick and Galan's attention was drawn towards the sight of Eder scaling the pillar, their eyes locking onto him simultaneously. *Fuck!!!! What now? Wait, Garrick is here? Why is he here? I'll bet he can't explain his way out of this, Aria!*

In a swift and calculated motion, Galan seized the opportunity presented by the momentary distraction and broke off a piece of the gazebo's roof tile with a deft hand. With precise aim, he propelled the tile towards the house, striking Dana's room with a resounding impact. Capitalizing on the ensuing chaos, Galan wasted no time, swiftly leaping off the gazebo and deftly maneuvering over the wall into the neighbor's yard.

BODHI

AGE: 27

SIGN: ARIES

FUN FACT: "YES I ONLY HAVE ONE NAME..."

Chapter Sixteen

The sudden knocking sound of the tile startled the inhabitants of the house, jolting Dana, Aria, and Malek into a state of surprise. Their eyes widened in disbelief as they laid eyes upon the unexpected sight of Garrick standing in their yard. Garrick wasted no time, his decisiveness propelling him to give chase to Galan.

Meanwhile, Galan sprinted with fervor, driven by the need to elude capture. He swiftly hurdled over the adjacent wall, descending into the street below, hoping to disappear into the anonymity of the surrounding area. However, his escape was abruptly halted as Eder, acting with remarkable reflexes, managed to grab hold of Galan's ankle, immobilizing him and preventing further flight.

With a resounding impact, Galan collided with the unforgiving sidewalk, his body absorbing the harsh landing. Seizing the opportunity, Eder swiftly moved to restrain Galan, unleashing a flurry of punches aimed at his face in an attempt to subdue him. However, Galan's resilience and strength shone through as he swiftly regained control, overpowering Eder and forcefully kicking him away. As Eder picked himself up from the ground, determination etched across his face, he wasted no time resuming the pursuit. He leaped over the railing that lined the street, descending to a lower level of the town.

Gracefully landing on a nearby roof, Galan continued his sprint, relentless in his quest to evade capture. Eder, undeterred, followed in hot pursuit, his agile form leaping from house to house, resolute to close the gap between them.

With unwavering determination, Galan propelled himself into a full sprint, his adrenaline-fueled energy pushing him to his limits. With awe-inspiring agility, he effortlessly cleared a twelve-foot gap, catching onto a ledge of the upper level of the town and swiftly pulling himself up. His fluid movements allowed him to deftly navigate over railings, maintaining his momentum as he sought to distance himself from his pursuers.

Eder, however, struggled to replicate Galan's grace. While attempting to make the jump, he faltered, grappling to pull himself up on the ledge. In that crucial moment, Garrick soared over Eder, demonstrating his agility and nimbleness as he smoothly cleared the railing. With a tenacious tone, Garrick urged Eder to keep up, his words a mixture of encouragement and urgency.

Garrick's keen eyes locked onto Galan, observing his evasive maneuvers as he slipped between buildings. Galan, desperate to impede his pursuer's progress, hurled objects in Garrick's path, but the agile pursuer remained undeterred, skillfully navigating the obstacles. Now, in the open street, Galan made a daring leap down to a lower level of the town.

In a calculated move, Maeve, driving with unwavering focus, accelerated and collided with Galan as he emerged from the alley. Despite the impact, Galan reacted swiftly, minimizing the damage by using his acrobatic skills to jump and hit the windshield. Propelled several feet forward, he executed a controlled tuck and roll, mitigating the impact of the fall and swiftly recovering to continue his frantic escape.

As Galan rose to his feet, prepared to resume his desperate flight, he was caught off guard by Garrick's sudden appearance from the alley. Garrick hurled the stone he had picked up toward Galan with lightning reflexes, aiming to impede his escape.

However, in a display of extraordinary dexterity, Galan's attention swiftly shifted to the incoming projectile. With almost effortless grace, he extended his hand, snatching the stone out of the air, leaving Garrick and Maeve stunned by his unexpected feat. Galan, seemingly unfazed by the astonishment around him, casually tossed the stone a couple of feet into the air before plucking it from its trajectory.

In a shocking turn of events, Galan unleashed the full force of his arm, hurling the stone with tremendous power toward the car's windshield. The cracked glass could not withstand the impact, shattering as the stone burst through, striking Maeve. The unexpected attack sent shockwaves through the vehicle, leaving a trail of chaos and confusion in its wake.

"No!!!" Garrick cried out.

As the chaotic battle continued to unfold, Eder emerged from another alleyway, launching himself at Galan with a powerful punch. Though staggered by the blow, Galan remained resolute and seemingly unaffected by the attack, his determination unwavering.

Garrick, fueled by a furious resolve, charged forward with relentless aggression. Having regained his balance, Edere quickly joined the fray, rushing towards Galan once again. However, Galan seized the opportunity, swiftly grabbing hold of Eder and utilizing his momentum to throw him into the path of Garrick's oncoming attack. In a display of acrobatic agility, Garrick leaped over Eder, driving his knee forcefully into Galan's chest, causing him to fall flat on his back.

Yet, Galan was quick to react, utilizing the momentum of his fall to execute a swift roll, springing back onto his feet with a remarkable speed. Without wasting a moment, Garrick launched into another ferocious assault, unleashing a series of rapid kicks aimed at Galan's side. Galan, while successfully guarding against the onslaught, still experienced the jarring impact of Garrick's strikes, each blow resembling the force of a sledgehammer. The pain surged through his body, and he could feel his arm beginning to swell.

Aware of the odds stacked against him in the two-against-one scenario, Galan made a swift decision. Recognizing the urgency of the situation, he wasted no time, promptly turning on his heels and embarking on a desperate sprint, fleeing from the relentless pursuit of his adversaries.

"Stay with Maeve!" Garrick shouted at Eder as he chased after Galan.

Fuck! This is bad. Not only did he see me, but he also got a picture. Fuck! Even with this mask, they could guess who was behind it; my eyes would be a clear giveaway. I need to lift his phone off of him, but this fucker can fight. I can spar in my gym, but he is world-class. Brains over brawn, Galan; outsmart his ass. He only has on a T-shirt, no pockets there. He has three pockets on his jeans, two side pockets, and one in the back. Where would he keep his phone? Damn, I have nothing on him apart from that night he caught me outside Aria's house. If it's one-on-one, I might be able to at least escape. I'm not a world-class kickboxer, but I can hold my own better than the average man.

Galan came to an abrupt halt, pivoting to face Garrick head-on. Anticipating Garrick's next attack, Galan braced himself as Garrick leaped once again, aiming to deliver another knee strike to the chest. However, Galan reacted with remarkable agility, ducking and rolling underneath Garrick's airborne assault, evading the blow and quickly rising back to his feet.

With both combatants now facing each other, the tension between them palpable, a brief moment of respite settled upon the battleground. Galan's eyes locked onto Garrick, his focus unyielding. At the same time, Garrick, undeterred by his previous unsuccessful strike, prepared himself for the next exchange. The atmosphere crackled with anticipation as the duel continued, each participant poised and ready to unleash their next move.

Scan him; look for his phone. His dominant leg is the right one, but it seems flat. It's a bit too dark to tell, but the streetlights would cast a shadow if there was any object in there. Garrick turned to Galan, facing full frontal. *Fuck, no shadow on either side... He must have it in his back pocket, then. It's not easy to get behind a fighter; they are trained to keep their opponent in front of them.*

"Galan, right?" Garrick said.

He doesn't know for sure... That's why he's asking. I've got this; let's see how well you know German, bitch.

"Was möchten sie? (What do you wish?)" Galan called out in a deep voice.

"The fuck?" Garrick replied.

Seizing the opportunity presented by Garrick's momentary surprise, Galan swiftly closed the distance between them. Lowering his body, he executed a well-timed tackle aimed at Garrick's knees, intending to disrupt his balance. As Garrick instinctively flipped over Galan's head in an attempt to evade the tackle, Galan skillfully slipped the phone out of Garrick's back pocket, utilizing the motion of his own rise to conceal the action.

With the phone now in his possession, Galan capitalized on the momentary advantage. *Fuck yeah!*

Garrick swiftly regained his footing, springing to his feet without missing a beat. Galan, aware of the relentless pursuit, continued his desperate flight, fleeing with all his might. The chase unfolded through several blocks, with Garrick steadily gaining ground on Galan's retreating figure.

However, when Galan reached the inclined portion of the mountain, his intimate knowledge of the terrain came into play. Exploiting the natural advantage of the uphill terrain, he was able to widen the gap between them, leaving Garrick struggling to keep up. Galan deftly navigated the familiar paths, utilizing his expertise to his advantage, defying Garrick's relentless pursuit.

As the dense woods enveloped Galan, he skillfully maneuvered through the wilderness, every twist and turn familiar to him. Garrick, frustrated by the loss of his target, let out a scream of vexation as Galan vanished from his sight. Unbeknownst to Garrick, Galan circled the mountain, cunningly resurfacing closer to the entrance of Salt Pine Acres.

They would go to the apartment next if they thought it was me. Going there is not the play. My car is still there, so that's enough reason to come back, but I need to get out of town for now.

Galan noticed the group of late-night employees waiting at the shuttle stop. *That's it! I can get down the mountain with the shuttle and into the city for now.*

Having successfully eluded his pursuers, Galan made his way down the mountain with a sense of haste upon spotting the approaching shuttle. Joining the other four employees, he boarded the shuttle and disembarked at the base of the mountain. From there, Galan hailed a cab, swiftly making his way into the city towards the nearest hotel.

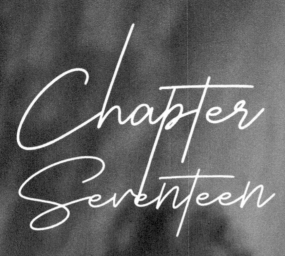

Chapter Seventeen

Now relishing in the privileges afforded by his newfound wealth, Galan checked into a luxurious room situated on the top floor of the hotel. With a touch of sophistication, he requested that the front desk deliver several bags of ice to his room. As he removed his shirt, Galan examined the telltale blue-black marks adorning his arm and side, remnants of the assault inflicted by Garrick. Gently touching the tender areas, he winced in pain, the visible swelling serving as a reminder of the intensity of the encounter.

Within twenty minutes, room service arrived with a cart laden with multiple bags of ice. Galan wasted no time, promptly filling the bathtub with a chilly mixture of ice and water. Submerging himself in the frigid depths, he sought relief from the throbbing ache and swelling, the coldness providing a soothing balm for his weary body.

That was a close call. It's too much of a coincidence that they found someone snooping around just a day after they caught me the first time. Even if they can't prove it was me, they have enough reason to sell it. It was dark, but if they got a good look at my eyes, then that was a pure giveaway. Think back to the alley where Garrick called your name. It was dark, and the streetlights were directly above us. Thus, a shadow would have been cast over my eyes. So, there is a good chance he didn't see my eye color. When I caught the rock he threw at me, he was a little distance away, plus whoever I hit in the car drew their attention from me. So, what are the odds they were trying to see my eye color?

Now, it's just their word against mine. The beauty of Salt Pine Acres is that it was built to keep its residents out of the public eye. There are no police, cameras, or security inside the town. Just two gates to get past that are only accessible with a resident's badge or a visitor's pass. They won't be able to bring in any law enforcement. No one has jurisdiction in Salt Pine Acres. It truly is a town of no consequence. I just need a proper alibi and a reason to return to Salt Pine Acres that won't raise suspicion.

Fuck, these bruises are a pain. Garrick is a bigger problem than I anticipated. Honestly, I always thought I could take on a professional fighter and win; it looked so easy on video. You can see their flaws and openings there, but it's different in the actual fight. Wait... Galan, you genius, that's it! Garrick's fights are all online. Study all of them and find his weaknesses so that you won't be completely useless the next time he becomes a problem.

Galan retrieved his phone from the nearby ledge. With a newfound determination, he quickly accessed a pay-per-view fight website, subscribing to gain access to a treasure trove of recorded fights. Galan's intention was clear—he aimed to download and study all the fights in which Garrick had participated. With a few taps on the screen, Galan set in motion his plan to unravel the enigma that was Garrick. Armed with the wealth of information contained within those fight recordings, Galan sought to understand his opponent on a deeper level, uncovering patterns, techniques, and weaknesses that could potentially be exploited.

Garrick and Eder carefully attended to Maeve's injuries, their hands gently extracting the shards of glass lodged in her shoulder and chest. "You ok, Maevy?" Garrick asked.

"I think the stone dislocated a rib when it hit me. Get me to the emergency room; the staff will take care of me," Maeve stated through clenched teeth.

"Galan, you son of a bitch!" Eder bawled.

"Easy, I don't think it's him. This might actually be someone else," Garrick informed them.

"Are you fucking kidding me? Who else could it be?" Eder replied.

"He spoke German, Eder. There is a possibility it's not him," Garrick remarked.

"Fuck. We already made a false accusation against him. If we aren't sure and he turns out to be innocent, then the Scarlets are going to act out against us," Eder exclaimed.

"What do you mean again?" Maeve asked curiously.

"Aria told Dana that Galan was a predator and was trying to get with her. I hastily confronted him, and it came to blows. Turns out Aria was misinformed, and Dana and Galan had nothing going on," Eder explained.

"Misinformed by who?" Maeve inquired.

"She was talking to Bodhi at the time when she mentioned it," Eder recalled.

"What time exactly?" Maeve questioned.

"I'm not entirely sure. After Garrick's little drama at the café, you and Bodhi left, and only he returned. So, maybe a couple of hours after that? Why?" Eder asked.

"That's about the time Galan dropped me off. I told Aria he was bad news," Maeve stated.

"So, what?" Garrick inquired.

"I know Aria; she is sneaky. She must have known I was lying about what I said and pitched it to Bodhi to see if it was true," Maeve replied.

"I don't know if she said it to Bodhi, but she said it to Dana in private. So, if you were lying about the accusation of Dana and him, why did she trip off?" Eder wondered.

"Something must have happened to make her think there was some truth behind it. She wouldn't question it unless she had reason to believe it was true. Galan must have slipped up," Maeve assumed.

"No, he didn't. Dana called him, and when he showed up looking for her, Aria snapped. He didn't do anything, so that's why he got away with it," Eder explained.

"Can we finish this conversation another time? Maeve is bleeding a lot here!" Garrick exclaimed.

With a sense of urgency and determination, Garrick swiftly assumed the role of the driver, taking charge of the situation. Despite her own injuries, Maeve directed Eder on how to apply pressure and prevent further bleeding, showcasing her strength and resilience in the face of adversity.

Garrick pushed the limits of their father's car, his foot heavy on the accelerator as he navigated the winding roads down the mountain. Time was of the essence, and he skillfully maneuvered, ensuring they reached the hospital as swiftly as possible. Their journey, while marked by urgency, was aided by Eder's proactive action of arranging a police escort ahead of time.

As they approached the city's border, the squad cars awaited them, ready to clear the path and provide a swift and safe passage to the hospital. With the squad cars leading the way, their emergency lights flashing in unison, Garrick and the others followed closely behind, maintaining visual contact, as they raced towards the hospital.

A sense of haste permeated the air as the car screeched to a halt at the hospital's entrance. Maeve's critical condition prompted the medical team to speedily prepare the emergency room for her arrival. A dedicated team of doctors and surgeons stood poised at the entrance, their anxiety evident as they awaited the patient's arrival.

Thanks to Maeve's instructions and Eder's quick actions, the bleeding had been successfully stopped, providing a vital lifeline in the midst of the crisis. The rapid journey down the mountain had allowed them to reach the hospital in under an hour, maximizing their chances of securing the urgent medical care Maeve required.

With an efficient and coordinated effort, Maeve was promptly transferred from the car to the waiting medical team, who wasted no time rushing her into the emergency room. Garrick and Eder, filled with concern and apprehension, were instructed to wait outside as the medical professionals focused on attending to Maeve.

Garrick and Eder paced impatiently around the car. Losing his temper, Garrick kicked the back of the vehicle. "Garrick, calm down, mate. Taking your frustration out on the car isn't going to do anything for her," Eder shouted.

"She's all I have, Eder! If something happened to her, I would lose my mind!" Garrick furiously responded.

"I know it's been hard since your parents passed away, mate. I get it; I really do. I care about Maeve as much as you do, maybe even more, mate. But she needs us right now; we cannot beat ourselves up, not now," Eder said, grabbing onto Garrick.

Garrick pushed Eder away from him. "Fuck off, like hell you care about her!" Garrick yelled.

"This is your fucking problem, mate. You let your anger get out of control; we wouldn't be here right now if you had just stayed in the car. That man would have eventually left the property, we would have gotten the jump on him, and Maeve would have been safe in the car. You need to control yourself, mate, or else the people around you will get hurt. I get it; you're upset. But that's not a reason to act out and risk the safety of everyone around you," Eder stated.

Eder got in Garrick's face as he continued talking. "We don't know for sure if it's Galan who did this, but we can't find out with you raging. We make one false move, and he walks free, whether he is guilty or not. Then Maeve would have ended up in this situation for nothing, and you would have blown your shot with the girl you really love for nothing. Let's do this as a team, mate. Leave Maeve out of this. You and I could take him. I can get Dana to give us something that will prove it was him, and Maeve and I will vouch for you with Aria. We can do this," Eder declared, raising his fist to Garrick. Garrick bumped their fists and calmed down.

"What the fuck do we do now?" Garrick asked.

"For now, we just need to get through this night. I'll let Aria and Dana know Maeve is in the hospital," Eder exclaimed.

Chapter Eighteen

Aria's emotions were in turmoil, a mix of anger, fear, and shock, as she grappled with the sight of Garrick's presence in her backyard. The unexpected intrusion had left her feeling violated and vulnerable. Dana and Malek, understanding the depth of Aria's distress, stepped in, offering comfort, their words aimed at soothing her frayed nerves and providing reassurance. Hans returned to the house and parked on the street.

"When will I have some peace! I just want to be left alone. Why does he follow me everywhere? I'm going to Dad; he will make sure Garrick never sees the light of day again!" Aria fumed.

"Galan tried to warn me earlier, and I got so caught up with other events that I didn't remember to mention it," Dana remarked.

"What? Are you fucking kidding me, Dana?!" Aria screamed.

Feeling Malek's comforting embrace, Aria's tense body gradually relaxed. "Shh, please, love," coaxed Malek.

"You remember when you saw Galan pull me aside for a 'private' conversation, and you accused me of sleeping with him and thinking something was going on between us? That's when Galan told me that he was on his way to the lookout when he saw Garrick sitting outside our house in a car. He even confronted Galan," Dana explained.

"Why didn't he come to me?" Aria asked, annoyed.

"Because you were in tears and surrounded by your 'friends,' and he didn't want to make things worse by bringing it up in front of everyone. So he asked me about it, and I told him I would handle it. And then you went and accused me of that shit, and I never got the chance to," Dana retorted.

"Why was he even by our house?" Aria wondered.

"He told me he was coming by to drop off my phone," Dana exclaimed. "You know, Aria, your 'friends' are the reason these things happen. They bring problems wherever you are. If you weren't so blind and didn't let them manipulate you like they clearly do, we would live much more peaceful lives. If it weren't for them, you wouldn't have had a problem with Galan and would have known about Garrick sooner. Even if I had forgotten, I'm sure he would have told you. Maybe you should think before you keep blindly following them."

"Dana, please! Before anybody says something they regret, let's calm down for a moment, ok?" Malek intervened.

Dana's phone rang, interrupting them. Eder had messaged her, 'Maeve had an accident. We got attacked, and she was struck by a rock thrown through the windshield. She lost a lot of blood and is in the hospital now. I'm here with Garrick."

Dana looked at her phone, her face etched with frustration. "What is it?" Aria asked.

"Here," Dana said as she extended the phone toward Aria. Feeling Aria's reaction, Malek instinctively tightened his embrace.

"Oh, my God!" Aria cried out.

"I'll see if Hans is back yet," Dana stated.

"Do you want me to go with you, love?" Malek asked, looking into her eyes.

"No, I don't want you mixed up in this. Hans will drop you off at the hotel on the way," Aria replied.

"Are you sure, love? I want to be there for you," Malek responded, stroking her hair.

"I know, but my life is crazy, and I like that what we have isn't. I wouldn't risk it for anything in this world," Aria said to him.

Feeling the weight of the moment, Malek tenderly pressed a kiss to Aria's forehead. As the trio settled into the backseat, Aria turned to Hans, conveying the need to prioritize dropping Malek off at the hotel before proceeding to the hospital.

Galan kept adding ice to his bath; the swelling had significantly reduced. During this time, he had watched a lot of Garrick's fights. After a marathon of videos, Galan took a break and pulled up Aria's page, scrolling through to see if he had missed anything about Malek. *There's nothing here; she is clearly hiding him. Is she serious about him? Is that why she isn't showing him off? Or is it because she isn't sure? You didn't taste like you were sure about him. You can't make up your mind; is that it? It must pain you to have to choose and be unsure. I should have told you I would stay for you. Maybe it's my fault. You think I wasn't serious about you, but I promise I am.*

Galan looked up Malek's page. *What is it about you? Do you really deserve her?* Galan was stunned when he saw that Malek had just then checked into the same hotel he was staying at. *You... Are... Here??? Is the ice water messing with my head? No, that's a picture of him holding a room key card at the front desk. Of course, your dad must own this place, Aria. If my guess is correct, you will put him in the best rooms, and the luxury suites are on my floor. Are you with him? I need to know. Maybe we can finish what we started earlier.*

Galan got out of the bath. *Fuck, I can't wear the same thing from earlier. If Aria sees me in this, I will be caught for sure. This is a luxury hotel; I wonder if they have a clothing rental service or a shop on the compound?*

Galan rang the front desk. "Hi, I was wondering if this hotel has a clothing rental service?" Galan asked.

The front desk receptionist responded, "Yes, Sir, we offer designer wear clothing options. Would you like the casual or business options?"

"Can't go wrong with a black suit. I'd like something in size forty, medium," Galan replied.

"Coming right up, Sir. For your convenience, we will send multiple options in your requested size to choose from," answered the receptionist at the front desk.

"Perfect, thank you," Galan said and hung up. *This guy is probably in his room by now. There's no chance of them coming out of there in a hurry. But why come here? Unless... The car incident. There must have been someone in the car, so when I threw the rock, it messed them up. It could also be that she feels unsafe in her house because they caught Garrick there. I hate that you don't feel safe in your own house, Aria. I'm sorry; I'll help you through this; you won't have to worry.*

Hmm, where are you? You wouldn't leave without your little sister. As Galan reflected on the past, a specific memory resurfaced—the night he had taken Dana's phone home with him. At that moment, he had seized the opportunity to open up the phone and discreetly insert a tracking chip, unbeknownst to Dana. Now, armed with his own phone and a GPS application, he accessed the tracking feature to unveil Dana's location.

However, as Galan examined the map displayed on his phone, confusion washed over him. *Where are you headed? Why are you going into the city at this hour? Aria wouldn't let you go alone, and Eder was with Garrick. Does that earlier incident have something to do with this? Wait, there is a hospital a couple of blocks ahead... So, it is about the person in the car. Who was in there? I know both of you were safe in your house, but did you get in the car and chase after me with them? Please don't tell me I hurt you or your sister; that can't be! I mean, it was dark, and I couldn't get a clear vision of who was in there.*

Stop, stop, Galan; you wouldn't hurt them; i couldn't be them. You are not a monster; you wouldn't do that! Keep it together. This Malek guy wouldn't be posting about the hotel if they were in trouble, or would he? Is that who he is? Is he a bigger monster than Garrick? I need to know. I don't like how I felt thinking you might have been hurt. I need to make sure this guy doesn't hurt you, too.

As Galan answered the knock at the door, his thoughts momentarily interrupted, he found himself face to face with an attractive young woman, pushing a rack of clothing. Despite his wet and dripping state, he couldn't help but notice her smile, which hinted at a shared sense of amusement. Politely exchanging greetings, Galan allowed her to enter the room, feeling a tinge of embarrassment about his current attire.

Engaging in polite conversation, Galan found himself drawn to the woman's charm and the natural ease with which they communicated. At that moment, he momentarily forgot his initial purpose of spying on Malek, instead enjoying the lively banter and friendly interaction that unfolded between them.

As they spoke, the woman sought to understand the purpose behind the clothing selection, aiming to assist Galan in choosing an outfit that would suit his needs. With his innate charm, Galan engaged in the conversation effortlessly, allowing himself to be swept up in the enjoyable exchange.

After a few minutes of browsing through the options, the woman skillfully picked out an ensemble that would complement Galan's physique and style: a flared lapel shirt, a stylish blazer, and a pair of sleek black slacks. However, Galan's oversight became apparent when he realized that he hadn't considered the need for shoes, a detail that had momentarily slipped his mind.

Watching his sneakers muddied from his run in the mountain, Galan said apologetically, "I'm so sorry, but I forgot to ask for shoes to complement this look."

"That's not a problem; I'll be right back. The store is just a few floors down," the woman answered.

"I'm Galan, by the way. Sorry, I didn't get your name," said Galan, smiling at her.

"You don't remember my name? I said it when I answered the door," the woman responded flirtingly.

"No, I'm sorry, I don't remember," Galan remarked.

"Ok, I'll tell you, but don't forget it this time," the woman answered. "My name is Nikki."

"Well, Nikki, maybe I can accompany you to the store. I wouldn't want you walking all the way back here," Galan replied.

"Sure, I would appreciate that," Nikki smiled. Walking barefoot alongside the woman, Galan couldn't help but share a laugh about his absent-mindedness, finding a lighthearted moment amidst the unexpected turn of events. Their shared laughter echoed through the hallway as they approached the elevator together, their camaraderie evident.

However, as the elevator doors slid open, Galan's composure wavered upon the sight of Malek stepping out. Determined to maintain his focus, Galan averted his gaze, fixating his attention straight ahead as if intentionally avoiding any direct interaction.

Though their paths intersected in this fleeting moment, Galan chose to keep his distance, aware of the complexities and uncertainties that lay between them.

Chapter Nineteen

*T*hat's him! And he's alone with no bags; did he check in earlier? Or was he just randomly brought here in the heat of the moment?

"Hey, nice suit, man," Malek complimented him.

"Why thank you," Galan responded with a smile. *Chatty, isn't he? Maybe this elevator door will stay open long enough for me to see which room he enters.*

Galan and Nikki entered the elevator. As the doors began to close, Galan noticed Malek had stopped and turned at the first door after the elevator before the closing doors blocked his view. *First room off the elevator, I can find him there. I will need to remember that.*

As the elevator came to a halt two floors down, Galan and Nikki stepped out onto a different level. The hallway unfolded before them, lined with a series of enticing stores and gift shops on either side, each offering a unique array of items. Nikki beckoned Galan to follow her, guiding him with the rack of clothing she pushed along.

Walking together, they navigated the hallway, their steps accompanied by the soft hum of activity emanating from the various shops. The allure of the surroundings was evident, with prestigious brand names and designer wear adorning the shelves, showcasing an array of coveted garments. Galan observed the limited selection, appreciating the high-quality craftsmanship and exquisite designs that filled the store.

With a purposeful stride, Nikki led Galan to the back room, rolling the rack inside. As she disappeared momentarily, attending to the organizational aspects of the store, Galan stood on the cold white tiles, relishing the cool sensation under his bare feet.

"Follow me for the shoes," said Nikki, smiling as she walked past him.

Galan followed eagerly; his softened footsteps were accompanied by the elegant tapping of her shoes ahead of him. "Here are some of the finest shoes anywhere," Nikki informed him, motioning to the line of shoes. Galan looked at the wall of shoes in awe.

"Personally, you can't go wrong with a pair of Chelsea boots," Galan stated, pointing to a black-on-black boot with a suede finish on the top shelf.

"Great choice; let me get the steps so I can reach that for you," answered Nikki.

Standing at six foot two, Galan had a reach of just over eight feet. "No need," he replied, easily reaching the desired footwear.

"Okayyy, maybe you should be in here more often," Nikki replied, looking at him.

"I'm tempted to be," Galan flirted.

Nikki looked at him and smirked. She watched Galan as he sat down and put on the shoes.

"So, Mister, when will you make it up to me for forgetting my name?" Nikki teased, approaching with her arms folded and smiling.

"I'm sure we could discuss it over a drink," Galan replied as he stood up.

"I don't get off until tomorrow, but I don't think I want to wait that long," Nikki responded, getting dangerously close to him.

No, this went too far. Reel it back, Galan.

"I know we have a nice little flirt going on right now, but I am interested in someone, and I don't think it fair to you if I led you on," Galan explained.

"I see, but I'm not the type of girl who wants to be owned. My life is inside the walls of this hotel, so if you are leaving this place behind, I don't mind being a memory," Nikki countered.

"I don't have it in me to do that. I believe in devoting oneself to that person in all aspects. I think you deserve to be more than just a fleeting memory. If I had come here one day earlier, I'd have obliged," Galan told her calmly.

"Whoever she is, I'm a little bit jealous. Enjoy your stay, Sir," Nikki remarked.

Galan felt a rush course through his body. Calling him 'Sir' had set off his libido. The look on Galan's face morphed from calm and happy one minute to lustful the next. Nikki felt a chill from the way he looked at her. She gulped and unfolded her arms. She walked closer to him and placed her hand on his bicep, "Sir…."

Nikki barely got the word out. Leaning over her, their lips met. Nikki was stunned for a moment. Having not expected his advances, she pulled away from his lips for a second and smiled with her eyes closed. Draping her arms around his neck, Nikki pulled him down harder. Galan lifted her, holding her tightly. Nikki climbed higher, looking down as she pulled his hair and slid her tongue into his mouth.

Galan, stop! Stop; this isn't what Aria would want. You are blowing your chances with her. Not like this; this isn't you. You're a nice guy; you're loyal, and you wouldn't do this. Control yourself!

Galan sucked on her neck. "What happened to being devoted to someone completely," Nikki teased.

"She's not mine yet. I think a good memory of a time before that devotion would be nice, don't you?" Galan murmured.

Footsteps approaching alerted them to the presence of others. Galan quickly slipped into a dressing room, still holding Nikki in his arms. Another member of staff had entered to get some articles of clothing. Hidden behind only a curtain, Nikki giggled in the dressing room. Galan covered her mouth to keep them from being caught. Slowly lowering his hand from her lips, he kissed her gently.

"I don't think I can keep doing this," Galan whispered, "I don't want your boss to wonder where you disappeared to. The things I'd do to you, I need a little more room and time than what we have right now." He gently put her back on her feet. Tucking a loose strand of hair behind her ear, he leaned in and kissed her cheek. Galan looked deep into her eyes and said, "I still need to make it up to you for forgetting your name."

Brushing his thumb over her lips, Galan smiled and walked away, leaving her in the dressing room. Taking a moment to compose herself, Nikki rushed outside to find him. However, the store was empty, apart from the other staff members walking around.

Galan re-entered the elevator and returned to his floor. He looked at the door of the first room after stepping off the elevator. He could hear someone moving around inside. *Good, he is still here.*

Galan swiped his card and entered his room. Picking up the phone, he called the front desk again. "Hi, could you send up another suit for me, shoes included this time, sized to fit someone who is five foot seven, medium-build? White shirt, black blazer, include a tie," Galan instructed.

"Coming right up, Mr. Rain," said the receptionist.

"Can you put it in a gift box with a card, please?" Galan asked.

"Yes, we can. Someone will bring that up shortly," the receptionist replied.

"Wonderful, you can leave it at the door, thank you," Galan replied before hanging up.

As Galan opened the door in response to the knock, he discovered an exquisite dark blue box adorned with shimmering gold sequins, elegantly wrapped in a golden ribbon. Attached to it was a blank card awaiting his attention. Intrigued, Galan brought the package into his room, feeling a sense of curiosity and anticipation.

Taking hold of a pen, Galan carefully inscribed a note on the card, his words reflecting a mixture of contemplation and intention. Once satisfied with his message, he ventured outside, cradling the package in his hands. Purposefully, he made his way to Malek's door, positioning the gift at its foot. With a gentle knock, he sought to alert Malek to the unexpected delivery. Retracing his steps, Galan returned to the confines of his own room.

Malek heard the knock at the door and curiously walked over. "Yes?" he called out in his deep Arabic accent. When he heard no answer to his call, Malek opened the door. "Hello?" he asked again, looking around, confused. Stepping outside, his foot tapped the box on the floor. He looked at the box curiously before scanning the halls left and right to see if the person who had left the package was still around. He hesitantly picked up the box and read the card, 'Thanks for the compliment. Hope this gets you some, too. From your neighbor two doors down. Cheers.'

Galan had returned to his room and was adjusting his clothes after his encounter with Nikki when Malek knocked on his door.

Not expecting any visitors, Galan walked over curiously to the door and opened it. "Hey, I see you got my gift," Galan stated upon seeing Malek.

"Hi, I'm sorry to bother you, but I can't accept this gift," Malek replied.

"Did you not like it?" Galan inquired.

"No, it's not that. It's a beautiful suit, but this is not something I can afford for myself, so I cannot accept it as a gift," Malek answered apologetically.

Who is this guy? That's a seven-thousand-dollar suit.

"Are you sure I can't convince you to reconsider?" Galan asked.

"I can't take this from you. I can't wear something like this, knowing I have a family to provide for back home. I'm sure my mama would love to see me in something like this, but I couldn't, with a clear conscience, walk around in it knowing that if I did have the money to buy it, I would have preferred to use it to help others," Malek responded.

Fuck, even I'm in awe of this guy. Could he be for real? No chance someone like this exists. Why would he be with you then? I need to know if this is just a front.

"I think kindness is something that's rare in the world now. You saw me earlier and said, 'Nice suit,' when most people would have made fun of the fact that I was not wearing any shoes. It took nothing to be kind to me, the same way it takes nothing away from me to return that kindness. If it's not something you would wear often, then maybe save it for a special day?" Galan suggested.

"I don't know. This seems to be too much," Malek said hesitantly, looking at the box.

"Tell you what, if you agree to take this, I'll write you a cheque for your mom. Not a crazy amount, but enough to take care of her comfortably for the rest of your life," offered Galan.

"Why would you do that for me?" Malek asked, shocked by his offer.

"Because kind-hearted people always want to help. They make the world a better place, or at the very least, they brighten the lives of the people around them. The opportunity to be part of something like that is worth more than any figure I can write on a cheque," Galan smiled.

Malek sighed, giving heavy consideration to Galan's offer. "Thank you, but I would have to decline," Malek politely refused.

Interesting.

"I work hard, and I study harder to make my parents proud, and part of that is that I earned all the things I have acquired. It's how my father raised me and what my mama fell in love with, so that's the son I strive to be. I think money would change who I am, and I like the person I am right now. I would like to make changes and help, but I want to do it on my own merit," Malek answered as he handed the box to Galan.

Galan couldn't help but smile as he accepted the gift back. "It was nice meeting you, um—" Malek said.

"Galan, Galan Rain," answered Galan.

"Malek Zakaria," replied Malek, slowly stepping back and walking back to his room.

"Malek! Are you busy?" Galan called out after him.

"Not at the moment," Malek responded.

"I don't suppose you drink?" Galan asked.

"I don't consume alcohol," Malek exclaimed.

"I figured as much. How about coffee?" Galan inquired.

"I could go for a cup of coffee; it might be a long night for me," Malek stated.

"Great, you're buying then," Galan chuckled.

"Sure, let me get my wallet," Malek laughed.

This guy is something else. But everyone has a past; everyone is hiding a darkness inside. As perfect as you are on the surface, I need to see deeper because if you are a threat to Aria, I cannot allow you to get any closer. Galan tossed the gift box on the bed and stepped outside, closing the door. Malek went into his room and picked up his wallet, phone, and flannel shirt before entering the elevator with Galan.

Chapter Twenty

Aria and Dana rushed to the hospital, their faces marked with deep concern. As they neared the main entrance, they spotted Garrick and Eder anxiously waiting outside. Dana's eyes lit up with relief as she hurried into Eder's open arms, finding comfort and solace in his embrace. Aria's attention was fixed on Eder, her worry evident as she addressed him, "How is she?"

"We don't know yet; they won't allow us inside," Garrick replied in his stead.

"You! I don't want to hear another word out of your mouth, Garrick! The police are on their way, and I'm going to make sure you get put where you belong," Aria screamed.

"What the fuck were you doing snooping around our house, you sick fuck?" Dana pressed.

Eder gently released Dana from his embrace, "Listen, if it wasn't for Garrick, you both could have been the ones that ended up in the hospital instead. Please go easy on him, Aria."

"What does that mean?" Dana inquired.

"I don't want to hear a word out of his mouth, Eder," Aria belted.

"Then allow me to explain. Please, just hear me out. Maeve would have asked the same," Eder implored.

Aria's frustration bubbled up like a tempest, causing her to clench her arms tightly across her chest as if trying to contain the whirlwind of emotions within her. With an exasperated scoff, the weight of worry and impatience echoed in every fiber of her being. Sensing the crackling tension in the air, Garrick, ever perceptive, silently excused himself, turning on his heels and retreating to the car. With an empathetic understanding of Aria's emotional mix, Eder pressed on, determined to bridge the gap between them.

"Garrick told me that someone sketchy was creeping around the neighborhood at night, especially around your house. When he told Maeve and I, we came up there to make sure that creep didn't return or at least catch him in the act," Eder explained.

"You mean Galan, don't you?" Aria stated.

"Y… Yes. Wait, you knew he was snooping around your house?" Eder asked.

"Galan was not snooping; he was trying to return my phone after I left it at the café. He drove up here the night we had finalized the deal with him. What bullshit story did that lying asshole tell you?" Dana scolded.

"That's all he said. He just said he saw Galan here," Eder explained.

"Bullshit, Garrick had no right to be there in the first place. He is the reason I came here because everywhere he followed me, disaster and pain followed as well. He had no right to be there; end of the discussion," Aria ranted.

"I understand, but it's a good thing he was. While there, he found someone hiding in the backyard. When we tried to capture him, the stranger ran off, and we lost him. It's because of Galan that Maeve got hurt. It came to blows once we cornered him, and he threw a rock, smashing the front of the car and injuring Maeve," Eder explained.

"That's bullshit; Galan isn't here anymore. He had a flight out of the country that he should have boarded by now. The only person we saw was Garrick, and given his track record, I wouldn't be surprised if he did this to Maeve. I have seen that side of him, so I know what he is capable of," Dana raged.

"D, come on, he saved my ass back there too. We are not claiming it's Galan. The person had his face covered, and Garrick said he spoke German the one time he spoke. But if I'm being honest, I think it's Galan, too. Unfortunately, we have no proof of it. All I'm asking is that you let us handle this if Galan shows his face again. We only want to confirm our suspicions. Just give us a chance to get some sort of proof to prove we were right," Eder begged.

"Are you kidding me? After your earlier accusations, you really want to go down this road again, Eder?" Dana asked, a hint of annoyance creeping into her voice.

"We are not accusing him; we just need to be sure. On behalf of Maeve and myself, I'm asking you to believe that Garrick was only trying to protect you both. Please, he saved my life tonight; I owe him at least that much. That guy could have harmed you both if it wasn't for Garrick. And I don't know what I would do if I lost you, D," Eder declared with a resolute tone, firmly gripping Dana's hand.

Aria's frustration and disappointment formed a potent mixture, swirling and bubbling at the surface of her emotions. She drew in a deep breath, attempting to steady herself, but her trembling head betrayed the intensity of her inner turmoil. With a tinge of raw disgust etched across her expression, she directed her gaze towards Garrick, "I stand by my original statement. I don't want to hear anything he has to say. And he had no right to be there either. But for Maeve's sake, let's put it aside for tonight only. I don't want to see Garrick again after this is over," Aria stated.

"Garrick will be with me. I'll make sure he behaves. He is trying to turn over a new leaf, but let's make sure this Galan guy is dealt with first. I have a hunch he won't leave yet and will show up again. We can put this to rest, then. If we are wrong about this, Garrick and I will be the first to apologize to him. And you will never see Garrick again; he will stay gone," Eder agreed.

As Eder finished his compelling explanation, he turned towards Garrick, acutely aware of the gravity of the situation. Their eyes locked in a moment of profound connection, and Eder could sense Garrick's readiness to cooperate, like a silent pact forged between them. With a shared understanding that transcended words, Garrick nodded affirmatively, his gesture signaling a resolute agreement to Eder's proposed terms.

"Fine, seems like a win either way," Aria answered.

Dana pulled Aria aside. "We have just been through this. Do you really think Galan would be involved?" Dana asked seriously.

Ugh, why is everyone going on and on about Galan? Everywhere I turn, I hear that name. Why is everyone but me obsessed with this guy? He's nothing special; get over it! I swear to God, if someone mentions that name again, I will lose it. He was a convenient 'Hi, bye,' but that's it.

"Honestly, D, I don't really care to hear Galan's name anymore. Ever since we met him, there has been so much negativity in our lives coming from all directions. I'm not saying he's a bad person, but I would be content if we never saw him again," Aria replied.

"Where were you when Malek arrived at the café?" Dana suddenly inquired.

"What? What do you mean?" Aria felt her nerves tangle in a web of uncertainty. Her heart raced, and her palms grew clammy, unsure of what to say or how to react.

"I know you, Ari, better than anyone. I have watched you my whole life. I looked up to you. I know you were with Galan when I called. Please don't lie to me like I am an idiot," Dana remarked. Eder's gaze remained fixed on Garrick, his arms folded in a stance that mirrored Aria's earlier display of frustration. The charged silence seemed to stretch, and with each determined stride, he closed the distance between them. In this pivotal moment, Eder couldn't help but catch snippets of Dana's nearby voice, her urgency seeping into his consciousness. As

Dana's voice grew louder, Eder's senses sharpened, absorbing every word, every nuance.

"Could you say that a little louder? I don't think the whole hospital heard you," Aria snapped.

"I don't care what you do, Ari. I am not perfect, either. I make mistakes daily, and you are always there for me to help me through them. But I really like Malek. I haven't seen you this happy in all my years knowing you. Please, be good to him; he is one of the good ones. And as for Galan, he has done nothing but worship the ground you walk on. I see the way he looks at you; I'm not blind. But he doesn't deserve to be hurt, either. Be honest with him. Honestly, I would rather have him around us than all of your friends combined. I know he may not be your type, but that doesn't mean you can dismiss him as a person. Ordinary people cannot do what he did, which says a lot about him. Or at least enough to give him the benefit of the doubt," Dana stated.

My baby sister isn't such a baby anymore. I know in a world of uncertainty that if there was one person who would always want the best for me, it would be you, D.

Despite the prevailing tension and uncertainty, a flicker of warmth and relief crossed Aria's face. Her frustration momentarily subsided, making room for a genuine smile to spread across her lips. With a renewed sense of hope, she embraced Dana tightly, "Thanks, D."

Closing the distance between them, Eder approached Garrick with a sense of urgency, as if every second counted. Leaning in closer, he whispered softly, "Listen, mate, we have a problem, but I can't tell you here." Garrick's gaze shifted from him to Aria, a flicker of curiosity and concern crossing his eyes.

With Eder and Garrick locked in their silent exchange, Dana approached with cautious steps, "Aria is gonna go inside and see if she can see Maeve. We will let you guys know as soon as we hear something." Eder leaned over and kissed Dana on the cheek before Aria and Dana proceeded inside.

"Ok, look, I overheard Dana saying that Galan and Aria might have hooked up," Eder stated.

As Eder struggled to get the words out, his attempt to communicate was abruptly interrupted as Garrick exploded into a full-blown tantrum. "Hey! Focus, mate. This is our chance. We can kill two birds with one stone here. Not only do we have something against Galan, but we also finally have something we can use to eliminate Malek from the picture. If that news gets out, it could break what they have. Malek will be out of the picture, and it won't be long until Galan is, too. Aria could be yours again. You just need to keep yourself in check and let the chips fall where they may. Be patient, mate," Eder announced with a measured tone.

"I'll kill him," Garrick's frustration lingered, and he muttered under his breath, his words barely audible.

"I'll help you hide the body, but all in good time, mate. We can make this work for us," Eder reached out, and the two of them bumped fists. "Right now, let's hope Maeve gets better. This, at least, we can't let go unanswered."

EYLA WHITLOCK

AGE: 25

SIGN: AQUARIUS

FUN FACT: "I BAN PEOPLE FROM MY BOOKSTORE IF I SEE THEM 'DOG EAR' THE CORNER OF BOOK PAGES."

Chapter
Twenty-one

Galan and Malek found themselves perched on the balcony of the hotel's rooftop café, their eyes fixated on the breathtaking cityscape stretching before them. Galan couldn't help but be drawn to Malek's captivating presence. There was an air of confidence about him, an aura that effortlessly attracted attention.

As they sat there, girls approached Malek, charmed by his magnetic personality. But despite the attention, Malek handled each encounter with grace and finesse. He politely declined their advances, leaving them captivated even in their moment of rejection. His ability to navigate social interactions with ease was nothing short of impressive, and it left a lasting impression on both Galan and those who sought his company. "This happens a lot?" Galan questioned.

"At first, when I moved out here with my mom and younger brother, but after a while, they stopped trying," Malek answered.

"Where did you live before?" asked Galan.

"My mother grew up in Sudan, and my father was from Egypt, but he grew up in America. He met my mother while visiting and volunteering in Sudan. He fell head over heels in love and asked her to return to America with him. When I was twelve, my father passed away while volunteering to build schools in impoverished countries. He fell off a ladder and hit his head on an exposed metal beam on his way down. He bled out before anyone could find his body," Malek lamented.

"Oh man, I'm sorry to hear that," Galan replied.

"Thank you. Now that it's just me, my mom, and my brother, I took up the responsibility to provide for them and ensure my brother has a good life. College and all that," Malek continued.

Is that his angle? Is he with you for the money? To support his family? I mean, that's noble and all, but someone should want you for you, Aria, not your money. But he's under my skin. If he wanted money, he would have accepted it when I offered. Or did I not offer enough? Tossing back the small fish and waiting for the big one? If he got a hold of your dad's money, life would basically be free for him; nothing he could ever want would be out of his reach.

But still, he doesn't seem like that type of guy. I see how he talks, the pain behind those words; you don't fake that kind of love. Maybe I'm getting too soft; it's possible he doesn't have a mother or brother he cares about and just practiced this speech over and over. I need to be on my 'A' game for you, Aria. I underestimated things before, but I will not anymore. I can't focus on you until I clear the path ahead; then, you can run into my arms forever.

"Not to pry, Malek, but can I ask you something? Why didn't you take the money earlier when I offered it? It would have been enough to get your brother a college education, and your mom would live comfortably, at least," Galan asked.

Malek smiled and replied, "My father taught me something when I was a child. I had a toy that was sold out, and the neighbors weren't able to afford it. He told me one day that it was my purpose in life to bring joy to people and help those I could in any way I could and that it was my duty. He told me that he could not accept a gift in good conscience, knowing it could go to someone who needed it more. Accepting your generous gifts would be selfish. That money could be better utilized by those who need it. I can work hard because I was blessed in my life to be able to do that for myself; others aren't as fortunate, and many didn't have the resources and opportunities I had growing up."

"And here I am; my journey was all about making it for myself, my goal, my dreams," Galan replied.

"Like I said earlier, money might change people, and I wouldn't want to lose the gifts my father left me with for such selfish reasons. This is how I want to carry on his legacy," Malek responded.

"So, tell me, what would your dad do if he saw you in this fancy hotel, sipping coffee by the poolside," Galan asked, chuckling.

"He would be happy, not about the hotel but because I was here. He would sit me down and lecture me for being in a fancy hotel and tell me all the things I could have done with the money it would cost to be here," Malek answered.

"So, what would he be happy about?" Galan asked curiously.

"That I have found someone who sets my soul on fire. I'm here because of love," Malek replied with a smile.

"What is love?" Galan exclaimed.

"Baby, don't hurt me...," Malek finished, chuckling.

Fuck, he passed the vibe check test. Damn, nobody ever gave the correct response for that when it mattered. But this guy...

The sound of laughter echoed through the night as Galan and Malek shared a genuine moment of joy. Their infectious laughter seemed to blend harmoniously with the bustling city sounds, creating a symphony of happiness. With cups of coffee held in their hands, they raised them in a toast, celebrating the camaraderie and the simple pleasure of being together.

"The only acceptable response to that question," Galan stated.

"Really though, I am here to support my girlfriend. I worked overtime for almost a year to be able to come to visit her. Once I had the money to travel, I waited for the right moment. When she told me she was celebrating something big, I figured this was the time to surprise her," Malek explained.

"So, she didn't know you would be coming here?" Galan asked. *Is that why she was with me? She didn't expect you? No, that can't be right; she had asked Dana if he was already there at the café, so she must have known.*

"I was trying to surprise her, but I couldn't get in to see her without her approval. They are pretty strict where she lives about who comes and goes. I spoke to her sister to get me permission, but I guess she figured it out," Malek replied.

"So, how did you end up here? I guess you got in late and checked in here instead of going to her?" Galan inquired innocently.

"No, actually, I saw her today. I came here afterward; my mother would have my head if she knew I had spent the night with a woman outside of marriage. She raised me better than that," Malek replied.

Smart. He's not lying, but he's not giving away any vital information, only vague answers. I mean, of course, he wouldn't tell a stranger, but it's still amazing how well he dances around my questions.

"I'm glad to hear that you found your life's love. Me? I've never had it when it was real. I worshiped the ones I dated before, and it did nothing but cause me pain. I gave them everything I had to offer, and in the end, it felt like what I was worth was absolutely nothing. I'm careful of who I let in now; pain like that changes you. The darkness it puts you in is scary. Not because it's dark but because you start to find comfort in the darkness. It's not a feeling I wish on anyone," Galan explained.

"I'm sorry you had such bad experiences. I don't think I can relate, but I can give you some advice my father would have given me. People deserve better from you; even if you don't believe they deserve it, it's your duty to be the best version of yourself for them. That is what love should be. The willingness to wear your wounds with a smile and love them as though you are not wounded," Malek advised as he placed a reassuring hand on Galan's shoulder.

As Galan's thoughts swirled in his mind, he couldn't help but ponder the profound advice bestowed upon him by Malek. The words resonated deeply, stirring a sense of purpose and determination within him. A smile slowly spread across his face as if a light had been switched on inside him, illuminating his features with newfound clarity.

The warmth of the moment extended beyond the coffee in his hands; it was a warmth that emanated from the genuine appreciation he felt toward Malek's guidance. In Malek's words, Galan found not just encouragement but also a belief in his own potential. "I would have loved to meet your father; he sounds like an amazing person," said Galan.

"And what of your family, Galan?" Malek asked.

"My family? I was kicked out of my house at six because my parents were alcoholics. For fun, my mother would tell me she didn't love me and that I was no longer a part of her family when she was intoxicated. She made me sign a 'contract' stating that I wasn't her son anymore. I was taken in by the neighbors, but that's a whole different story. I don't think I can talk about that right now," Galan answered shakily. "I grew up without knowing if anyone loved me or even wanted me. Anytime I got the slightest bit of attention I was so deprived of, I clung to it hard. And I got hurt because I overestimated my value in people's lives, believing I was actually worthy of their time and attention."

BROKEN TOYS

As Galan poured out his painful experiences, Malek sat there, his eyes widening in shock. The weight of Galan's words crashed over him like a relentless wave, leaving him speechless and struggling to comprehend the depth of the pain his newfound friend had endured. The raw honesty of Galan's narrative tugged at Malek's heartstrings, evoking an overwhelming mix of empathy and sorrow.

Tears welled up in Malek's eyes as he grappled with the unimaginable hardships Galan had faced. In stark contrast, Galan seemed surprisingly nonchalant as he recounted his story, as if he had become detached from the emotions surrounding his own experiences. Malek couldn't help but admire Galan's strength despite the heavy burden he carried within. It was evident that Galan had developed a resilient facade, perhaps to protect himself from the pain or to cope with the scars of his past.

"Hey, let's not sour the night with that stuff; here's to new beginnings," Galan declared with a smile.

"Can I ask you something, Galan?" Malek asked.

"Sure, what's up?" Galan replied.

"Why do you still smile even after such things happened to you?" Malek inquired.

The weight of the question hung in the air as Galan sat in silence, contemplating his response. "I guess I'm just a hopeless romantic. Believing that out there is someone sent here for me, and one day, I will find them. A soulmate, a best friend, a wife. The small chance of finding love is enough for me to cling to a better tomorrow," Galan responded with a smile.

"I think you will find it one day; you seem kind and might even be the strongest person I know. I don't know of anyone who could endure such pain and still manage to smile, not even my late father. I think he would have been in awe of you, as I am, Galan," Malek stated.

For a fleeting moment, a smile graced Galan's face, a glimmer of something hidden within his gaze as he stared out into the night sky. With a sense of finality, he emptied his cup of coffee, savoring the last drop as he stood up. "It's been a pleasure meeting you, Malek. I wish you the best; I truly do," Galan finally broke the silence. His voice carried a tone of sincerity and appreciation as he spoke. As he extended his hand towards Malek, who was touched by Galan's words and the warmth in his eyes, he rose from his seat, meeting Galan's gesture with a firm, heartfelt handshake.

"Likewise," Malek answered, looking at him.

I don't think he would hurt you, Aria, and I really care about you. I will not stand in the way of this love. I want you to be happy, even if it isn't with me. It was fun knowing you. For a shining moment, Aria, my life had some meaning. Thank you for reminding me that happiness still exists.

Galan made his way up to his room, his mind still preoccupied with the encounter from earlier. A curious sight caught his eye as he opened the door— a card lying on the floor. Picking it up, he found a phone number inscribed on it, accompanied by a short but intriguing note that read, 'Thanks for the memories. I get off at three A.M tomorrow morning if you still want to make it up to me.' Galan smiled. *I think it's time I moved on. Let her be happy with Malek. I can chase my own happiness.*

BROKEN TOYS

Sitting in his room contemplating his next move, Galan decided to take the plunge and compose a text message to the number written on the card. After a few moments of contemplation, he began typing, 'I'm not sure how I can make it up to you. Stop by when your shift ends, and I'm sure we can work it out.' With a sense of anticipation and a flicker of hope, Galan hit the send button.

Feeling a tumultuous mix of emotions, Galan found himself perched on the edge of the bed, his mind consumed by thoughts of Aria. The profound weight of their connection lingered like a haunting melody playing on repeat. Seeking a distraction, he reached for his phone. He absentmindedly opened the security app to a flood of live camera feeds from Grounded Coffee House. For a moment, he hesitated, torn between curiosity and desire. But something had changed within Galan. He realized that relying on the surveillance feed was becoming a crutch, a way to hold on to the past instead of embracing the present. With newfound resolve, he took a deep breath and tapped the 'Disconnect' button, severing his connection to Aria as he embraced the idea of Malek making her happy as he chased his own.

This is behind me now. New beginnings are ahead. The only way to be the man she deserves is to let the right person love her.

Feeling a profound need for solace and a change of perspective, Galan gently tossed his phone onto the bed and wandered out onto the balcony. The bustling city below greeted him with its myriad of lights, an electrifying display of life unfolding beneath the night's embrace. He inhaled deeply, taking in the energy that surrounded him, but deep down, he craved a moment of stillness, a connection with nature.

His eyes were drawn to the right, where a majestic mountain stood tall and imposing in the distance. Its peak adorned with twinkling lights, the mountain seemed to hold a mystique that transcended the urban landscape. At that moment, Galan found himself transported, imagining himself standing atop the mountain's lookout point.

In his mind's eye, he saw the world from that elevated perspective, gazing out at the vastness of Salt Pine Acres. The tranquility and serenity of the place washed over him like a gentle breeze that whispered of untamed beauty and untapped peace. He envisioned lush greenery embracing the mountainside, a sanctuary for weary souls seeking respite.

Why is it always me? Why do I always have to step aside to let them be happy? Why can't they pick me? Why can't I be their choice?

Emotions surged within Galan, a tumultuous wave crashing against the shores of his heart, threatening to engulf him entirely. The weight of his feelings became almost unbearable, and as tears welled up in his eyes, he felt the raw vulnerability taking hold of him. Clinging to the balcony rails with a grip so tight his knuckles turned white, he fought fiercely to contain the flood of emotions within.

Droplets of tears cascaded down his cheeks, each one carrying a story of its own, tracing a silent path of vulnerability. At that moment, he allowed himself to be fully human, to embrace the intensity of his emotions without judgment or restraint. The tears became a poignant reminder of his capacity to love and feel deeply.

With a shaky inhale, he attempted to steady himself, but the tremor in his body remained, a physical manifestation of the storm raging within. His shoulders quivered with each deep sniffle, and it felt as though the weight of the world was bearing down on him.

Amidst this tempest of emotions, however, Galan found a flicker of solace within his heart. Something shifted within him as he raised his gaze to the majestic mountain in the distance. The mountain stood tall and steadfast, a symbol of resilience and strength but also a reminder of the vastness of the world beyond his immediate turmoil.

At that moment, a small smile slowly formed on his face.

Take some comfort in the fact that you will be the reason she is happy, Galan.

Chapter Twenty-two

Suddenly, Galan heard a sound coming from the room. Startled by the unfamiliar sound, Galan's heart skipped a beat, and he quickly turned around, retracing his steps back into the room. The ringtone persisted, growing louder as he moved closer to the corner near the balcony. He cautiously approached the wicker basket where he had casually tossed his clothes.

The vibrating sound became more pronounced, emanating from within the basket. Galan's curiosity heightened as he cautiously reached in and pulled out his jeans. As he rummaged through the pockets, a realization suddenly struck him like a lightning bolt. His hand froze mid-air, gripping something unexpected buried within the depths of his pocket.

At that moment, Galan's mind raced.

Oh, fuck! Garrick's phone. He still has a picture of me in Aria's backyard. Is he stupid enough to leave his phone without a password? Maybe I can figure this out. He is obsessed with Aria; maybe that's his password. Let's try '2742.' No, wait... What if it has one of those apps that takes a picture and tags your location when you try to access it? I can't take chances; I need to get rid of the phone. That picture is the only proof they have. So long as I can keep that from them, I'm good.

Garrick found a temporary seat on the car's hood, engaging in a conversation with Eder just outside the hospital, "I don't need the phone. That son of a bitch must have slipped it off me at some point. But all that stuff is backed up to my account. I can always pull that picture later with the time and location. I just need to get to a laptop; we can give it to Anthony so he can work his techy magic and enhance the picture for us."

Eder was struck by a thought, "Mate, how much of his face was showing?"

Garrick thought about it before replying, "Maybe just his eyes and above? Why? Does it matter?"

"It might. I socked Galan pretty hard earlier; if the bruise from earlier is showing, that can be something else we use to identify him by. Also, doesn't he have grey eyes? That's not common in this town," Eder surmised.

"That's perfect! How he was positioned with his back against the wall left him exposing the left side of his face as he peeked around the side of the gazebo wall," Garrick stated as he fist-bumped Eder.

Aria and Dana stood shoulder to shoulder, their eyes unwavering as they peered into the operating theater through the window. Inside, Maeve's life hung in the balance as her colleagues and seasoned medical professionals labored diligently to remove the shards of glass embedded in her face, neck, and shoulder. The procedure was meticulous and time-consuming, a delicate dance of skill and precision as they painstakingly extracted almost one cup's worth of glass fragments.

As the surgery reached its conclusion, the transformation in Maeve's appearance was stark. Her once unblemished features were now covered in stitches and bandages, a testament to the extensive work that had been undertaken to repair the damage. The physical toll was evident, a haunting reminder of the gravity of the situation.

Time crawled slowly in the waiting room as hours passed like an eternity. Aria's heart ached to be by Maeve's side, offering support during this trying time. With bated breath, she received the long-awaited permission to enter Maeve's room, where her friend fought a battle not only against physical wounds but also the emotional aftermath of the traumatic event.

Dana, ever the steadfast friend, made the difficult choice to remain in the waiting area. As she waited, she took out her phone and composed a text message to Eder. Dana informed him that Maeve had successfully undergone the surgery and had been transferred to a private room, and visitors were now allowed.

Aria spoke softly as she settled beside her friend. She gently took hold of Maeve's hand, offering a warm and reassuring squeeze, "How are you feeling, sweetie?"

Maeve groaned and shook her head in disappointment, feeling frustrated with her current situation, "I'm hardly in any pain. I'm just pissed that this happened. These scars won't fully heal, so I'll need surgery to cover the wounds properly."

"Typical Maeve could have died but is instead worried about how pretty she would look after the fact," Aria chuckled, stroking Maeve's hand.

"I hate this, Ari," Maeve whined.

"What were you thinking? What were the three of you doing there in the first place?" Aria questioned.

"Are you blaming me for this?" Maeve responded.

"Don't do that. I'm not Bodhi, and I'm not Eyla. Don't play the victim with me. Why were you with Eder and Garrick, and what were you guys doing? If you cannot give me a straight answer, I will walk out of here. I came to make sure you were ok, and now I know you are. So, do not insult my time," Aria responded sharply.

Feeling shaken by Aria's demeanor, Maeve took a deep gulp, gathering her thoughts as she contemplated her next words. "We were trying to catch Galan creeping—" Before Maeve could continue, the room was abruptly filled with the rush of Garrick and Eder entering, their urgency evident in their expressions. Dana followed closely behind them; her presence added to the sudden flurry of activity. The trio's arrival interrupted the conversation, shifting the focus and dynamics of the room.

"Finish what you were saying, Maeve," Aria's insistence brought an immediate shift in the room's atmosphere, causing tension to fill the air. The discomfort was palpable for both Garrick and Eder, who found themselves at the receiving end of Aria's seriousness. This change in her demeanor unsettled them, as they had grown accustomed to her more lighthearted nature. Aria's direct and serious approach to addressing them created a sense of unease. "And if your story varies from what Garrick and Eder told us, this friendship may end right here and now," Aria stated nonchalantly.

As Aria continued to speak, Eder and Garrick exchanged subtle glances, their eyes briefly meeting in a silent acknowledgment of the tension in the room. Meanwhile, Dana stood nearby, her arms folded across her chest, attentively observing the interaction between Aria and Maeve.

"Aria, why are you behaving this way?" Maeve asked, shaking.

"Do not dodge the question. What I asked is very straightforward. I will not ask you again, Maeve. My main concern was your safety; now that you are safe, you owe me an explanation. I know that's your dad's car out there; he used to take us for long drives all the time in it. Eder's car isn't outside, which means all three of you were together. Now speak up, or I will walk out of here and leave this friendship behind me," Aria claimed.

Aria maintained a calm demeanor, her gaze shifting from one person to the next as she spoke. Her measured tone conveyed a sense of composure, commanding the room unrivaled.

"You wouldn't believe me anyway. I lied about Galan and Dana earlier, so you have no reason to believe me now, and that's my fault. It makes no sense to give you an answer when your mind is already made up. I'm sorry I lied about Galan. I just sense that he is trouble. Maybe not right now, but he is, and it's why we were at your house. I had my suspicions, separate from Eder and Garrick. They told me someone was stalking you. I wanted to believe it was Galan, and if we got proof that it was him, I wanted to be the one who confirmed it for you because I proved myself unworthy before. After Eder and I made mistakes and knowing you would never hear Garrick out, we decided to do it on our own. We'd hoped to earn your forgiveness, but my motives were selfish. I wasn't doing this for you; it was really for me," Maeve explained.

Aria let go of Maeve's hand; she stood up slowly, walked to Dana, and turned to face the others. "Alright," Aria answered.

"Alright? What does that mean? Alright?" Maeve asked.

"I asked for the truth, and I got it. I knew this was about nobody else but yourself, but you did shock me. I never expected you to cut your bullshit. I am not happy about any of this; I firmly believe I should have been told about this before anything else. The fact is, it's my life and my sister's. Had something happened to Dana or me because this was kept from us, this would be an entirely different story. You owe us an apology, but not now. I don't want some pitiful apology for being in the wrong. We'll be willing to hear you out when you understand what you did was beyond stupid. And this obsession everyone seems to have about Galan fucking Rain has to end," Aria insisted.

"Hold up, Aria. I have something further to say about that," Eder interjected.

"I am disappointed, Eder. I expected better from you. Garrick is an asshole that can't help it. Maeve is manipulative and will say whatever she needs to. But you, I expected better from you. Of all the people in our circle, you have been the most level-headed, and seeing you come to blows was a shock," Aria exclaimed.

"Exactly, isn't that weird?" Eder asked. Everyone stood still and silent. "Listen, I am not obsessed with this guy, but you have to admit that problems follow whenever his name is mentioned. Think about how many people have met you and Dana. Now, tell me, has anyone gotten under your skin like him? How often have Maeve, Eyla, and Bodhi been so cautious of someone? When have I ever been in beef with anyone? I deal with social media trolls every day. I get hated on daily, and it doesn't bother me. But something about that guy doesn't sit well with any of us.

"The thing is, you guys didn't hear what he said to me. Galan started talking about Dana and me being sexually active. He doesn't know me, and we had no beef prior to this, right? But off the top of his head, he was ready to accuse me of having sex with an underage girl. When he encountered Garrick outside your house, he was aggressive then, too. Think back to the café when Garrick made trouble and the way he was back then. He approached us all the same, and he smiled when I struck him. Something about him is sketchy, and no one standing in this room can deny it," Eder ranted. "I am not accusing him of this. All I'm saying is that we should be a little more careful around him, and if we see him again, let Garrick and myself work him for answers. Let us prove that we are all not crazy," he pleaded.

"That's a good theory, but Galan left town. He moved on to start a new life after he sold the café. His flight is probably already in the air," Dana stated.

"Maybe, but I don't think it's the last we have seen of him," Eder countered.

"How about this. We will drop this whole thing if we don't see Galan within the next week. But if he shows his face in Salt Pine Acres in the next seven days, let me and Eder handle this. If we are wrong, I promise I'll leave you alone, and you never ever need to hear my name again," Garrick implored Aria.

Worry etched on Maeve's face, her gaze shifted towards Garrick, expressing her concern for the unfolding tension. The atmosphere in the room grew increasingly tense as Aria's piercing stare directed toward Garrick intensified, reflecting her inner frustration and disappointment.

The weight of silence hung in the air, stretching the seconds to what felt like an eternity. Finally, breaking the stillness, Aria spoke. "Fine, you have one week, but if you don't hold up your end of the deal, I will see to it that you never see the outdoors again. I will not spare you because you're Maeve's brother. I have suffered enough of your presence in my life," Aria barked.

Garrick chose to maintain his silence, his gaze locked onto Aria as he offered a subtle downward nod, an acknowledgment of her words and an indication of his willingness to listen and reflect. The atmosphere in the room remained charged with emotions still simmering beneath the surface.

Just then, Maeve's senior, carrying her file, entered the room. "This is quite a crowd in here. Are you all aware that there is still a very real coronavirus pandemic raging?" asked the doctor.

"We're sorry; it's just that Maeve is like family to us, Doc," Aria replied sweetly.

"Well, Ms. Scarlet, this isn't your lake house; this is still a hospital. And I need only her immediate family in here right now. I know you are all very close, but I cannot break the rules for the friends of my trainees. Garrick can stay; everyone else needs to leave. Visiting hours are not active," the doctor responded.

Aria, Dana, and Eder swiftly exited the room, bidding Maeve a quick wave of support before leaving her in the care of her senior and the medical staff. Walking side by side, they made their way down the steps; Dana turned to Eder and asked, "How are you going to get home?"

"I found my way here. I can find one home. Besides, Garrick could use the company," Eder answered.

"Since when were you and Garrick this close?" Dana asked suspiciously.

"It's not like that. I reached out to Garrick first; I just don't want to abandon him now after what happened to Maeve," Eder explained.

"So, you're concerned about Maeve?" Dana snapped.

"D, nothing is going on with Maeve. Relax, it's just been a hell of a night, love," Eder clarified.

"Yeah, it has been, and I noticed you haven't checked on me once in all that time. But you're at Maeve and Garrick's side all night, barely speaking two words to me," Dana responded.

"D—" Eder exclaimed.

"You know what, just don't. Something has been off with you. You were too quick to believe I would cheat on you. And you have been ignoring me recently. Something is up; I can feel it. God knows what you've been doing with Maeve and Garrick suddenly, and I just want no part of it. When you get your shit together, Eder, then we can talk. Leave me the fuck alone until you figure it out. I am not doing this with you," Dana seethed before walking off and entering their vehicle.

"Dana, please," Eder pleaded, desperate to catch up with Dana, his voice filled with urgency as he called out to her. He hurriedly closed the distance between them, driven by his need to address something important. However, before Eder could reach Dana, Aria swiftly interjected herself between them, effectively halting Eder's pursuit.

"Don't make this any worse," Aria's quiet words hung in the air, leaving an air of finality as she stepped away, making her way toward their car. Without further hesitation, she entered the vehicle, ready to depart. Hans, their driver, swiftly responded to Aria's signal, starting the engine and driving away, leaving Eder standing outside the hospital.

"Fuck me!" Eder mumbled to himself in a state of quiet determination as he made his way towards Garrick's car. Aware of the shards of glass scattered within, he took it upon himself to clean out the remnants, carefully clearing the vehicle of any potential hazards. It was a task he undertook while patiently waiting for Garrick's return.

After a tense half-hour had passed, Garrick emerged from the hospital, his footsteps carrying him toward the car. As he approached, he discovered Eder seated in the passenger seat, one foot casually leaning through the open window.

Garrick got into the driver's seat and closed the door. "Come on, man, take your foot off my door," he called out.

"Sorry, mate," Eder replied, scrambling to pull his foot back inside. "What did they say?"

"She's going to be fine; she will take about two to three weeks to heal, but the lacerations weren't too deep," Garrick answered.

"That's great news, right?" Eder asked.

"Yeah, that was a close call," Garrick stated.

"Dana wants a break from me," Eder informed him.

Garrick turned to him, "What?"

"She's suspicious of me. I have been acting out of sorts, and she noticed. She doesn't know what's up, but she knows there's something going on," Eder explained.

"Fuck," Garrick muttered.

"We need to get rid of Galan fucking Rain, Garrick. I don't care anymore whether it's him or not who did this to Maeve. None of this would have happened if he hadn't weaseled his way into their lives. With or without proof, he has to disappear. You with me, mate?" Eder extended his arm to Garrick.

"Yeah, I got your back. We can't move any guns inside the town, but with two of us against him, we can take him. Nobody will find the body once we toss his cold dead corpse over the lookout," Garrick stated, grabbing Eder's hand.

"Then, that's it, mate. Galan Rain is a dead man," Eder exclaimed with a smile.

Chapter Twenty-Three

A new day dawned, and the sun's rays painted a vibrant tapestry as they danced through the half-open blinds of the hotel window. Galan stirred from his peaceful slumber, his eyes adjusting to the gentle morning light. An arm casually draped across his naked chest. Suddenly, a faint yet persistent knock at the door disturbed the tranquil morning calm. Galan's senses sprang to attention, and he gracefully slipped out of bed, the smooth fabric of his robe caressing his skin as he approached the door. With a gentle turn of the handle, the door revealed Malek all packed.

"Hey, Malek," Galan uttered, wiping his eyes and yawning.

"Sorry to wake you, Galan. I just wanted to say I was leaving and that it was really nice to meet you," Malek said. With a warm smile spreading across his face, Malek extended his hand to shake Galan's.

"Likewise, man," Galan smiled.

"I wanted to ask you something if that's ok?" Malek asked.

"Sure, man, what's up?" Galan inquired.

"Can we talk inside?" Malek requested.

Wrapped cozily in the covers, Nikki, Galan's mischievous friend, sauntered up behind him with a playful smirk dancing on her lips, "He's a bit busy at the moment."

"Oh, I am so sorry. I didn't mean to intrude," Malek remarked quickly.

Galan turned around, his eyes meeting Nikki's playful gaze. Without a word, he pulled her closer, wrapping his arms tenderly around her waist. With a gentle touch, Galan traced his fingers along the contours of Nikki's back, feeling the warmth of her presence against him. Then, he leaned in, their lips meeting in a soft, affectionate kiss.

"Give me a few minutes. I'll be back soon," he told her. Galan turned to Malek, "Let me get some clothes on, and I'll be with you shortly." As Galan closed the door behind them, a playful and passionate energy enveloped the room. He tried to hurry to get dressed, but Nikki had other mischievous ideas in mind. As he fumbled with his clothing, Nikki couldn't resist teasing him, making the process of getting dressed a delightful challenge.

With a teasing glint in her eyes, Nikki playfully undid the buttons he fastened, kissing his chest and disrupting his hands as she went. "Stop," Galan commanded.

"Yes, Sir," Nikki answered.

"Good girl, wait for me in bed. I won't be long," Galan stated.

With a lingering smile, Nikki gracefully returned to bed, reclining amidst the soft sheets with an air of allure. She looked up at Galan with a playful glint in her eyes, her lips slightly parted in a seductive gesture that spoke volumes without a single word.

Still buttoning his shirt, Galan couldn't resist the magnetic pull of Nikki's gaze. He moved toward her with measured steps, savoring the moment and the tantalizing anticipation that filled the air.

As Galan reached the edge of the bed, he paused for a moment, his eyes locked onto Nikki's. His smile deepened, reflecting his appreciation for the allure she emanated. With a final button secured, "Kneel," Galan's eyes locked with Nikki's. His voice was low and inviting as he gently instructed her, standing at the side of the bed. Nikki crawled to the edge of the bed and gracefully got onto her knees, her eyes never leaving his. Their proximity brought them almost at eye level. Galan's touch was tender as he traced the edge of the bed with his fingers, a slow and deliberate movement that traveled from the bed to Nikki's thighs. He spanked her and grabbed hold of her petite butt.

"You're mine, understand?" Galan whispered.

"I understand," replied Nikki.

Galan's eyes gleamed as he leaned in, a playful grin spreading across his face. There was an undeniable spark between them, and he couldn't resist teasing Nikki in the most alluring way.

He lightly sucked on her bottom lip, his lips playfully nibbling and tugging, eliciting a gasp of surprise from Nikki. The moment was charged with electricity, and Galan relished in the sounds she whispered.

As Nikki gasped, he couldn't resist the temptation to entangle his hand in her long black hair, pulling her head back ever so slightly. His lips left her mouth to trail a line of teasing kisses down her neck, causing her breath to quicken.

Moving with a deliberate yet playful rhythm, Galan continued his trail of kisses, guiding them lower until he reached Nikki's enticing curves. His lips hovered over her nipples, and he couldn't help but tease her further with a devilish grin.

"I'll be quick," Galan moaned as he let go of her and walked toward the door. Malek stood in the hallway, waiting for Galan's return. "Sorry to keep you waiting," Galan said.

"No, no, I'm sorry. I didn't realize you had company," Malek gushed.

"It's all good, man. So, what did you want to talk to me about?" asked Galan.

"Well, I'm about to do something really big; remember I told you I was here for a girl?" Malek explained.

"I do remember," answered Galan.

"Well, I think it's time for me to get serious with her, and I want to take things to the next level," Malek continued.

"I'm listening," Galan curiously responded.

"I'm going to ask her to marry me, and I would like your contact information so I can invite you to the wedding if she says yes," Malek finished.

No fucking way. I didn't know it was this serious! I thought this was new; it had gotten this far? You should be happy for her, Galan, for them. Malek is such a nice person.

"Oh, of course, man. I would love that. Give me your phone, and I'll put in my number," Galan replied.

Malek handed Galan his phone to enter his contact info and name.

Nikki's playful nature came to life as she stumbled upon Garrick's phone in the laundry basket, the glowing screen catching her attention in the dimly lit room. Her curiosity piqued, she couldn't resist taking a peek at the notifications, but the password screen lock thwarted her attempts to unlock it fully.

A mischievous idea crossed her mind, and with a sly smile, she decided to leave a little surprise for Galan to discover later. Quickly mastering the shortcut to open the phone's camera, Nikki struck a playful pose, the hotel robe artfully draped around her shoulders. She captured the moment in a topless photo, ensuring a hint of mystery and allure.

With a chuckle, she tucked the phone back inside Galan's hoodie, the same spot where she had found it. The photo nestled safely within, waiting for him to stumble upon it when he eventually scrolled through his camera roll.

As Galan entered the room, his eyes were immediately drawn to Nikki standing by the glass doors, gazing out into the city beyond. Her presence captivated him, and he couldn't resist the impulse to be closer to her.

With a playful grin, he gently tugged at the partially wrapped hotel robe around her shoulders, causing it to fall softly to the floor at her feet. The action revealed more of Nikki's figure. Galan moved closer to her, his pelvis lightly pressing against her back. His fingers trailed through her hair, pulling it aside to reveal her soft, delicate neck. As his lips brushed against her shoulder, he kissed her neck and moved to her ear. Wrapping his hand around her throat, he whispered, "Open," in her ear.

Nikki opened her mouth and stuck her tongue out. "Good girl," Galan said as he took two fingers, placed them on her tongue, and slid them inside her mouth. Nikki sucked and made his fingers wet. Pulling her closer, Galan took his wet, dripping fingers from her lips and moved his hand down her body. He tapped her pussy, circling her clit. Nikki's moan was his guide as he paid attention to her responses to every delicate movement. Making small circular motions, he then slipped his fingers inside her. Galan felt her warmth as he entered her.

"Do you want me?" Galan asked.

"Yes," Nikki replied.

"Excuse me?" Galan responded.

"Yes, Sir," Nikki corrected, looking up at him.

"I don't want to be just a memory. I want you, all of you," Galan whispered.

"Why?" Nikki asked, gasping from the pleasure surging through her.

"Does it matter?" Galan replied.

"Yes. Yes, it does," Nikki answered.

"I guess I never had a memory quite like you. I think I want to hold on to that," Galan told her.

Nikki smiled, "I know rebound sex when I see it. I don't think you want me; you just want to get over whatever you are running from!"

"Is that a no?" Galan remarked.

"It's a no for now until you know what you want. Then, you can ask me again. And when I know you will be completely mine, I'll say yes to you. You're free now; use that time to work through this, and if you still feel the same way, come find me right here," Nikki replied.

As Galan's mind wandered to thoughts of Aria, everything that made him fall for her flashed and replayed in his mind like a montage. He couldn't shake the feeling that he was betraying those memories by being with Nikki.

With a heavy sigh, Galan abruptly stopped what he was doing, stepping away from Nikki to gather his thoughts. Confusion and guilt clouded his expression as he wrestled with the emotions tugging at his heart.

Sensing his turmoil, Nikki tried to reach out to him, seeking reassurance or understanding. But Galan was quick to react. Catching her hand in his, he gently but firmly stopped her from touching him. "Let me," she pleaded.

Nikki's heart sank as she looked into Galan's eyes, witnessing the turmoil and sorrow that clouded his usually vibrant gaze. She was taken aback by the depth of emotion she saw in him, and it left her at a loss for words. "I'm sorry, but I don't let anyone touch me unless I think they can be mine. You're right. I need to work through this; it wouldn't be fair to you. And it's really not fair to me because I do like you, Nikki. And not as a rebound; I saw you as more than that. But I have things to work through, and once I do, I will come back for you," Galan whispered.

Galan softly kissed her forehead, saying, "I'll head to the gym; you can stay here until your shift begins."

"It's fine. I have a room here," Nikki told him. As Nikki gathered her belongings and made her way to the door, her heart weighed heavy with the realization that Galan was struggling with emotions beyond their connection. Standing by the door, fully dressed and ready to leave, she turned to face Galan one last time. Her voice was gentle yet firm as she spoke, "You were more than just a memory, too." With a heavy sigh, Nikki stepped out of the room.

Galan stood there, leaning against the wall, his gaze fixed on a point in the distance.

I let myself get too attached. I let people in too easily, and all I'm left with is the pain of knowing I wasn't good enough for them to choose me. Am I not good enough? What's wrong with me? Why am I never the one they choose?

Oh, fuck! I need to get back to the apartment before that timer goes off!

Galan's heart raced as panic coursed through his veins, urging him to gather his possessions in a frenzied rush. With trembling hands, he hastily stuffed his weathered clothes into a bag, not sparing a moment to organize them properly. Time was of the essence.

Leaving the room hurriedly, he navigated the hotel's corridors like a man possessed, his footsteps echoing with urgency. In the lobby, he wasted no time and swiftly called a cab. The seconds felt like minutes as he anxiously waited for the vehicle to arrive.

Finally, the cab pulled up to the entrance just a few tense minutes after Galan's request. Without a moment's hesitation, he darted out the door and into the waiting vehicle. "Gates of Salt Pine Acres," he instructed upon entering.

I wasn't supposed to be gone for this long. Fuck, how could I forget! If I don't reset the locks on that door... Calm down, Galan. You were there at roughly four p.m. yesterday. You've got all day to make it back before the locks release. You were in such a rush yesterday that you forgot to reset the timer. Fuck, Galan, what is this girl doing to you? Look at you; this isn't you! You are a wreck. You need to make peace with her and find closure so you can move on. God only knows what would happen if that room was left unlocked...

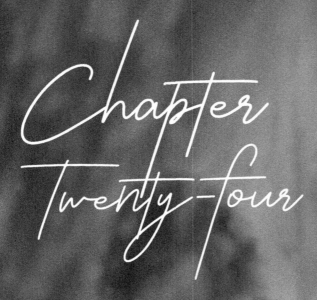

Chapter
Twenty-four

Garrick and Eder settled comfortably into the car's seats, their hunger driving them to indulge in a hearty breakfast sandwich. "I'll head back to Salt Pine Acres. Dana was pissed at me, but I need to remain in her good graces," Eder informed Garrick.

"You need a ride?" Garrick offered.

"Nah, I'm ok, mate. A tow truck service is bringing my car up here in a couple of minutes," Eder replied.

"Ok, good. The guys at the garage will come and change out the windshield for me sometime today. I wouldn't leave yet. Maeve's doctors said she should be good to go after her second check-up today," Garrick mentioned to Eder.

After savoring their satisfying breakfast, a tow truck rolled in, with Eder's car securely attached to the back of it. The arrival was prompt, only a few minutes after they had finished eating. As the tow truck driver carefully unloaded Eder's car at the hospital, Eder bid farewell to Garrick, who remained behind at the medical facility. The engine roared to life, and with a determined look in his eyes, Eder drove away from the hospital and set his course for Salt Pine Acres.

After a couple of hours had passed, Malek finally arrived at Grounded Coffee House, driven by Hans. As he stepped out of the car, he could hear the bustling sounds of the café as Aria and Dana efficiently attended to the morning rush of customers.

Aria, standing behind the bar, happened to glance up just in time to catch sight of Malek entering the café. Her face lit up with delight as she recognized him. Unable to contain her excitement, she swiftly made her way from behind the counter and practically leaped into his waiting arms, embracing him in a warm, heartfelt hug.

Malek's smile widened as he reciprocated the affectionate gesture, cherishing the familiar comfort of Aria's embrace. "I missed you," Aria whispered into his ear.

"I missed you too, my love," said Malek.

Dana came over, excited to see him as well. "Heyyy, you made it," Dana exclaimed.

"Hey, D," Malek called out with a beaming smile as he pulled her into a warm, one-armed hug.

"How was the hotel?" asked Dana.

"It was nice. I've never seen such a great view before," answered Malek.

"If you think that's great, Aria should take you to the lookout at night," Dana told him.

"Heyyy, leave something for me too, D," Aria chuckled and kissed Malek.

"Fine, make yourself at home. If you need anything and we aren't around, you could ask Alliyah; she's great," Dana stated as she walked away.

"You know she doesn't like anyone, right?" Aria pointed out.

"Really?" Malek responded.

"Yes. But she's very fond of you, as am I," Aria exclaimed with a smile and kissed Malek again. "Have you had breakfast yet?" she inquired.

"I have not. I was hoping we could have breakfast together," answered Malek.

"Of course you did, boo," Aria remarked, beaming. "Come on. Hans will take us to the diner at the Gates," she told him.

Aria turned to Dana and called out to her. Using her hands, she signaled they were going out for a moment. Dana understood and gave her a thumbs up as she continued tending to the customers.

As Aria and Malek got in the car, Hans took them to the diner, where they enjoyed each other's company. Aria's infectious smile never seemed to fade, and she held onto Malek as if he were her lifeline, reveling in the comfort of his presence.

Time seemed to slip away as they chatted, laughed, and caught up on each other's lives. Aria couldn't help but admire Malek; his vibrant personality and genuine kindness always left her in awe. Her cheeks began to ache from smiling so much, a testament to the joy he brought into her life.

Meanwhile, Galan had reached the Gates of Salt Pine Acres, arriving shortly after Eder, who hadn't noticed him in passing. Galan was focused on reaching his apartment and quickly made his way through town. Carrying a black bag containing his belongings from the previous night and Garrick's phone, he walked with determination, his mind preoccupied with what lay ahead.

Upon arriving at his apartment building, Galan ascended the stairs and approached a particular room down the hall. With a deep breath, he placed his hand on the door's palm scanner, activating the security measures. The screen displayed 'Auto Release Lock Reset,' indicating a successful authentication, and a new countdown of twenty-four hours started.

I was supposed to leave this behind me with everything else. What am I even doing here!?

The sound of water cascading from the showerhead provided Galan with a brief respite from the turmoil in his mind. As the water dripped off his bent head, he stood motionless, lost in thought. The minutes felt like an eternity as he grappled with the weight of his emotions.

Eventually, Galan turned off the water, wrapping a towel around himself. With a sense of purpose, he walked to the end of the hall and placed his palm on the scanner of the locked room. As the door opened, he stepped inside, closing it behind him, shutting himself off from the outside world.

Inside the room, time seemed to blur, and several hours passed in introspection and reflection. Galan's heart and mind were heavy with the burden of whatever he had discovered or experienced inside those walls. When he finally emerged, he locked the door again, sealing away the room's secrets.

Returning to his own room, Galan moved sluggishly, physically and emotionally drained. He sat on the edge of his bed, feeling the weight of the world upon his shoulders. Overwhelmed by the flood of emotions within him, tears streamed down his cheeks, a cathartic release of pent-up feelings.

I can't give up on you yet, Aria; I can't. I have to fight for you. I need to show you I am good for you. I need you to tell me it's not me so that even if you don't choose me, I have that closure to move on. I don't think I have what it takes to recover from this, but I must. That's what love is; it's handing someone a loaded gun that can destroy you and trusting they won't use it on you. No one has had that kind of power over me since 'Her,' and I can't imagine my life with that pain again. I trust you, Aria.

Galan's mind seemed to be on a relentless quest for answers as he swiftly picked up his phone and opened the security application. The prompt for a fingerprint scan verification appeared on the screen, and without hesitation, he proceeded to unlock the secret compartment in his dresser.

Revealing a hidden space filled with various items, Galan's hand searched until it found a piece of latex film labeled 'DS' in the top corner. As he held the small square in his hand, memories flooded back to the night he had secretly obtained Dana's fingerprint from her phone. Galan placed the piece of latex film on the phone's screen, aligning it carefully. He pressed his thumb down firmly, using Dana's fingerprint to gain the necessary security access. The phone recognized the print, granting him the access he sought.

He cast the phone's screen onto the television in his room, where multiple video feeds were displayed. Galan's gaze scanned each feed intently, searching for any sign of Aria. His heart pounded, the tension and anticipation evident in his every move.

Where are you?

Eder sat at the bar of Grounded Coffee House while Dana tried to keep busy in his presence. "Talk to me, D," Eder begged.

"The time for talking to me was last night, Eder. But you had other priorities," Dana barked.

"I'm sorry. I know I messed up. I was just in shock that something like that had happened. I guess because I was in the middle of the chaos, I felt a little more affected because she was with us," Eder explained.

"You shouldn't have been anywhere near those two, period," Dana snapped.

"You're right, and I'm sorry. The idea of someone wanting to harm you really made me do some stupid stuff, but I promise it was for you," Eder apologized.

"I don't need someone to protect me. I am not the fragile child people make me out to be," replied Dana.

"How can I make it up to you? Please tell me," Eder pleaded.

"Get out of my face, Eder. Let me have just one day away from all this," Dana responded.

"D—" Eder beseeched.

"I said get out, Eder. This is my place of work; I don't need your shit ruining this, too," Dana fumed.

With his hands raised in a gesture of apology, Eder quickly backed away from the bar. "Sorry," he muttered, his voice tinged with regret, before turning and walking out. Though momentarily affected, Dana shook off the incident; she composed herself, wearing a warm smile, and seamlessly resumed attending to the other customers in the café.

Leaving Grounded Coffee House behind, Eder's mind seemed preoccupied with something as he stood outside, scanning the surroundings. His eyes settled on Galan's condo complex, a tall structure that loomed over the other buildings, standing further into Salt Pine Acres. Eder got into his car and began driving towards Galan's condo. The engine hummed softly as he navigated the now familiar streets of Salt Pine Acres. As he approached Galan's condo complex, he parked, got his phone, and called Maeve. "Hello?" Maeve answered.

"Hey, love, I've got a question for you. Galan offered you a ride home, right? Do you remember what kind of car he drives?" Eder asked.

"Yes, of course. He drives a twenty-eighteen muscle car, matte black, custom kit, wouldn't be hard to miss in Salt Pine Acres," Maeve replied.

"I see it parked out front of his apartment building," Eder mentioned.

"Wait, is he in Salt Pine Acres now?" Maeve inquired.

"Well, I'm about to find out, love," Eder responded.

"Don't do anything stupid; wait until you're with Garrick to engage him," Maeve advised.

"Ok, ok, I'll keep my distance until Garrick gets here," Eder answered.

Galan stood at the window, peeking through the blinds to the street below. *What have we here? Eder Barlow? Why are you stalking me? Do you think I wouldn't find it suspicious that you drove into town from the café? The only thing here is me; you have no reason to come this way with Dana in the café. Hmm, maybe this is a blessing in disguise.*

Unlocking the secret compartment in his drawer once more, Galan opened the blacked-out container, revealing the array of paper-thin buttons within. With a calculated tap on one of the buttons, his phone emitted a soft tone, and the screen came to life, activated by its hidden functionality.

Time was of the essence, and Galan hastily threw on a suit of clothes. He knew that every second counted, and he couldn't afford to be delayed. Taking the elevator down, he prepared himself for the encounter that awaited him outside.

Eder, ever watchful, noticed the movement of the elevator but couldn't identify the person inside. With a sense of caution, he swiftly put his car in reverse, backing up slightly to create a safe distance from the apartment building. His instincts were sharp, and he remained alert to any potential surprises.

As Galan stepped out into the street, holding his phone up, his gaze met Eder's car.

"Oh, fuck me!" Eder muttered, realizing he had been caught. He drove up to Galan and got out of the car.

"Eder, what the fuck are you doing here?" questioned Galan.

"What do you mean, mate?" Eder asked innocently.

"Ok, cut the bullshit. Let me just warn you that this entire exchange is being recorded. Now, why were you parked outside my apartment building?" Galan repeated.

"I can explain," Eder claimed.

"Is this about yesterday? Did you come to finish the job? And what, no backup this time?" Galan provoked.

"Wait, what! So, it was you!" Eder answered, stunned.

"Of course, it was me! Who else would it be? You're lucky you had backup then; else, I'd have fucked you up!" Galan's retort echoed with triumph. With a decisive tap, he halted the recording on his phone, muttering under his breath, "Finally, I've got enough here!"

"What do you think you're going to do with that, mate?" Eder inquired.

"Just insurance… I'm warning you, I am in no mood for your shit. The next time, you won't be so lucky," Galan replied swiftly, closing the distance between him and Eder. "You see that café?" Galan pointed urgently in the direction of Grounded Coffee House. As Eder turned to follow his line of sight, Galan deftly flicked the paper-thin button into the backseat of the car, where it landed noiselessly on the floor. "The next time you cross that place and come this way, I won't be so understanding. I do nothing but keep to myself. I will not tolerate bullies!" Galan finished.

"Bullies? After what you did, can you really stand here and threaten me?" Eder questioned him.

"What are you talking about? It was a misunderstanding, you asshole. There was nothing going on between Dana and me. They cleared that up, so why are you still on me for that?" Galan snapped.

Eder's eyes widened in astonishment, and he instinctively took slow steps backward. "You... You're right. I'm sorry, mate. I don't know what came over me," Eder replied with a hint of unease in his voice as he climbed into his car and started the engine.

Galan leaned on the window. "Listen, I really don't want any trouble, and I think a lot of this is because you don't know me. Maybe we should get a fresh start. I've got some errands to run; if you're free, wanna tag along?" Galan offered.

Eder: *If I can stay with him, I could buy enough time to get him in the same place as Garrick. This might be the break we were hoping for.* "That sounds good, mate. Sure, let's put all this behind us," Eder answered. As Galan and Eder locked eyes, a warm smile spread across Eder's face, and he extended his hand toward Galan, and they shook on it.

"Ok, well, I've got some stuff to finish at home first. How about I pick you up in the next hour?" asked Galan.

"Next hour sounds good to me, mate," Eder replied.

"Alright, see you then, man," Galan tapped the top of the car, a signal for Eder to depart. With a nod of farewell, Galan turned and strolled back to the elevator. Eder steered his vehicle away, making his way back to the familiar ambiance of the café. As he parked outside, Eder grabbed his phone and dialed Maeve's number.

BROKEN TOYS

In the hospital room, Garrick remained faithfully by Maeve's side, keeping a watchful eye on her as she rested. Suddenly, he noticed her phone vibrating with an incoming call from Eder. "Hello?" Garrick answered.

"Mate, I think I just solved all our problems," said Eder. "Galan just asked me to run errands with him so we could 'start over.' I'll keep you updated so we can ambush him."

"What! Is Galan back in Salt Pine Acres? Who else knows?" questioned Garrick.

"I don't think anyone else is aware of this. I haven't heard a word from Dana, and he hasn't been in the café today," Eder responded.

"Great, keep it that way. If nobody knows he is here, then nobody will know he is missing," Garrick stated.

"Alright, bet, mate," Eder ended the call and sat in his car parked outside the café, where he had a clear view of Dana inside. She was engagingly interacting with the customers, her infectious smile brightening the atmosphere around her.

Chapter Twenty-five

As Eder ended his conversation with Garrick, Galan stood in the kitchen, his attention drawn to the phone resting on the counter, listening to every word they said. *What... The... Fuck! When did this happen? Did they plan this since Garrick caught me in the backyard last night? Were they all there to "ambush" me? I think my attention has been too diverted. I have been looking at all the wrong things. When will I learn that the obstacles in the way are*

EDER BARLOW

AGE: 22
SIGN: LEO
FUN FACT: "I DON'T POST ABOUT MY ROMATIC RELATIONSHIPS BECAUSE MY FAN BASE CAN BE REALLY JEALOUS AND VINDICTIVE."

more important than the destination? I wish I was recording that.

Dammit, had I been paying better attention, I might have caught on to them earlier. I thought it was all just a coincidence when they ran into me last night. Fuck, these assholes were a step ahead. If I keep playing like this, I am setting myself up for failure. I know I fall in love too quickly and get blinded by it. I can't keep making that mistake. This is a wake-up call. The people around you are dangerous, Aria. They are very dangerous. Something needs to be done. I need to put an end to this.

With a sense of urgency, Galan reached for his phone, lifting it from the kitchen island. His fingers swiftly dialed Alliyah's number, and he anxiously waited as the phone rang. After a few rings, she picked up the call. "Hey, Ally, it's Galan. Is your boss around?" he asked. Alliyah walked over to Dana, holding her phone out to her.

"Hello?" Dana answered curiously.

"Hey, Dana, it's Galan," Galan replied.

"Galan? What an unexpected surprise? What can I do for you?" Dana inquired.

"Actually, I might have a surprise for you," Galan told her.

"I'm all ears," Dana responded.

"Well, I need to run some errands today; one of them is on the way to a supplier for the café. How would you like to get some face time with the owner of the biggest coffee and premium ingredients importer? I'll be in the area, so I wouldn't mind dropping by and introducing the new owner of Grounded Coffee House," Galan explained.

"What? I thought you left already; didn't you have a flight last night?" Dana questioned.

"I did, but I had to reschedule to tie up some loose ends, which is what I'll be doing today. I can be at the café within the hour; I'll pick up you and Eder, and we can step out for a quick run," Galan exclaimed.

"Eder? What? Why?" asked Dana.

"That's kind of a long story," Galan chuckled.

"I am not excited to be in the same place as Eder right now, Galan. I'll have to pass," Dana responded.

"Well, how about you and me? As long as you let Aria know, or if she wants, she can come too," Galan replied. "But it's entirely up to you. I would prefer if Eder tagged along or someone else just to avoid any more drama, you know?"

"Thanks, Galan, but I think I'll pass. I think I've had enough drama to last a while," Dana politely refused.

"Not a problem. If you need anything in the city, shoot Eder a message, and we can grab it on the way back. He will be with me for the day," Galan remarked.

"Sure, have fun," Dana replied as she hung up and handed Alliyah the phone.

Good, now we have accountability. If anything goes wrong, Eder will be tied to me last. Once I inform him that Dana knows my whereabouts and who is with me, he will have a harder time doing whatever the hell he thinks he is going to do. I would have preferred Dana with me. You wouldn't dare make a move with her around, but beggars can't be choosers.

Galan observed the video feed on his phone. From the café's front door camera, his eyes locked onto Eder, sitting in his car, twirling his phone.

What is my other contingency? You're a famous social media personality; therein lies your weakness. You can't make a mistake with your great fans all watching. You wouldn't dare risk your reputation by being the last person to be seen with me. That's my second safety. I'll get it on video that I am with you and tag you. Garrick, again, is a pain in the ass, but I have no way of linking him to this. I don't have any proof the call even happened. I guess I only need to worry about the devil I know, for now.

In the back office, Dana retrieved her phone from the desk, her mind filled with a sense of urgency as she thought about the situation with Galan and Eder. After a moment of contemplation, she decided to reach out to Aria. Meanwhile, Aria was engrossed in a heartfelt conversation with Malek, wholly engrossed in their time together. Her phone vibrated inside her bag, but she remained oblivious to the call as the two were lost in the moment. "Damn it, Ari! Pick up," Dana mumbled.

"Hi, it's Aria. Leave a message," Dana heard as her call went straight to voicemail.

"Ari, something is going down. Eder and Galan are going to run errands. I don't like this; I think they are making their move against Galan! Call me back as soon as you get this," Dana's voice trembled slightly, the weight of uncertainty clearly evident in her tone.

"Fuck, what the hell is Eder up to?" mumbled Dana. As the anxiety gnawed at her, Dana's concern intensified, and she couldn't suppress the urge to seek comfort and guidance from Aria. Frustration consumed her as she repeatedly dialed Aria's number, hoping desperately for her sister to pick up. However, with each attempt, it went straight to voicemail, leaving Dana feeling more isolated and unsettled.

"Fuck it, Ari! Fuck, fuck, fuck!!" Dana exclaimed. Frustrated by the lack of response from Aria, Dana decided to reach out directly to Galan. With trembling fingers, she dialed his number.

"Dana?" Galan answered.

Feeling overwhelmed by the gravity of the situation and her own emotions, Dana froze on the phone, unable to find the words to convey her concerns to Galan. The weight of uncertainty and fear gripped her, causing her to panic. In a moment of distress, she hastily hung up the phone. "Fuck!!! Why did I do that?" she mumbled.

Galan looked at the video feed on his phone of Dana in the office. *Why did you call? You seem really jittery. Why are you acting this way? Unless… You know? Are you in on this? Are you all conspiring against me? Say it's not true, Dana.*

Dana called Aria again; this time, Galan had eyes on her. "Ari, you need to pick up. I am freaking out about this Eder and Galan thing. Pick up!" Dana panicked.

I don't think you do, but you know something to be this worked up. I must be missing something. Fuck, it's like no matter where I turn my attention, I miss the shit that would be useful. I need some face time with Dana. Maybe I can get her to crack under pressure if this is getting under her skin. I'll slip over there through the back; Eder won't know I'm there, so there'll be nobody to run interference.

Galan's determination to find answers propelled him into action. He quickly got up from where he was and made his way to his room, intent on changing into something more appropriate for the situation. His mind was filled with concern for Dana, and he felt a pressing need to understand the events unfolding at the café.

Once he was dressed, Galan hurriedly got into his car and drove to the back entrance of Grounded Coffee House. With a sense of urgency, he took out his phone and called Dana, hoping to speak to her directly and get to the bottom of what was happening.

As Dana's phone rang, she felt a mix of relief and hesitation. She answered the call, and Galan urged her to step outside using the back entrance, where he was waiting for her. Dana's confusion and wariness lingered, unsure of what Galan's arrival meant and whether it was connected to her earlier call.

Her desire to reach Aria for guidance and support persisted, but when she dialed Aria's number once more, disappointment washed over her as there was still no answer.

"Fuck," Dana remarked as she took a moment to compose herself before finally deciding to confront the situation and meet Galan outside. With a mix of curiosity and trepidation, she walked towards the back door, her heart beating a little faster with each step.

As Dana reached the back entrance, her eyes widened in surprise as she found Galan leaning against the wall just outside. His presence caught her off guard, as she hadn't anticipated him being so close to the door.

"Hey, you ok?" Galan quickly asked as she flinched.

"I'm fine," Dana replied.

"Didn't mean to scare you," Galan stated.

"You didn't. I'm just having a rough day, that's all," Dana responded.

"Alright, if you say so, but is everything ok?" Galan repeated.

"Everything is fine. Why?" Dana inquired.

"It's just that you called and didn't say anything, and you were ranting about Eder and stuff before that, so I just wanted to make sure you were good," Galan explained.

"I said I'm fine. I just butt-dialed your phone, that's all," Dana replied angrily.

"Why are you so tense?" questioned Galan.

"I hate being interrogated like this," answered Dana.

"You mean you don't like someone being concerned about you?" asked Galan.

"I never asked for your concern, and I do not need anyone to worry about me!" Dana barked.

As Eder overheard Dana's voice outside, his curiosity was piqued, and he became more alert. He carefully glanced around, trying to pinpoint the source of the sound. Eventually, his eyes caught sight of Galan's car parked on the street at the back of the café, visible through the alleyway that separated the café from the neighboring building.

"Ok, ok, message received. I'm sorry I bothered you," Galan apologized.

"Why are you still here, Galan?" Dana couldn't help but ask.

"I'm sorry?" Galan turned around as he walked away. He faced Dana once more.

"Where were you last night? And why are you still in Salt Pine Acres?" Dana repeated.

As Dana's questions hung in the air, Galan hesitated, taking a moment to gather his thoughts before responding. His mind raced with the complexities of the situation, unsure of how much to reveal and how best to address her concerns.

"Answer me!" Dana shouted.

As Eder heard Dana's voice once more, he became determined to find out what was happening at the back of the café. He swiftly exited his car and hurriedly ran towards the back entrance, driven by a sense of urgency to address the situation firsthand.

Meanwhile, Aria and Malek had just pulled up behind Eder's vehicle, unaware of the unfolding events. Aria noticed Eder quickly leaving his car, his demeanor expressing concern and a sense of urgency. She exchanged a worried glance with Malek, who was equally puzzled by the sudden turn of events.

Not wasting any time, Aria looked through the café's glass windows to see if she could spot Dana. "Is everything ok, love?" asked Malek.

"I need to find Dana," Aria's concern for Dana pushed her into action. Without a moment's hesitation, she hurriedly entered the café, gently pushing the door open. The interior greeted her with the familiar aroma of coffee and the soft buzz of conversations, but her focus was solely on finding her sister.

As she scanned the room, Aria's eyes couldn't find Dana.

Feeling overwhelmed by the situation and Dana's raised voice, Galan took a step back, giving her some space. "Calm down; what's wrong?" asked Galan nervously. "What did I do?"

"Don't come near me. Why the fuck are you hiding in these backdoor alleys trying to talk to me? What do you want, Galan?!" Dana yelled.

"Why are you coming at me like this? What have I ever done to you?" Galan questioned.

"You stay away from us, from all of us. You hear me! I don't want you anywhere near Eder, my sister, or her friends. Just stay the fuck away, you hear me!?" Dana shouted.

As Eder rushed around the corner of the alley, he found Dana in the midst of expressing her frustrations to Galan. His arrival added another layer of tension to the already charged atmosphere. Galan turned towards Eder, his body language showing confusion and a clear message that he was not responsible for the situation.

With raised hands, Galan attempted to signal to Eder that he had no part in whatever was causing Dana's distress. His head shook subtly, indicating he was just as clueless about the unfolding events as Eder.

"Get away from her!" Eder growled.

"Excuse me?" Galan replied.

The sudden escalation of events caught everyone by surprise. Eder's emotions got the better of him, and he impulsively rushed toward Galan, pushing him away from Dana with force. Galan stumbled backward, unable to maintain his balance, and tripped on the uneven sidewalk. With a jolt, he fell and rolled into the street.

"Oh, that fucking does it!" Galan exclaimed. In a sudden explosion of rage, Galan's restraint shattered, and he lunged toward Eder with all his might. Eder, quick to react, met Galan's charge head-on, aiming a powerful tackle at his hips. The impact sent them both tumbling to the ground in a chaotic entanglement of limbs. Eder found himself on top of Galan, unleashing a torrent of punches in his fury.

Galan instinctively shielded his face with both hands as the blows rained down, attempting to fend off the onslaught. Amidst the chaos, Dana, filled with alarm and concern, mustered her strength and intervened, pulling Eder away from Galan with all her might. However, in the heat of the moment, Eder's focus shifted to Dana, and he jerked his arm, unintentionally pushing her away.

The realization that he had nearly harmed Dana pierced through Eder's fury, and for a moment, his attention wavered from Galan. He turned his attention to her for a split second. That was all it took for Galan to scramble back to his feet and barrel toward Eder. But before contact could be made between them, Aria stepped in between them, and Galan skidded to a stop. Her wide eyes were filled with fear as she stared into the wildness of Galan's expression, contemplating what might have happened if no one had been able to intervene. His once soft grey eyes held a devilish intent in his fit of rage.

"Galan! Get the fuck out of here!" Aria groaned.

"Ari!" Dana said.

"Are you kidding me? I'm the one who was attacked again, yet I'm the bad guy here?!" Galan shouted.

"I was only protecting Dana!" Eder countered.

"Zip it, both of you. Galan, get the fuck out of here now, or I will take legal action and make sure you never get anywhere near my family and me again. Are we clear?" Aria declared.

"Oh, I don't believe this. I'm sorry I came over here because Dana rang my phone and hung up without saying anything after she said she didn't want to be around Eder. I'm sorry I offered to help with the café and supplier relations, but let me tell you something: I have done nothing but mind my business since day one. Not only has Eder attacked me twice, but he was also stalking me outside my apartment," Galan exclaimed, his anger now taking an unexpected turn. With a swift motion, he retrieved his phone and eagerly played a video for everyone to watch.

Aria and Dann turned to Eder. "Eder!" they called out in sync.

"And like an idiot, I wanted to put it behind us and try to get along with him, your friends, and you, but all I have ever received were insults and drama. And now you're here threatening legal action? Go ahead. I have been harassed in my hometown and outside of my house for no good reason by people who have no right to be here. I'm more than happy to make this whole thing public," Galan fumed.

"Wait, stop. Everybody, just take a breather," Dana exclaimed.

"Why should I? I have received nothing but threats since meeting you people. What have I done?" Galan argued.

"Please just come inside the café; we can work this out," Dana pleaded.

"No, I'm good. I think I've reached my quota of threats for the day. I'm not gonna listen to that in the place I built from the ground up," Galan retorted as he turned and walked to his car.

"Galan!" Dana called out.

"Let him go," Aria said, holding her back.

As Galan got into his car and drove off, the tension hung heavily in the air. The dust had not yet settled from the altercation, leaving the group with a sense of unease. Still visibly upset, Dana stormed back inside the building, her emotions raw from the events that had just transpired. Aria, recognizing the need for support, followed closely behind her, offering a comforting presence.

Meanwhile, Eder, trying to find a way to ease the tension and perhaps seek some guidance, pulled out his phone and dialed Maeve's number once again. "Hello?" Maeve answered.

"Maeve? How are you feeling?" asked Eder.

"I'm doing ok. Just annoyed by these wounds," Maeve replied.

"Ok, I'm happy to hear that. Where is Garrick?" Eder asked.

"Garrick said the guys came to replace the windshield. He's out there with them right now," Maeve responded.

"Do me a favor, love. Tell Garrick to call me as soon as he comes back in. Things got a little complicated just now," Eder stated.

"Why, what happened?" Maeve inquired.

"Galan and I had a little scrap. He was hiding in the back alley with Dana, and she started screaming at him. I didn't think. I just got in the middle, and it came to blows," Eder explained.

"Are you ok?" asked Maeve.

"I'm fine. I wasn't hurt. Aria broke up the fight, but they seem pissed," Eder informed her. "This means our plan is off. Galan left, and it looked like he had gone back to his apartment. I messed up a chance to get rid of him. Garrick is going to freak; he told me to not do anything without him," said Eder.

Malek stood at the partially open door as he searched for Aria, unintentionally overhearing Eder's conversation.

Chapter Twenty-Six

"Plan?" Malek mumbled.

"Listen, Maeve, I'm gonna go. Dana is pretty upset. I should go and comfort her. When Garrick returns, tell him to get down here immediately. We have to do this today while he is still here. If Galan leaves, we don't know when we will see him again, and most likely, he won't be coming around the café again," Eder remarked.

"Ok, I'll get someone to find Garrick immediately. Be careful, boo," Maeve replied.

"I will, my queen. I love you," Eder responded.

"What?" as Malek mumbled to himself, his pace quickened, and he continued walking away. "I need to tell Aria." Startled by Dana's sudden action,

Malek found himself yanked into her office. His heart raced as he looked at Dana.

"Dana?" said Malek, surprised.

"You will say nothing about this to her. Do you hear me, Malek?" asked Dana.

"Did you know this has been going on all this time?" questioned Malek.

"Yes, we both know they are planning to do something to Galan, but I don't need you to get in the middle of this. Aria likes you; I mean, really likes you. Stay out of all this. Don't let her choose between her friends and you; she will always choose them. It's a sick co-dependency between her and her friends. Promise me you'll take that to your grave; I haven't seen anyone make my sister happier than you, and I refuse to let their shit jeopardize what you have. I've got this. Trust me, I just need you to be you, ok?" Dana pleaded.

"Are you sure? Dana, this isn't fair to you. You are such a wonderful person; you don't deserve that..." Malek was cut off.

"I can handle it. I promise I know what I'm doing. Please promise me you won't breathe a word of this to Aria," Dana affirmed.

As Malek looked at Dana with a touch of sorrow, he could sense the weight of the situation and the emotions that she was carrying. Without hesitation, he pulled her into a warm and comforting hug as he answered, "Ok, I promise, D."

Eder walked in on Dana and Malek. Dana was still in Malek's embrace when he called out, "Dana?"

Dana pulled away from Malek and looked at Eder. "What the hell are you doing in here, Eder? Was I not clear about our situation?" Dana snapped.

"Our situation? What is this? Was I interrupting something?" Eder growled, approaching Malek.

"I beg your pardon?" Malek responded.

Dana got between them, "What the fuck do you think you're doing?"

"Me? What the fuck do you think you are doing with your sister's boyfriend, D?"

"What the fuck is that supposed to mean, Eder?" Dana shouted.

"You hypocrite! How dare you say that about her when you are the one...." Malek began but was interrupted by Aria's entrance.

"Hey!" Aria shouted as she burst through the door. "Eder, get out! Now!"

Eder looked from Malek to Aria before scoffing and storming out of the room.

"Can I have a word with my sister, alone, please, babe?" asked Aria gently.

"Of course, my love," Malek said as he left the room and closed the door behind him.

As Aria walked over to the desk, she took a seat on its edge. Using her feet, she pulled a nearby chair closer, gesturing for Dana to have a seat.

Still feeling a mix of emotions from the intense events that had unfolded, Dana walked over and settled into the offered chair. She took a deep breath, trying to steady herself.

"D, talk to me. Every time I turn my back, something happens. What is going on with you? I'm worried; I haven't seen you like this since we were kids. Why are you acting out this much? I just want to understand so I can help you," Aria stated.

"Did you get my message?" asked Dana.

"No, I didn't," Aria replied.

"Eder was going to do something today. Out of nowhere, he and Galan were going to run 'errands.' That's not a coincidence; you know what they said back at the hospital," Dana explained.

"Can we not make this about Galan, please? I have heard that name enough times to last a lifetime," Aria remarked.

"What is with you? Why have you been so cold to Galan since we met him?" Dana inquired.

"Galan is nothing but a businessman. You had a transaction with him, and that's the end of that relationship. He's not a friend," Aria stated.

"Galan has shown more support than anyone else. You know it's funny; he showed up here because he thought something was wrong, and I hate that he was right. He has been there every single time I needed him, and he has always ended up somehow being the one in the wrong. Listen, Eder was up to something. I can only assume Garrick is in on it, too. I had a bad feeling when I heard Galan was going to be alone with Eder today, and I wanted to warn him. I made such a big fuss so they wouldn't be near each other. I didn't expect Eder to show up and attack him. I was just going to tell Galan to stay away from us, but things got out of hand," Dana explained.

"What were you thinking?" asked Aria.

"I tried calling you! I needed some advice, but you weren't available," Dana told her.

"You're blaming me for this?" Aria inquired.

"I am not! I did what I had to do. Despite what you and everyone else think about Galan, he has been nothing but helpful and sweet to me from the start. Even when I was being a bitch to him," Dana retorted.

"Oh my God…," Aria gasped.

"What?" Dana replied.

"You have a crush on Galan!" Aria claimed.

Dana's cheeks turned a deep shade of crimson, an immediate and unmistakable sign of her embarrassment. The words she intended to say seemed to get caught in the tumultuous whirlwind within her throat, leaving her momentarily speechless. Flustered and restless, she abruptly rose from her chair, her footsteps echoing as she paced the room. Each step seemed to match the erratic beat of her heart.

"I do not!" Dana protested, her voice trying to convey a sense of conviction. However, her rapid breathing betrayed the intensity of her emotions, subtly revealing a contradiction between her words and her inner turmoil.

"D, he's way older than you. He's older than me! You know that's not right. You're sixteen, and he's twenty-five," Aria pointed out.

"I said I do not have a crush on him!" Dana blushed.

Eder stood seething in the hallway just outside the office, unintentionally eavesdropping on Dana's conversation. As he listened to her words, an overwhelming rage built up inside him, making the vein on his forehead visibly bulge. His emotions were so intense that he could hardly control himself.

His eyes scanned the hallway, searching for an outlet for his anger, and they landed on a table nearby. On it were several trays with coffee machine parts drying. Without a second thought, Eder grabbed a metal piece from the table and fueled by his fury, he hurled it with all his strength at the ceiling. The metal piece collided with a glass segment that ran just below the ceiling, creating a deafening crash that reverberated through the entire office space.

The loud noise immediately drew the attention of the staff, including Dana and Aria, who rushed to the scene. Realizing the gravity of what he had done and not wanting to be caught, Eder quickly slipped into another room before anyone could spot him. He needed a few minutes to regain his composure, so he took a moment to breathe deeply and collect himself.

Back in the main area, the staff was now gathered, trying to assess the situation and clean up the broken glass and metal parts scattered on the floor. Eder knew he had to act swiftly to avoid being questioned, so he decided to make a discreet exit. Sneaking out the back door, he managed to elude the attention of Aria and Dana, who were still preoccupied with the aftermath of the incident.

As Eder walked towards his car, his phone rang. It was Maeve calling. He got into his car and answered the call.

"Yeah?" answered Eder.

"Garrick isn't here. I asked someone from my training team to go find him, but he and the car were gone. The security said they left the compound, but Garrick left a message for me. He said he was heading home first before coming to Salt Pine Acres. Try calling the house and leaving a message with the maid; he will get back to you once he gets there. Unless he is already there. You know he drives like a maniac," Maeve informed him.

"Ok, thanks, love. I'll get on that," Eder replied.

"Keep tabs on Galan. Don't let him out of your sight. If he leaves Salt Pine Acres, tail him," Maeve instructed.

"I don't think that's possible, love. He spotted me within a few minutes of parking outside his apartment. I don't think I could follow him without him noticing me," Eder explained.

"Then stay near the café. The only road that leads out the gates passes by the café. If you can't keep watch while he is there, just make sure he doesn't leave. Garrick will be there as soon as he can," Maeve advised.

"Will do, love. Hope you feel better soon," said Eder, hanging up at the end of his sentence.

Galan sat alone in his condo complex's dimly lit parking garage, his car engine idling softly. He listened intently to the audio of Eder's conversation with Maeve, the words flowing through his phone speakers. *I see. Those fuckers are out for me. I could stay in my apartment and wait them out. There's no way they'll get past the security on the elevator. But how long can I wait them out? If I hide out here, it will only give them a reason to believe I am guilty of something. I have to carry about my day as I normally would. I cannot be swayed by their threats. If I avoid them, I only stand to prove them right. They must suspect me from that night at the house. I need to think this through. The only way to avoid their suspicion is to act as though I am not trying to avoid anything.*

Think! There isn't much to do in this town except eat, exercise, and enjoy the majestic view and mountain air. I am not an indoor person, so hiding inside now is a bad idea. I need to get out. I can go to the lookout, run my exercise route, and get my caffeine fix at the café. No more friendly banter; just be a customer. What are they going to do? Chase me out? No, they wouldn't; reputation is everything to them. I need to get Garrick and Eder off my back. If I can sway their suspicions off of me, I'll be in the clear. Then I can work my way back to you, Aria. I can finally get closure to this little dance we have been doing.

Garrick pulled into his driveway, the revving engine signaling his return home in his dad's car, now boasting a brand-new windshield. As he stepped out of the car and approached the front door, the familiar comfort of home enveloped him. Upon entering the house, he was promptly greeted by the maid, who informed him that Eder had left him a message. "Thank you. Did my package arrive?" Garrick asked.

The maid nodded yes and pointed to the sofa in the next room, where a package rested on it. Garrick walked over and opened the box. The new phone he had ordered the night before while at the hospital using Maeve's phone had arrived.

"Great," Garrick muttered and turned it on. As he made his way to his room, he had a clear purpose in mind. He needed to find a particular Rolodex tucked away in his nightstand drawer. With a sense of nostalgia, he retrieved the small index file and opened it up to the section marked with the letter "A." His finger glided along the names until he reached "Anthony." Garrick located Anthony's contact details. He skillfully inputted the phone number into his new device and called Anthony. He answered.

"My man! I need a favor. Are you in the lab right now?" asked Garrick.

"I'm out on the job building a server for a company. What do you need?" Anthony inquired.

"Not in any rush, my man. My phone got stolen or lost; I'm not quite sure. But I got a new one, so can you do that thing you did before and pull all the data from my old phone and copy it to this new one?" Garrick wondered.

"That's easy enough. I just need some time, alright. Maybe later when I'm back?" Anthony suggested.

"Not a problem, man. I'll drop it off at the lab in a couple of minutes," Garrick informed him.

"No need, my friend. Times have changed; all I need you to do is text me your email address and then link your phone to that email. Once I pull the data, I can use your email to export your entire database to your new device," Anthony explained.

"Damn, alright, man. I'll text you that information now. I owe you one, Anthony," Garrick stated.

"Anytime, my friend," Anthony responded.

Garrick flipped through the Rolodex once more, now searching for Eder's name. The smooth pages glided beneath his fingers, each turn bringing him closer to the "E" section.

Eder sat comfortably in his car, immersed in the rhythmic tunes of his favorite music. With one hand on the steering wheel and the other holding his phone, he casually scrolled through his social media feeds, relishing the online interactions with his ever-growing community of followers. A sudden interruption caught his attention as he navigated through the virtual landscape—a mysterious unknown number flashing on his phone's screen. Curiosity piqued, he decided to answer the call. With a swift gesture, he lowered the volume of the music, eager to find out who might be on the other end of the line. "Hello?" Eder answered.

"Eder, it's Garrick," said Garrick.

"Oh, hey, mate. Where are you calling from?" asked Eder.

"I got a new phone. I heard you left a message for me; any update on Galan?" Garrick inquired.

"Yeah. Unfortunately, mate, we hit a bit of a rough patch. Galan and Dana got into a heated argument earlier. I got involved, and it came to blows. Aria and Dana are pretty upset. Some other shit happened, but that's not important right now," Eder explained.

"Damn it, Eder, I told you not to engage him without me," Garrick growled.

"I know, mate. I'm sorry," Eder replied.

"Look, stay away from him. Wait for me. I'm on my way. Don't let him leave!" Garrick instructed.

"What are you gonna do, mate? I can't stalk him and risk getting caught again. Even if you get here, it's no use unless we get face time with him," Eder told him.

"Leave that to me. I've got an idea. You just have one job; keep Galan there. You got me?" asked Garrick.

"Yeah, I got you," said Eder.

"Good, I'm on my way. Be there within the hour," Garrick responded.

Galan, still seated in his car, listened to their conversation. *Garrick, you are the only problem I*

really have. Eder can be easily dealt with. Aria's other friends can be quickly dealt with as well. But you, you pose a problem. But despite being such as big of a pain in the ass as you are, you have a weak spot, Aria herself. That café is a safe house when it comes to you. As long as I can spend my days there, you can't touch me.

"Let's see how well your plans work, Garrick," Galan mumbled.

Chapter Twenty-Seven

Garrick arrived in Salt Pine Acres just before lunchtime, the sun shining brightly overhead. He pulled up beside Eder's car and smoothly rolled down his window. Catching Eder's attention, he gestured for him to do the same. Garrick invited Eder to join him, and without hesitation, Eder switched cars. The duo set off towards the scenic lookout; upon reaching their destination, Garrick skillfully parked the car, turning to face Eder, "Is he still here?"

"I believe so. I didn't see Galan drive past me at the café," Eder replied.

"Great, we have a plan. This guy has been around Aria. I caught him sneaking around her house before, and I'm pretty sure that was him the night we chased someone from the property. And today, he was even caught with Dana—" Garrick began.

"Right, so?" Eder interjected.

"Wherever she goes, he follows. Maeve had an idea; she wanted to throw a party at Aria's house. She said she could get her hands on surgical equipment, anesthetics, and things we could easily conceal. If he shows up at her place, all we need to do is inject a dose of the anesthetics in him, and we could toss his ass over the lookout. That way, nobody would ever find him," Garrick finished.

"I don't think that would work. Aria and Dana had a bad falling out with him today," Eder explained.

"We don't need him to be invited; he just needs to snoop around," Garrick clarified.

"Why would he? After almost being caught, I don't think he would risk it again, mate," Eder exclaimed.

"Dammit, Barlow, what's your great idea then?" Garrick fumed.

"Hey, take it easy, mate. I'm not trying to be negative here. I'm trying to be smart about this," answered Eder.

"If you have a better plan, I would love to hear it," Garrick sarcastically remarked.

"Galan always seems to have a way out; every time we thought we had him, he was one step ahead. There is always something we seem to miss because we're too hasty. I think if we are going to get rid of Galan, we need to hit him when he would never see it coming," Eder declared.

"That's not a bad plan, but how do we do that?" asked Garrick.

"I don't know. I'm not used to planning murders, mate," Eder confessed.

"Why do you sound like you're having second thoughts about this?" Garrick inquired.

"Do we really have to kill him? Can't we just get rid of him? Chase him out of town or something?" Eder wondered.

"Don't be a pussy, Eder. That guy put Maeve in the hospital and is standing in the way of us and the Scarlet fortune," Garrick responded.

"We don't know that for sure, mate," Eder claimed.

"Are you kidding me? Get your head out of your ass, Barlow, or we both lose out on our futures! If we succeed and things go as planned, we'll both get our hands on the Scarlet fortune. Then, our great-grandchildren's great-grandchildren could buy companies on a whim every day and not put a dent in their finances. Think of the bigger picture, Barlow. This isn't about us; this is about the future generations," Garrick stated.

"Wow, after all that talk last night about Maeve and me only going after their money!" Eder scoffed.

"That should have been us. We grew up together, and our parents were business partners. They were on their way to conquering the world together until Aria's father started cutting backroom deals and exploiting contracts with our family. When his first major deal went down, they sold a company for eighty billion dollars. But my parents received a couple million from that deal. Aria's dad exploited my father's trust when signing the contracts, limiting what my parents would make when the company sold.

"We should have been set up for life after that deal; they owe us. But it's not just about the money;

the money is for Maeve. I fell for Aria. I really did, and she broke my heart. I have been trying to piece it back together ever since so I can win her back. I know I messed up big time. I had no right to hit her. After that moment, I knew I needed to stop the steroids and fights altogether. I am trying to change, but there are some habits I can't shake," Garrick explained as he looked over to the glove compartment on the passenger side. "But this isn't just about me; this is for Maeve, too. So, I will do this with or without you," he declared.

Eder took a moment to let it sink in, "Alright, mate, I've got your back. I'll do it for Maeve."

"For Maeve," Garrick echoed and fist-bumped Eder.

The sudden roar of a powerful engine caught their attention, and they turned to see Galan's arrival. His vehicle pulled up a few spots away, and he gracefully stepped out. In one hand, he carried a paper bag and in the other, a refreshing bottle of water. With an air of ease, Galan strolled towards the benches situated closest to the lookout, seeking solace in the shade provided by a nearby shed.

"Eder, are you seeing this?" asked Garrick.

"What do we do?" Eder wondered.

"I don't see anyone else around. We could take him now; there are two of us!" Garrick responded.

"What happened to not being so hasty? What if he escapes us again and goes to Aria and Dana, and they get law enforcement involved? That whole no police thing is only applicable to the residents of Salt Pine Acres. You and I have none of the perks of this place," Eder stated.

"Come on, this is an open shot! If we don't take this now, we may not get a chance like this again. We don't need to hurt him. We just need to toss his ass over that railing he is sitting eight feet from. There are no cameras in Salt Pine Acres; everything is off the grid here. It's smack in the middle of the day, and everyone is occupied or on lunch, which means they are near the gates or in their houses and not here. Just follow my lead!" Garrick remarked as he jumped out of his truck.

"Garrick! Aw crap, mate," Eder muttered as he exited the vehicle behind Garrick.

Garrick and Eder stealthily approached Galan, who was facing away from them. Galan took a bite of his sandwich and kept calm at the sound of approaching footsteps. Garrick and Eder came up behind him and quickly noticed Galan's phone camera was on.

"Galan?" Eder called out nervously, looking at Garrick in a panic.

Galan wiped his mouth with a tissue and calmly opened his water bottle. "Come to try me again?" asked Galan with a smirk.

"What are you doing out here?" Eder inquired.

"You know I am really sick of people who don't fucking live in this town asking me what I am doing here!" Galan snapped.

Garrick and Eder walked around to the front of the bench.

"Every time I seem to leave my apartment, I find one of you. Trouble always ensues, and somehow, I end up being the bad guy. So, I decided to take a different approach; every time I leave my house, I'll have my phone on a live feed. Nobody will see it right now, but once it stops recording, there will be a prompt to opt out of posting it for the public. And only I can cancel it. On the off chance that something were to happen to me, they would know about my last moments. And it's not just video, but audio as well. Even if they don't see you, they'll hear you in great clarity," Galan warned while sipping his water.

Eder looked over to Garrick; Garrick's eyes met his. "You're the freak who was snooping around Aria's house and going behind her back doing God knows what with her sixteen-year-old sister, Galan Rain. Also, we know, without a shred of doubt, that you were the one sneaking around Aria's house last night," Garrick declared with a smirk.

"Interesting, you're trying to use my safety precautions against me. Not a bad attempt, but here's the kicker. Eder Barlow is dating a sixteen-year-old while he is twenty-two. I've heard rumors about him and Dana having sex, and I've heard there was proof. That sounds a lot like statutory rape, and considering where she is from, the age of consent is eighteen. And Garrick, you have been stalking Aria, hiding outside her house, and threatening locals, i.e., me. As for snooping around Aria's house, I don't know what you're talking about," Galan firmly stated.

"Really? Because I have a picture that clearly caught you hiding in her backyard! Your face was fully exposed; you have no excuse to worm your way out of this one," Garrick exclaimed snidely.

"Is that so? Where is your proof? Because you see, I do have proof of the things I've claimed. If I am not back home in twenty-four hours to reset the timer, all that information, along with my proof, goes public. You should stop bluffing, or at least have the means to back up your claims," Galan retorted.

With clenched fists, Garrick snarled, "You little asshole."

"Listen, I told Eder this before when he was spying on me in my home, but I don't want any trouble. Despite what you think of me, I am a nice person. I may not like you, but that doesn't mean we have to be assholes to one another. We can all get along without the need for all this posturing. Stay out of my way, and I will have nothing to do with you. This is your last warning; I will not be so civil the next time you two jackasses threaten me. Are we good?" asked Galan as he stood and looked at Garrick.

Garrick walked up to Galan, getting in his face. "Garrick, leave it alone. Let's go, mate. He's not worth it," Eder exclaimed. Concerned about the escalating tension, he quickly intervened by grabbing Garrick's shoulder, attempting to hold him back. Fueled by his emotions in the heat of the moment, Garrick resisted Eder's efforts and squared his chest defiantly in Galan's direction.

"I'll overlook this. I think Dana and Aria are upset enough, so as a show of good faith, I didn't see you here today," Galan expressed as he walked off and got back into his car. He started his vehicle and drove back to his apartment.

"Fuck, that could have gone badly," Eder mumbled.

"On the contrary, that couldn't have gone better!" Garrick replied with a smirk.

"What do you mean? You heard him; he has proof that could sink the both of us. You know, if anything gets leaked, Dana and Aria will not have anything to do with us again. They wouldn't want to be associated with our bad reputations," Eder commented.

"True, but Galan finally made his first mistake. Now we know it was him last night. And we have the proof that he put Maeve in the hospital," Garrick answered.

"What are you talking about," Eder inquired.

"Did you see how calm he was until I said I had a clear photo of his face fully exposed in my possession? How was he so sure I was bluffing?" asked Garrick.

"Because… He knew you lost your phone that night! Garrick, that's brilliant!" Eder responded.

"Now that we have that, we can bring him down. He wants to be civil? We can do civil. But I wonder if Aria and Dana would react the same when they find out what he was really doing last night!" said Garrick with a smile.

"What do we do now?" Eder inquired.

"Now we need to be smart about this like you said. Both of us had run-ins with him before; they won't take our word for it. We need to gather the support of the people Aria would die for. We need to convince Eyla and Bodhi. He won't be able to dismiss all five of us. He's smart, but he can't outsmart all of us. We end this today. Let's go see Maeve; we need to gather all the stuff she can get for us. The Scarlets could cover up his death; we just need to convince them that Galan is a monster. I've seen them do this before; they covered up my parents' death, after all," Garrick explained.

Eder looked on in shock, "What?"

"When the Scarlets sold the company and cut my parents out of the deal, they weren't happy about it. My parents had evidence that could have proved the Scarlets cut them out of the deal; they were only seeking their fair share, but that wasn't good enough for the Scarlets. Our parents disappeared soon after. It took a while for Maeve and me to come to terms with the reality of the situation.

"Suddenly, Aria's father was interested in us and ensured we were cared for as kids. To this day, he can't look either of us in the eye. And the way he spoke, it was like he knew my parents weren't alive anymore. Just like Galan, the only way you're that certain of yourself is when you know about the situation first-hand. I saw the same smug look in his eyes; that son of a bitch knows we can't pin it on him. The difference now is that I am not a child anymore!" Garrick clarified.

"You sure we can do this, mate?" asked Eder.

"Yeah, we got this. Come on, let's go get Maeve," Garrick answered.

With the tension at the lookout behind them, Garrick climbed into his truck with a resolute expression. Eder wasted no time and quickly joined Garrick in the vehicle. Without any hesitation, they sped away from Salt Pine Acres as they drove toward Maeve's location.

Chapter
Twenty-eight

Galan arrived back at the apartment. Stepping out of his car, he noticed a figure standing near the elevator. Squinting to get a clearer view, he approached the person cautiously, unsure of their identity. With a calm yet cautious demeanor, he asked, "Can I help you?"

Stepping into the light, Aria walked up to Galan.

"Aria? What are you doing here?" Galan remarked, confused.

"We still have some unfinished business left, don't we?" answered Aria.

What the fuck? Does she mean the last time she was here? What about Malek? What is happening right now?

"Didn't you tell me off earlier today?" Galan inquired.

Approaching Galan, Aria gently extended her hands towards his chest, but Galan swiftly intercepted her, gently catching her hands in his own. She looked up at him, her eyes filled with lust, before asking in a soft, demure tone as she bit her lips, "Did I hurt your feelings? Let me make it better."

This is it, the moment you've been waiting for. No obstacles, just you and her. Make it count!

"Aria, I'm…." Aria covered Galan's mouth, silencing him.

"Shh, not a word," Aria replied as she walked to Galan's car. Opening the passenger side door for him, Galan entered first. She then got on top of him and closed the door.

Dana gracefully exited the café, her determined steps leading her toward Galan's apartment. She took a moment to compose a sincere text message, expressing her intention to visit him and offer a heartfelt apology for their earlier encounter. Meanwhile, Malek sat leisurely in the café, savoring his lunch as Aria had excused herself briefly to fetch something from home, assuring him of her swift return.

As Dana rounded the corner onto Galan's street, her sharp eyes caught sight of Hans' car parked just outside the condo complex, raising curiosity about his presence in this seemingly unexpected encounter.

"What? Is Aria here?" Dana mumbled.

Dana attempted to reach Galan by placing a call, but his phone remained engaged in recording mode, frustrating her attempts to connect. Letting out an exasperated grunt, she reluctantly hung up as the call was redirected to his voicemail. Undeterred, Dana proceeded to the building's elevator, hoping for an alternative means of communication once inside.

Upon stepping into the open parking garage, Dana immediately sought a way to contact Galan's room, but the options were limited. The only available method was a thumbprint scanner to gain access through the doors, akin to the standard security setup for all the residences in Salt Pine Acres.

Dana's curiosity turned to concern as she heard a muffled scream echoing through the expansive parking garage. Her instincts kicked in, and she swiftly turned her gaze towards the source of the sound. There, in the dimly lit corner of the garage, a parked vehicle seemed to be the epicenter of the commotion.

Driven by a mix of apprehension and determination, Dana decided to investigate further. Carefully hugging the wall to remain inconspicuous, she tiptoed toward the moving car, her senses heightened with each step. As she drew nearer, she could now discern the silhouette of someone inside the vehicle.

The moans and screams grew more intense, and the sound of the car shaking became clearer. Dana stopped one car before and peeked over the trunk of the vehicle. She gasped as her eyes fell on Aria riding Galan in his car. Soon after, the car's shaking came to a halt. Dana was shocked by what she'd witnessed. In a panic, she took her phone out and snapped a picture of Aria and Galan in the car making out.

Dana, still hidden, observed Aria exiting the car and quickly leaving the parking garage. Suspicion gnawed at her, wondering about the connection between Aria and Galan's unexpected encounter. Remaining discreet, Dana cautiously peeked under nearby cars, tracking Aria's movements through her feet as she walked away and eventually departed the garage.

A couple of minutes elapsed before Galan finally emerged from the vehicle. Dana's heart raced as she watched him straighten his attire and run his fingers through his hair, trying to appear composed. Without wasting any time, Galan approached the elevator and used his thumb to unlock the door. Stepping inside, he swiftly pressed the button to close the doors.

Just as the elevator doors were about to seal shut, Galan's eyes caught a glimpse of Hans driving away. However, before the doors could fully close, Dana made her move, dashing into the elevator.

"Dana?!" Galan asked, startled. "What the hell are you doing?"

"We need to talk," Dana stated.

"You know a phone call would be sufficient, right?" Galan remarked in a panic.

"I tried, ok, but it kept going to voicemail. But this is important; I had to do this in person," Dana replied, blushing.

Oh fuck, my phone's still recording... I forgot to switch it off...

As Dana and Galan disembarked from the elevator, they entered his apartment on the top floor. While Dana's attention was absorbed in exploring her surroundings, Galan seized the opportunity to discreetly act. Swiftly but subtly, he retrieved his phone, putting an end to the recording he had been making earlier. He decided not to share the video online and instead chose to save it privately.

Concealing his actions, Galan skillfully returned the phone to his pocket, hiding any evidence of his previous recording. Turning to face Dana, he wore an enigmatic expression, masking whatever might be going on in his mind. He realized that Dana's presence and their encounter in the elevator raised questions that demanded an explanation.

With a deep breath to steady himself, Galan addressed Dana, "So, what did you need to talk to me about?"

Dana stood in silence, her thoughts swirling like a storm. Galan, perceptive as ever, noticed her contemplation and approached her with a concerned expression. "Dana?" he said, his voice gentle, as he positioned himself in front of her.

"This was a mistake," Dana exclaimed. In a sudden panic, she swiftly turned on her heels and hurried back towards the elevator doors. "Talk to me. What's wrong? You've been acting strange lately," Galan expressed.

"That's the problem! You're the only one who seems to notice when something is off with me," Dana gushed.

Dana turned to face him, her gaze averted, unable to meet his eyes directly.

"What's on your mind?" Galan softly prompted.

"Why my sister?" asked Dana.

"Sorry?" said Galan.

"Please don't treat me like I'm stupid. I know you're hooking up with Aria. Why her?" Dana sternly questioned.

Galan found himself at a loss for words, his confusion evident as he scratched his head. He gave her some space and walked over to the kitchen, retrieving a bottle of water from the fridge. "Can I offer you something to drink?" he offered.

"I'm fine. Stop dodging my question, Galan; it's important," Dana answered.

As Galan approached Dana, he noticed her arms tightly folded, a clear sign of her discomfort. She continued to avoid making eye contact with him, further deepening the mystery of her inner turmoil. With a mixture of empathy and determination, he positioned himself across from her, leaning casually against the wall.

The silence between them hung heavy, like a thick fog blanketing the room. "I honestly don't know what it is about Aria that drew me in. It just happened. I saw her, and at that moment, she seemed sad. I wanted to be the reason she smiled again. It's a feeling I have been trying to shake, but no matter what I try, it always comes back to her," Galan explained.

"What about me?" Dana asked quietly.

"I'm sorry?" Galan responded.

"It's always Aria. Everyone sees her, but nobody ever sees me. What's wrong with me that you can't see me the way you see her?" Dana stated while staring at the floor.

"Dana—" Galan replied softly.

"No, don't do that," Dana snapped.

"Don't do what?" Galan inquired.

"I'm always just the kid sister, a child. Nobody sees me the way they see Aria, Maeve, or Eyla. I'm tired of being treated like a child. I want more; I deserve more," Dana declared sadly.

"What about Eder?" Galan questioned.

"Eder is fucking Maeve. I knew those two were hooking up, or rather, they never stopped," Dana answered.

"What? If Eder is doing that, why are you with him?" asked Galan.

"Because he is the only one that gives me any kind of attention. So, even if I'm not the only one, it's still something," Dana explained.

"Why would you settle for something like that? You're such a great person. You deserve someone who doesn't treat you like an option; you shouldn't have to settle for anything less. There are people out there who would kill for someone like you, someone who can give you the attention you crave," Galan replied.

"Maybe if they took their eyes off my sister, they would see me," Dana grumbled as she looked up at Galan.

"I'm not that kind of person. You're just a kid. I couldn't do that to you; it's not right," Galan responded.

"I'm close to seventeen, and sixteen is the age of consent," Dana stated.

"Just because the law says it's ok doesn't make it alright. A good man would know that and not exploit your need for attention. What Eder is doing is sick and wrong, and it makes me sad to know that's what you are going through. But even if age wasn't the issue, you would still be the girl I chose after it didn't work with your sister. You deserve better than that; I couldn't do that to you.

"I think you are really special. You're mature and brilliant, and you are going to do great things. I truly believe that, and I hope you stop settling for anything less than what you deserve. Tell you what, if anyone breaks your heart, or I see any tears from those big bright eyes, I'll end them without hesitation," Galan professed.

Dana unfolded her hands and walked over to Galan, "I just want to be seen by someone who sees me the way you do." In a sudden rush of emotions, Dana found solace in Galan's presence. Without a word, she embraced him tightly, seeking comfort in his warm embrace. Her tears flowed freely, and he could hear her soft sniffles as she buried her face in his chest. Galan's heart ached for her, and without hesitation, he wrapped his arms around her.

"Come on, I'll take you back to the café," Galan whispered.

"Can I stay here a little bit longer?" asked Dana softly.

"Your sister is going to wonder where you are. I think I've been accused of enough things," Galan responded.

"Please, Galan, please let me," Dana softly pleaded, squeezing her arms around him tighter.

Galan looked down at her and felt her grip tighten. "Ok, you can stay for a little while longer," he conceded. "I'm nothing special, you know. I'm not sure what you see in me. I'm so fucked from my past relationships that I'm barely a person anymore. I'm just a broken toy, hoping one day someone will want to put the pieces back together," Galan continued.

Dana looked up at him with watery eyes. "Maybe you're not the only one that's broken," she whispered.

She's just a kid; she shouldn't have to feel like this.

GARRICK WILDER

AGE: 27
SIGN: TAURUS
FUN FACT: *UNAVAILABLE* (HE HIT ME ON
THE HEAD WITH MY MIC. I HATE IT HERE.)

Chapter Twenty-nine

With utmost tenderness, Galan reached up and gently wiped the tears from Dana's cheeks. "Come on, how about I make you something to eat?" he offered.

As Galan stepped into the kitchen, he decided to channel his concern into a simple act of kindness. With a thoughtful smile, he turned on the stove. "This is a big hit in the café: grilled chicken breast, glazed in a smoked honey sauce, pickles for some sourness that balances the sweet, lettuce, tomatoes, and smoked gruyere cheese. Toasted and pressed on both sides; seasoned with black truffle salt and done," Galan explained while preparing the sandwich for Dana. The sweet aroma of the honey glaze sizzling on the pan filled the air, enveloping the kitchen in a tantalizing fragrance that seemed to wash away the heaviness of the moment. The sound of the crackling pan added a subtle rhythm to their conversation.

"Tell me what you think," Galan said warmly, sliding the plate across the smooth kitchen island to her side.

"Excuse me, I'm a lady, not an animal. I would like a knife and fork, please," Dana teased.

As Galan turned around, his eyes caught a glimmer of playfulness. He reached into a nearby drawer next to the stove and retrieved a knife and fork. With a mischievous grin, he tossed the knife gently into the air, its gleaming blade flipping and spinning gracefully. Dana's unease was evident as she watched the knife dance, her heart skipping a beat with each twirl.

However, Galan's smile reassured her. With a calm and practiced motion, he deftly caught the knife just above the plate, holding it between two fingers on the blade's end. His fingers moved with a swift elegance as he twirled the knife through his hand, displaying a skill that spoke of both confidence and control.

As the knife came to rest, Galan lightly pressed it into the sandwich, the crunch of the hard-toasted bread mixing with the softness of the filling. The sound echoed in the kitchen, and Dana couldn't help but be captivated by his flair and finesse.

"Are you insane? What if you got hurt?" Dana asked anxiously.

"Before I built Grounded Coffee House, the building was a butcher's shop for exotic and sought-after cuts of meat, mostly A5 Wagyu. There wasn't a lot to do while maintaining the building. So, I'd clean surfaces and sharpen the knives when I got bored. Eventually, I started playing with them to pass the time. Getting comfortable with the knives is what played a major part in the food menu chosen for the café. I figured coffee alone would get boring, so I did my research, and through trial and error, I came up with a food menu to pair well with the coffee," Galan explained.

"You really put a lot of work into this place haven't you?" Dana remarked.

"I did; I needed this. Failing was never an option. I couldn't go back to the life I had, and I refused to keep living that way. I worked my ass off to build this. It's hard to just walk away from it. Even though there has been so much drama since handing over, I couldn't stay away. The café played a part in me coming back, too," Galan continued.

Dana picked up the knife and cut off a small neatly sliced piece of the sandwich. With a hint of anticipation, she brought the fork to her mouth and tasted the flavors that Galan had artfully combined. "Wow, this is good—Oh my God!"

"There is the kick of flavor; the honey sauce is robust on the first bite, and as you chew, the pickles seep through, and the salty cheese just explodes on your tastebuds. That's what people come back for: the passion that goes into making these things. It's not just about following the directions on paper. The more you understand what you are serving, the more innovative you can be. It's all about paying attention to the customers, the compliments you get, why you get them, what it was paired with, and if it was eaten alone. What is the pattern? What is the common variable?

"That is what your job is. You have a team of talented staff to cook and prepare everything for you but the more hands-on you get, the better you'll understand your products and your customers. As you see the opportunity for improvement, you'll start learning about what people want and need. And it's up to you to take that chance to give them what they want or show them what they need," Galan explained.

Dana took another bite and soaked in what Galan was saying to her. She took a deep breath and looked at Galan, "Teach me, stay here in Salt Pine Acres. Be my mentor, and we can make Grounded Coffee House into a global phenomenon together," Dana exclaimed.

Galan smiled and leaned on the kitchen island, "As much as I would love to see Grounded turn into something greater, I've wanted to leave this place for a while. I've never felt like I fit in; I felt like there was nothing here for me. Grounded was my ticket out of the life I was in. So, when it became a success, I planned a new beginning—a way to leave everything behind and start fresh," Galan informed her.

"And what if Aria picked you? Then what?" asked Dana. "Would you stay then?"

The room fell into a hushed silence as Galan bowed his head, a mix of emotions flickering across his face. He knew that what he was about to say might challenge everything he had shared earlier.

"You would do it for her, but you wouldn't for me," Dana's whispered words conveyed a sense of emotional turmoil that mirrored Galan's own internal conflict. As she got up from her chair, a subtle tremor in her movements betrayed the weight of her thoughts. She took a few steps, attempting to walk away from the intensity of the moment.

Galan caught up to her; he reached out and gently took her hand in his, "Dana, it's not like that."

Dana yanked her hand away, "That's what they always say, but the fact is, I am never given the same chance that everyone else seems to get. You would chase her, knowing she would never choose you; you would let her treat you like shit just to be close to her. She doesn't deserve you; I would be good to you. I would never do what she is doing to you, Malek, and the guys before. There is a reason Garrick didn't work out; there is a reason she has been single all this time. It's because Aria will always do what Aria wants. She gets whatever she wants, and it doesn't matter who gets hurt in the process as long as she gets what she wants. Take your own advice; don't settle for someone who doesn't deserve you," Dana ranted.

"D—" Galan said.

"No!!! Don't call me that. That's only for people who are like family to me, and I don't want you thinking of me like that," Dana remarked.

"I'm sorry, Dana," Galan corrected.

"I would like to leave, please," Dana responded.

Galan nodded in agreement and scanned his thumb on the elevator panel. The doors opened, and Dana hurriedly stepped inside. She turned to him with a sweet and tender expression as they entered. "Walk me back to the café?" she asked, her voice filled with a gentle plea.

Galan stepped onto the elevator next to Dana and pressed the button to go down to the ground floor. As the elevator descended, the atmosphere was filled with an awkward silence that seemed to stretch on forever. Neither Galan nor Dana dared to meet each other's gaze, the weight of their emotions hanging heavily in the air.

Galan's mind was a whirlwind of thoughts, and he found himself revisiting Dana's offer to be partners at Grounded Coffee House.

If I stay, I get more face time with Aria. Showing up before always led to something awkward. But if I'm there and working closely with Dana, I can get more face time. Plus, Dana knows her sister better than any of Aria's friends would have. Dana is my ticket to your love; maybe it's not a bad idea. Also, being a business partner means Eder and Garrick can't approach me carelessly. Dana is the ultimate shield; Aria won't let them get near her. This might be a blessing in disguise.

The elevator reached the ground floor, and the doors slid open. Dana exited and turned to Galan, who was lost in thought. "Hey, you are coming?" she asked.

Galan snapped out of it, "Sorry, yeah, I'm coming." Galan stepped off and followed her, "You know we could take my car instead of you having to walk—"

"I would rather not sit in the car you just fucked my sister in," Dana snarked.

Oh, fuck! She saw us!

"No comment," Galan replied playfully.

Dana couldn't suppress a deep sigh as she distanced herself from Galan, her demeanor growing noticeably cold during their walk back to the café. Undeterred, Galan followed closely behind, adjusting his pace to match her tiny steps.

Feeling the weight of the silence between them, Galan finally decided to break it. "Has Aria called you to find out where you went?" he inquired.

"Aria is too busy fawning over Malek to worry about where I am and where I am not," answered Dana.

"That can't be true," Galan responded.

"Here, check my phone and prove me wrong!" Dana remarked. Her frustration was evident in her sharp response as she swiftly retrieved her phone from her pocket and tossed it to Galan. Caught off guard, he stumbled slightly but caught the phone, careful not to drop it. As he tapped the home button to turn on the screen, his eyes scanned the display, revealing an absence of notifications from anyone.

The lack of messages seemed to intensify the tension between them, leaving Galan uncertain about how to proceed.

"You can catch a knife flipping out of the air, but a phone made you stumble?" Dana stated. "See, I told you! I know my sister; what she has with Malek is unlike anything she has ever had. But that scares her. She has never experienced the happiness he brings her, and she is falling into old habits because she doesn't know how to deal with it. It's the reason she is hiding and hooking up with you. Right now, it's you; if you left, she would hook up with someone else. And it's not because she cares or likes you, but because you are nothing more than a fix to satisfy her needs.

"Aria was never planning to settle down with someone. Life for her is so hectic she barely has time for me or anyone else. Since Malek came into the picture, she stepped away from her life of fame. She came here for peace and to free up her time so she could spend it with him without worrying about the public eye. I have never seen Aria do this for anyone. She loves her life; it's why she can't let go of her old habits, even for Malek. But he is changing her, and soon enough, she will let go. That boy is a Godsend, and he is exactly what she needs," Dana explained.

I see; then I don't have much time. I need to show Aria that I am the one for her before she completely falls for Malek. He doesn't know what she wants; there is a reason she is sneaking around with me. He wouldn't even spend the night because his mother would be upset. He isn't dangerous and spontaneous; he isn't willing to break the rules for you. It's why you came back to me. It's ok, Aria; I will fight for you. May the better man win your heart!

"I see," Galan replied.

"You don't seem upset that she's just using you," Dana commented.

"I told you, I'm barely a person anymore. I've been through so much pain that I'm numb to it now. I just hope one day I feel something again, and maybe I can find that with her," Galan responded.

"And what if she breaks your heart the way the rest did?" asked Dana curiously.

"What else do I have to lose?" Galan's attempt at a smile was evident. Dana couldn't help but notice as he began to speak; his eyes betrayed a deeper emotion as they glistened with unshed tears.

The remainder of the walk was shrouded in silence, both Galan and Dana lost in their thoughts. They marched on with their heads down, eyes fixed on the sidewalk, each seemingly absorbed in their own world as they strolled down the street.

Approaching Grounded Coffee House, Galan suddenly came to a halt, breaking the rhythm of their footsteps. He turned to face Dana, "Well, I hope you enjoy the rest of your day."

BROKEN TOYS

"You sure you don't want to come inside? You didn't get to eat back at your place," Dana exclaimed.

"I don't want to make things weird right now. If what you said is true, then Aria seeing me in there might not be the best thing right now," Galan explained.

"You have a point. Thanks for walking with me," Dana kindly stated.

"You're welcome," Galan replied.

"I hope you seriously consider my offer; I think we could do great things together," Dana commented.

"You mean Grounded, right?" Galan asked.

As Dana smiled and playfully shrugged her shoulders, she pushed open the café door and entered, still carrying the unspoken word 'Bye' on her lips as she mouthed it to Galan through the glass door. Galan returned her smile and replied with a brief wave as he turned to head back home.

Chapter Thirty

*G*arrick and Eder finally made it to the hospital later that day. As they entered the lobby, they spotted Maeve seated patiently, waiting for Garrick to pick her up after her second check-up had cleared her for discharge. Garrick's truck pulled up at the hospital entrance. Eder promptly hopped out of the front passenger seat, then courteously opened the back door for Maeve, gesturing for her to get in, following right behind her.

"How are you feeling, Maeve?" asked Garrick.

"I'm not in any pain unless I move too much, then it agitates the wounds. But as long as I'm relatively still, I don't notice it," Maeve replied.

"Well, good. We have some news that'll cheer you up," Garrick stated.

"Oh?" said Maeve.

"Garrick caught on to Galan. He basically confirmed our suspicions when he called Garrick's bluff," Eder explained.

"What do you mean?" asked Maeve.

"Galan knew I didn't have my phone with any proof of him being on the property. The only way he could be so calm about it is because he had to be sure the phone was no longer in my possession," Garrick clarified.

"Then let's go after him. We have good reason to act, right?" Maeve inquired.

"Yeah, we do. But it's just us. This accusation may not be well received since Eder attacked Galan twice, and all three of us got caught lurking outside Aria's house. That's where you come in; we need Bodhi and Eyla to back us up. Think you can make that happen?" asked Garrick.

"Done. Seeing me wrapped in these bandages will surely sway them to go against Galan. Besides that, it won't be too hard convincing them because they both already hate him," Maeve answered.

"Good, he can dismiss us three, but he can't fight five claims all at once. The moment Aria sees him as a threat, we can make our move. Did you get the stuff we'll need?" questioned Garrick.

Maeve opened her handbag and revealed several bottles of anesthesia and syringes.

"No scalpels?" asked Eder.

"Those are stored separately. I only had access to these because we fund this department and help buy these items, so I can get access to stock easily. I mean, it's a big hospital; things go missing all the time," Maeve exclaimed.

"That will do; I still don't think we need those. Eder and I could take him as long as he has nowhere to run. Regardless, I'd rather be safe than sorry," Garrick stated.

"There is still one problem, mate. He said he has things on us that could run our reputations into the ground. If we get caught up in any online scandals, it's over. We could kiss the Scarlets' goodbye. Not to mention, I am a public figure; it would tank my reputation," Eder informed them.

"I've got that covered. All we need to do is get his phone. Anthony could disable anything he has and wipe his devices clean, that phone and anything else he might have it linked to," answered Garrick.

"Are you serious, mate?" asked Eder.

"Oh, one hundred percent. You've got nothing to worry about," Garrick replied.

"So, it's on, then? We take down Galan Rain tonight?" Maeve remarked.

"How are we going to get to him? His apartment is like a fortress; the security systems are top-notch," stated Eder. "Could Anthony do something about that?"

"No, not a chance. Anthony isn't some secret agent; he's just a brilliant I.T. guy. He can do small things, but breaking a security system? Highly unlikely," Garrick replied.

"Then we draw Galan out," Maeve answered.

"How do we do that?" Eder speculated.

"We are going to throw Aria a proper congratulations party for her and Dana at their place. Leave it to Eyla, Bodhi, and myself to get Galan to the party," Maeve responded.

"Guys, I think we have quite an opportunity on our hands; we could kill two birds with one stone,"

Garrick claimed as all eyes fell on him. "If we can get Malek there too, we could take him out the same way; we have a lot of this stuff. We could hit them both and toss them over the mountain's edge. No one would even see it coming."

"Don't you think that's being a bit too greedy? It's going to be hard enough to get one person. How can we slip out with two of them without anyone noticing? That's crazy, mate," Eder pointed out.

"What if we hit everyone?" asked Garrick.

"What?" Maeve exclaimed.

"At some point, we will toast their new journey with the café. What if we spike the toast and knock everyone out? Then, we could easily toss Galan and Malek over the side of the mountain. No trouble, no witnesses," Garrick explained.

"Are you insane? If they ingest anesthetics, the complications could kill them if we don't get the dosages correct. It's impossible to regulate it if you spike a drink," Maeve commented.

"I guess it's a good thing we have a medical prodigy to help make sure that doesn't happen, huh? Come on, Maeve, we have the chance of a lifetime; we can't miss this," Garrick whined.

"This is too much, guys. If we get this wrong and accidentally kill Aria or Dana, we could all kiss our freedom goodbye. You know how her dad is…," said Eder.

"The only people who are gonna die are Galan and Malek. There must be something, Maeve; just think," Garrick remarked.

"Eder's right. It's too much of a risk. Going after both of them is risky; I won't put Aria in danger like that. Eyla and Bodhi would never go for that, one monster at a time. Let's hit Galan first; he's the one we have the least access to. Last I heard, he was leaving town. That could still happen at any time because we have no idea why he is still here. Malek, on the other hand, goes wherever Aria goes. We can always get rid of him easily," Maeve stated.

"Guys, Galan is smart. Don't you think Garrick being at the party would send off red flags? Dana is also on the outs with me at the moment. I wouldn't be able to attend unless I apologized to Dana, and she won't want to see me right now," Eder expressed.

"Fuck, you're right; we would have no business being there. Eder, you, and Maeve could still get away with being there, you just need to kiss ass and grovel, and Dana would be ok. But it would be a big giveaway, especially after today's encounter. Do you think the both of you can pull this off without me?" asked Garrick.

"No, but I bet Bodhi, Eyla, and I could. All we need to do is hit him with a shot of the anesthetic. Once he goes down, we can bring in the two of you and prove he was dangerous to Aria. With Eyla and Bodhi backing up what you have to say, Aria will listen and do whatever it takes to protect her family," stated Maeve.

"Guys, maybe we are getting ahead of ourselves. Why don't we just go to Aria beforehand? We have the proof; there is no reason she won't believe us. We acted without consulting them before. Don't you think it builds credibility to do it this time? Let's just say we do pull it off; she will still know we planned this without her. That may not bode well for us; we need to let them in on it," Eder suggested.

"Are you sure you're up for this, Barlow? You have been fighting this ever since we started," asked Garrick.

"No, Eder has a point. If Aria found out that we thought Galan was dangerous and didn't tell her, she would have our asses for it, especially if Dana got caught up in the middle. I think it's the safe move," Maeve exclaimed.

"Are you kidding me, Maeve?" asked Garrick. "And what happens if she doesn't go for it?"

"Then it will be her fault when 'Galan' kills Malek," Maeve responded with a sinister smirk.

"You know you scare me, right?" Garrick smiled.

"You in, babe?" Maeve asked Eder.

"Alright, I'm in," answered Eder.

"Then it's on, Maeve; get Bodhi and Eyla on a call. Fill them in, and let's get this done," Garrick instructed.

As Dana stood behind the bar, her phone still in hand, she found herself captivated by Galan's social media account. The professionally-taken picture of him, standing confidently at Grounded Coffee House in a sharp suit, left her in awe. Her gaze was fixated on the image, and a mix of emotions swirled within her.

Unbeknownst to her, Aria and Malek emerged from the back room, walking past Dana on their way to the front of the café. They exchanged a curious glance, noticing the slightly distant look on Dana's face. "Since when do you keep your phone while working?" Aria teased. Malek's arm around her

"Just finished a call with a supplier," Dana lied, quickly locking her phone to hide her screen.

"Did you have lunch? Malek and I are going to the diner; I'm starving," Aria claimed.

"I'm good; you two enjoy," Dana replied.

"Alright, see you in a bit," answered Aria, stepping outside the door with Malek.

Dana waved at her before looking down at her phone and unlocking it to see the image of Galan again.

Dana opened her messages and texted Galan. 'Aria isn't here; it won't be weird if you came inside now.'

Galan replied, 'I would, but the café is such a far walk!'

Dana chuckled, 'I can come to get you if you prefer.'

Galan responded by saying, 'A gentleman would never let a woman come alone.'

Dana smirked and sent a winking emoji.

'I should have phrased that very differently….' Galan commented.

'I kinda liked how you phrased it the first time,' Dana texted back.

Ignoring her statement, Galan responded, 'You have customers to tend to, no phones!'

Dana chuckled and messaged, 'I'm working on expanding a more personal touch when dealing with cute customers.'

Galan replied, 'When you find one, let me know.'

Dana rolled her eyes and smiled. 'Fine, I'll go, but I really hope you rethink my offer to return to the café. I think you and me can do a lot of things.'

Galan responded to her message, saying, 'I'm definitely thinking about it; give me till tonight to give you an answer?'

Dana's heart raced; she leaned off the bar and gulped. 'Tonight is fine.'

Galan sent Dana a smiling emoji.

As Dana smiled and blushed at her phone, Alliyah returned from a table and caught sight of her trying to conceal her emotions by covering her face with her device. Intrigued, Alliyah couldn't resist teasing Dana a little, "Everything ok, boss?"

Dana, unable to remove the smile from her face, answered, "Everything is fine; I just got some good news."

As Galan walked upstairs, his gaze fell upon the locked door at the end of the hall. A smile tugged at the corners of his lips. He continued down the hall and entered his bedroom. Feeling a wave of exhaustion wash over him, Galan flopped onto his bed like a falling leaf, surrendering to his weariness. His body felt heavy and drained, and it didn't take long for sleep to claim him. As Galan dozed off, little did he know that Garrick's plan was quietly being put into motion.

Chapter Thirty-one

The day flew by, and as the sun dipped below the horizon, darkness began to weave its way through the gates of Salt Pine Acres. Garrick, Eder, and Aria's inseparable trio of friends made their way into the Salt Pine Acres. Dana was occupied with the evening rush at the café while Aria and Malek were at her house. Dana witnessed the convoy of vehicles as they drove past Grounded Coffee House headed to Aria.

Aria had received a message from Maeve earlier, hinting at a surprise planned for her and a matter of importance that required a face-to-face conversation.

Perched by the pool's edge, Aria and Malek found themselves in awe of the breathtaking scenery sprawled before them. Their spot provided a vantage point atop the mountain, offering uninterrupted views of the surrounding landscapes. The sun's last rays painted the heavens with a captivating palette of red and orange hues, blending harmoniously with the dark clouds that veiled the sky.

As the distant rumble of Garrick's truck echoed through the air, Aria became uneasy.

"Stay here and look cute, ok, boo? I'll be right back," Aria leaned in and softly whispered her excitement to Malek, who responded with a knowing nod as he remained engrossed in reading a book.

As Aria strolled toward the front gate, her heart danced with a mix of curiosity and joy, eager to greet her arriving friends. Eyla, Bodhi, and Maeve dashed in with beaming smiles, and before Aria could even utter a word, they enveloped her in warm, tight hugs.

"Oh my God, Maeve, how are you doing, sweetheart? You must be in pain," Aria exclaimed as she hugged Maeve.

"I could be better, but it could have been worse, so I'm thankful for small mercies," answered Maeve.

Eyla was distant and quiet, shying away behind Bodhi and Maeve. Aria walked between them and hugged Eyla, "How are you, doll?"

"I'm ok," Eyla replied.

"Still being a baby because I snapped at you?" Aria joked.

"No," Eyla chuckled.

"You know I love you; you just get on my nerves. That's what best friends are for. You know my life would be boring if I hadn't met you," Aria

As Eyla returned Aria's hug with a genuine smile, the warmth of reconciliation filled the air around them, reaffirming the strength of their bond.

Eyla's smile brightened as she warmly reciprocated Aria's hug. Meanwhile, Garrick and Eder entered the compound shortly after. Aria glanced up at them but avoided making eye contact with Garrick. With a sense of tension lingering in the air, she approached them, "Why are you two here?" she questioned them.

"That's what we need to talk to you about, Ari," Bodhi responded in their stead. "Garrick, how about you explain this!"

Aria turned to Bodhi in confusion and back to Garrick. "I just want to say I am sorry; I shouldn't have been stalking you outside your house. I know it was wrong, and I had no business being there. That being said, had I not been there, I wouldn't have caught Galan lurking around and peeking inside your house," Garrick replied.

"This again? Are you kidding me?" asked Aria, frustrated.

"Hear him out, Ari. I think you should hear this," Bodhi gently stepped forward, coaxing Aria as he placed his reassuring hands on her shoulders. Aria looked up at Bodhi, her eyes reflecting a mix of emotions, and hesitated for a moment. Taking a deep breath, she turned back to Garrick.

"That was the first thing. The second is that Eder had a run-in with Galan. He was also wrong on his part, approaching Galan like that. It was a misunderstanding; we found that out afterward because there wasn't anything going on with him and Dana," Garrick continued.

Bodhi added, "Maeve and I also played a part in that. I carelessly played along with Maeve's lie and stirred up trouble. When we met Galan, we thought he was a nice guy, so we felt territorial and tried to scare him off. We apologize for that; it wasn't our place. We had no right, and we are sorry."

"Truly, we're sorry, Ari," Maeve chimed in.

"However, those mistakes led us to Eder and Galan's first interaction. Although we were in the wrong, Galan was defensive about it. He insinuated that Eder and Dana were sleeping together, and he was leaning towards using that information to tarnish Eder's reputation. That, in turn, would have dirtied Dana's in the process and, ultimately, your family's reputation," Garrick stated.

Aria's eyes narrowed, and her eyebrows furrowed, signaling the rising tide of anger within her. Garrick pressed on, "Fast forward to the night Maeve, Eder, and I was camped outside your house after Eder came to us with this information. We were contemplating how to tell you, but we were also hoping we would run into Galan snooping again so we could have some hard proof.

"Unfortunately, that night, we had a run-in with someone hiding in your backyard. Eder, Maeve, and I chased him across the town, and I eventually lost him in the mountains and woods. In the middle of all of that, he had thrown a brick through our car's windshield. He damaged Maeve, stole my phone during our scuffle, and disappeared. I had snapped a picture of the person before the chase began, but my flash accidentally fired, alerting him of what I'd done, which is why I assume he took my phone in the middle of our little scrap.

"At first, it was just a hunch that the masked person was Galan, so we'd asked you for a few days to prove it was him. We've got it now," Garrick explained.

"You have hard proof Galan did this? Really?" said Aria skeptically.

"It's true," Eder replied. "Keep going, mate," Eder said, patting Garrick on the shoulder.

"After the hospital, we were pissed that something like that had happened to Maeve. We had our suspicions, but to be honest, we weren't completely certain because the person spoke to me in German, I think. A part of me wanted to believe it was Galan. I just wanted a reason to beat the fuck out of this guy," Garrick remarked.

Aria shook her head in disappointment, "Typical Garrick, raging and not thinking before he does something stupid."

"Ari, let him finish," Bodhi exclaimed.

"I deserved that; I know what I did to you was unforgivable. I never should have put my hands on you, and for that, I will never forgive myself. But I am hoping what we are about to do will be a step in the right direction to make up for my mistakes," Garrick stated.

"I'm listening," Aria replied sternly.

"Well, according to you and Dana, Galan was supposed to leave that night, right? That's why you dismissed the idea of it being him, and that's fair. But he was here today; Eder had another run-in with him, and he recorded Eder 'stalking' him outside of his apartment. He even threatened to use the footage to blackmail him," Garrick informed her.

"I expected better from you, Eder. You, of all people, how could you do something so stupid? You are constantly in the public eye; your platform on social media has the influence of millions around the world," Aria exclaimed.

"Fast forward to a while after that, where you found Galan and Dana arguing behind the café, and you and Eder had to intervene. Why was he even there? Why not come in through the front of the building? Why sneak around the back like that? After Eder told me he was still in town, we needed to confront him about the night we chased him. But for some reason, Galan was waiting with his phone at the ready, recording everything the moment we showed up. He threatened us, saying that if we tried anything, he would leak information about Eder, Dana, and me, tarnishing all of our reputations. He said that if something happened to him, he would not cancel the video from going public once it stopped recording," Garrick continued.

"What about Dana?" Aria grunted.

"Galan said he had proof that Eder was sleeping with her and blackmailed him with a rape scandal. He was willing to damage the reputation that Dana had worked so hard for, and indirectly yours," Garrick answered solemnly.

"What!" Aria shouted.

"Keep it together, Ari," said Bodhi.

"But he slipped up," Garrick continued. "We had no hard proof that Galan was the one we had chased last night. But the moment he threatened Dana, I wasn't going to let him do that to her or you. So, I bluffed about having a photo of him the night we found someone creeping around your backyard. He calmly called my bluff and even smiled like he knew I was lying!"

"Are you joking? That's your proof? That Galan was calm about it?" snapped Aria.

"Galan was calm because he knew he'd lifted my phone during our scuffle. He knew I didn't have it in my possession, so I didn't pose a threat to him. He didn't deny it happening; he only denied me having the proof. He's smart, and he knows we can't pin this on him, but it's because of that arrogance that he showed his hand. I don't know what he has on Dana, Eder, myself, or anyone else here. But even if he starts rumors, it's enough to put a strain on your family's good name. We don't want that for Dana or you," Garrick claimed sympathetically.

Aria stood her ground, her breaths coming heavily as waves of rage washed over her. The mere thought of someone threatening her family ignited an inferno of emotions within her. "How sure are you? Why should I trust you?" she asked.

"Because I'm not doing this for you. He hurt my sister, and I wouldn't wish the same to happen to Dana or you. Something didn't sit right with me the night we met, with none of us actually. We all got a bad vibe about him. Tell me you don't feel it, too!" Garrick probed.

He's right. I have been on edge about Galan since the start. I am not leaving anything to chance; if he really is a danger to Dana, I wouldn't be able to live with myself if she got hurt because of him. What does he have on Eder and Dana? Why is he blackmailing them? I knew something was off about that guy; I've always been drawn to those sick motherfuckers. I should have known he was trouble the moment he fought the urge to fuck me in public. This is my fault, too; I couldn't let go and stop my bad habits. I have Malek now. I had no business running around with him. That's on me, and if he hurts Dana, that will be my fault. I need to be a big sister right now and put a stop to this!

"Fine, let's say he is everything you claim he is. What are you going to do about it?" Aria inquired.

"The less you know, the better. We just needed you to be in on this before anything goes down. We didn't want to do this behind your back," Garrick answered.

"So, what? You just expect me to leave the safety of my family up to you?" questioned Aria.

"No, to us," Eyla replied.

"Galan is smart. He will smell a rat if Eder and Garrick are anywhere near him. All we need is for you to get Galan here, and we can take care of the rest," Maeve explained.

"What do you mean here?" asked Aria.

"We are throwing you a proper celebration for the grand reopening of Grounded Coffee House right here at your place. Get Galan here and leave the rest to us," Maeve responded.

"Can you handle that?" asked Bodhi.

"Yeah, I can do that," Aria agreed. "What about Eder and Garrick? What are you two going to be doing?"

"We are going to make ourselves scarce. We're counting on you guys to get this done. We would be just down the mountain at the employees' housing units, out of the way, just in case Galan gets uneasy about seeing us in the town," Garrick informed Aria.

"What if something goes wrong?" Aria queried.

"Trust me, that'll take minimal effort. Just keep Galan occupied and leave the rest to us. Once it's done, call Eder and me, and we'll take it from there," Garrick responded.

"We won't let him hurt Dana or you. We love you guys and will do anything for you," Maeve added.

As Aria looked at Bodhi, Garrick, and Eder, her thoughts couldn't help but drift to Dana, the weight of concern evident in her gaze. Aria gave them the green light to proceed with their plan. As night fell, the world around them was swiftly engulfed in darkness. Dark clouds loomed, obscuring the setting sun, and distant rumbles of thunder echoed through the air, adding an ominous tone to the unfolding events.

With everything settled, Garrick and Eder hopped into Garrick's truck and set off on their journey. Meanwhile, Maeve, Bodhi, and Eyla started preparing for the upcoming celebration, eager to make it a memorable event. Aria bid them farewell and made her way to the café to have a conversation with Dana, leaving Malek with her friends at home. As Garrick and Eder passed by the café while leaving Salt Pine Acres, Eder turned to Garrick, curiosity shining in his eyes, and said, "Your plan worked like a charm, mate. Making it about Dana really set Aria off!"

"I know Aria well enough to know that what she cares most about in this world is her little sister. In all my time with her, the one thing she has never compromised on was her sister. She would do anything for Dana; she is the definition of overprotective. I figured the best chance we had was if we focused on Galan being a threat to Dana. If I'd made it about Aria or our suspicions, Aria's hatred would trump our plans. I needed her to listen, and thankfully, I know exactly what sways her the most," Garrick explained.

"You think they can pull this off?" Eder wondered.

"I have total faith in my sister. We have done everything we ever needed to get where we are. There's not a doubt in my mind she will see this through," Garrick replied.

"I know we haven't seen eye-to-eye much. When this is all over, I just want you to know that it doesn't change a thing," said Eder. Garrick turned to him as he continued, "I will never forgive you for abusing Aria. I don't care that you're Maeve's brother; I can't just pretend you are not an evil person for that, mate."

"You think I don't know what I did was wrong? Of course, that haunts me every single day of my life! I didn't want to do that; I lost control. I was so shot up on steroids and testosterone boosters I'd lost my head. What she did hurt me, but that didn't give me the right to put my hands on her," Garrick responded.

"What did she do that you felt the urge to beat her unconscious like that, mate?" asked Eder curiously.

Garrick sat in solemn silence, the weight of his thoughts palpable as he clutched the steering wheel with an unwavering intensity. Moments stretched into eternity as he wrestled with the emotions that had engulfed him.

Finally, after a deep, contemplative sigh that seemed to echo through the depths of his soul, he found the strength to respond. "Aria isn't the type of girl you can settle down with. I wanted something more, but she didn't. She was free, and she did whatever she wanted. She would tell me, 'Let's not put a label on what we are,' so that she could sleep with other people. Technically, she wouldn't be cheating because we weren't 'officially together.' I wasn't going for it. I wanted to spend my life with her, but she didn't want to break up; she wanted me to be the one to end it so she could say it was my fault.

"She would pick fights to make me lose my temper and then act like I was the crazy one. She got joy from being the one in control. Whenever I got upset and raised my voice, she would smile uncontrollably because it meant I'd lost control. So, she could now hold the moral high ground and tell me I was behaving crazy. I held out well for a while; I tried to keep it together, but that got her very upset. She didn't have her workaround to sleep with other guys, nor was she getting the upper hand in the power dynamic; we were just equals, both trying to make it work. Then she found out I was using steroids for my fights, and she started getting me these crazy strong concentrations. She made it look like she was being supportive by giving me the best tools to succeed at what I was doing.

"Those new steroids came with severe side effects of uncontrollable raging testosterone, mood swings, and crazy episodes of anger. Everything would upset me; I would be walking in the street, and someone would simply look in my direction, and I would lose my shit. I would only think of running up to them and kicking them in their stupid fucking faces.

"Unfortunately, it got addicting. I couldn't stop using it, and I started overdosing. It got to a point where I was an entirely different person. Aria stopped loving me, but I was still trying. She was done, but she didn't want to end it; she wanted me to be the reason it ended. So, she cheated on me with someone and made sure I caught them. I fought that anger for as long as I could, I really did, but then I blacked out in a rage. I don't remember anything much of that night, but I know I was kneeling over her unconscious body with a bloody knuckle. I had hit her until she stopped moving," Garrick's emotional dam finally crumbled under the weight of the memories. As he recalled the traumatic incident, his voice trembled with a mixture of sorrow and raw emotion. It was evident that the wounds were still fresh despite the passage of time.

Garrick's anguish became overwhelming, rendering him speechless amidst the sniffles and erratic breaths that escaped him. His emotions became too much to bear, and with a sense of urgency, he pulled his truck to the side of the road. Tears streamed down his face like a river, blurring his vision as he unbuckled his seatbelt and stumbled out of the vehicle.

He felt the need to escape the confined space, seeking solace under the night sky. With teardrops falling to the cold asphalt beneath him, Garrick stood in the stark illumination of his truck's headlights, the darkness surrounding him like a shroud. Eder acted swiftly, exiting the truck and approaching Garrick with a mix of compassion and worry etched across his face. But as he drew nearer, he witnessed Garrick's pain manifesting in a physical form. The world had become too much for him to bear, and in an outburst of frustration, he began striking the unforgiving ground with his clenched fists.

Reacting instinctively, Eder moved swiftly to prevent any further harm. He knew he had to stop Garrick from hurting himself, so he courageously rushed in, tackling his friend to the ground. As they grappled on the ground, Eder's grip on Garrick's arms was firm but gentle, offering both support and restraint.

"Easy, mate, easy!" Eder squeezed tight to stop his frantic movements.

"Let go of me!" Garrick screamed.

"It's ok, mate, it's ok," Eder said calmly.

"It's not! I loved her, Eder! I loved her with everything I had, and it wasn't enough," In the midst of his tears and distress, Garrick's determination surged within him. With an unexpected burst of energy, he managed to overpower Eder's grip, breaking free and rolling away from his restraint.

Surprised by the sudden turn of events, Eder raised himself onto his elbow, watching Garrick as he moved to a hands-and-knees position. The intensity of the emotions had not subsided entirely, but Garrick was trying to regain control over his breathing and composure.

"You have to take it easy, mate," Eder repeated firmly.

As Garrick's intense emotions continued to surge, his arm trembled uncontrollably. Feeling the weight of the world on his shoulders, he surrendered to the overwhelming emotions, collapsing onto the cold asphalt before finally rolling onto his back. He gazed up at the expanse of the dark sky above, the stars flickering like distant beacons of hope. The two friends lay side by side on the road, finding comfort in each other's presence.

Sniffling, Garrick reached up with a trembling hand, gently wiping away the lingering tears from his eyes. "I have to get her back, Eder. You don't love someone like that, and just let go! I will be whatever she needs me to be if it means I can have her again," he stated.

"So, this isn't just about the money?" Eder inquired.

"That's what I fooled myself into thinking. Maybe if I could focus on something else, it would stop the pain. But the truth is, I couldn't give a fuck if I ever got a cent from their fortune. I just want Aria back; I lost too much already, and some things you just can't replace," Garrick replied.

"Why? You sounded miserable while you were with her! What are you going back to?" Eder wondered.

"I would take being miserable with her than being happy without her any day. I fell hard for her, she was my first love, my first kiss, my first everything," answered Garrick.

"Weren't you with Eyla before Aria?" Eder probed.

"That's true, and everyone thinks Aria and I met after Eyla and I were done. Truth is, Aria and I met at Bodhi's mother's estate, and in one night, she did what Eyla couldn't do in six months," Garrick responded.

"You slept with her that night?" questioned Eder.

"Among other things, but I fell for her the moment I laid eyes on her. She made me feel seen for the first time, she made me feel wanted, and her lips were the sweetest I have ever tasted. I was young and somewhat of a romantic. The way things happened when we met was like something out of a novel. I'd never made that connection with Eyla, not before that night. When Aria showed me what true passion was, I tried to replicate it with Eyla, but it wasn't even close. Neither Eyla nor anyone that came after ever lived up to what I felt for Aria in that one night," Garrick explained.

As the night sky grew restless, a sudden rumble of thunder echoed through the air, heralding the arrival of rain. Fat droplets fell from the heavens, pitter-pattering on the ground and washing away the traces of emotion left on the asphalt.

Eder, feeling the first raindrops on his skin, swiftly rose to his feet. His hand outstretched, he extended it towards Garrick, offering him support to stand once more. "Come on, mate," he said.

As Garrick gazed up at Eder, their eyes met with a profound understanding that words could never fully express. Feeling Eder's reassuring grip, Garrick firmly clasped his friend's hand, allowing himself to be pulled up from the ground. "Let's get out of here," stated Garrick. Both of them swiftly got into his truck and continued down the mountain.

Chapter Thirty-two

Galan stirred from his slumber, jolted awake by the resounding booms of thunder. He peered out the window, greeted by a somber sight of darkened skies and a relentless downpour. With a groggy yawn, he reached for his phone, sat up in bed, and gently rubbed his eyes to shake off the sleep.

As he unlocked his phone to check the time, the clock showed just past seven, and he noticed a series of unread messages from Dana, patiently awaiting his attention. But before delving into them, he decided to open the security app, hoping to catch a glimpse of Aria at the café. The café's surveillance footage appeared on the screen, and he scanned the area eagerly. There was no sign of Aria at first, and just as he was about to close the app, his heart skipped a beat as he spotted her arriving outside the café, accompanied by Hans, both seeking refuge from the rain. Galan's face lit up with joy, witnessing Aria's arrival.

Unable to contain his happiness, he smiled warmly and cast the application to the television, allowing himself to immerse in the moment and get a better look at her. *There you are, beautiful; you look so sexy with your wet hair flowing down your shoulders.* As Galan basked in the warmth of seeing Aria on the café's security footage, memories of their times together flooded his mind. He couldn't help but reminisce about the moments they had shared in the comfort of his apartment and the intimate moment in his car.

As Aria walked up to the bar, she caught Dana's attention and waved her over. However, Dana was in the midst of serving another customer, so she mouthed a reassuring message to Aria, indicating she'd be there shortly. Understanding the situation, Aria took a seat on a barstool and patiently waited for Dana to finish up.

As she sat there, lost in her thoughts, Aria was approached by Alliyah, one of the friendly staff members at the café. Alliyah smiled warmly and asked if she could get anything for her.

Aria thought for a moment, "Hey, can I ask you something about Galan? You've worked with him the longest, haven't you?"

"I did. What can I help you with?" said Alliyah.

"What was he like? What kind of person was he?" Aria probed.

"Umm, let's see… He was a really focused person. Whatever he set his eyes on, he wouldn't stop until he got it. Most people would be discouraged when they run into problems and have major setbacks, but not him. He saw it as a challenge, like a game almost, and he would keep going despite the hiccups," Alliyah answered.

"What about him as a person? Did he ever seem odd?" Aria prodded.

"What do you mean by odd?" asked Alliyah.

"Well, did you ever feel uncomfortable around him? I don't know how to explain it, but I was almost scared when I first met him, like a weird gut feeling," Aria replied.

"I don't think I can relate; Galan has always been sweet to all of us. He took us out for team lunches, celebrated birthdays, and acknowledged hard work. As a boss, he was amazing. He really understood his customers, and in a way, he understood his team. He knew us really well, what we struggled with, and what we excelled at. He even set us up for success by playing to our strengths and helping us where we needed it. I don't think anyone here would say he was scary in any way, maybe a little intimidating at best. He kept his calm always; even under pressure, he wouldn't budge," Alliyah responded.

"Maybe it's just me overthinking things, then. He acted weird around me, so maybe I just read too much into it," Aria stated.

"Weird how, if you don't mind me asking?" Alliyah inquired.

"One time, I almost touched him, and he grabbed my arm before I could," Aria explained.

"Oh, I guess that is a weird thing about him. Ha-ha, yes, Galan did mention that to us. He had rules stipulating that we should not be too formal and treat him like an equal. He asked us to never call him 'Sir' or touch him to get his attention. Galan told us to call out to him if we needed his assistance. It's a quirky little detail, but most successful people have them. I think he gets annoyed if we do those things. It happened before when someone new was hired. They slipped up and called him 'Sir,' and he did a weird twitchy thing like he was annoyed and tried not to say anything. But he handled it calmly. We wear these name tags, so people call our names instead of 'Sir' and 'Ma'am.' Galan said it's important that customers and staff feel comfortable," Alliyah replied.

It's not just about business; he did the same thing when I touched him. He wanted me to call him 'Sir.' So, that's what turns him on; it's a big trigger for him, interesting. Is the reason he got physical on the stairs because I touched him? Hmm…

"I guess that makes sense. I kept calling him 'Sir,' so he might have been annoyed. I thought he was acting weird, but that actually clears up a lot. Thanks, Alliyah," Aria replied.

"Any time," Alliyah smiled and walked away.

As Galan sat in bed, he found himself captivated by the lively conversation unfolding at the café. *Why are you suddenly inquiring about me? Are you falling for me? Why do you want to know more? You know you can ask me anything, Aria. I would be honest with you; you don't need to hide and ask about me. I guess this means there is hope for us after all!*

Galan smiled. He stood up and walked to the door. Leaning slightly outside, he looked down the hall toward the locked door. *I will never need to go back again. I can finally leave this behind me. Once these twenty-four hours end, that room will stay locked indefinitely.* Galan stepped back into his room and put his hand on the television. *I will fight for you, Aria. I will make you smile as brightly as you once did.*

❧

Dana sat beside Aria on a stool. "What's up, buttercup?" asked Dana.

"You're in a chipper mood," said Aria, smiling.

"Maybe…," Dana replied with a blush.

"What has you so smiley?" Aria teased.

"I don't want to say until it happens for sure, but I might get Galan to come back to the café and be my business partner," Dana answered excitedly.

Aria's smile quickly flew off her lips, "What are you talking about?"

"I think Galan would be a good mentor for me. He can teach me how to do this and help make the café even better than I could alone," Dana answered while heavily blushing.

"Why didn't you come to me about this?" Aria asked sternly.

Dana, still smiling, was confused by her sister's tone, "What?"

"Why would you make a decision like that without consulting me first?" Aria snapped.

"When have I ever needed to consult with you before I did something? Why are you being like this?" Dana inquired, still trying to keep her smile.

"D, I think you should call off whatever you think you are going to be doing with Galan," Aria responded sternly.

Dana's smile died; she looked at Aria dead in her eyes and said, "I don't think you're qualified to tell me what I can and cannot do."

"Listen to me, Galan is bad news; trust me," Aria pleaded.

"Is that why you snuck away to fuck him in the parking garage of his condo complex today? Or are we going to pretend you are not falling into your old habits with him like you do in every other relationship?" asked Dana.

"W… What are you talking about?" Aria stammered, shocked

"Oh, please don't treat me like I'm stupid," Dana responded.

"I don't know where you got that idea from, but I promise you, there is nothing going on between Galan and me. Where did you even get that ridiculous thought from? Did he tell you this? Let me see your phone; are you still talking to him?" Aria probed.

"Oh, you want to see my phone? Sure, here you go," Dana took out her phone from her apron and opened it to the image of Aria and Galan in his car.

Aria gasped and jumped off her seat, slowly covering her mouth and backing away. She snatched Dana's phone out of her hand and deleted the picture. "Where the fuck did you get this?" she snarled.

"Wow, after promising me that you didn't do anything, Ari? I told you I am not a fool, and I am sick of you trying to interfere in my life. How can you sit here and lie to my face while being a hypocrite and then asking me to trust you? Some sister you are," Dana replied in a rough tone.

Aria pulled Dana off the stool and into the back room. Dana yanked her hand away once in the back. "Let go of me!" Dana all but yelled.

"Let's not do this out here; get in your office," Aria ordered.

"No, let's do this right here. Since you came with your shit here, so much has happened since I got this place, and it's all been because of you and your co-dependent group of asshole friends. You don't get to tell me what I can and cannot do!" Dana growled.

In the midst of the tense moment, lightning suddenly flashed outside, casting an eerie glow that illuminated the hallway. The sudden brightness briefly revealed Aria and Dana's expressions, frozen in their contemplative exchange. The flickering shadows danced across the walls, adding an almost surreal element to the scene.

As the lightning subsided, a loud clap of thunder followed, breaking the silence that had enveloped them.

"Dana, I am trying to protect you; you have to believe me," pleaded Aria.

"Just like I should have believed you a minute ago when you promised you weren't with Galan?" Dana barked.

"I'm sorry I lied to you, but you have to listen to me, D. You need to stay away from Galan," Aria replied frantically.

"No, I am done listening to you. You didn't care enough to find out where I was today when I left the café. As long as you are getting what you want, your world doesn't include me. At least Galan is honest about it," Dana countered.

"You were with Galan today?" asked Aria in a shaken voice.

"What if I was?" Dana replied sternly.

Aria stepped back and turned away. "You have to believe that I am just trying to protect you," Aria responded, her gaze avoiding Dana.

The sudden lightning strike unexpectedly impacted the café's electricity, causing a brief dip in power. During that momentary darkness, Aria's gaze instinctively shifted upward, drawn to a subtle red glow on the ceiling. As the lights flickered back on, the red glow faded, but it was still faintly visible, a lingering trace of something mysterious and unusual. Aria blinked, trying to make sense of what she had just witnessed. Her curiosity was piqued, and Aria's eyes remained fixed on the corner of the ceiling where the red glow had appeared. There, she noticed a broken piece of glass, its sharp edges reflecting the light from the overhead fixtures.

"What the hell are you doing?" Dana asked as Aria took cautious steps towards the corner of the room, her eyes fixated on the broken piece of glass on the ceiling. Dana's curiosity got the better of her. She followed Aria's gaze and looked up, trying to decipher what had captured her sister's attention.

Dana saw the broken glass fragment in the corner of the ceiling, its jagged edges reflecting the light. She couldn't help but wonder why this seemingly inconspicuous piece had drawn Aria's interest so keenly.

"Isn't that what we cleaned up earlier?" Dana inquired.

"I was wondering where that glass came from. You see this band of glass that wraps the ceiling in all of the rooms, but it didn't come to mind earlier when we were trying to figure out what had broken," answered Aria.

"What are you looking at, though?" questioned Dana.

"I saw a glow coming from inside there; what the hell is behind that glass?" Aria wondered.

"I think we have a ladder in the storage room. I'll go get it so we can get a better look," Dana replied as she walked off and stepped into the next room.

Galan stared at the video feed, "What is she looking at? Why does it seem like she's looking directly into the camera? That can't be; it's a one-way mirror, so there's no way they could see what's behind this." Galan's heart raced with concern as he watched the scene unfolding before him. His panic only intensified as Dana hurriedly rolled a ladder out of the storage room. Aria, seemingly determined to unravel the mystery of the broken glass and the red glow, climbed up the ladder. She stood precariously on the highest rung, trying to reach the corner of the wall where the broken piece of glass was situated. Aria's eyes came into the camera's frame, and for a moment, their gazes locked. Galan felt a pit in his stomach, seeing her looking directly at the camera. It was as if she knew he was watching.

"Oh, fuck!" Galan panicked and grabbed his phone quickly, disabling the security cameras.

As the light next to the camera went dark, Aria's curiosity deepened, sensing that there was more to the situation than they had initially realized. Determined to uncover the truth, she instinctively reached for the broken piece of glass and pulled at it, revealing another hidden camera behind it. The revelation sent shivers down her spine, and she exchanged a stunned look with Dana. Aria grabbed her phone and carefully inserted it into the opening left by the removed glass. She snapped a photo of the inside of the panel, capturing the concealed camera in all its secrecy. Safely descending the ladder, Aria approached Dana and showed her the photo on her phone.

"What is that?" asked Dana.

"You tell me!" said Aria.

"It looks like... Cameras?" Dana replied.

"Still think I'm lying about Galan?" Aria probed.

"This doesn't prove anything; what are you trying to say?" Dana responded defensively.

"Are you kidding me? There are cameras hidden in the—" Aria stopped talking when she noticed Alliyah walking around the back. She grabbed Dana by the wrist and pulled her into her office, locking the door behind them. "Listen, Ga—" Aria began, but when she looked up, she noticed the same glass panel wrapped around the office. "We can't talk here; outside, now!" Aria instructed.

Dana was dragged outside; Aria was getting flustered. Standing under the awning of the back door, heavy drops of rain splattered on their feet. "You're acting like a crazy person, Ari. There has to be an explanation; maybe we should just go and ask Galan instead of jumping to conclusions," Dana suggested.

"No! You are not to go anywhere near Galan! D, this is much more serious than you realize!" Aria claimed.

"Then why don't you tell me! Clearly, you know something I don't. Did sleeping with him give you some insight into something I can't see because haven't slept with him yet?!" asked Dana.

"Yet?" Aria barked. She walked closer to Dana and said, "Oh my God, you really do have a crush on him—"

"And what if I do, Aria?! Ever since I met Galan, he has noticed me. Even when you and Eder missed it, he knew when something was wrong just from hearing my voice. There has never been someone who took the time to pay attention to me that much. I deserve someone who can hear my silence. Not just when I scream!" Dana cried out.

"D, he's not the one for you; he's dangerous. Galan threatened Eder, saying that he had proof of you and him sleeping together. I'm starting to think it wasn't a bluff. I know you two were in the storage room having sex. If you really believe Galan isn't dangerous, walk with me to the storage room; let's see if that glass panel is built into the ceiling there too," said Aria, with tears welling in her eyes.

"No, Galan wouldn't do that. They went after him; they are the ones who have been trying to make him out to be a bad person, but he's not," Dana belted.

"Then prove me wrong. Walk with me to the storage unit; if there are no cameras in there, I will let this go. And I promise I will never stand between you and Galan if I am wrong about this," replied Aria, a tear running down her cheek.

Dana was hesitant; she looked at her sister in tears and contemplated her proposal. "Fine, if this proves you were wrong about him, I will do it since you feel so strongly about it. But when you are prover wrong, I don't want to see any of your friends again. Not Bodhi, Garrick, Eyla, Maeve, or even Eder," Dana responded.

"Deal," answered Aria.

"Then, let's go," Dana agreed.

Malek Zakaria

AGE: 21
SIGN: PISCES
FUN FACT: "I LIKE TO READ SPICY BOOKS IN
PUBLIC AND TRY TO KEEP A STRAIGHT FACE."

Chapter Thirty-Three

The weight of uncertainty hung heavily in the air as Aria and Dana approached the café's storage unit. The apprehension was palpable, and Dana's nerves were on edge. Her mind raced with thoughts and fears, her heart beating rapidly with every step closer to the door. She couldn't shake the nagging worry that something ominous might be lurking inside.

Dana's palms grew sweaty, and her breaths became shallow as she clung to the hope that her worst fears wouldn't be realized. "Please don't be in there," she silently pleaded, the mantra echoing in her mind.

Aria put her hand on the door's handle and looked at Dana with a hint of sadness in her eyes. Aria opened the door to the storage unit without peeking inside, keeping her gaze locked with Dana's. "Have a look," said Aria.

Dana's anxiety surged as she stood before the storage room, hesitant to look inside. The possibility that the glass panel might indeed be in there made her heart pound in her chest. Aria's unwavering eye contact was unsettling; the unknown still gnawed at her.

As Dana took a deep breath and prepared to enter the room, hoping to find answers and validate Aria's concerns, a voice broke the tense atmosphere. Alliyah peeked into the back and called out to them both.

"Hey, boss, we are heading out for the night. See you tomorrow," Alliyah cheerfully informed the team, her warm smile spreading as she playfully waved alongside the rest of the staff.

"Bye, everyone; thanks for a great day today," Dana said in response.

Aria waved at them as they left.

Dana purposefully drew out the moment as she seized this opportunity, savoring the suspense. Deep down, she was well aware of what awaited her inside the room.

Meanwhile, Aria's curiosity got the better of her. As she peered into the storage room, a sudden realization struck her. She glanced back and forth between Dana and the room, a silent question evident in her eyes.

Aria: *She is going to hate me for doing this to her, but it's my job to protect her.*

Dana clutched at every precious second she could but knew she had to confront it head-on, like ripping off a band-aid. Hastily, she stepped into the room, her eyes immediately scanning the ceiling to confirm the presence of glass panels. Just as Aria had warned her, they were there. Her heart sank, and a torrent of emotions overwhelmed her.

In an instant, the heavy door to the storage room swung shut with a resounding thud, the lock clicking ominously into place. Startled, Dana whirled around, desperation etched across her face. She dashed to the door, frantically trying to turn the handle, but it remained stubbornly immovable. Panic rising within her, she pounded on the door with all her might, screaming for Aria to release her, yet her pleas seemed to vanish into the void.

Inside the storage room, Dana soon realized the room's peculiar locking mechanism. As the door closed, the auto-lock feature engaged, so the door could only be opened with the key from the outside. "I'm sorry, D. Please, believe that whatever I do, I do for you," said Aria in tears as she removed the key from the lock.

"Let me the fuck out, Aria!!!" Dana screamed.

"I will. I just need to do something first," Aria answered.

"Aria, let me out now!" Dana yelled.

"I'm sorry, D," Aria whispered, stepping away from the door.

Dana's heart pounded in her chest as she took a step back, the realization hitting her like a cold wave. She instinctively reached for her phone, intending to call for help, but her pockets yielded nothing but emptiness. Panic escalated as she frantically searched, only to remember that she had handed her phone to Aria earlier to show her the picture of her and Galan in his car.

"Aria, let me out!!! Don't leave me in here! Aria!!!" Dana bellowed.

BROKEN TOYS

As Aria deliberately placed Dana's phone on a nearby table beside the door, she couldn't help but feel a mix of conflicting emotions. She understood the gravity of the situation, yet her determination to carry out her plan persisted.

With a deep breath, she retrieved her own phone and dialed Garrick's number.

Garrick answered, "Aria?"

"You were right; Galan is trouble. We just discovered that this place is filled with cameras in every room. He's not bluffing about having proof of Dana and Eder," Aria replied as she stormed out of the café.

"No way! Cameras aren't allowed in Salt Pine Acres. Isn't that the point of this place, to be off the grid?" asked Garrick.

"That's the least of our worries. Who knows what else Galan knows; he must have been watching us from the very beginning!" Aria responded.

"That sick fuck, I knew it!" Garrick remarked.

"Get your asses back to Salt Pine Acres now! I am not taking any chances," instructed Aria.

"I know you're pissed, but that's not a good idea. Galan is smart; if he sees us, he will be too suspicious, and we may not get it done," Garrick told her.

"There is a new plan; this mother fucker has been watching us since we got to Salt Pine Acres. He is already a step ahead of us, so we need a new plan. Galan has one soft spot: me. Just follow my lead, and I'll handle the rest. You need to tell me what the plan is now! Now, Garrick!" Aria commanded.

Garrick and Eder looked at each other. They nodded in unison, silently agreeing to fill her in. "Ok, Ari, Maeve and the others have syringes filled with a general anesthetic to knock him out. The plan is to hit him when he wouldn't see it coming; injecting him anywhere would work, but hitting the artery in his neck would act the fastest. The idea is to use the toast for the new owners of Grounded Coffee House and make everyone drink. Once they throw back the shot, he would reveal his neck. We'll have someone placed just behind him who can inject the syringe the moment he does," Garrick explained.

"Oh my God, it's good that you didn't go through with that plan because it wouldn't have worked. Galan doesn't drink alcohol, so he wouldn't have taken part in the drinking. This is why you need to cut the secrecy," Aria declared.

"What do you suggest?" asked Garrick.

"Galan drops his guard around me. I know what makes him tick; I can make him vulnerable. Stay close enough to the gates so that when we need you, you and Eder can be here in a matter of minutes," Aria replied.

"You know we've got that covered," Garrick answered as he revved his truck's engine.

"Listen, Dana is caught up with Galan. This has to end tonight," Aria exclaimed.

"We won't let you down," Garrick agreed.

Sitting in the car being driven back home, Aria hung up the phone and looked ahead. *Hang on, D, we just need a little time.*

"Hans, take me to Galan's, please," Aria instructed.

"Yes, Ms. Aria," Hans replied.

Aria and Hans arrived at Galan's condo complex a few minutes later. While still in the car, Aria dialed Galan's number, her fingers trembling slightly. The phone rang, each ring echoing with a sense of urgency. As she called, she peered through the car window.

"Hey, Aria," Galan answered.

"Hi, Galan. Look out your window for a moment," Aria replied.

Despite the heavy downpour outside, Galan made his way to his bedroom window, his curiosity piqued by the sight of a familiar car parked below. He peered through the rain-streaked glass, squinting to make out the figure beyond the blurry windshield, faintly making out Aria waving at him.

"What a nice surprise; I'll be down soon," Galan informed her.

"Don't keep me waiting," Aria chuckled.

Galan hurried down the elevator. *Why the fuck is Aria here? She must be here because of the cameras; she has to be! I need to keep calm about this. Fuck!*

Galan descended the elevator, his hair disheveled from sleep and his eyes still bearing traces of puffiness. He had rushed down as quickly as he could after Aria's call. Stepping out of the car, Aria braved the rain, running through the downpour to reach the parking garage where she knew Galan would be arriving.

As the elevator doors slid open, Galan was greeted by the sight of a soaked and determined Aria, raindrops dancing off her. *Damn, she looks so good with that wet hair; the things I wanna do to you, Aria...*

"Why did you get wet in the rain? I would have come to you," said Galan.

"It's fine. I don't mind getting a little wet," Aria flirted, biting her lips.

Aria noticed Galan's body tensed when she did that. Aria: *I knew it; it does trigger him!*

"To what do I owe the pleasure?" Galan asked, leaning on the elevator.

"Dana, actually," Aria replied.

Surprised, Galan repeated, "Dana?"

"Yes. So, we had a bit of a rough opening celebration, as you know. It was a really tough day, and tempers were flying, so Dana didn't get to properly celebrate her big accomplishment. Eyla, Bodhi, and the gang are helping me throw her a party to fix that. It's just us; Eder will not be there because they had a falling out last night when Maeve ended up in the hospital. I'm inviting you because Dana seems fond of you. I'd like to have at least one person she is somewhat close to there to celebrate it with her," Aria explained.

Galan: *So, this isn't about the cameras; did they not find it? She looked directly into the lens, but maybe the glass didn't break enough to reveal the camera? Something is fishy here, fuck. I would have seen what followed if I hadn't panicked and switched them off. Fuck, I have a bad feeling about this. Aria arrived just after she found a camera in the café and is now talking about a party for Dana. But earlier today, she practically ran me out of the premises when Eder and Dana were yelling at me. Something isn't right about this; you were just warning Dana about me, so why do you suddenly want me in the same room with her?*

"I don't think that's a good idea, Aria. Dana asked me to return to the café as a partner and mentor. I told her I'd think about it, but I don't think I have an answer for her yet. If I go, she will want me to give her an answer, and I don't want to ruin her celebration with a rejection. It's not her, but people have constantly been coming after me. Maeve, Eder, Garrick, and even you have all done nothing but assume I would do something to Dana for whatever reason. You can't expect me to forget all that because you're batting your eyes at me.

"I would have liked to be there and celebrate with Dana; that girl is going to reach heights you cannot imagine. She has such drive, passion, and willingness to do better. But at the risk of any more accusations and drama, I'll pass. I'll give her my answer tomorrow. I wouldn't want to put a damper on the celebrations," Galan responded as he turned to open the elevator doors.

Aria: *Fuck, fuck, fuck. That's not a bad reason to decline. Dammit, I need to get him there by any means possible.*

"Galan—" Aria called out.

Galan stopped and turned slightly.

"Eder and Garrick got into our heads; well, actually, mostly just mine. They convinced me something was going on with you and Dana. They even had this crazy theory about you being the one who put Maeve in the hospital last night. Dana is my baby sister, and I will do anything under the sun to protect her; you have to understand that," Aria continued.

"You know, Dana doesn't believe that. She told me that you are so occupied with your own happiness that you don't care about her. I'm paraphrasing, but that's essentially what she said," Galan countered.

"That's not true," Aria replied defensively.

"That's what she believes. Whether it's true or not, it's what's ingrained in her mind. Maybe you should work on that a bit with her. I'm not saying you're a bad sister, but Dana feels like no one sees her," Galan informed her.

Aria: *He completely ignored the thing I said about Garrick and Eder. Garrick was right; he knows. That's why he can keep calm about it.*

"Why didn't you ask anything about Maeve being in the hospital or about Garrick and Eder?" Aria questioned. *Fuck, why did I say that? I'm letting my emotions cloud my judgment, and I'll give away my plan.*

Galan turned around and walked up to her. "Garrick and Eder having a lot of things to say about me isn't anything new. I am trying to move past that right now. I don't know if you know, but those two tried to ambush me today while I was having lunch on the lookout. Unlike your friends, I am not someone who wants conflict and drama. I've had enough pain to last a lifetime, and I am actively trying to avoid that every single day.

"Maeve being in the hospital is news to me. Until a few moments ago, I didn't even know she was admitted to a hospital. As for the claim that I put her there? That sounds like some half-assed story from Garrick and Eder or possibly Maeve herself. This is why your sister thinks so little of you; you are more concerned with your friends and the things you have going on than her. All you had to say about my earlier remark about Dana were three words, but you are determined to look further into some bullshit claim from your friends about me?

"If you do not get your shit together, Aria, that child will lose her way. Dana might fool everyone else with her maturity, but she's still just a kid. Somewhere in your climb to fame, the friends you keep seem to have made you lose sight of that. Be a better sister to Dana before she tries to fill the void you left in her heart with someone as damaged as I am. There are a lot of monsters in the world, and most of them smile while sitting at your table," Galan retorted.

Aria was stunned. For a moment, she questioned everything. She even thought about calling off the plan. What Galan had said had hit close to home. *What have I done? Dana would never forgive me for what I did. But I can't be distracted now. Galan's lying; he must be. The evidence points to him. He could ruin our reputation, and I will not let anyone threaten our family; I can't. I've worked too hard for this. We have to do this tonight; get it together and follow through with the plan!*

"Galan, Dana is falling for you," Aria mumbled.

Galan looked at her.

"I felt threatened when I found out. I know what I did with you, and the thought of you doing those things to her was unacceptable. When the accusations came flooding in, I took it and ran with it because now I had a reason to push you away from her," Aria explained.

"She's a kid, Aria. She's sixteen!" Galan remarked in disgust.

"That's not what bothers me. As much as I wanted to keep you away from her, I think I really just wanted you for myself," Aria whispered as she walked closer to Galan and held his hand.

Galan looked into her eyes. "Aria…." he said softly.

Aria: *There it is, his weak spot.*

"Leave with me; let's disappear together! Just the two of us!" Aria exclaimed.

"I've wanted to leave this place for a long time now," Galan responded.

"Then let me take you anywhere you want to go. I'm done with everything. I just want to be happy, and I feel safe when I'm with you. I feel complete, like I've found the piece of my life I've been missing," Aria replied softly.

"What about Dana?" Galan inquired.

"Dana will thrive here. This is where she belongs, but this isn't what I want," answered Aria.

"What do you want, Aria?" asked Galan.

Aria placed her hand on Galan's chest and slowly moved it up his neck, settling on his face. "I want you, Sir," Aria whispered, pressing her body against Galan's and biting her lip. Galan stood frozen; the sound of his breathing grew heavier. "Be mine, all mine," Aria sighed as she pulled his head down and whispered in his ear.

Galan's body burned with lust for Aria. Unable to resist, Galan leaned in to kiss her, but Aria placed her finger on his lips, stopping him. "Say that you are mine," said Aria.

Galan: *Say it, Galan. Say it, and she's yours!*

"I… I am all yours," Galan gulped.

"Then leave with me tonight," Aria repeated.

"I will follow you through the fires of hell if that would make you happy," Galan replied.

"Help me do this for Dana. One last thing for her, and then we can disappear, just you and me. I know you mean something to her; it's what she would have wanted. It's what I want," Aria muttered.

Galan looked at her in her eyes and nodded 'Yes.'

Aria kissed him gently. "Go get changed. I have to help them get ready at home. See you at my place, ok?"

"Ok, I'll see you soon," Galan agreed.

As Aria abruptly let go of Galan and dashed back into the car through the pouring rain, he stood there, momentarily stunned and catching his breath. His heart pounded in his chest, and the intensity of the moment left him speechless. Galan leaned against the wall of the glass elevator, trying to steady himself and make sense of what had just happened.

He was left with a mixture of emotions, the encounter with Aria leaving him both exhilarated and breathless. Galan couldn't help but smile as he felt a rush of happiness wash over him. With a calm determination, he scanned his thumb to unlock the elevator doors, the digital display showing him that it was now ready for use.

Stepping into the elevator, Galan couldn't resist glancing out through the glass wall. Through the rain-streaked windows, he caught a glimpse of Aria's car driving away and disappearing around the corner. The sight of her departure only fueled his elation, leaving him feeling on top of the world.

As the elevator ascended to his apartment, Galan couldn't contain his joy. He blushed, feeling a touch of shyness as he ran his fingers through his hair, the encounter with Aria replaying in his mind like a sweet melody.

Galan's heart raced with excitement as he sprinted up to his room, the wide smile on his face a reflection of the euphoria that enveloped him. He could hardly contain his happiness, yet he paused just shy of his door, unable to resist stealing a glance down the hallway. His gaze fell upon the locked room. *I can finally leave this all behind me. I can finally turn over a new leaf.*

Chapter Thirty-four

Breathless from her swift return, Aria hurried inside her home. As she stepped through the door, Maeve and Eyla greeted her with concern evident in their expressions.

"What's happening? Garrick called and said the plan changed!" Maeve stated.

"Your genius plan wouldn't have worked; Galan doesn't drink," Aria explained.

"So, what are we going to do now?" asked Eyla.

"Give me the syringe. I'm the only one who could get close enough to Galan to inject him," Aria claimed.

"That's it? How can you get near him with Malek here?" Maeve questioned.

"Oh fuck, I forgot Malek was still here. Listen, you need to get him out of here before this all goes down. Bodhi, can you take him back to the hotel?" asked Aria.

"Not a problem," Bodhi replied.

"After we do the shots, we will 'wrap' things up with the party and get him out as soon as possible," Aria instructed.

"Where is Dana, by the way?" Eyla inquired.

"I don't want Dana anywhere near this when it goes down," Aria exclaimed.

"Don't you think it's a little odd to have a celebration for Dana without, you know, Dana?" Bodhi remarked.

"I'll say she's just running late at the café, but we can start early. I'll toast to something, like maybe Galan for founding the café, I don't know. I'll think of something," Aria replied.

"Ari, we can't just leave this up to chance; we need to get this right," Maeve stated.

Aria turned to Maeve, enraged, "Don't question what I will do for my family, Maeve."

"Is everything okay, love?" Malek asked, peeking through the door with a smile.

Feeling a sense of comfort from Malek's presence and his lighthearted response, Aria's worries began to ease. She couldn't help but reciprocate his smile, "Everything is fine, my love," she answered.

"Come with me; let me steal you away for a bit," Malek said as he extended his hand.

Aria walked to him and took his hand in hers. "I'll return her soon," Malek called out to the rest of them.

BROKEN TOYS

In Malek's comforting embrace, Aria felt a profound sense of calm wash over her. His presence and support had a soothing effect on her, easing the remaining tension from her shoulders.

As he lifted her chin gently, Aria looked into his eyes, finding reassurance and warmth in their depths. His tender gesture of kissing her on the forehead made her heart flutter, "I have something to tell you, but I don't know if this is the right time."

"Tell me," said Aria softly.

"Well, I didn't just come to support Dana and you with the opening of the café. I had something else I have wanted to do for a long time, and I think I finally have the courage to say it," Malek answered.

Aria looked at him eagerly, "I'm listening."

"I just need to wait for Dana to get back home. I wanted to run something by her before I could do my part," Malek continued.

As Malek enveloped Aria in a warm hug at the front door, her smile brightened even further. She held him tight, cherishing the closeness between them. In the embrace, Malek softly whispered words of love into her ear.

Aria's smile grew wider with each heartfelt word, her heart swelling with affection.

Clad in a refined dark suit, Galan braved the relentless downpour as he made his way to Aria's house. As his car came to a stop in front of the elegant residence, his gaze locked onto a heartwarming sight: Aria, nestled in Malek's embrace, radiating an unparalleled joy that left Galan feeling a profound sense of emptiness within himself. Never before had he witnessed such a radiant smile on her face; it was as if all the stars in the cosmos had converged to illuminate her happiness.

Malek is here? Why is he here? She must not have wanted to do this tonight; she must have felt like she was about to lose me when I refused her. No, no, Aria, what did you do? Malek is a good person. He shouldn't be hurt like this. Are you going to choose me in front of him? I can't do this; I actually like Malek. I'll have to diffuse the situation if it arises; I won't hurt anyone tonight. Tonight is for Dana; tomorrow can be for us, Aria. I am a patient man. I can wait one more day. Let's just try to get through tonight.

Galan leaned forward, pressing firmly on the car's horn to signal his arrival to Aria. The blaring sound pierced through the heavy rain and the quiet ambiance of the neighborhood, announcing his arrival. "Oh, that's one of the guests. How about you wait inside, love, while I help get everything ready, and after, we can celebrate together?" Aria remarked.

"I would love that," Malek replied as he turned and made his way back inside the house. Galan watched him disappear through the door before mustering his resolve.

Determined to face whatever awaited him, he opened the car door and stepped out into the relentless downpour. The rain soaked through his dark suit, and he felt the cool droplets tracing rivulets down his face. Ignoring the discomfort, Galan hurriedly crossed the distance to the front door, his footsteps echoing on the steps. Each stride mirrored the quickened pace of his heart as he ascended the stairs with a sense of urgency. "You made it," Aria smiled.

Aria: *What horrible fucking timing. Couldn't he have arrived a few minutes later?*

"Of course I did. I wouldn't miss it," answered Galan.

"You got all wet in the rain; it's going to ruin your nice suit," Aria exclaimed.

"I left the hydrophobic one at home. To be honest, I haven't been able to think straight these past few days," Galan said, smiling at her.

"Well, come on in; everyone is already inside," Aria responded.

"After you," Galan said, offering a small smile as he gestured for Aria to enter the house first. He opened the door wider to let her pass, allowing her a moment of privacy before he followed suit.

Aria stepped inside, her expression betraying a mix of emotions, and her eyes met those of Eyla and Maeve. A tense silence enveloped the room, making it palpably awkward. Galan followed closely behind, feeling the weight of the atmosphere settle upon his shoulders like a heavy shroud.

"Hey, everyone, Galan is here. Galan, you've met everyone already," Aria said.

Galan waved at them and said, 'Hi.'

"That hair is looking much better than last time," Bodhi added to break the ice.

"Thanks, I had a good stylist fix me up," Galan replied.

"Good? Don't insult me," Bodhi teased.

"Amazing stylist, my apologies," Galan corrected, chuckling.

"That's better," Bodhi snickered.

Galan couldn't help but notice Maeve's intense glare directed his way as if her eyes were shooting daggers at him. He could sense the animosity in her gaze, and it added another layer of tension to the already fraught atmosphere. "Oh my God, Maeve, what happened to you?" asked Galan.

Maeve's eye twitched. Bodhi and Eyla grew nervous. "I was attacked by a coward, a real sociopath, scum of the land," Maeve muttered.

"I see that. You're all wrapped in bandages. Are you in any pain?" Galan inquired.

"The pain meds are helping me manage it. It's really the emotional trauma: I am having trouble dealing with knowing such a sick, poor excuse of a human being is still out there, roaming free," Maeve vented.

Galan: *Come on, don't talk about your brother like that!*

"Damn, I'm sorry this happened to you, Maeve. It must be hard to feel safe after something like that," Galan remarked.

"It has its moments," Maeve replied.

"Alright, that's enough of that. Tonight is a night of celebrations. We are here for one thing and one thing only: to celebrate Dana and her grand reopening of Grounded Coffee House," Bodhi stated.

"Where is Dana? I don't see her?" Galan exclaimed, looking around the room.

"She should have been here already, but she told me she had some stuff to clean up. We found some broken glass near the ceiling, so she wanted to take care of that before she closed up to avoid anyone getting hurt," answered Aria.

Aria: *If he was looking at us when we found the camera, at least he wouldn't think I was hiding it. I hope that didn't give it away; I really hope when the lightning dipped, the power shut off the cameras. I know I saw those lights go out.*

This is harder than it seems. How the fuck do I act? I don't know what he knows. How do I figure out if he knows I know? He makes it look so easy. I'm over here blurting out things to not seem suspicious when I might be giving myself away. When he came off the elevator, he looked as though he was asleep, so maybe he didn't see anything prior to that.

Fuck, this is so nerve-wracking. Try to keep calm; if Galan was on to me, he would not have come... But wait, he was initially not going to... Oh my God, I am going to lose my mind! What kind of person can do this and not be bothered? I have never been so flustered in my life. I've stood in a room with the most powerful people in the world and kept them on their toes. So, why am I losing myself over a nobody?

Galan: *So, they didn't find out about the cameras? I panicked for no reason. Damn, well, better safe than sorry. But what does it matter now? After tonight, we will disappear together. I wouldn't need to have eyes on you anymore because you won't ever leave my sight, Aria. I promise I will always look after you.*

"Well, how about a toast?" Maeve suggested. "Anyone? Aria, how about you go?"

"Actually, I would like to say something if that's ok," Malek called out. As he stepped into the room, the attention of everyone present shifted towards him. He had changed into a new suit, his appearance sharp and confident. His entrance seemed to add another layer of complexity to the already charged atmosphere.

Aria's hand froze midway as she was about to retrieve the syringe from the back of her jeans. The sound of Malek's voice made her hesitate, and she turned her gaze toward him.

Aria: *No…*

"Galan? Is that you?" Malek asked. Beaming with surprise and joy, Malek turned his gaze towards Galan and, with a friendly gesture, pointed at him.

"Malek!" Galan greeted. He gracefully traversed the room and extended his hand toward Malek. Galan pulled Malek into a heartfelt embrace, catching everyone off guard. The room was filled with astonishment, and Aria, in particular, felt a chill run down her spine, her blood turning cold at the sight of this surprising and unexpected turn of events.

Aria: *No… No, no, no, no. What is happening right now?*

Chapter Thirty-five

"What are you doing here? I can't believe you're here right now," Malek exclaimed.

"Well, I actually almost wasn't. Aria insisted I attend this little celebration for Dana," Galan replied.

"You and Aria know each other?" Malek inquired.

"By circumstance, yes. Dana bought the café from me, so that's how we met," Galan answered.

Aria's heart pounded like a drum as she entered the room, only to find herself engulfed in a swirling whirlwind of emotions. The sight of Galan and Malek, their faces adorned with beaming smiles and animated expressions, sent her nerves into overdrive.

The room seemed to sway around her, adding to the disorienting feeling that had settled deep within her chest.

"I see where your knowledge and love for coffee comes from. This is so amazing. I'm so glad to meet you again," Malek responded excitedly.

"This is amazing, man. You look good," Galan complimented him, placing his hand on Malek's shoulder.

"Thank you. This suit belonged to my father. He wore it for a very special occasion, which brings me back to what I have to say," Malek responded, and he turned to Aria with a smile that melted her heart. "My love, I never imagined what my life would be like. The future I saw was filled with possibilities, filled with hope. Hope that one day, I'll find happiness in being a good son and making my mother proud and that I'll find happiness in the simple mercies of life. My father once told me that there are things in this world that are so precious and worth any sacrifice," Malek continued, his heart pounding with nervous excitement. With a deep breath, he gently took Aria's hand, feeling the warmth of her touch. Slowly, he lowered himself onto one knee, his eyes locking onto hers, sparkling with affection and admiration; her hand rested softly between his.

"The moment I met you, I understood why I have never made sacrifices before. You gave my father's words meaning, just like my mother gave his life meaning. I don't want my life to begin and end with you; what I feel for you, my love, I don't see an end to it. I will love you beyond the shackles of death. I will find you in our next life and keep my promises. Wherever our souls may end up in the vast universe, know that I will never stop looking for you.

"I cannot imagine my life without you. I haven't been able to for a very long time. I would trade that future I once saw in a heartbeat if it meant I could be with you for a moment in the present," Malek declared. He reached into his shirt pocket, took out a red velvet box, and looked at Aria. "This is my sacrifice; I surrender my life to you. Aria Scarlet, will you marry me?" Malek carefully opened the box, revealing a breathtaking diamond ring that sparkled under the soft glow of the room. The beauty of the ring took his breath away, and he couldn't help but admire its exquisite craftsmanship. Even by Aria's high standards, he knew this ring was incredibly extravagant.

Aria's heart sank the moment she laid eyes on the ring. "Baby, how could you afford this?" she gasped softly.

"This is my family's entire life savings. I meant what I said; I will give anything for you, my love. I wouldn't have been able to do this without the love and support of my family. They are finally ready to let me go because they know there is not a doubt in my mind I have found the one precious thing on God's green earth worth giving everything for," Malek replied with a smile.

Aria's breathing grew untamed, her chest rising and falling with deep, rapid breaths as she struggled to contain the flood of emotions overwhelming her. Eyla, Bodhi, and Maeve exchanged concerned glances, silently communicating their support for their friend in this pivotal moment. Each of them understood the weight of what was happening and how much it meant to Aria.

Ever the stoic presence, Galan stood across from them, positioned directly behind Malek and in Aria's direct line of sight. He had seen countless emotions in his lifetime, but there was something unique about witnessing this vulnerable side of Aria.

Galan: *Oh my God, I can see it in her eyes; this isn't just some guy to her. She's... In love. The moment he entered the room, her entire demeanor changed; she stopped being the biggest presence in the room within seconds of hearing his voice. I know that kind of passion all too well; it's how I used to be with 'Her.' This kind of devotion and love is not something you come back from. She loves him too much. If he breaks her heart, she won't ever recover from it. He will destroy her emotionally and mentally. I can't watch this happen; she will lose herself when she rejects him to disappear with me.*

Beaming, Aria said, "Yes, I will marry you, Malek!"

Galan: *What!*

"Oh, my God!!! Ari!!!" Maeve, Bhodi, and Eyla exclaimed in unison. Aria's friends bombarded her with unbridled enthusiasm and joy, surrounding her in a tightly-knit circle of love and excitement. They showered her with hugs, congratulations, and unrestrained screams of happiness. Galan, observing from across the room, couldn't help but be taken aback by this sudden turn of events.

Bodhi popped open a bottle of champagne, filling each glass with effervescent bubbles, making sure to include Galan. Amid the laughter and chatter, Malek took Aria's hand, their fingers entwining with a loving touch, and he gently slid the exquisite ring onto her finger. Aria beheld the breathtaking ring. Her eyes widened with awe, and a radiant smile adorned her face, illuminating the room with the brilliance of her happiness. But amidst the joyous scene, Galan's heart ached. He couldn't help but notice Aria's beaming smile.

Galan: *It's brighter than it was before. What happened to the girl who was faking her smiles? I was supposed to be the one who made you smile again. I don't understand; how could I lose. Moments ago, you promised me a life together. Was all that a lie? What have I done to deserve this? I have done nothing but dote on you—*

Malek went to Galan and hugged him, "She said yes!"

"Congratulations, man," Galan raised his glass and cheered with Malek. "I'm happy to be part of this."

"It must be fate that we met. I'm happy I met you, Galan; you were the reason I had the courage to do this. I was scared to make this leap until you spoke about love. Despite all the things you had been through, it didn't stop you from trying to find it. When you said, 'Believing that out there is someone sent here for me, and one day I will find them,' I realized something. Even though you don't know what the future holds, regardless of your past, you weren't afraid to take that leap of faith for the chance to find true love. And here I was. I had found the love of my life, my soul mate, my best friend, but I was scared. You reminded me of my father for a moment; he was always the strongest person I knew, and, at that moment, I looked up to you. I wanted to be that fearless in my pursuit of love. I am so thankful we met," Malek remarked.

Sensing Galan's quiet contemplation, Aria approached him with concern evident in her eyes.

Standing just behind Malek, she paused and directed her gaze toward the enigmatic figure before her. Galan returned her worried look with a serene smile and gently bowed his head in acknowledgment.

"Congratulations, Aria," Galan's congratulatory words carried a sense of genuine warmth as he offered his heartfelt wishes to her. Reaching out to her with one hand while still holding his drink in the other, he invited her into an embrace.

Aria hesitated for a brief moment, her eyes subtly avoiding Maeve and the others. However, in that fleeting hesitation, Galan's presence provided a sense of understanding and comfort that she couldn't deny. Finally, she wrapped both arms around Galan's neck and hugged him tightly, seeking solace in the familiar and enigmatic presence that had always intrigued her. In that embrace, her hand rested gently on the nape of his neck.

Meanwhile, growing frantic, Maeve and the others noticed that Aria wasn't holding the syringe she had been entrusted with.

"What is she doing?" Maeve turned to Bodhi and Eyla once again, trying to convey her concern in hushed tones. However, Bodhi's response remained the same as before. He looked at Maeve with curiosity, subtly shaking his head, and shrugged his shoulders, expressing the same level of confusion. "I knew this would happen. I always have to do the dirty work myself," Maeve mumbled to herself as she quickly marched off to another room, needing a moment of privacy to make a phone call. She took out her phone and dialed Garrick's number, her fingers trembling slightly with nervousness.

"Talk to me. Is he down?" asked Garrick.

"Get your asses here. Aria isn't going through with the plan," Maeve replied.

"What!? What is happening over there?" questioned Garrick.

"No time to explain, you idiot. Just get here as quickly as you can; it's about to go down," Maeve instructed. As she angrily ended the call, frustration and worry etched across her face, she stormed back into the living room where the others were gathered. Her emotions were running high, and she struggled to contain her anger and concern.

Aria, sensing Maeve's distress, immediately noticed her approaching Galan with her hand hidden. In a quick and instinctive move to divert any suspicion, Aria rushed up to Maeve and enveloped her in a tight, supportive hug. It was a subtle yet deliberate act to shield Maeve's actions from prying eyes.

With her arms wrapped around Maeve, Aria whispered softly, "Not now, not while Malek is here. Call it off," Aria whispered.

"He did this to me, Aria! How long are we going to wait? Who does he have to hurt before you take action? Dana? Another one of us? Your fiancé?" Maeve grilled quietly.

"I am trying to keep Malek out of the crazy in my life. I always protected him from it. It's not his burden to bear; it's ours. We don't do this now, not while he is here," Aria replied sternly.

"Then, at least take him into a different room. Garrick is on his way with Eder; we will get rid of him in no time. Do it for Dana," Maeve advised.

Bodhi hugged Aria and Maeve, "I'm so happy right now. I cannot wait to design your look for the wedding!" said Bodhi excitedly. Toning his voice down, he said, "Guys, it's now or never."

Aria nodded 'yes' and walked over to Malek. Turning to Galan, she said, "Sorry, I need to steal my fiancé. I don't feel like sharing him with everyone; this is my moment. Dana should be here soon; come find me then."

"By all means, don't let me get in the way," Galan responded with a smile.

Aria took Malek into her room and turned on the privacy glass walls. Galan looked at the others before turning to the door. "Hey, guys, I think I'm going to head out. I feel a bit out of place at this celebration."

Galan walked to the door and put his hand on the handle when Maeve approached him quickly. "Galan, wait. You don't have to go; at least wait for Dana," she suggested.

"I thought I was a predator who was set on Dana?" Galan snarled. "Isn't that what you told Aria?"

"Let's talk outside," Maeve replied.

"No, we don't have anything to say to each other. What exactly have I done that you all are so hard on me? Tell me, please," Galan probed.

"You don't understand, Galan," Maeve responded.

"What don't I understand?" Galan asked.

"We really did like you, but we knew it would never work with Aria. We were trying to protect you," Maeve explained.

"Protect me? By making heinous accusations about me, lying to my face, coming into my home, insulting me, and calling me a nobody? What have I…?" Galan quickly stopped himself from talking and turned to the door. *Fuck… They never told me that, I have no reason to know that piece of information. Shit, shit, shit, let's just hope they missed that. Fuck, Galan, get yourself together. You are not thinking straight; you are too concerned about Aria and Malek!*

"I'm sorry, Galan. What we did was horrible, but it was not meant to hurt you. We have just seen this enough times to know that the guys never heed the warnings. Aria has a hold over them; they do not listen to reason. We just wanted to save you from this pain," Maeve answered; she reached out to Galan with an air of urgency. However, before she could reach him, Galan, ever perceptive, sensed her approaching presence. In a swift and unexpected move, he turned towards her and swiftly grabbed her hand.

"Please, don't…," Galan began. Looking down at her hand, he saw the syringe clenched in her fist. "What the hell is this?!" he growled.

Maeve used both hands to try to drive the needle into Galan's neck, pushing her entire body to overpower him. Galan held her back, but Bodhi and Eyla rushed in to assist her, their hands hidden behind their backs.

Galan: *What the hell is in these needles? What are they trying to do? Do they all have one? Was this whole thing a trap?! No, I don't believe that; Aria could have done something to me multiple times. She could have done something earlier, too, when she invited me here. She wouldn't; it's her friends. It's always been them. They have been out for me since the very beginning!*

Bodhi and Eyla thrust their hands from behind their backs in Galan's direction. Galan, in turn, swung

Maeve into them, causing them to stumble for a moment. "Aria!!!" Galan yelled.

Malek and Aria, sitting on the bed with their hands in each other's, were startled by Galan's scream.

"Stay here, love. Please, please, don't leave this room," Aria begged.

"What's going on out there?" asked Malek, worried.

"Please, for me, stay here," Aria repeated as she got up quickly and ran outside.

Bodhi, Maeve, and Eyla united their strengths, forming a formidable trio against Galan. Swiftly, Galan launched a vicious kick at Bodhi, sending him crashing to the ground. Pain seared through Bodhi's body, but he refused to yield. Unfazed, Eyla and Maeve stepped forward, syringes poised, determination in their eyes. Galan's eyes flickered with amusement. In a blur of motion, he intercepted their syringe-wielding hands, thwarting their attempts to subdue him. The air crackled with tension as the three faced their relentless adversary. Bodhi rose, gritting his teeth against the pain, and adopted a measured approach. He circled behind Galan, intending to immobilize him with a chokehold. Galan retaliated, slamming his head back with force, breaking Bodhi's nose. Blood streamed down his face, but Bodhi clung steadfastly to his grip. With every ounce of willpower, Eyla and Maeve pushed onward, their eyes locking with determination as they struggled to overpower Galan.

"ENOUGH!!!" Aria screamed. "Get your hands off of him!" Malek panicked when he heard Aria's scream.

"Aria, what the hell are you doing? He's a freak!" Maeve shouted.

"Get your hands off of him, now. NOW!!!" Aria commanded.

Galan's breaths came in heavy gasps as he felt the sudden release of pressure. Confused and wary, he cautiously looked around at Bodhi, Maeve, and Eyla.

"Aria, what the fuck are you doing?" questioned Maeve.

"Get out—" Aria groaned.

"Excuse me?" said Maeve.

"I said, get out. What the hell do you think you are doing?" Aria growled.

"Aria, he's dangerous. He is a danger to you, to Dana… To Malek," Maeve pleaded.

"One more word out of you, and I will make sure you never see the light of day again. Now get the fuck out of my house. We are done; I don't ever want to see your faces again," Aria snarled as she went to Galan and pulled him behind her. "You've stood in the way of my happiness for the last fucking time."

Galan: *She did pick me…*

"Ari, please," Bodhi begged.

"I said get out," Aria gritted her teeth, "Don't make me repeat myself!"

Bodhi, Eyla, and Maeve backed away in disbelief. Seeing the rage in Aria's eyes, Bodhi held Eyla and Maeve and whispered, "It's over. Let's go." Bodhi opened the door and pulled them out of the room.

"How can you do this to me? I have been with you forever," Maeve said in dismay.

"You've stood in the way of my forever. I will never forgive you for that," replied Aria. "Now, leave."

Bodhi reached in front of Maeve and pulled the door shut.

Galan: *You chose me…*

Aria turned to Galan and asked softly, "Are you hurt?" as she stroked his face with her finger.

"I'm ok," Galan responded. The world disappeared around him as he spoke those words to her.

"I'm so sorry," Aria gushed.

"It's ok," Galan whispered.

"Kiss me, please, Sir," Aria begged.

Galan closed his eyes and leaned in. Aria drove the syringe into his neck and emptied the dose into his carotid artery. Gasping, Galan pulled away quickly.

"Aria?" Galan called out. His head began to spin, and his vision began to blur. "Aria… No…." Galan swayed and fell onto the wall.

"I hope you burn in hell, you sick fuck. This is for preying on my family!" Aria stated.

Galan tried to run to the door but stumbled with every step he took. Galan opened the door and ran outside, tumbling down the steps and into the rain. He landed on his back. Before losing consciousness, Galan caught a glimpse of Eyla, Bodhi, and Maeve standing over him, smiling. Eder and Garrick stepped in over him. "Gotcha!" said Garrick, moments before he stomped on Galan's face and knocked him out.

Aria walked to the door, looking at the five of them standing over Galan. Garrick looked up at Aria and nodded at her. Aria returned the gesture. "Get rid of him."

Malek peeked out from behind Aria and asked, "Love, what's going on?" Aria's blood ran cold.

"Baby, I told you to stay inside," said Aria in a shaky voice.

"Oh my God, is that Galan? What happened?" Malek ran outside; Aria grabbed him and tried to hold him back. "Love, he's bleeding; we need to help him!" Malek remarked.

"Baby, I didn't want you getting caught in any of this. You should have stayed inside," Aria repeated.

"Galan Rain isn't who you think he is. He is the reason I was put in the hospital; he did this to me," Maeve pointed at her bandages.

"And he's been having sketchy conversations with Dana," stated Eder.

"He was stalking Aria outside her house. He threatened to blackmail her family and destroy their reputation," Garrick added.

"Last night, when we caught Garrick in the backyard, it was because they'd found someone snooping around. Galan has been stalking us; he is dangerous. Garrick, Eder, and Maeve risked their lives to protect us from him," Aria explained.

Malek turned to Aria and held her face in his palms, "My love, it couldn't have been Galan. Last night, Galan was with me at the hotel."

"What?" Aria asked, her brow furrowing with confusion.

Bodhi, Maeve, and Eyla exchanged puzzled glances, unsure of how to respond. The unexpected turn of events had caught them off guard, and they struggled to make sense of Malek's statement.

"It's true. When I arrived, Galan was with a woman. I complimented his suit, and he later came back, and we hit it off. Galan couldn't have been guilty of any of those things; he's a kind soul. I would know; I've seen who he really is. Galan isn't stalking you; he was with a woman when I left this morning. Why would he do that if any of these things are true?" Malek questioned.

"No, that can't be. I fought him with my bare hands," uttered Garrick.

"Garrick, you and Eder said you were completely positive about this," said Aria.

"We are. There has to be some mistake. Galan must have been stalking Malek, too, and followed him to the hotel. He does that; he digs up dirt on people and uses it against them," Garrick retorted.

"Nobody knew Malek was here. Even if Galan was spying on the cameras when he arrived, there is no way he would know about the hotel. We only dropped Malek off there because Maeve was in the hospital. There are dozens of hotels in the city. It could have been any one of them he chose. Dad owns them all, so we, too, could have chosen any one of them. And we don't need to book our rooms; we dropped him off with our authorization for the room," Aria exclaimed.

"I met Galan when I first arrived; he was already there and had gotten a suit from the hotel store. He even went and got me one, but I refused it. How could he have known I would be there on the same floor, no less? None of it would have happened if I hadn't given him a compliment on his suit. Galan is a sweet guy. He was moved by that single act of kindness and wanted to return the favor. He spent the entire night with me, talking about life and family.

You didn't hear the things I heard; the person you are describing is not the person on the ground now. Please, help him," Malek pleaded.

"Garrick, he might be right. How would Galan have even gotten there? When you lost him in the mountains, didn't you go back to his place before returning to us? You said his car was still at the apartment," Eder stated.

"Are you kidding me, Eder? You know it's him!" Garrick growled.

"Mate, what if we were wrong? Even if we could pin everything else on him, he has an alibi for the night Maeve was attacked. You said it yourself; the guy who fought you spoke German," Eder countered.

"Love, please, I can vouch for Galan. He wouldn't do any of those things," Malek claimed.

"Baby, even if we take away the night of the attack, he still spied on us. And he still threatened Eder and Dana," Aria replied.

"Then, for me, will you give him a chance to explain himself? If he is guilty of those things, we can take this to the police," Malek declared.

Aria looked at them, soaking in the rain. "Get him inside. Maeve, wake him up," she ordered.

"What? You're going to listen to him? Aria, you know better," Maeve wailed.

"I also knew better, yet I trusted you all. But you were wrong about him; who knows what else we were wrong about! Malek is right; give him a chance to explain himself, at the very least. We already have a track record for misunderstandings. Get him inside. We can restrain him," Aria said as she took Malek's hand and led him back inside and to her room.

"How the fuck did we miss this?" asked Garrick.

"What is it about Galan fucking Rain that has everyone fooled like this," questioned Maeve.

"I say we drop his ass off the side of the mountain now. This is pointless," Garrick remarked.

"You do that, and Aria would never forgive you. Not to mention Malek might not take that well," Eder responded.

"Fuck that guy. Who cares what he thinks? Aria is not in her right mind; she's like a puppy whenever he speaks," Garrick retorted.

"Get him inside. Let's not make this worse; we're all involved here. Don't go making any rash decisions. If Malek blabs about this, it might be worse than what Galan was planning to blackmail us with," Bodhi pointed out.

"That's right… His phone! He blackmailed us with information on his phone," Garrick beamed.

"What about it?" asked Maeve.

"Let's unlock it. There must be something in there we can use. If he really wasn't bluffing, then he has all that stuff. We find it, expose him, and flash his phone. It's most likely connected to an email or a main account. Anthony showed me how to flash everything associated with any linked devices that share the same network and account. Once we prove he is guilty, it's game over for him," Garrick explained.

"Alright, that sounds like a plan. Help me get him up. Maeve, Eyla, go find something to tie him up with. Eder, help us carry him inside," said Bodhi.

"Got it," Eder replied. The three of them lifted Galan and carried him inside. Maeve and Eyla dragged a chair to the center of the room and got rolls of duct tape.

The guys sat Galan on the chair, taping his hands behind his back and his feet together. Meanwhile, Aria and Malek sat in her bedroom talking.

"Baby, things aren't as simple as you might think. There is no police here. We can't make reports or provide evidence of anything. Our reputation is worth everything; without it, I could lose a lot, and my dad and Dana could also. The safety of my family comes first, and now you are my family. So, there is nothing I won't do to protect you," Aria explained.

"I heard you out there and the way you spoke to Galan before you injected something into his neck. Who are you?" asked Malek.

"I am the same person, baby. Please believe me. I told you I would do anything to protect the ones I love. I believed Galan was a threat; I would do anything to stop him and protect you. I wish you weren't caught up in this; I never wanted you to be a part of this life," Aria professed.

"But, my love, you are my life now. I want to share my life with you, the good and the bad. I wouldn't love you any less," Malek told her as he took her hand.

"I don't deserve you," Aria whispered.

"Are you kidding me, my love? You deserve everything you want; all I can ever do is wake up every day and try to be worthy of you," answered Malek.

Aria kissed him; she wrapped her arms around Malek and straddled him at the edge of the bed. Aria began ripping his clothes off while undoing his belt. Malek stopped her. "Love, it's not that I don't want to. It's just that I want our first time to be special. And maybe with fewer people around," said Malek.

Aria leaned to his ear and whispered, "Having people around makes it all that more fun," as she tried to undo his pants. Malek wanted to stop her, but she wouldn't let him. He eventually gave in and let her have her way. He stopped resisting; he loved her too much. This was what she wanted, and all he desired was to give her whatever she sought. After Aria took her top off, a loud banging at the door startled them.

"Aria, you need to see this!" yelled Maeve.

Aria: *Why does everyone have such horrible fucking timing?* "Coming!" she answered. Aria put back on her top. Malek buttoned his shirt, leaving the tie and jacket off. Once they were decent, Aria and Malek stepped out into the living room. Galan was tied up on a chair, dripping wet. "What is it?" asked Aria.

"It's Galan's phone; there is an app on it for a camera security system, but it's password protected, so we can't get in," Garrick replied.

"How did you unlock his phone? Try the same password?" Aria suggested.

"We used facial recognition to open his phone, but this is protected by a fingerprint scan. The weird thing is it won't open; we tried scanning it twice," Garrick told her.

"Maybe it's because he's soaking wet? Dry his fingers and try again," Aria advised.

"No good; if we try opening it again, it might lock down the entire system. Then we won't be able to get in at all. That's usually how these things work, three times, and it locked," Garrick responded.

"Then wait till he wakes up. See if you can find anything else on his phone in the meantime, anything at all," instructed Aria.

"Try his gallery. Check his videos and pictures; he said he had proof, right? That's where it would be," Eder suggested.

Garrick clicked the gallery application. "It's locked, with a PIN, fuck."

"Wait, look there, mate. What is that timer?" asked Eder, pointing to the bottom of the screen where they saw a running timer with a twenty-four-hour countdown.

Garrick tapped the timer, opening another application. One of the screen options read 'Disable timer security lock.' "It's the timer he told us about that would leak the videos and stuff if he didn't cancel it," Garrick said as he clicked the button. A message popped up: 'Disable all security measures' and 'Disable this file only.' Garrick pressed the 'Disable all' button. 'Scan fingerprint to confirm' appeared on the screen.

"Fuck, it won't work," Eder muttered.

"Wait, this is a different app. We would have three tries here, separate from the other one. This is clearly something different; it's worth a shot," Garrick replied as he scanned Galan's fingerprint. With the fingerprint verified, the lock was removed from the gallery, but it did not undo the PIN lock on the application. "Damn, well, at least that's one problem out of the way. If we keep his phone, there won't be anything for him to use to blackmail us."

"Maeve, how do we wake him?" asked Aria.

"The anesthetic is not on an IV like we administer at the hospital. Once it stops flowing through his body, he should come around in a couple minutes. I can't really say how long he will be out. It could be five or ten minutes more; he's already been out for about fifteen. Maybe we can try some sort of stimulus to wake him," Maeve advised.

"Oh, we can certainly do that," Garrick smirked as he hit Galan with a right hook punch.

"Hey, man, what are you doing? You could hurt him like that!" Malek exclaimed.

"Oh, he deserves this. Look at what he did to my sister. He's lucky I don't hit harder," Garrick retorted.

"Garrick!" Aria belted.

"You know what, you're right," Garrick turned back and kicked Galan across the chest, sending the chair and him flying backward and falling over.

Galan let out a muffled grunt, his labored breaths filling the air. His body convulsed, and he collapsed to the ground, struggling with each breath. Maeve reacted swiftly, her instincts kicking in as she rushed to his side. With a calm demeanor, she began to assess the situation. She knelt beside Galan and carefully placed her ear on his chest, listening intently for any irregularities in his heartbeat. Her fingers gently searched for his pulse on his neck, her training guiding her through the process. "His heartbeat is strained. I need to give him CPR. Bodhi, come here and do the chest compressions. Pump to the beat of that old Bee Gees song; keep it steady," Maeve stated. With Bodhi's assistance and Maeve's instruction, they performed CPR, and in a few minutes, Galan slightly regained consciousness. He began coughing uncontrollably. "Lift him back up!" she advised.

Bodhi and Eder worked together to carefully lift the chair back to its original position, ensuring Galan was stable as his coughing gradually subsided. However, the effects of the injection left him disoriented, and his head spun with dizziness. His eyes rolled back, and he struggled to open them or take a steady breath, causing immediate concern for Maeve and the others.

Maeve remained composed, gently encouraging Galan as she guided him through the process of regaining consciousness. Her soothing voice served as an anchor for Galan, helping him focus and regain control over his breathing. Despite still feeling the effects of the anesthesia, Galan slowly but steadily started to regain full consciousness, thanks to Maeve's patient coaching.

As the anesthesia-induced haze began to lift, Galan's awareness returned, but he was still feeling the effects of being immobilized. Panic crept in as he realized he couldn't move his hands or feet; Galan became frantic.

"What the hell? Why... Can't I move?!" Galan stuttered.

"Easy, you won't be going anywhere. Calm down and do what we say; this will be over before you know it," Garrick stated.

"Aria, get him something to drink; anything that is high in caffeine would help him come back around quicker. He is still loopy," Maeve advised.

"On it," Aria hurried to the kitchen and grabbed an energy drink from the fridge. She returned shortly after with the drink and straw in hand. "Come on, Galan, drink this. You will feel better."

Aria placed the straw in Galan's mouth, and he began to drink, coughing every few sips. Maeve explained the shot they'd given him was messing with his motor functions, so he would have some trouble until it was completely out of his system.

"Wh… What did… You do to me…," Galan muttered.

Chapter Thirty-Six

Galan's heart raced as he found himself tightly bound, his hands and feet entwined with unforgiving duct tape. Each attempt to break free only seemed to make the situation more challenging. The tape constricted around his wrists and ankles, leaving him feeling trapped and vulnerable. With each tug and twist, Galan could feel the sting of the tape against his skin.

"Struggle all you want; you can't squirm your way out of this," Garrick smirked.

"Let me out, or I swear to God!" Galan fumed.

"Or what? You're gonna go crawling back to Aria?" Garrick mocked.

"That's enough. Don't get Galan any more riled up; we just need to ask him a few things. If he's not willing to cooperate, he can spend the rest of his life in prison," Maeve stated.

"I didn't do anything. Let me go!" Galan demanded.

"Leave him alone. He won't help us if we rile him up anymore," Aria exclaimed.

Malek walked up to Galan. "Hey, are you ok?" Malek asked sympathetically.

"No, I'm not! The room is spinning, my face is killing me, plus my arms are tied behind me in an awkward position, and it's getting rather painful," Galan snapped.

"It's going to be ok; I'll make sure they won't hurt you. I will not let something like this go on and say nothing; I've got your back," Malek assured him.

Garrick and Eder stepped in front of Galan. "Alright, mate, don't make this harder than it needs to be. The faster we get answers, the faster we can end this," Eder declared.

"I'll be straight with you; we know you are guilty. We know you're a sick fuck, and we have the proof to back it up. The only reason you are still here is that Malek thinks you deserve a chance to explain yourself. And honestly, if his influence didn't affect Aria's decisions, you would be dead by now," Garrick stated.

"Garrick!" Aria exclaimed.

"I don't give a fuck anymore, Aria. We had a plan; this isn't the first time you couldn't commit," Garrick shot back.

"Garrick, what are you doing?" Maeve inquired.

"Let's be real for a moment, Maeve. Let's just say Malek was right. If so, Galan walks free, and we all deal with Aria's hatred. But if he was wrong, then do we just pretend none of this happened? Malek isn't going to sweep this under the rug, and when it comes down to it, Aria will choose him over anyone. No matter how this goes, we have no place in her life anymore. This story ends with Aria and Malek. So, let's cut the shit," Garrick snarled.

"What the hell are you talking about?" asked Aria.

"Galan, here's your first question. How many times have you fucked Aria?" questioned Garrick, his gaze unwavering as he locked eyes with her.

"Garrick, what the fuck are you doing!?" Maeve repeated.

Eder pulled him away. "Mate, what does this have to do with the plan?" he whispered.

"There is no plan anymore, Eder. Aria made her choice; there is nothing left for us," Garrick explained.

"What the hell is wrong with you?" Eder questioned.

"Since we all want the truth, right, we are the ones being blamed for this? Then let's talk truth; answer the question, Galan. You answer that question, and I will let you go," Garrick declared.

Galan looked at him; he understood his pain. He, too, knew what it felt like to be on the short end of Aria's love, along with the betrayal he felt and the deep sorrow. Galan leaned back in the chair and looked from Aria to Malek. *You'll do this to him eventually; neither you nor he will come back from that pain. I will grant you the mercy of sparing you from that, Malek. I wouldn't wish this on anyone.* "We didn't," Galan confidently answered.

"Bullshit! I know her, Galan. I knew her better than anyone. I know her patterns; I know her tells.

Look at her; she looks like she has seen a ghost! That's not the look of someone who has been loyal to her man," Garrick responded.

"You're wrong; it's true that I have feelings for her, but I got shot down. I tried, but your meddling always got in the way. Whenever I believed I was making any headway, you and your friends broke the little trust we had. If I had some time away from all of this, I might have been able to at least get the chance to ask her to be mine. But as of right now, that's nothing but wishful thinking. I didn't know about Malek and her, but that's just a testament to how little we actually got to connect with each other. We barely got to talk about ourselves; it was mostly disproving rumors. So let's get this over with; ask your questions," Galan replied.

Garrick grabbed Galan's suit and leaned him back on the chair's back legs; Eder and the others quickly pulled him off of Galan.

Aria: *He could have ended my relationship with Malek had he told the truth. Why didn't he? Is he really not a bad person? What have I done?*

"That's enough, Garrick. What the fuck is wrong with you?" asked Bodhi.

Fueled by a surge of adrenaline, Garrick swiftly pushed Bodhi away and, with a well-aimed kick, incapacitated him, rendering him unconscious. Recognizing the danger, Eder rushed to restrain Garrick and calm him down. Despite his efforts, Garrick's strength proved formidable, and he managed to lift Eder off the ground as he struggled to keep him at bay. With a mighty effort, Garrick broke free from Eder's grasp and, employing a cunning move, seized Eder's clothing from behind, using it to pull him forcefully toward the ground, sending him crashing down with a resounding thud. All the while, Galan, determined and unwavering, had been tenaciously attempting to free himself from the constraints of the duct tape throughout this intense altercation.

"Don't fucking touch me. This 'friendship' we had expired the moment Aria decided to take matters into her own hands," Garrick snapped.

Maeve ran to Garrick and pushed him away. "Stop! Now!" Maeve yelled.

"It's over, Maeve; there is nothing left," Garrick hissed.

"I said stop. We have one job right now: to prove Galan is who we say he is. Keep it together, and let's just do this. Don't try to drag us all down because you have nothing to fight for," Maeve retorted. "I get it; you love Aria, we all do, but be a decent human for once, and don't make this about you," Maeve continued.

"You know what, I'm done. I'm not going to stay here and watch this anymore. At least this time, when Aria's life gets fucked up, everyone won't blame me," Garrick's rage boiled over as he stormed out of the house, slamming the door shut behind him before climbing into his truck.

The tense atmosphere lingered inside as Maeve, feeling the weight of the moment, turned to Aria and Malek. Her heart raced, searching for the right words to mend the situation and restore some sense of peace. "Forget Garrick; we don't need him. I know everything he does. Let's just get this over with," she stated.

As the dizziness slowly subsided, Galan felt a renewed sense of determination surging through him. The water soaking his clothes inadvertently played a crucial role in his liberation, causing the tape to lose its grip and become increasingly pliable. Galan seized the opportunity, wiggling his hands relentlessly until they were almost free. Summoning every ounce of strength left in him, he powered through the last stubborn bits of tape, and with a triumphant snap, his hands were finally liberated.

Aria and the others stood in awe, taken aback by Galan's resourcefulness and resilience. They couldn't believe their eyes as they witnessed him breaking free from his restraints. Eder, reacting swiftly to the unfolding scene, instinctively rushed to Maeve's side, shielding her protectively behind him.

Galan, now free, wasted no time. He carefully removed the remnants of the tape from his wrists and took a moment to regain his composure.

"Easy… I just wanted my hands to stop hurting so damn much. If it makes you feel better, I'll leave my legs taped together. Can I finish that drink, Aria?" asked Galan.

As Aria processed the intense series of events, her emotions were in turmoil, leaving her momentarily speechless. She stood there, trying to gather her thoughts and feelings, while Malek fetched a drink and handed it over to Galan, who graciously accepted it. Galan took a sip, feeling the cool liquid soothing his parched throat after his ordeal.

"Thanks, Malek," Galan replied, quickly finishing off the energy drink.

Chapter Thirty-Seven

Garrick sat in his truck, the leather seats creaking as he clenched his fists in a fit of uncontrollable rage. Frustration and anger boiled within him, and he unleashed his emotions upon the dashboard and the empty seat beside him as if they were the cause of his torment. A primal shout escaped his lips, echoing into the silence of the vehicle.

His attention shifted to the glovebox, and he stared at it intently as if seeking solace or answers within its confines. But before he could open it, his phone started to ring persistently, accompanied by a series of incoming messages. He sighed in annoyance, his anger momentarily diverted.

Reluctantly, he retrieved his phone and saw a notification indicating that his account had been synced. Curiosity piqued, he opened the app and scrolled through the images, his eyes eventually landing on the particular photo taken on that fateful night. The image was overexposed, ruined by the harsh reflection of his phone's camera flash against the glass wall of Aria's house. At that moment, Garrick's anger escalated beyond its usual threshold. But as quickly as his fury had erupted, it subsided, giving way to a profound sense of helplessness. He realized that his anger stemmed from the powerlessness he felt in the face of his own inadequacies. No matter how hard he tried or what he did, it never seemed enough.

Garrick pressed 'back' on the picture and noticed one that was taken after the photo of Galan. Curious, he opened the image and found a picture of a topless girl standing in front of a beautiful sunset, wearing a robe that she had loosely wrapped around her shoulders. "What is this?" Garrick muttered. He zoomed in on the image, trying to see the hotel's name printed on the robe. "No way... I've got you, you son of a bitch!" Garrick's heart pounded in his chest as he hurriedly got out of the truck, leaving the engine running as he ran back towards the house. With a determined expression, he reached the front door and, without hesitation, burst through it. "Sorry, I lost my temper back there. I know I'm not wanted here, but I'll be quiet. I would just like to see this through; I'll just observe. I'll even stand where no one can see me in the corner," Garrick claimed.

"I think you should leave," Aria replied.

"Please, Aria, I will walk out of your life. You will never have to see me again. I promise I will keep away from you. I just want to see this through. Ask him about our claims; I won't oppose anything he says or try to convince you otherwise. I just want to see how this ends, ok?" Garrick pleaded.

Aria's mind raced with conflicting thoughts as she pondered Garrick's words. While part of her wanted to be understanding and supportive of Garrick's feelings, another part couldn't shake the worry about the potential risks involved. If Galan broke free, having Garrick around was their best bet at taking him down.

"Fine, but when this is over, that's it. I don't see you ever again," Aria acceded.

"You have my word, Aria," Garrick replied as he positioned himself in the corner of the room; he observed the scene unfolding before him.

"Alright, let's start. The first accusation was you blackmailing Eder about sleeping with an underaged girl," Maeve began.

"Are you asking if I really did that? The answer is yes; I was never hiding that fact. I was just never asked about it. As funny as it may seem, you tend to retaliate when someone threatens you and puts their hands on you. But why does that matter? What does it prove?" asked Galan.

"It proves you have been stalking Aria and Dana, and you knew the age difference," Maeve exclaimed.

"Are you kidding me? Look at Eder! Aside from the fact that he is a prominent social media influencer that any idiot with a phone would have known about, he has exceptional muscle tone and facial features not common for a child, which is what Dana is! You can clearly tell the age gap, and it's big enough to be obvious she is underaged. After all his accusations against me, I find it fitting that he felt what it was like for people to talk about things they didn't know about," Galan remarked.

"Didn't know about? Well, that's funny, but we will get to that bit in a minute. Let's talk about the night Garrick found you snooping around here," said Aria.

"I told you, I wasn't snooping. I live in this town; Garrick does not. Of the two of us, I am the only one who should have been here that night," Galan remarked.

"So, you admit to being outside Aria's house that night," Maeve smirked.

"Yes, I even told Dana. In fact, all of you had a problem with me talking to Dana after Garrick caused a scene in the café. But that's what we were talking about; I told Dana that I ran into some guy sitting in a car outside of their house the night before when I was trying to return her phone," Galan explained.

"Aha! That's not what you told Garrick. You said you stopped because you were conducting business, and you didn't want to drive and do that," Maeve stated.

"And? If you got stopped by a strange guy who doesn't live in your town, a town that is highly exclusive, are you going to tell that stranger what you are doing in detail?" Galan inquired.

"He has a point, Maeve," Aria agreed.

"Alright, let's move on to when you threatened Garrick and Eder, then. Why were you recording when they approached you? You again threatened to tarnish the good reputation of the Scarlets in order to get to Eder and Garrick," Maeve claimed.

"Well, Maeve, maybe you should ask your boyfriend, Eder, why he was stalking me outside my apartment building earlier that day," Galan countered.

"What… What do you mean, boyfriend?" Maeve stammered.

"Interesting that you didn't focus on the information you asked me for, but rather that I pointed out you and Eder share some relationship," Galan pointed out.

"We do not," Maeve denied.

"I saw the way he ran to your side when my hands got free. It makes sense; one minute, he was ready to fight Garrick in the café, but they have been together every single time after that. How odd. What would Dana's boyfriend and Aria's ex be doing roaming about together? If I understand this correctly, Garrick abused steroids, raged out, and put his hands on Aria. So, why would Eder be friends with someone like that? Unless, of course, it had something to do with Garrick's sister. Aria mentioned that Eder and Dana were not on good terms. If I had to guess, I'd say that brilliant girl figured it out, too," Galan calmly replied.

Aria looked over to Maeve, who was panicking exactly as she had earlier when they accused Galan of sleeping with her.

Aria: *That manipulative little bitch…!*

"You don't know what the hell you're talking about!" Maeve refuted his statement.

"It's frustrating when someone doesn't know the whole story but jumps to conclusions, isn't it?" Galan remarked.

"We are not jumping to conclusions. You were there that night! You were the one who did th to me; you were there in the backyard. Garrick saw you; we have proof!" Maeve declared.

"Then, by all means, Maeve, present your proof," Galan suggested.

"You smug son of a bitch. You know there is no proof because you stole Garrick's phone, which had the picture of you in Aria's backyard. But that is something only the person who was there would know. Yet when Garrick threatened to use the proof, you knew he didn't have it. That's why you are so calm about all of this. You know we can't pin it on you, but that's your mistake," Maeve snarled.

"Alright, let's play this out. Let's say that it was me. What time did this occur?" Galan questioned.

"Got you! You can't deny it because you know you were there! You seemed to have an answer for everything else, but suddenly, you want to role-play?" asked Maeve.

"I didn't deny the other claims. I had my reasons for every single one. However, this one, I had an alibi. I was supposed to fly out of here, but I stopped off at a hotel until my flight at midnight. I couldn't wait to leave and put this place behind me. Malek can confirm I was there before he got there, so go ahead and play out the events of that night for me. Poke holes in my alibi with that top-notch evidence you seem to have," Galan taunted.

"It was just after closing up the café," Maeve informed him.

"Alright, that's a good start. There was a lot of time before my flight, so your claim is valid thus far. Keep going," Galan said.

"Fast-forward to the end... Garrick chased you into the woods on the far end of Salt Pine Acres, near the hiking trail, and lost you in there. You disappeared then, and we lost sight of you. That was enough time to get from Salt Pine Acres to the hotel and arrive before Malek," Maeve declared.

"That's actually not a bad scenario, but answer me this. How did I go from the mountain to the hotel?" Galan inquired.

"You tell me!" replied Maeve with a smirk.

"Alright, where were you when Garrick chased this storybook version of me?" questioned Galan.

"We were in the car, tending to my wounds, so I didn't bleed out," Maeve replied angrily.

"Where exactly were you?" Galan repeated.

"We were on the steps to the lower level of Salt Pine Acres," Maeve answered.

"Alright, that's near Grounded Coffee House. That road is the only way in or out of Salt Pine Acres. Now, tell me, did you see me leave through the gates?" asked Galan.

"No…," replied Maeve uneasily.

"Alright. And since you believe so strongly that it was me that night, it would only make sense that you went to my apartment to see if I was still in town. Did you?" Galan probed.

"Why does that matter?" Eder interjected.

"Well, if you did, you would have noticed that my car was parked in the garage," replied Galan.

"What does that prove?" Maeve questioned.

"Well, for the average car, it takes about two hours to venture down that mountain, and at night, it might take longer due to how dark the road is. So, with my car still at home, how did I beat Malek to the hotel? You guys were guarding the gates, right?" Galan guessed.

Maeve began to twitch in frustration. "We can't account for the time between then. Garrick was rushing me to the hospital," Maeve answered.

"Alright, how long did that take, then?" Galan remarked.

"Garrick took less than an hour to get to the hospital," Maeve answered.

"That doesn't surprise me; you drove my car like a bat out of hell down that mountain. So, I would imagine he could also make great time," Galan replied.

Maeve, who had been observing the situation alongside Garrick, couldn't help but feel her frustration growing. Galan's calm demeanor seemed to be a facade, and it only added to her sense of unease.

"How did Malek get to the hotel, Aria?" Galan inquired.

"Hans dropped him off while we were on our way to the hospital," Aria answered.

"When did you tell Aria that Maeve was going to the hospital? Did you leave together?" Galan probed.

"No, we told her after we got there," Eder responded.

"Then that gives me a one-hour head start. So, if I left after you guys, that means I would have been halfway down the mountain by the time Aria left. So, technically, your claims are still valid," Galan stated.

"I don't understand. Why are you trying to prove you did it?" asked Eder.

"He's not; he just knows we can't figure it out. He knows there is something we cannot account for, and that's why we can't pin this on him. He has a great alibi; his car was home, and he was at a hotel,"

Garrick responded. "He's toying with you; he's making us look like a bunch of idiots because we don't have all the answers. Move on, Maeve. You don't have him."

Galan: *That's right; a bunch of rich assholes who never had to work a day in their lives wouldn't know a thing about the employees here or how the bus systems work.*

Galan looked over at Garrick. He seemed defeated; his hyper demeanor shriveled.

Galan: *There goes your case. You have one more option, but even with that, you will ultimately lose. If you call me out on the cameras, it's game over!*

Maeve looked flustered and turned to Aria, "You're up, Ari."

Aria stood in Malek's arms. "Galan, we found cameras in Grounded Coffee House. Every single room has cameras built into them. How do you explain that?" questioned Aria.

Galan looked at Aria. "I am not a trusting person, Aria, and neither was the guy who owned the butcher's shop before I bought the building. This happened before Salt Pine Acres became the off-the-grid town that it is today. I couldn't watch the entire building at once, just floor by floor, so I used the security systems to keep my eyes on all three floors at once. When I bought the place, I upgraded his system, hiding it behind a one-way glass in the ceiling. I've always kept tabs on my building twenty-four-seven. It's partly why I became so successful. I was able to see my staff, learn from them, and ultimately, bring out their best potential. Soon enough, I applied it to the customers, and it's what created Grounded Coffee House's unmatched service and quality goods.

"But you are right. The café isn't supposed to have them because Salt Pine Acres has a rule against it. Nobody else but me knew about it, which is why you didn't know about it until now. If word got out about that, everything I'd built would have come crashing down, so I kept it to myself. If you or Dana knew about it and blabbed to someone like Eder, Maeve, Eyla, or Bodhi, they could blackmail you and destroy what Dana was trying to do. I figured the best way to protect you from that was for it to remain hidden. No one would ever know or find it," Galan explained.

"So, you admit to spying on Aria and Dana all this time! And don't even lie; we have you dead to rights. The app is on your phone," Maeve's smirk was a mixture of satisfaction and triumph as she revealed Galan's phone. Garrick's attention was momentarily diverted from the intensity of the moment when he received a message on his own phone. He quickly checked it. Garrick's focus quickly returned to the present as he pocketed his phone.

"Let's hear it now!" said Maeve.

"Well, that's fun. Nothing like invading the privacy of others! If you know there is an app, I can only assume you used facial recognition to open the lock on my phone. Did you try to open the app?" Galan questioned.

"We did, but it failed because you were soaking wet, and your fingerprint didn't register," answered Maeve.

"No, it didn't fail because my hands were wet. It failed because it will not open to my fingerprint," Galan replied.

"What? What sense does that make," Eder interjected.

"The day I signed over the business, the ownership of the security system changed too. It won't open to me anymore; it opens to—" Galan began before he was interrupted.

"It opens to Dana…," Aria whispered.

Chapter thirty-eight

As all eyes turned towards Aria, the atmosphere in the room became charged with concern and worry. Aria's shocked response caught everyone off guard. The weight of the discovery seemed to crush Aria, triggering a panic attack. Her breathing became rapid and shallow, her chest tightening with each breath. Her hands trembled, and her body felt as though it had betrayed her, spiraling into a state of uncontrollable panic. Malek, who had been standing nearby, acted swiftly. He moved closer to Aria and enveloped her in a comforting embrace, providing a sense of security and stability amidst the chaos.

"That's not true… That can't be…," Maeve stammered.

"Then prove me wrong. If you scan Dana's fingerprint and it doesn't authorize the application, I guess you'll know that I was lying about it," Galan commented.

"No, it could be a trap. We've already tried twice. Suppose we try a third time, and Galan is lying about Dana's print being able to open it. In that case, his phone will go into a lockdown that only he can open," Eder stated.

"Then, how about this: if Dana's print doesn't open the app, carry out your original plan. Whatever you were going to do when you injected me, I won't resist," Galan offered.

"Either he's bluffing, or he knows it will work," Maeve expressed.

"How mistrustful you must be. I am outnumbered seven to one, bound to a chair, and you have my phone in your possession. What advantage do I have to be lying right now? You think I'm bluffing? Then call my bluff; what have you got to lose?" questioned Galan.

Galan's gaze shifted towards Garrick, who stood quietly in the corner, radiating an aura of remarkable composure amidst the mounting frustration that had gripped everyone else in the room. As the weight of the situation settled upon him, Galan took a moment to gather his thoughts, and then he began to speak, "Well, come on then, where is Dana? Let's get her to scan her fingerprint."

Aria's emotions reached a breaking point, and she couldn't contain her feelings any longer. With a deep, trembling gasp, tears welled up in her eyes and overflowed, cascading down her cheeks. "Dana... No... What have I done," Aria muttered through labored breaths.

"Aria, what's wrong? What about Dana?" asked Galan.

As Maeve and the rest of the group noticed Aria's outpouring of emotions, their attention shifted toward her. Meanwhile, Bodhi, who had been unconscious, showed signs of stirring, his eyelids fluttering as he started to regain consciousness.

"I didn't want her to be a part of this… She has a crush on Galan, so her judgment would have been skewed—" Aria began.

As Galan's eyes fell upon Aria, his previously calm and composed demeanor underwent a sharp transformation. Anger flashed in his eyes, and his voice carried a mix of concern and frustration. "Aria, what have you done to Dana?!" he demanded, his words laced with intensity.

As Aria met Galan's accusing gaze, her vulnerability was evident in the single tear trickling down her cheek. Her voice trembled with emotion as she struggled to find the strength to speak. Sensing her distress, Malek tenderly embraced her, offering reassurance and support.

In the hushed room, all eyes remained fixed on Aria, understanding that whatever she had to say would likely unravel a deeply troubling mystery. The weight of the moment was profound as they awaited her whispered revelation, "I locked Dana in the storage room so she would be safe until we got rid of Galan—"

Galan's anger reached its peak, and his heartbeat thundered in his ears, drowning out all other sounds. "This has gone too far. I don't care what you did to me, but how dare you do that to a child?" he growled, his voice laced with a mix of fury and anguish. The room trembled with the intensity of his emotions, and the others were taken aback by the unyielding determination in Galan's eyes. In a swift, powerful motion, Galan broke free from the restraints of the duct tape that had bound his feet. Even Garrick's calm demeanor faltered for a moment, caught off guard by Galan's fierce reaction.

As he approached Aria, still trembling in Malek's embrace, Galan couldn't bring himself to look directly into her tearful eyes. The weight of the moment was crushing, and he whispered, "You monster…," to Aria before marching to the door.

"Hey, where do you think you're going?" Eder called out. He quickly stepped forward and positioned himself firmly in front of the door, effectively blocking Galan's path.

"I'm gonna go get Dana," Galan replied.

"Oh, he's not going anywhere," Bodhi said as he and Maeve got between Galan and Eder.

"I'm only gonna say this once. If you don't get out of my way right now—" Galan stated before he was interrupted.

"You'll what?" asked Eder.

"You better cherish the breath you take, or it will be your last… Now get out of my way," Galan remarked calmly and slowly.

"I have one more question before you leave," said Garrick.

"Fuck you and your questions," Galan barked.

"Oh, my question isn't for you," Garrick responded. He turned to Malek and took out his phone. "Malek, can you tell me if you know this person?" asked Garrick, showing him the nude picture of Nikki.

Stunned by the picture, Malek turned away immediately. "I don't know her name, but that was the woman Galan was with at the hotel. The morning I left them, she came to the door looking like that when I was saying goodbye to Galan," Malek answered.

"Thanks, Malek," Garrick replied.

"What does that have to do with anything? We know he was at the hotel with a girl," Eyla claimed.

"That's right, he wasn't lying about that. But the strange thing is that this was taken on my stolen phone after I took a picture of someone in the back of Aria's house," Garrick declared.

Galan: *What... When did this happen?*

———

Galan's mind was momentarily transported back in time to the events that had unfolded at the hotel. The flashback engulfed him, and vivid memories flooded his consciousness. He could see himself entering the room, the memory as clear as if it were happening again in the present.

In his mind's eye, he saw Nikki standing near the balcony's glass doors, and a pang of realization struck him. She was standing next to the basket where Garrick's phone was hidden in his hoodie.

———

Galan: *Fuck... You don't need to unlock someone's phone to open their camera if you know that the shortcut to open it is to quickly tap the home button twice. I didn't think she had it at any point.*

"We've got you now, you sick fuck," Garrick snarled.

Maeve's eyes widened in shock as she desperately reached for the syringe concealed within the depths of her back pocket. The glint of determination in her eyes betrayed her intentions. But before she could execute her plan, Galan's swift reflexes intercepted, seizing the needle from her grasp.

Without hesitation, Galan took matters into his own hands, thrusting the needle toward Maeve's eye in an audacious move. Time seemed to slow as the needle pierced the air and found its mark. Maeve let out an agonizing scream, a chilling sound that sent shivers down their spines.

Reacting instinctively to avoid drawing attention to their sinister act, Galan quickly muffled Maeve's screams by clamping a hand over her mouth. "I'm pretty sure that was supposed to go into the bloodstream, oops," he remarked.

Bodhi and Eder stood rooted in shock, their hearts pounding in their chests as they witnessed the unfolding chaos. Garrick's anguished cry for Maeve echoed through the room, propelling him into action. Without hesitation, he lunged toward Galan. Galan thrust Maeve into Garrick's arms before executing a ruthless kick into her back, sending them crashing through a nearby table. Glass splintered and shattered around them as they hit the floor, leaving them momentarily stunned.

Meanwhile, Malek, quick on his feet, seized Aria's hand and pulled her towards safety in another room, locking the door behind them. Aria's heart pounded in her chest as she glanced back, the adrenaline fueling her senses as she clung to Malek's reassuring presence. Bodhi and Eder, now finding themselves at the forefront of this chaotic scene, mustered their resolve and took on the responsibility of blocking the exit. As he prepared to make his escape, a sudden intervention halted his path. Eyla, fueled by a mix of fury and justice, appeared from the shadows and thrust the final syringe into Galan's shoulder.

Galan's reflexes were lightning-quick as he reacted to Eyla's attempted injection. With a powerful kick, he sent her crashing into the wall, halting her attempt to deliver the contents of the syringe into his body. Breathing heavily, he yanked the syringe from his shoulder, relief flooding through him that he had escaped its effects.

Swiftly tucking the syringe into his jacket pocket, Galan turned his attention to Bodhi and Eder, who were bravely standing in his path, blocking his escape route. With a fierce determination, he lunged at them, resolute to break free from this perilous situation.

In a chaotic frenzy, Galan managed to overpower Bodhi and Eder, using his strength and agility to force the door open. The three of them crashed onto the front porch, the impact sending shockwaves through their bodies.

Seizing the opportunity, Galan wasted no time in regaining his footing. He sprinted down the stairs, adrenaline coursing through his veins, and leaped into his waiting car. The engine roared to life as he swiftly started the vehicle, the sound echoing through the tense air.

Without a second thought, Galan floored the acceleration, the tires screeching as he peeled away from the scene. The car's engine roared with ferocity as he turned the vehicle around and sped down the street.

Garrick's heart pounded in his chest as he scrambled to his feet amidst the wreckage of shattered glass. Fear gripped him as he saw Maeve lying unconscious on the floor, her body limp and bleeding from the sharp shards that had penetrated her skin.

"Oh my God, Maeve!!!" Eder's heart raced, and his breath came in short, panicked gasps as he peeked through the broken door alongside Bodhi.

"I have to get her to the hospital. That thing almost killed Galan, so who knows what it would do to someone as tiny as her," Garrick remarked.

"Let's go, come on!" Eder agreed.

"No, get Aria and Dana out of here," Garrick instructed.

"You've got it, mate. Just go and get Maeve to the hospital," Eder responded.

As Garrick drove off with Maeve in the front seat, Eder wasted no time rushing to the vehicle behind them, where Hans was waiting. He urgently relayed the situation, instructing Hans to prepare the car for a hasty departure from Salt Pine Acres. The urgency in Eder's voice left no room for questions or hesitation.

Hans nodded, understanding the gravity of the situation. He swiftly made his way to the car, ensuring it was ready for a quick escape. Time was of the essence, and they couldn't afford to waste a moment.

Garrick's truck roared through the stormy night, the rain pounding against the windshield like an incessant drumbeat. The howling wind added to the sense of urgency as if nature itself was in sync with the turmoil of the night's events.

In the distance, Galan's car revved its engine, and his gaze shifted between the GPS on his dashboard and the small car icon representing his vehicle. He was tracking the movement of his phone, which was in Maeve's possession.

Galan: *I could hear your engine from two streets down. Let's see what you can do against this beast!*

As Galan's car shot forward, he felt the adrenaline coursing through his veins. The sound of Garrick's truck grew louder, and he could feel the tension building with each passing moment. Garrick's truck zoomed past the entrance to the alleyway, leaving Galan with little time to make his move. With determination burning in his eyes, he slammed his foot on the accelerator, urging his car to go faster. The engine responded with a roar, mirroring the storm's fury that raged around them.

As he approached the next street, Galan risked a quick glance between the gaps of each house. To his surprise, he realized he was almost neck and neck with Garrick's truck. The sight fueled his determination, and a sinister smile crept across his face. He relished the thrill of the chase, knowing that victory was within reach. Garrick's truck was now coming up on the last stretch of road leading to the gates of Salt Pine Acres.

"Hold on, Maevy. Hang on just a little bit for me; just stay with me oka…," Garrick started saying. The sound of metal on metal reverberated through the air as Galan's car slammed into Garrick's truck at the final intersection leading to the gates of Salt Pine Acres. The impact was forceful and unexpected, sending Garrick's truck into a spin on the wet roads. In the chaos of the collision, the tires lost traction, and the vehicle careened out of control.

As the truck veered wildly, its momentum took it straight into the gates of Salt Pine Acres. The once imposing structure buckled and deformed under the massive impact, its sturdy frame unable to withstand the force of the collision.

Garrick's truck lodged sideways into the gates, blocking the only way out of Salt Pine Acres.

Galan revved his engine. "One down," he muttered. Making a U-turn, he drove back to the café. The doors were open, so Galan ran inside and went directly to the storage room. Dana was sitting in a fetal position on crates of coffee beans, rocking back and forth in anger.

When Galan came breaking through the door, Dana hopped off the crate and ran to the door to see what had made that noise. "D!" Galan called out.

As Dana spotted Galan in the storage room, her emotions surged from fear to relief. Tears streamed down her cheeks, her heart aching with a flood of emotions. Without hesitation, she ran towards him and jumped into his arms, "You ok?" Galan asked, holding her tightly.

Dana was overcome with emotions, rendering her unable to find her voice.

"It's ok; I've got you. I've got you," Galan gently stroked the back of her head as he locked eyes with her, speaking in a soothing, soft tone, "D, I need to get you somewhere safe."

Dana nodded in agreement, her emotions still preventing her from finding the words to express herself. Galan tenderly set her down and hurriedly led her out of the café, hand in hand. They quickly reached his car and discreetly navigated through the less-traveled back streets, heading back to his apartment.

"What happened? What did they do to you?" asked Dana worriedly.

"They tried to kill me," replied Galan nonchalantly.

Dana gasped, "They did what—"

"They injected me with this," Galan revealed the syringe to Dana, holding it in his hand with a serious expression on his face.

"What is that?" Dana gasped.

"That is a nasty little gift from your old friend, Maeve," Galan answered. "I don't know exactly what it is, but I was unconscious within seconds of being injected... By Aria...."

Dana looked at Galan in horror. "Wha... What?" she stammered.

"I should have known nobody could love someone as broken as I am. I let her toy with me, and for once in my life, I thought someone had finally chosen me. But like every other time, it was always the next guy," Galan remarked.

"Galan...," said Dana softly.

"My priority right now is you; I need to keep you safe from these monsters. I'll take you to my place; once you're inside, you can leave at any time. There is an override switch to the elevator in the kitchen. No one but me can get into the apartment, so you will be safe there," Galan explained.

"What are you going to do?" asked Dana worriedly.

"Don't worry about me," Galan answered.

"Please don't go. Stay with me, Galan," Dana pleaded.

"I will never forgive them for what they did to you, for what they did to me. Now, they are going to know what it's like to lose what little hope you have to hang on to," Galan replied as he pulled into the parking garage.

"Please, Galan, don't leave me," Dana begged him.

"They took everything from me. This was my chance at a new beginning. This was my one hope for a new beginning. She broke me, Dana—" Galan got quiet for a moment before saying, "I don't want to feel anymore."

Dana undid her seatbelt, hopped over to the driver's side seat, and got on top of Galan.

"Dana, stop," said Galan.

"Let me," Dana whispered.

"Please, Dana, don't," Galan responded.

"Let me love you; let me show you there is still hope," Dana replied.

"There is nothing left to love, Dana. You don't deserve the part of me that was shattered," Galan whispered. Dana held his face in her hands and leaned in close.

"Maybe I like broken toys…," Dana said softly. She leaned in to kiss him, but Galan placed his hand on her cheek and stopped her. Tilting her head down, he kissed her forehead and held her in his arms.

"You deserve someone who wouldn't do that to you," Galan murmured in her ear. "I will wait for you; it's what everyone else should have done."

Dana broke down into tears in Galan's embrace.

"I will come back for you, I promise. But I cannot forgive what they did to me, and I refuse to let them get away with what they did to you. Take the keys to my car; if I am not back in one hour, leave this place and don't look back. I will come for you no matter where you go," Galan told her.

"Promise me you will come back," Dana softly replied.

"I promise," Galan answered. He gently lifted her chin, looked into her eyes, and softly wiped away her tears.

"Come on, let's get you to the apartment," Galan suggested.

Galan and Dana swiftly exited the car and made their way to the elevator. Ascending to the top floor, Galan led the way to his apartment. He wasted no time, shedding his wet clothes and selecting a fresh, elegant black and white suit from his wardrobe. As he stood in his boxers, preparing to dress, he sensed Dana's gaze on him. Looking towards the slightly ajar door, he caught a glimpse of her peering in. Blushing, Dana quickly turned away when Galan noticed her.

Galan got dressed and walked down the stairs in his suit and tie. "Why did you change?" asked Dana, gawking at him from head to toe.

"Hydrophobic suit means no soaking wet clothes to slow me down. It also means I won't get blood on my suit," Galan replied.

"Blood!" Dana exclaimed.

"They worked me over pretty good last time. I bled all over myself. This time, I won't need to worry about the cleaning bill," Galan responded.

Galan walked to the elevator, pressing the override button on his way past the kitchen, "See, if you want to leave, I am not keeping you here. You can stay here as long as you need to. You have my keys; if I don't return, run far away."

Galan excused himself for a moment and discreetly stepped into the kitchen. He reached for a knife, carefully sliding it into the inside pocket of his jacket, keeping it concealed from Dana's view.

As Galan entered the elevator, Dana called out, "What if this is the last time I ever see you. How will I live with myself if I never know the taste of your lips!"

"Easy! Take comfort in the fact that I cared enough and was willing to wait," Galan responded with a warm smile just as the elevator doors closed.

Chapter Thirty-nine

Aria and Malek arrived at the café, filled with concern for Dana. Without hesitation, they hurried inside, searching for any sign of her. Their hearts sank when they discovered the back room and storage room doors had been broken down. "No…," she whispered, horrified.

"What is it, love?" asked Malek.

"It's Galan. He took her—" answered Aria.

"Call the police," Malek advised.

"You don't understand. No law enforcement has jurisdiction here. The people here control everything: the hospitals, the police, the schools, the media, everything. Their contributions fund everything; this place exists for people who want to escape the regular world. Here, you are completely secluded; there is nothing here we can do. We need to get out of here, but I am not leaving without Dana," Aria explained.

"We will find her, don't worry, my love," said Malek.

As Aria and Malek rushed outside, they heard the sound of a honking horn. Their eyes fell upon Hans in his car, fear apparent on his face as he rolled down the window. He screamed at Aria, "Ms. Aria, look!" In shock and horror, Aria followed Hans' pointed finger, her eyes widening as she saw the scene illuminated by the car's headlights. There stood Garrick in the pouring rain, dragging Maeve's lifeless body across the road, sending chills down Aria's spine.

"Oh my God—" Aria gasped and ran to them. "Maeve!!!" Aria let out a heart-wrenching scream as she ran towards Garrick and Maeve. Her eyes widened at the sight of the blood-smeared and injured Garrick, with his head bleeding and clothes torn. Maeve's body was in a horrifying state, with wounds reopened, leaving her covered in blood and scars.

"Maeve!" Aria cried out and tightly clung to Maeve, pulling her close.

"She's gone, Ari…," Garrick wailed.

"No, don't say that; she will wake up!" Aria exclaimed as she tapped Maeve's face. "Wake up, sweetie. Come on, you promised you would be with me forever!"

Malek came up behind Aria and pulled her into his arms. "Love, I don't think she made it," he whispered.

"She's alive! She has to be; she wouldn't leave me like this!" Aria screamed.

As the reality of the situation weighed heavily on Garrick, he collapsed to his knees, succumbing to the overwhelming grief. Maeve's lifeless body lay beside him, a haunting reminder of the tragedy that had unfolded. The blood trickled down her cold skin, forming a sorrowful trail onto the rain-soaked asphalt, mirroring the anguish and pain that engulfed them all in that heart-wrenching moment.

"We can't stay here. We have to leave," Malek advised.

"We can't; Galan ran me into the gates. The truck is wedged into it, and it won't budge," Garrick informed him.

"No. There must be another way out, a back road or something—" Malek hopefully suggested.

"There isn't, love. This is the only road in or out of Salt Pine Acres," Aria informed him.

"Then what do we do?" Malek inquired.

"We'll leave by air; we have a fleet of helicopters, most of which are in the hotels and penthouses that Dad owns. We can have one here in an hour tops," Aria exclaimed. "Get up, Garrick. Help me get Maeve into the car."

With strength fueled by sorrow, Aria helped Garrick to his feet, and together, they carefully lifted Maeve's body off the ground. Gently, they placed her in the backseat of the car, treating her with utmost respect and care. Malek took the front passenger seat next to Hans while Garrick and Aria settled into the backseat with Maeve's lifeless form,

"Hans, contact the nearest fleet member; I need a helicopter in the air as soon as possible," Aria commanded.

"Aria, I need to grab something," said Garrick. "Hans, can you back up to the gates?"

As Hans skillfully reversed the car, Garrick swiftly jumped out and hurried over to his truck. He

reached through the passenger side window
searching inside the glove box. His hands found a
black pouch, and with determination in his eyes, he
secured it before returning to the car. "Alright, we're
good," Garrick told them.

"Gar, is that…?" asked Aria.

"Yeah, it is. Galan will die tonight for what he
did to Maeve; I don't care anymore. I wanna make
sure he never comes back from what I am about to do
to him," Garrick replied.

"Garrick, Dana is missing. Galan must have
gotten to her," Aria informed him.

"We will get her back. Let's get Maeve to the
house, and then we can go find Dana," Garrick
advised.

"What's the plan, my love?" asked Malek.

"The house is the safest place in Salt Pine
Acres right now. Galan can't get inside. You will stay
there with the others. Garrick, Eder, and I will go find
Dana," Aria explained.

"You can't ask me to do that. We are in this
together," Malek remarked.

"No. I never wanted you to get mixed up in
any of this. I wouldn't be able to live with myself if
something happened to you because of me. This is my
mess, my mistakes. I need you safe. Don't argue with
me on this," Aria replied. Garrick held Maeve close
in his arms, their heads touching as if seeking solace
in the midst of sorrow. As Hans drove into the
driveway, the trio carefully carried Maeve's lifeless
body inside the building. Eder and the others, who
had been waiting anxiously, were visibly torn and
heartbroken upon seeing Maeve's bloodied form.

"Nooo. What the hell happened?!" Eder cried
out. Eyla and Bodhi could no longer contain their

emotions, and they broke down into tears, seeking support in each other's embrace.

"Galan happened. You're coming with us, Eder," Garrick answered. He took out the black pouch, filled a needle with the steroids inside, and injected a massive dose into his quads.

"You're juicing again?" asked Eder.

"I'm leaving nothing up to chance. Come on, we don't have time to waste. The gate to the town is blocked, so we can't leave. A helicopter is on its way. We need to find Dana and bring her back here before then. If we see Galan, between you and me, we will rip that mother fucker apart," Garrick snarled.

"The rest of you inside. Galan could be anywhere out there. Take no chances. He can't get inside the house, so you will be safe here," Aria told them.

"You can't expect us to sit here and do nothing while you go out there with that psycho!" Eyla commented.

"You're not doing nothing. Stay here with Maeve; I don't want her to be alone when the helicopter arrives. It will land on the roof, so call and let me know when it gets here if we are not yet back," Aria instructed.

"Then let me go with you! The more people we have when Galan shows up, the better our chances of taking him down. If Dana is with him, then all the more reason to keep him busy and make sure you and her get back here safe," Bodhi responded.

"Yeah, I agree. I have nothing left to live for. I've made peace with that. We stop Galan at any cost," Garrick agreed.

"I'm with you, mate, for Maeve," Eder declared.

"For Maeve," everyone replied.

"Load up. Let's go," Garrick commanded.

With a sense of urgency, Aria, Bodhi, Eder, and Garrick hurried out the door and piled into Aria's car, their hearts pounding with concern for their friend Maeve. Hans backed the car out of the driveway, following their instructions to head to Galan's apartment.

The storm raged on outside as Galan stood on the roof, his knife gleaming ominously in the lightning-lit darkness. His clothes billowed in the strong winds and heavy rain. Galan took out the latex film of Dana's fingerprint from his pocket. Meanwhile, Malek, deeply concerned, entered Aria's room. His eyes fell upon his father's jacket and tie carefully placed on the bed.

"I wish you were here, Dad; I really wish I could talk to you one last time. Maybe you would know what to do in this situation," Malek stated. In the dimly lit room, at that very moment, Galan's agile figure moved swiftly towards Malek, silencing him with a firm yet gentle hand pressed against his lips. A glimmer of cold steel caught the faint light as Galan pressed the sharpened blade against his throat. "Shh, shh, shh, shh, you should be more careful what you wish for, Malek. Life has a way of giving you exactly what you've asked for," Galan whispered.

In a state of sheer panic, Malek's heart raced, desperate to warn Eyla of Galan's ominous presence lurking within the house.

"Come now, Malek, don't do something stupid. I'm not here to hurt you. That's not my intention. No, I'm here to save you," Galan said softly.

"Mmm?" Malek mumbled.

"I know what it's like to fall for someone like Aria. In fact, I've been there more times than anyone should. But, you see, I'm a hopeless romantic. I really do believe that one day, someone will choose me. I believe people can change for that special someone, and I've always tried my best to be that person. But look where it got me. I really do like you, Malek; you were the most genuine person I'd ever had the pleasure of meeting. I want to save you from the damage she will cause. People like you shouldn't be turned into people like me. Walk away from this. She will bring you nothing but pain. Let it go and move on with your life," Galan stated.

Although Galan's hand covered his mouth, Malek mumbled, "She is my life." Galan was barely able to make out what he said.

"That's what I said every single time. I'm sorry, Malek, but I will not watch you make the mistakes I made," Galan responded.

Malek mumbled through his hand, "I am nothing like you. What we have is real, and she will never hurt me," he answered.

With a forceful thrust, Galan flung Malek against the sturdy door, the impact reverberating through the room. Malek's muffled protests only grew louder beneath Galan's unyielding grip, his attempts to break free becoming increasingly desperate.

In an unsettling display of menace, Galan wielded the glinting knife with unwavering precision, its razor-sharp tip ominously pointed at the center of Malek's head; the cold metal hovered dangerously close. "You think you're something special? Do you think there is room for good people in this fucked up world? If you are so desperate to have your heart ripped out because you loved the wrong person, then let me help you. Why wait? I'll show you exactly what happens to guys like us," Galan retorted.

Just as the air thickened with tension and Malek found himself at the mercy of Galan's sinister intentions, a faint sound of footsteps echoed through the hallway. Eyla, oblivious to the unfolding danger, came strolling down the corridor.

"Malek? Are you ok?" Eyla called out.

Galan held his finger to his lips. "Shhh," he whispered. Amidst the escalating peril, Eyla's path took her toward Aria's room, but the activated privacy walls shrouded the interior in secrecy, rendering her unable to peer inside. Unaware of the clandestine activity within, she continued walking. Galan's calculating gaze penetrated the privacy walls, fixated on Eyla's figure, unaware of Malek's intention. With a silent determination, Malek's fingers grazed the switch, poised to deactivate the protective barrier that concealed Aria's room.

"Malek?" Eyla's voice carried a mix of curiosity and concern as she approached the door, attempting to catch a glimpse of what lay beyond the opaque glass wall. Her brow furrowed in confusion, sensing that something was amiss. But before her intuition could unravel the mystery, Malek sprang into action.

In a swift and calculated move, Malek's hand darted towards the tablet mounted on the wall, deftly flipping the switch. The once opaque walls transformed, now becoming transparent and revealing the shocking tableau inside. Eyla's eyes widened, and her breath caught in her throat as the truth unfolded before her.

There, within the unveiled room, stood Galan, his sinister intentions laid bare for Eyla to witness. The knife held menacingly against Malek's head sent a jolt of fear through Eyla's veins, and her heart pounded in her chest. At the sound of Eyla's piercing scream, Galan's attention snapped away from Malek. His cold, calculating gaze locked onto Eyla; meanwhile, Malek's hand began to withdraw from the tablet, but Galan's keen eyes caught the subtle movement.

In a heart-pounding frenzy, Eyla dashed into the adjacent kitchen across the hall, her breath hitching with terror. Galan, releasing his grip on Malek's neck, turned his focus to the defenseless Malek. A malevolent grin painted across his face as he covered Malek's entire face with his palm, stifling any chance of outcry.

With malicious intent, Galan yanked Malek away from the door, positioning him to the left, just inches away from the transparent glass wall. In one savage motion, he slammed Malek's head into the unforgiving surface. A sickening thud echoed through the room as the impact sent shockwaves of pain through Malek's body.

Blood spattered like macabre artwork on the once pristine glass wall, a gruesome testament to the brutality of the act. Malek, now unconscious, crumpled down the wall, his lifeless form falling gracelessly to the floor.

With adrenaline coursing through his veins, Galan hastily made his escape, fleeing from the room where the gruesome act had just unfolded. As he darted through the house, his gaze caught sight of Eyla through the translucent kitchen wall. Her phone clutched tightly in her hand; she was quick-witted enough to dial Aria's number in a desperate bid for help.

Upon spotting the device, a menacing growl rumbled from deep within Galan's throat, "End the call now, or Aria will be cleaning the insides of Malek off the walls!" With the blade of the knife gripped tightly in his hand, he scraped the menacing tip against the transparent glass separating him from Eyla.

As Eyla's desperate call reached Aria on the other end, Eyla heard her voice faintly. Eyla's eyes darted between the phone in her hand and the lurking shadow of Galan just beyond the glass wall. Her voice trembled, but she mustered all her strength and screamed into the phone, "GALAN IS IN THE HOUSE!!!"

Chapter Forty

"Fuck!" Galan muttered as his frustration escalated. His kicks grew more forceful until the door finally gave way, splintering under the relentless assault. The sound of the door breaking echoed through the house, signaling the shattering of its sanctuary.

In the chaos of breaking down the door, Galan momentarily lost sight of Eyla, her quick thinking affording her a chance to evade his clutches. Taking cover behind the kitchen island, she kept her breaths as quiet as her pounding heart, eyes fixed on the scene unfolding before her.

With nerves of steel, Eyla seized the opportunity when Galan's attention was diverted. In a burst of agility, she dashed out the other door and into the hallway, her instincts urging her to find a place of safety.

Galan's focus was now firmly locked onto Eyla's fleeting figure. Fueled by a twisted determination, he chased after her, the sound of his footfalls echoing through the house.

Aria and the others arrived at Galan's condo complex and tried to find any clues that could lead them to Dana. In the midst of their search, the sudden ring of a phone pierced the tense silence. Eyla's panicked voice echoed through the garage, her scream cutting through the air like a chilling siren. "Garrick, he got inside the house!" Aria screamed.

"What, how the fuck did he get inside?!" asked Eder.

"Doesn't matter; let's go, Eder! Aria, his car is here. He may have Dana somewhere close by, or maybe he doesn't have her at all. Someone should go back to the café in case she's there somewhere; someone else can stay here and try to get inside his apartment!" Garrick suggested.

"No! I'm going with you; Malek is back there!" Aria cried out.

"Aria, you need to find Dana! Let us worry about Malek," said Garrick.

"I wasn't asking! Bodhi, go check Grounded for Dana. None of us are getting inside this place without Galan's fingerprint, anyway," Aria instructed as adrenaline coursed through their veins; Aria, Eder, and Garrick wasted no time in heeding Eyla's urgent plea. With a sense of determination, they swiftly made their way to Aria's car. With her phone still clutched tightly in her hand, Aria dialed Dana's number once more.

As Dana's phone lay forgotten on the table beside the café's storage room door, its persistent ring filled the air, seeking someone's attention. After a few unanswered calls, a voice finally picked up on the other end with a hesitant, "Hello?"

"This isn't Dana. Who the hell is this?" Aria panicked.

"Hey, Aria. Sorry, it's Alliyah. I was just on my way out and heard a phone ringing. What happened in the café? Two doors are broken?" Alliyah asked.

"Alliyah? What are you doing there? Didn't you leave already?" Aria inquired.

"I did, but I forgot some stuff in the office. So, I came back not long after I left. I saw you leaving the premises on my way back in. I'll just get the next shuttle that leaves in a few minutes," Alliyah clarified.

Aria looked at Garrick and Eder, who were all listening to the conversation on the loudspeaker.

"That's how he got to the hotel without his car…," Garrick muttered.

"Aria?" Alliyah called out.

"Sorry, Alliyah. Um, have you seen Dana by chance?" Aria asked.

"Sorry, I haven't seen her since I got back. I'll just leave her phone at the bar on my way out. Got to go; my bus will be leaving soon. Have a good night," Alliyah replied.

"Alliyah, wait. The gates are blocked; you can't…." Aria tried to warn her, but the call ended too abruptly. "Shit."

BROKEN TOYS

As Hans swiftly approached Aria's residence, he hastily parked the car in the driveway. The trio of Aria, Eder, and Garrick swiftly exited the vehicle, their hearts pounding with trepidation. Aria deftly scanned her fingerprint to unlock the door, revealing a chilling scene that would haunt them forever.

Aria's horrified screams reverberated through the entire house, causing her to crumple into Garrick's supportive embrace, her gaze averted from the gruesome sight. With trepidation, Garrick and Eder braved a look inside, only to be met with a gut-wrenching spectacle that made Eder turn away and involuntarily retch.

Blood was splattered across the walls and floor, leaving a morbid trail leading to the dreadful discovery. There, they saw Malek suspended upside down from the railing, his lifeless form dripping blood from the end of his hanging tie. A grisly hole had been carved into his chest, revealing a gruesome scene where his heart lay in two grotesque halves, surrounded by a pool of crimson blood.

Aria's anguished cries filled the air, her desperate pleas for Malek's return seemingly unanswered by the unforgiving reality. Meanwhile, Garrick's gaze shifted upward, detecting a shadowy figure lurking behind an opaque partition upstairs. Determined to investigate, he gently released his grip on Aria, consoling her momentarily, and cautiously made his way inside.

The dimly lit interior revealed a ghastly tableau that horrified even the brave Garrick. There, against the wall, was Eyla, impaled by knives, her visage so marred it appeared as if her face had been brutally excised. Shock and dread consumed him, but he knew he had to remain strong for the sake of Aria and the others.

As Aria continued to sob uncontrollably, Eder tried his best to console her, though the heartache seemed insurmountable. Meanwhile, a putrid odor began to waft through the air, assaulting Garrick's senses. He instinctively covered his nose to shield himself from the pungent stench, further adding to the grim atmosphere that enveloped the house. "He did all this in a matter of minutes?" Garrick muttered. "Eder! Don't bring her inside! Listen, get her in the car. Go get Bodhi and get out of Salt Pine Acres. There is no time to wait for that helicopter. Climb the gates if you must. I don't care how; just get Aria out of here!" Garrick called out.

"I am not leaving without Dana!" yelled Aria through her sobs.

"Aria, listen to me; you need to run now. If that bus is coming here for Alliyah, then grab her, and you and Bodhi get out of here. Eder and I will finish this alone. We promise to find Dana. Galan can't be with her and hunt us at the same time. We'll find Galan and kill him, and then wherever Dana is, she will be safe. Right now, you need to go. We will find Dana and take the helicopter back to you. Meet us at the hotel," Garrick declared.

"No, I won't leave her!" Aria screamed.

"God dammit, Aria! Don't let Dana find you like these people! Go, now!" Garrick screamed.

"People… Is Eyla—" Aria began, covering her mouth in terror.

Garrick looked at her and turned away. He could not bear to tell her. "Please, Aria, do it for Dana. I promise I will do everything in my power to make sure this maniac is stopped. Go—" Garrick instructed. As Aria, tear-stricken and filled with sorrow, hurriedly made her way to the car, her heart weighed heavy with grief and fear. Without wasting any time, Hans quickly reversed out of the driveway, his driving spirited as he sped off toward the café where Bodhi and Alliyah awaited her company. Outside the house, Garrick emerged to join Eder.

"How very noble of you, gentlemen," Galan exclaimed.

The moment Galan's voice pierced the air, Garrick and Eder involuntarily shuddered, their nerves on edge. With their hearts pounding in their chests, the two friends instinctively moved closer to each other, their backs pressed together for mutual support. Their eyes darted around, searching for any sign of Galan's ominous figure, but he remained elusive, concealed within the shadows.

Galan, covered in blood, sat perched like a malevolent specter, a haunting figure against the darkened sky. Galan's piercing whistle cut through the air, demanding their attention, and they reluctantly turned their gaze upward and instinctively took a step back. Atop the roof, an eerie sight awaited Garrick and Eder—a chilling tableau that sent shivers down their spines. "Aria was never in any real danger, but it's sweet of you to think she needed your protection. Look what that did for Malek and Eyla," Galan remarked as the rain poured relentlessly, drenching Galan's bloodied form. The raindrops pelted down on him like a cleansing torrent, washing away the crimson stains from his skin.

"How are we getting up there?" Garrick asked Eder.

"I don't know, mate. I haven't explored the house enough to have the slightest clue," Eder answered.

"Well, this works in our favor. The longer he sits up there, the more time we give Aria and the others to escape. Let's wait him out," Garrick stated.

As the rain continued to lash down around them, a sudden scent caught Garrick's attention—a familiar odor that he had encountered earlier. At first, he had dismissed it, attributing it to the blood and the gruesome scene within the house. But now, as the same scent lingered in the air, he couldn't ignore the feeling that something was amiss.

Before he could share his suspicions with Eder, Galan's voice cut through the tension, interrupting any chance of conversation.

"You know, these buildings in Salt Pine Acres are kind of similar. They are all built to withstand disasters, such as hurricanes, earthquakes, and things like that. The structure itself is strong and will not easily fall," Galan began as he picked up a black tablet next to him. "I love these modern houses; the privacy glass is amazing. Among the other great features are the lights and door locks, all part of a fully automated network that controls the whole house. How unfortunate for you. Let me borrow a trick from an old flame with the help of modern tech." In a low, menacing voice, Galan continued to toy with their fears. Garrick's unease intensified as he observed Galan's focus shift to the tablet displaying the kitchen's controls. The pungent smell he had noticed earlier grew more potent, and even Eder began to sense the danger that lurked in the air.

As the horrifying truth unfolded, it became apparent that Galan had cut the gas lines, allowing the deadly fumes to seep into every corner of the house. A sense of horror gripped Garrick and Eder as they realized the extent of Galan's malevolence—his intentions were far more sinister than they could have ever imagined.

Galan's dark grin hinted at the impending doom he had orchestrated. With a chilling calmness, he pressed a button on the tablet, igniting the stove's burner. Within moments, the kitchen erupted in flames, and the fire swiftly spread, consuming the house with unstoppable fury.

Garrick's heart pounded in his chest as he witnessed the fire's rapid progression, devouring everything in its path with a ferocity that seemed otherworldly. The blast that followed was deafening, sending shockwaves through the Scarlets' property, causing glass to shatter and debris to fly through the air.

"How's that for burning in hell, bitch!" Galan muttered from atop the house.

The deafening explosion and the subsequent yellow glow of the fire ripped through the tranquility of Salt Pine Acres, jolting Aria out of her distress. Startled, she turned around, and her eyes widened at the horrifying sight that unfolded before her. The massive inferno towered above the houses, casting an ominous glow that pierced the night sky, alerting everyone in the town to the impending danger.

In the wake of the explosion, families from all corners of Salt Pine Acres rushed to their windows, desperate to make sense of the commotion that had disrupted their peaceful night. The glow of the fire acted as a chilling beacon, drawing concerned residents to its source.

The roaring flames devoured the Scarlets' house, their ferocity ascending to towering heights that seemed insurmountable. Galan observed the scene with an unsettling sense of satisfaction, his sinister plan having come to fruition. Knowing the dangers of staying amidst the blaze, he swiftly devised an escape route. With a cunning leap, he hurled himself off the edge of the building and dived headfirst into the pool in the backyard, seeking refuge from the encroaching heat.

The pool water greeted him with a brief respite, but the scorching intensity of the flames above began to warm the water rapidly. Galan wasted no time, springing out of the pool and vaulting over the fence, seeking temporary solace in the neighbor's property. Moving from one house to another, he made his way onto the street, his every move shrouded in darkness and rain.

Despite the relentless downpour, Galan could still sense the lingering warmth from the massive fire that raged behind him. The occasional lightning strikes illuminated the street, revealing three shadows cast upon the wet pavement.

Startled by the sudden revelation, Galan turned around to face the source of the additional shadows, only to find himself met with a dual assault from Garrick and Eder. The two friends had been tracking Galan with unwavering determination and now launched a surprise attack, tackling him with fierce intensity.

Reacting swiftly, Galan braced himself for the impact, shielding himself from the force of the collision. The trio tumbled down the rain-slicked street, entangled in a violent struggle. Galan's knife

403

was dislodged from his grasp amidst the chaos, sent flying away from them during their fall.

Galan: *What? How the fuck are they still alive and in one piece? That explosion should have shredded them with all that glass flying everywhere.*

Chapter
Forty-one

In a split second before the explosion, Garrick and Eder's senses were heightened as they detected the distinct smell of gas in the air. The realization struck them with a jolt of terror, and without hesitation, Garrick sprang into action. Pulling Eder with him, he instinctively guided them to take cover at the base of the steps just as the detonation erupted.

The force of the explosion sent glass shards and flames soaring into the sky above them, but their quick reflexes and strategic positioning shielded them from harm. As soon as the initial shockwave subsided, Garrick and Eder knew they had to move quickly. The intensifying heat radiating from the blazing house compelled them to flee, and they wasted no time in running into the street. The rain, pouring down with renewed vigor, acted as a fortuitous shield against the scorching heat, safeguarding them from the flames' wrath.

The torrential downpour offered a reprieve, not only for them but also for Galan.

Amidst the downpour, the three figures rose to their feet. Breathing heavily, the two charged at Galan. Galan, desperate to regain his weapon, attempted to make a run for his discarded knife. But with swift reflexes, Garrick intercepted him, delivering a powerful kick that sent the knife tumbling into the lower level of Salt Pine Acres, out of Galan's reach.

Eder wasted no time launching a barrage of punches at Galan, but the elusive antagonist expertly evaded them, staying just out of Eder's grasp. Garrick then attempted to come at Galan from above, but Galan had anticipated his move, meeting his attack with a forceful kick. The clash sent both Garrick and Galan tumbling to the ground, grappling fiercely in the rain-soaked street.

Refusing to be deterred, Eder sprang into action, delivering a powerful kick to Galan's gut, followed by a series of punches to his chest. Galan struggled to regain his footing, unable to mount an effective defense against Eder's relentless assault.

Seeing an opportunity, Garrick joined in the melee, both friends launching a coordinated attack against Galan.

Despite Galan's efforts to back away and evade their merciless assault, his footing faltered in the rain-soaked ground, making it difficult for him to

The relentless battle continued, with Galan displaying his adaptability and cunning in the face of Eder and Garrick's assault. As Galan decided to go low, he targeted Eder's shin, causing him to stumble momentarily, giving him an advantage in the close combat.

However, Garrick responded swiftly, aiming a kick at Galan to create some distance between him and Eder. Yet, Galan's agility and skill proved formidable as he deftly caught Garrick's foot between his legs and executed a roll, forcing Garrick to the ground.

Recognizing Garrick's expertise, Galan knew he had to release his hold quickly, avoiding any risk of a countermove from his skilled opponent. He regained his footing before Garrick and Eder and launched himself at Eder, aiming to incapacitate him swiftly and isolate Garrick.

However, an unexpected intervention occurred. Bodhi, arriving on the scene, charged at Galan with unwavering determination, using his shoulder to send Galan flying several feet away. Galan rolled to regain his balance, his resolve unbroken as he promptly got back on his feet.

Now, facing three formidable opponents—Bodhi, Garrick, and Eder—Galan braced himself, ready to confront the combined strength and perseverance of his adversaries. As lightning struck, momentarily illuminating the street in the flickering light, the adversaries stood shoulder to shoulder, facing Galan as the sky lit up once more, silhouetting Galan, his grey eyes peering through the shadows cast on his face.

"What were you saying about cherishing our last breaths?" asked Garrick.

"For someone who is a waste of life, you just don't die, do you?" mumbled Galan as the rain beat down on them.

"Are those your final words?" Eder questioned.

Galan smiled and said, "You two... For the things you've done, you will meet an end so grim the devil will crawl from hell to beg for your merciful deaths."

As the storm raged on, a spectacular display of lightning illuminated the night sky, and the deafening roar of thunder echoed through Salt Pine Acres. Galan's blood-soaked figure stood in stark contrast to the torrential downpour, creating an eerie and haunting sight.

His eyes locked onto Garrick and Eder, the adversaries ready to face each other once more in this climactic showdown. Despite the drenched rain washing away the blood from his skin, the crimson stains persisted.

As the commotion drew the attention of Salt Pine Acres' residents, they cautiously emerged from their homes, curious about the source of the chaos that had unfolded amidst the tempest. Their eyes fell upon Galan, the center of this destructive storm, and the three figures standing resolutely before him, ready to bring an end to his reign of terror.

The powerful rains had begun to tame the once-raging flames that had threatened to consume the town. With the fire's intensity subsiding, the surrounding area was now bathed in a reddish-orange glow, casting an eerie light upon Galan's figure.

In this surreal illumination, Galan appeared like a different person altogether. His intense gaze bore into Garrick and Eder, reflecting the malevolence that had consumed him. The blood that clung to his skin, a macabre reminder of the night's horrors, stood out in stark contrast against the relentless rain that sought to cleanse the darkness.

As the raindrops continued to fall with unyielding force, each figure seemed like a mere silhouette against the backdrop of the storm.

As the storm continued its relentless assault, Galan's stained figure raced through the rain-soaked streets, his eyes reflecting an intense determination. At the next deafening clap of thunder, he sprang into action, his mind set on reaching the lookout.

Garrick, Eder, and Bodhi pursued him, closing in on Galan as he fled. Garrick took the lead, his strides strong, closing the distance between them with every step. With Eder and Bodhi right on his heels, the trio pursued Galan with unyielding determination.

As Galan's form loomed ever closer, Garrick mustered all his strength and energy, pushing himself harder to reach him. With mere inches to spare, he launched himself into a desperate dive, aiming to grab hold of Galan and bring him down.

Reacting swiftly, Galan anticipated Garrick's move and dropped to the ground, assuming a crouched position. His right leg extended in front of him while his other leg and both hands braced behind, creating an improvised anchor to halt his forward momentum. The wet roads made maneuvering difficult, but Galan's quick thinking and skillful adaptation allowed him to achieve a similar outcome to what he had planned. His evasive tactic prevented Garrick's full grasp, but the near-contact left no doubt that Galan's time was running out.

In the midst of the chaotic scene, Garrick, in a careless maneuver, soared over his opponent and tumbled forward. But Galan, fueled by determination, instantly sprang to his feet and charged toward his comrades, Eder and Bodhi. Galan ran full tilt, Bodhi flanking on his right and Eder on his left.

As Galan closed in on them, he executed a remarkable display of cunning. A master of deception, he cunningly feigned a move to the left, tricking Eder into an attempted block. Like a lithe panther, Galan effortlessly evaded the attack, smoothly altering his trajectory toward Bodhi. Swift as a shadow, he maneuvered himself behind Bodhi, ensnaring him in a tight and unyielding chokehold.

Time seemed to slow for a fleeting moment as Eder turned his attention to his imperiled companion. But in that very instant, Galan's resolve turned resolute, and with a single decisive motion, he incapacitated Bodhi with deadly precision, breaking his neck and releasing and letting go of him.

Bodhi's arms went limp, and he slumped forward, crashing face-first onto the unforgiving ground. Galan swiftly reached out, seizing the back of Bodhi's head with one hand, and with a calculated movement, he swept his feet from under him. In an instant, Bodhi's head collided with the hard street, causing a gruesome split that released a torrent of blood, splattering the surroundings in a horrifying display.

As Eder stood there, stunned and paralyzed by the brutal scene before him, Galan's instincts kicked in. Without hesitation, he sprinted toward the spot where Garrick had discarded the knife moments ago. From the vantage point of the balcony, he noticed several curious onlookers gathering on their lawns, drawn by the commotion. Retrieving the knife was too great a risk.

Eder's eyes darted around; amidst the smoke and dust, he noticed a sizeable chunk of concrete lying nearby, and instinctively, he grabbed it, clutching it tightly in his trembling hands. Garrick, battered and bruised, struggled to his feet, coughing and muttering under his breath as he tried to regain his composure, "No, he's trying to split us up," Garrick's keen eyes quickly caught Eder's discreet action, holding the chunk of concrete behind his back. "Eder no!!!!!! Don't go after him alone!" Garrick shouted.

Eder's surge of confidence overshadowed Garrick's cautionary words, and with a rush of adrenaline, he disregarded the warning, determined to take on Galan himself. He charged forward, the chunk of concrete held firmly in his hand, and swung it with all his might towards Galan's head.

But Galan, a seasoned and formidable opponent, anticipated Eder's reckless attack. He caught Eder's swing with skillful precision, effortlessly using his opponent's momentum against him. In a swift and fluid motion, Galan deftly turned Eder around and forcefully slammed him into the unforgiving ground.

The impact was jarring, and Eder's breath escaped him in a painful gasp as the wind was knocked out of him. His grip on the chunk of concrete weakened, and it slipped from his fingers, clattering onto the street nearby.

"This would be too good of a death for you; you don't deserve to die quickly. You don't do that to kids and die an easy death—" Galan declared.

As Galan swiftly made his escape, Garrick immediately shifted his focus to Eder, who was still recovering from the impact of the fall. He hurriedly approached Eder, extending a hand to help him up before chasing after Galan.

"Go on, mate, I'm only holding you back. I'll catch up to you," said a winded Eder.

Chapter Forty-two

As the chase continued up the hiking trail in the mountains, Galan's familiarity with the terrain provided him a strategic advantage. Despite Garrick's enhanced stamina and strength from the steroids, Galan's knowledge of the area allowed him to stay a step ahead. He skillfully took routes that were challenging for Garrick to follow, and the steep incline of the mountain began to work against Garrick, causing him to gradually fall behind.

But Garrick's determination remained unwavering. He refused to give up the pursuit, pushing himself to the limit as he ascended the mountain. As the distance between them grew, Garrick's frustration mounted. However, he glimpsed Galan's destination and found renewed strength. The steroids gave him an advantage in terms of recovery, and soon enough, he caught his breath and felt a surge of energy.

Reaching the clearing, Garrick was met with a breathtaking view of the surrounding mountains, illuminated by occasional flashes of lightning. Galan stood at the other end of the clearing, breathing heavily; Garrick's eyes found him.

"You have nowhere to run now," Garrick exclaimed.

"Who's running? I just needed a little quality time with you, away from your little helper, Eder," Galan replied.

As the storm raged on, the mountain bore witness to a clash of titans. Garrick and Galan squared off in the clearing, their actions mirroring an unspoken agreement to settle their differences through sheer physical combat.

Garrick's determination blazed in his eyes as he shed his jacket, revealing his muscular frame. Galan, too, discarded his formal attire, showing off a physique that matched Garrick's in strength and power. The atmosphere crackled with tension as they prepared for the showdown, each fully aware of the stakes involved.

With a confident smirk, Galan extended his hand in a beckoning gesture, inviting Garrick to attack. In response, Garrick charged at him with a ferocity that shook the ground beneath their feet. He threw everything he had into his punches, aiming to land a decisive blow that would end the confrontation once and for all.

Galan proved to be a formidable opponent, skillfully meeting Garrick's attacks and blocking his attempts to strike vulnerable spots. Despite Garrick's relentless assault, Galan's defense held strong preventing any fatal blows from landing. The stormy weather mirrored the intensity of the battle. Trees shook as the two combatants slammed into them, and the ground beneath their feet churned with each forceful collision. Both refused to yield, their determination driving them forward despite the pain and exhaustion. Galan's punches seemed to have little effect on Garrick, almost as if he wasn't feeling a thing.

The brutal fight had taken its toll on both combatants, and the clearing bore witness to the physical and emotional toll it had exacted. Blood dripped from cuts and bruises on Galan and Garrick, evidence of the intense blows they had traded.

Despite Galan's efforts to defend against Garrick's attacks, the relentless assault had left him severely injured and weakened. His head wound bled profusely, and the pain seemed to blur his senses. As he fought to stay on his feet, Galan knew he was rapidly losing his ability to keep up with Garrick's unmatched strength and agility.

Garrick, on the other hand, seemed unfazed by the punishment they had inflicted on each other. His unique fighting style, honed through countless battles, had brought him to this pivotal moment. He recognized the signs of Galan's fatigue, knowing it was time to deliver the finishing blow.

With a confident smile, Garrick temporarily eased his assault, taunting Galan with a display of his agility. Galan's hands trembled, his defenses weakening, and he realized he was outmatched by Garrick's superior strength and technique.

Garrick sensed the opportunity to end the battle decisively, just as he had done in previous fights. He adjusted his stance, preparing for the signature uppercut that had proved devastating to defensive opponents. Closing the gap with lightning speed, Garrick launched his attack, but to his surprise Galan had evaded it with a swift and precise movement.

Galan: *I guess all those videos paid off. Maybe none of your opponents in the ring saw it, but I'm good at reading people. I saw your tell when you realized you had the upper hand. It's that slight sideways shift in your stance, so you get a little extra power when you turn into your uppercut. But therein lies your biggest opening; the momentum of that upward swing causes your entire side to be wide open.*

Galan's cunning nature had fooled Garrick, who believed that his opponent was truly on the brink of exhaustion. In reality, Galan had saved a reserve of strength, waiting for the opportune moment to strike back.

Taking advantage of Garrick's uppercut miss, Galan swiftly turned the momentum of the sidestep into a powerful cross-body kick. The impact was devastating, the force of Galan's kick connecting with full force against Garrick's right side, breaking his ribs with a sickening crack.

Garrick's body convulsed with pain, and he crumpled to the ground, unable to maintain his balance. He struggled to his feet, but the pain was too much to bear, causing him to collapse back onto his knees.

"Looks like you really are a washed-up fighter now. Pathetic," Galan smirked.

With a surge of energy fueled by his sheer determination to keep fighting, Garrick executed a breathtaking backflip toward Galan. Tucking his feet in at just the right moment, he propelled himself forward like a human projectile, aiming directly at Galan's chest.

The impact was immense as Garrick's feet connected with Galan's chest, driving him backward with force. Galan stumbled, his back slamming against a nearby tree trunk with a loud thud. The collision left him winded and disoriented, the pain coursing through his body.

Garrick chuckled menacingly, "You really thought you had me, didn't you? You think some wannabe tough guy can best me? You think I don't know my finisher has a major flaw? Of course, I would train to fight against people who could counter it, you fucking piece of shit!"

Galan gasped for air on the ground, holding his chest. In the moment of intense confrontation, as Garrick raised his foot to deliver what he thought would be a crushing blow to Galan, the tables turned in an unexpected twist. Galan revealed a concealed knife from his waist, swiftly intervening to protect himself.

As Garrick's foot came crashing down, it met the cold steel of Galan's knife instead of its intended target. The force of the impact caused the knife to be driven into the ground, piercing through the blade. Garrick cried out in pain as the knife found its way through his foot, causing him to stagger backward. Meanwhile, high on the mountain, Eder heard the cry of pain echo through the storm. Recognizing it as Garrick's voice, he instantly knew he had to find Garrick and Galan before the situation escalated further.

Galan got off the ground, "See, that's funny. You think your weakness was your finisher? No,

Wilder, it is your stupid fucking ego. That's the only time you truly drop your guard. I'd be stupid to come into this with just one weapon. I couldn't sneak multiple at my place, but I had an entire kitchen to raid at Aria's." Galan pulled out another knife. "You thought I was going to fight fair? This isn't the ring, asshole. This is life or death." Galan walked over, picked up his blazer off the floor, and draped it over his shoulder.

Garrick rushed at Galan, catching him off guard as he hadn't expected Garrick to run on his injured foot. Seizing the opportunity, Garrick swiftly grabbed hold of Galan's blazer and yanked it around his neck, attempting to strangle him. Galan struggled fiercely, desperately trying to break free from Garrick's grasp. However, Garrick's strength was too much for him to overcome, and he found himself lifted off the ground, the blazer tightening around his neck.

In a desperate attempt to defend himself, Galan reached for his weapon, but the distance between them was too great due to the position he was being strangled. As the lack of oxygen began to take its toll, Galan's vision started to blur, and the world around him started fading away.

As the adrenaline surged through his veins, Galan's desperation fueled his actions. Despite his fading strength, he swung the knife several times, each attempt missing Garrick by a hair's breadth. Gathering his last reserves of energy, Galan mustered one final swing and, with remarkable accuracy, sent the knife hurtling into Garrick's side, where he had been kicked earlier. The searing pain caused Garrick to loosen his grip on Galan, finally allowing his feet to touch the ground.

Seizing the opportunity, Galan wasted no time. With lightning speed, he spun around, swiftly unraveling the blazer from around his neck. Galan bound Garrick's hands together using the blazer, cinching it tight to ensure he couldn't break free. With Garrick's arms immobilized above his head and behind his back, Galan clenched the handle of the knife he had thrown earlier. With forceful precision, using his palm, he drove the blade into Garrick's side, eliciting a blood-curdling scream that echoed through the mountain, merging with the cacophony of thunder and the relentless torrent of rain.

Eder came up to the clearing and saw Galan and Garrick. He noticed Garrick was bleeding heavily and tied up with the knife stuck in his side.

"NOOO!!!!" Eder cried out.

He withdrew the knife that Garrick had kicked away from Galan on the street, which someone on the lower level of Salt Pine Acres had thrown up to him when Garrick gave chase to Galan. With adrenaline coursing through his veins, Eder rushed to confront Galan, fueled by a mix of anger and fear. In a moment of reckless abandon, he hurled the knife toward Galan, hoping to bring an end to the pursuit. However, Galan's reflexes were astonishingly swift as he deftly caught the knife between his fingers.

A surge of defiance flashed in Galan's eyes as he retaliated, kicking Eder with a force that sent him stumbling to the unforgiving ground.

Galan pulled on the blazer, and Garrick screamed in pain again. Galan took that opportunity to ram the knife down his throat while he cried out. He yanked the blade out of Garrick's mouth, and blood came gushing out along with it, silencing Garrick's screams. Galan stabbed him several times in his stomach and drove the knife in with one swift thrust. Pulling at his blazer, Garrick flexed backward again and flared his stomach forward. Galan ripped open his midsection. His innards spilled out in a clumsy mess; Garrick stood there silently trembling, blood splattering from his lips. Galan pulled the knife from his side, released the blazer, and walked a couple of steps behind him, draping the blazer over his shoulder again.

Galan turned to Eder, frozen on the ground in fear. Galan looked at Garrick and muttered, "You just won't die, huh? You pathetic waste of life." Galan didn't hesitate; he threw the knife at Garrick, standing just shy of two feet from him, bleeding out. The knife pierced Garrick's head; one-third of the blade was visible, protruding through his forehead. Garrick's body began convulsing, and his eyes struggled to focus on Eder, who was on the ground, moaning softly.

"Stop it, please!!!! Please, mate, stop! We're sorry. We're sorry!!!" Eder cried out.

"How are you holding on still? People don't bleed this much. You should have gone into shock when the knife pierced your foot, not to mention taking that kick and breaking your ribs; it's like it did nothing to you. You're on something, aren't you?" Galan suspected.

"Mate, please... He's done; please just stop!" Eder begged.

"You won't die, huh? I used to have that fire in me, that strong will to live. But I learned one heavy truth in life. Nothing makes you feel alive like love," Galan said as he walked over to Garrick. "The dark side of that truth is that nothing makes you die inside quite like having your heart ripped out." Galan punched into the gash in Garrick's stomach and reached into his chest. Galan felt the dying heart beating in his hand and looked Garrick in his eyes. "This is what love did to me. Consider this mercy; no one ever stopped the pain when I needed it." Galan pulled hard and yanked his bloody arm out of Garrick's body, holding his heart in the palm of his hand.

Galan caught his lifeless body and tossed it in the pond, where he went to cool down after every workout. The water turned a deep red tone with each passing second.

Eder was in shock. He tried to scream, but he was barely vocal. His voice was paralyzed by seeing Garrick die right before his eyes. He tried to get up, but his body wouldn't move. He crawled backward on his hands, trying to scream for help.

"I tolerate a lot in this world. I have taken so much shit and endured so much pain from so many people. But the one thing I will not let go unpunished is hurting children. Dana is only sixteen, you sick fucking piece of garbage. You don't understand the depths of pain you've created for her. You inflicted damage she will never heal from. All she will know is pain and trauma until the end of her life. I'm going to show you what that's like," Galan announced as he stabbed Eder in the ribs, puncturing his lungs. He grabbed Eder off the ground and plunged his head under the bloody water of the pond.

Eder struggled and fought for his life; his lungs filled with water, and he began to drown. Galan pulled him up and removed the knife from his ribs. The water in his lungs emptied outside the wound as well as inside his body. Galan stabbed him in the other lung and held his head under the water again, stabbing him in his arms and legs every few seconds. Eder thrashed and screamed wordlessly under the cloudy, red, cold water. Galan pulled him up at the last second.

Eder coughed up blood and water, struggling to breathe. He was beginning to slip into death. Galan dragged him by his hair and walked to the edge of the mountain. Looking down at the waterfall running red, he gouged Eder's eyes out and dropped him to the ground at the mountain's edge. "How dare you look at innocent kids as sex objects?! Maybe nobody ever taught you this, so I'll make sure it's the last thing you learn before you leave this world behind. A little lesson in consent…," Galan exclaimed.

Eder coughed and gargled blood and water. Slowly suffocating, he muttered through the coughing, "Please, kill me. Please end this."

Galan stooped down, lifted Eder by his hair, and looked into his bloody eyes. The simple touch of Galan's hand made Eder's blood run cold. "No… As much as you want this, it's too early for you to have that end. I will not kill you; you could choke on your blood for hours, maybe even days, and nobody would find you here. Or you can die of hunger or dehydration if you somehow manage to survive with your wounds. You just have to wait, which is what you should have done for Dana. You were so eager before. Why stop now? You couldn't wait, right? Then maybe you should crawl off that cliff and fall to your death," he remarked.

Eder cried out; he tried to scream but was in too much anguish. The way Galan spoke to him, the calm in his voice as he chose his words, shook Eder to his core. Eder mustered the strength and dragged his bloody, half-dead body a couple feet to the edge crying and bawling uncontrollably in the pouring rain. Galan didn't say a word and kept his glare on him. Eder looked over the edge at the darkness; though he was unable to see, he knew he was at the ledge of the fifteen thousand-foot drop and rolled himself off the edge without a second thought.

Galan quickly reached out and caught Eder as he fell off the ledge; Eder tried to scream. "This is what it feels like; remember this feeling for the rest of your worthless life, Barlow," Galan exclaimed as he dropped him off the edge.

Chapter Forty-Three

Dana's movements were filled with curiosity and excitement as she wandered through Galan's apartment, guided by an innate sense of exploration. Her fingers glided along the walls, leaving a gentle trace behind, while she playfully tapped random spots with her finger as if seeking hidden secrets within the walls. The sight of a spiral staircase leading upstairs piqued her interest, but her eyes briefly darted toward the elevator door. Despite the momentary hesitation, the thrill of the unknown pushed her to take the more adventurous path—up the winding steps she went.

Upon reaching the top, Dana found herself standing outside Galan's room. The door stood slightly ajar, a silent invitation for her to venture further. With a mixture of anticipation and respect for

Galan's privacy, she gently pushed the door open, revealing the space that held a piece of his world. The room was a reflection of him, and she absorbed its essence with every step she took.

Her hands roamed freely, delicately touching each object she encountered as if seeking to connect with the very soul of Galan through the things he surrounded himself with. Her fingers danced over books, memorabilia, and photographs, absorbing the stories they held. But when she stumbled upon his collection of colognes, her heart skipped a beat.

Carefully, Dana picked up one of the bottles and twisted the cap open, "Wait a minute, this is Aria's line, LVTCH." She popped the cap and inhaled the scent. "This is the tobacco fragrance. My God... No wonder you smell so delicious." With a playful glint in her eye and a mischievous smile, Dana couldn't resist the temptation to make the scent her own. The alluring fragrance enveloped her as she sprayed a few pumps on her wrist and neck. A delightful blush crept up her cheeks when the fragrance mingled with her natural scent.

Dana couldn't resist the allure of getting closer to Galan's world. With a playful audacity, she opened his closet, eager to explore the hidden treasures within. Her fingers danced along the hangers, pulling out a black hoodie that held the essence of his style. As she slipped into the cozy fabric, a sense of comfort and familiarity washed over her. Dana gazed at her reflection in the mirror, her smile growing wider as she admired how effortlessly the hoodie embraced her.

Feeling a surge of spontaneous energy, Dana hopped from the dresser to the bed, savoring the excitement of the moment. Playfully, she rolled around, hugging his pillows tightly, imagining they were an extension of Galan himself. In her whimsical fantasy, she could almost feel his presence, and it brought an inexplicable joy to her heart.

As Dana basked in this private reverie, a sudden and faint thud interrupted the peaceful atmosphere. Her playful demeanor turned curious, and she stilled her movements to listen attentively. "Galan?" she called out. Dana's heart raced with a mixture of disappointment and intrigue as she didn't find Galan waiting by the elevator. However, her adventurous spirit wouldn't be quelled so easily. Turning back toward his room, she couldn't help but notice a peculiar door at the end of the hallway. Unlike the others, it stood out with an air of mystery surrounding it, beckoning her to explore further.

Driven by her insatiable curiosity, she walked toward the unusual door, her senses heightened with anticipation. There was something special about it that caught her attention. As she drew closer, Dana noticed that this door was different from the rest—a sophisticated scanner was attached to it. The scanner's display glowed with an intriguing message: 'Security timer disabled.'

When Dana heard the sound again, she opened the door and walked inside. The room was dimly lit, and slow music was playing. She looked around as she took each step. It looked like a bedroom but was a little bit bigger than a normal one. From one corner of the room, Dana heard, "Does Sir want to play?"

Startled, Dana let out an audible gasp. The lights in the room were flipped on, and Dana could see a woman standing in black laced lingerie. She was just barely taller than Dana, at five feet one, with short, dark, curly hair. "Hi?" said the woman.

"Um… Hello… Who are you?" asked Dana while looking around skeptically.

"Why do you smell like Master?" the woman inquired.

"What are you talking about?" Dana remarked, backing away.

"You're not Aria. Why are you here?" questioned the woman.

"What do you know about my sister?" Dana asked in a shaky voice.

"Your sister… Oh my. Then you must be Dana," the woman replied.

"I am. Who are you exactly?" Dana inquired.

"I am Master's first love, Morrigan Paige, but please just call me Paige," answered Paige.

"I have never heard about you," Dana countered.

"Master doesn't speak about me," Paige informed her.

"Why do you call him 'Master?'" Dana inquired curiously.

"It's what he likes being called. I obey Master, and he rewards me," Paige replied.

"Reward you how? What is all of this?" asked Dana, gesturing around the room.

"This is Master's dark room. He comes here when his mind goes to dark places, and he needs to release his negative thoughts," Paige explained.

"Release how?" Dana asked skeptically.

"By cumming inside me… Over and over again," Paige stated, approaching Dana slowly. "I obey Master, and he rewards me by granting me the opportunity to console him in his darkest moments."

Dana gulped and backed away slowly. "That's not the Galan I know. He is sweet and kind," she claimed.

"You haven't gotten to see this side of him, but your sister has," Paige stated.

Dana looked stunned and afraid. Seeing this, Paige tried to comfort her. "Sweetheart, look around you. This room is built entirely for his pleasure. It's who he is, but he wasn't always like this. Come, sit with me, and I'll tell you all about him," Paige offered.

"Not in here. No offense, but I'd rather not be in a room in which you've had sex on every surface here," Dana responded.

"Then, let's take this outside if that makes you more comfortable," Paige replied.

"One more thing. Put some clothes on; I'd prefer not to see so much of you," Dana remarked.

"Maybe you can get me one of Master's shirts? I like the white ones," Paige informed her.

"Fine, let's get out here. My skin is starting to crawl at the thought of you two," Dana stated.

With a sense of urgency, Dana hurriedly left the dimly lit room, making her way into Galan's nearby quarters. She wasted no time, immediately searching through his closet, her hands swiftly selecting a clean, white shirt. Meanwhile, Paige stood at the entrance, her fingers gently tracing the door frame as her eyes wandered around the unfamiliar surroundings of Galan's room.

Dana turned back to Paige and tossed the shirt her way. "Please cover those up," she said. Paige put on the shirt while continuously eyeing the apartment. As they descended the stairs, Dana couldn't help but notice the curiosity etched on Paige's face. It seemed as if Paige was experiencing this familiar place with a newfound wonder, as though she were seeing it for the first time.

Paige walked to the sofa and sat down. "Join me," Paige suggested, patting the seat beside her.

"If it's all the same, I would rather stand," answered Dana.

"Feisty little thing, aren't you? It's no wonder Master is fond of you," Paige replied.

"What is that supposed to mean?" asked Dana.

"Master likes strong women, loud, fierce; it's why he is so attached to you. He speaks of you like a little sister," Paige explained.

"What were you saying about Galan?" Dana asked, changing the subject.

"Right, Master wasn't always this way. He was a kind soul, romantic, loving, and caring. Master's idea of love was that he wanted the first one to be the last. He gave himself wholeheartedly and devoted himself to the people he loved, all of them, even at the expense of his own happiness. I watched Master devote himself to women who used, cheated, lied, and destroyed him.

"Master wasn't always what he is today. From a young age, he was bullied for being chubbier than the average person, and he was mistreated because he came from a family that lived in poverty. All he had to offer was his love, but that was never enough. Master couldn't do fancy dates, flashy gifts, or dress dapperly. All he had was a hoodie and a good heart.

"It was enough to get their attention but not enough to win them over. Time and time again, Master went above and beyond for the ones he fell for, but they chose exes, strangers, and even his friends over him. I watched him beg for affection from the people he dated while they bragged about how they gave it to the people before him without even asking. It broke his spirit; every time it happened, he would feel less and less like a person. He was always the one who got refused and rejected. He begged for efforts that were given to the people before him and the people immediately after him.

"Do you know what that is like, the pain Master felt? To wake up every single day and feel like you aren't worth anything on this earth? It got to a point where he couldn't even pretend to love himself anymore. That sweet, loving boy was broken beyond repair. His beautiful heart wouldn't allow him to be anything less than he thought a woman deserved. Every single time they said that they were different and were not like the rest, he would always trust them. Despite knowing nothing but pain, he always hoped and believed each would be the 'One.' And not like those who came before and did nothing but rip his heart out and tear it into pieces.

"Master has tried to take his life many times. It reached a point where he couldn't take the pain; it seemed like there was no light at the end of the tunnel for him, no silver lining. He began chasing after exes, hoping that if they took him back, he would feel like he mattered to someone… Anyone. But that only led to more pain and heartbreak. Not a single ex took him back or even paid attention to him. Even though they cheated on him and hurt him, they didn't want him back. They acted like he was the biggest mistake of their lives, like he was a joke. The depression got worse, and the pit he was in got darker and deeper. Soon, there was no light in his life anymore.

"Master didn't want to give up; all he had was love. This one shining hope of redemption lay in the arms of someone who could make him feel again. After his exes didn't want him, he tried to find a workaround. Maybe if he found someone with the same name or bore the same resemblance, it would do something. He was hoping that whenever he called out their name, it would fill the void in his heart. But this only led to more rejections and heartbreak until very little was left. Master shut his heart off; he grew cold and emotionally unavailable. There was so little left that he wanted to protect it. He never wanted to stop loving or believing that out there, everyone had a soulmate, a special person. Master is a hopeless romantic in that sense. He refused to give up in the name of love.

"However, there were shining moments. There was someone who got past Master's darkness and reached him. He saw how much pain she had been through and the smile he could give her. He fell in love with this girl. Unfortunately, meddling friends and jealous exes ruined what could have been. They stopped seeing each other, and neither knew the real reason why. He was told a lie, and she wasn't told the truth.

"It wasn't until years later that he found someone who made it past his walls again. It didn't start out as love; he was heavily guarding himself, keeping himself emotionally unavailable. Until he got to know her. Master started keeping his phone on him all the time, hoping she would make the time to talk to him. He started to fall for her and wanted to make himself available for her, but he was too late. She left him hanging and disappeared. Master was devastated, but it was at this point that he knew he couldn't do it anymore. Just like the others, that girl moved on from him and did the things he had begged her for, willingly giving the effort he was asking for to other people. He was rejected, and they weren't. He was at his lowest point when she told him they meant nothing to her. He was now second to someone who meant nothing, so what did that make him?" asked Paige.

Dana stood speechless, listening to the things Galan had been through.

Paige took a deep breath, "That was only a piece of it. The pain that Master had felt began long before he started dating. It all started with his family. Master grew up without knowing what the love of a parent or family felt like. His parents constantly treated him like a nobody. One of his earliest memories is crying for his mother's attention and begging her for some sort of affection. She would tell him that he was no longer a part of her family and would write on a piece of paper that he was 'divorced' from the family. She would draw two lines at the bottom of the page, sign, and then make him sign his name on the line while he cried.

"He remembered her laughing hysterically while she did that. It was a routine for her whenever she got drunk. But it didn't stop there. She would also stick it on the fridge as a constant reminder to him. Around the age of six, his parents began drinking so much that they would beat him until he was bruised all over. It got so bad one night that they kicked him out of the house. He was only six years old! Master slept in an old rotting cupboard for over six months. They would refuse to feed him or let him into the house. He would go beg the neighbors for scraps, but it wasn't enough, so he broadened his search for food, walking around the village he grew up in, begging.

"He learned how to connect with people through that. It's why he is so good at it now. Things only got worse for Master after. He ran away from home several times and jumped off buildings in a suicide attempt more than once before he was eight years old. He tried overdosing on pills so much that he built a tolerance for it over time," Paige explained.

"Oh my God," Dana muttered under her breath at the horror Paige brought to light.

"I wish I could say that was the extent of it, but it goes deeper than that. Master was only nine years old when he met some new people in the village while going around and asking for food. They had a lot of children; among them was a girl barely older than he was at the time; she was eleven. Galan befriended them, and for the first time in his life, he had friends, company, and people who wanted to be around him. They would have him over for sleepovers and family cookouts. Master began to feel like he was part of the family. This girl was his first crush. She made him smile when everything was falling apart. But they were just kids, playing in the dirt and splashing in puddles.

"One day, Master went over to play, like they would every day. The girl wasn't there, and neither were most of her siblings. Her mother informed him they had gone to visit their dad for the weekend. She told Master he was welcome to hang around if he wanted; they had cable TV and games, which was something he didn't have growing up. So, he would sit and watch cartoons whenever they weren't there. Their mother would ensure he was well-fed and had snacks while watching TV. Master would often miss them since they would visit their dad every other weekend.

"One day, Master came over to watch cartoons, and their mother informed him she needed to step out for a minute to run to the store. She told Master to lock the doors so he would be safe inside while she was out. He did just that. He locked the doors when she left, sat in front of the television, and glued his eyes to his favorite cartoons. It was raining that day, so their mother got stuck at the store until the rain had eased. One of the girl's older siblings had returned home earlier than everyone else. Now, she was eighteen. So, she unlocked the door and found Master. Excited to see him, she ran to him, hugged him, and ruffled his hair. Soaking wet from the rain, she needed to change into dry clothes. But the television faced her room, and her door was broken, so she could not close it.

"She grabbed her towel and told Galan to turn for a moment so she could change. Master did as he was told. He turned and covered his eyes, listening to the cartoons in the background. Several minutes passed, and Master heard her call him. He uncovered his eyes and turned around to face the television. That's when he saw her standing in the doorway with her towel wrapped around her. She told him to come into her room for a moment because she needed to ask him something.

"Master obeyed and went into the room. She sat him on the bed and sat beside him. She told him she knew he had a crush on her little sister. Master grew nervous; he was trying to keep that a secret. She told him that she knew they had hugged each other and that if her mom ever found out, everyone would be mad at him. They might also never let th___ play together again if they knew what Master and she had done.

"Master was sad and afraid to lose his friends, especially his crush. So, he begged her older sister not to tell her mother. He said he really liked his friends and didn't know he was doing a bad thing. She told him she would not say a word but only if he did something for her. Master, of course, agreed. He would have done anything to keep his newfound friends. So, she told him to stand up. As he did, she laid back and undid the towel," Paige continued.

"No...," Dana gasped.

"I'll spare you the details, but she blackmailed him for years. It didn't stop until he was thirteen. She mostly forced him to perform oral sex; it was always about her pleasure. She would tie him up so he couldn't move unless she wanted him to. Then, one day, they moved away, but that's not what they told Master. That girl told him that he was the reason they were leaving. Master believed that, and the trauma from the things that she had done to him wrecked him as a child. There were many other things that followed, but those were by far the ones that yielded the most pain. He was sent out into the world already in a mess," Paige explained.

"How do you know so much? Where were you in all of this? You know all of his heartbreaks, so where did you fit into all of this? Let me guess, you were the little sister?" Dana asked.

"I was the first woman he ever tasted," answered Paige with a smile.

Dana's eyes widened, her arms unfolded, and she unconsciously took a step back. "Oh my fucking God. You were the older sister...," Dana exclaimed.

Paige smiled at her and bit her lips.

"You're a sick person; you're a child molester," Dana stated.

"That's funny, aren't you sixteen? Master is twenty-five; the age gap is exactly the same. The only difference is it's reversed," Paige countered.

"It's not the same! I am not a nine-year-old, and Galan wouldn't have done what you did," Dana cried out.

"What makes you so sure? I have seen all of them fall. Every single girl he has ever loved ended up leaving him, and he always came back to me. Master doesn't love me, but he knows I am his soulmate. And when Aria doesn't work out, he will be mine once more. I've listened to him talk about her; I could practically point her out in a crowd from how he described her. She will inevitably destroy him. Then, he will return to me, and I will love Master the way none of them ever could," Paige responded.

The sudden, violent tremor shook the apartment building, and Dana and Paige instinctively turned their attention to the ominous yellow glow seeping through the kitchen blinds.

"No… No, that's my house! Galan is there!" Dana cried out.

"What?" Paige remarked.

"Galan went to confront my sister and her friends; they had some plan to do something to him. They had locked me up in a room, but he came for me when he got away from them. He brought me here, told me to stay, and run if he didn't return," Dana replied, panicking.

"Calm down. Maybe Master isn't hurt. Where can we find your sister?" asked Paige.

I don't know. I don't have my phone," Dana panicked.

"You need to calm down. Master is fine. He would never harm your sister; I am positive he'd survived that blast. We need to find your sister. Where she is, Master will follow. Think, where would she be if she wasn't at the house?" questioned Paige.

"The Coffee House, no doubt," Dana replied immediately. "Come on, he left his keys. We can get there quickly."

Dana rushed to the kitchen and hit the override switch. As the elevator doors slid open, Dana stepped inside, motioning for Paige to follow. Paige dashed into the elevator just in time, and the doors closed shut behind her.

Chapter Forty-four

Galan descended the mountain with a determined gait, his breaths were heavy and labored. Despite the trail of blood washing off his skin, his attire remained remarkably pristine—his white shirt and black blazer a stark contrast to the turmoil surrounding him. The blazer was now unbuttoned, and the sleeves rolled up. Galan's exhaustion was evident as he reached the base of the trail and emerged onto the familiar streets of Salt Pine Acres. His body carried the marks of a fierce battle, battered and bruised from the ordeal he had faced. Yet, there was an unwavering resolve in his eyes, a determination that seemed to defy the physical toll.

Galan's attention shifted to the direction of the Scarlets' property. The fire, once raging, had

MORRIGAN PAIGE

AGE: 34
SIGN: SCORPIO
FUN FACT: *UNAVAILABLE* (SHE TOOK ONE
LOOK AT ME...I HAVE NEVER BEEN SO SCARED
AND TURNED ON IN MY LIFE...)

started to subside, leaving behind smoldering remnants. As the danger ebbed, the neighbors around the area began to retreat from their vigilant positions at the windows, slowly returning to the safety of their homes.

Galan: *Fuck you for what you did to me, Aria. I loved you. I was in love with you from the moment I met you. I did everything right. I jumped over every hurdle and crossed every bridge. Why would you do that to me? I don't care that you chose Malek over me, but how dare you make me believe there was hope for me! I was ready to give you everything. I was ready to fight for you. I could have waited as long as it took to win you over from Malek if I needed to.*

Galan could hear a helicopter approaching. *That's my ticket out of here. Thanks, Aria. You did one good thing for me. You gave me a way out of this godforsaken place. I can finally leave this fucked up life behind me.*

As the ground shook beneath him, Galan was thrown off balance by the force of the second explosion, which had erupted in the heart of Salt Pine Acres. His body hit the ground, but the adrenaline coursing through his veins pushed him to his feet once more. Ignoring the pain and disorientation, he ran toward the source of the blast with a mixture of fear and determination.

Turning the corner at full speed, Galan's mind focused on the unfolding scene before him. His heart sank when he saw Grounded Coffee House, a place that held cherished memories for many in the community, engulfed in flames and billowing smoke. The familiar and comforting sight had been transformed into a nightmarish inferno.

No, no, no, no!!!!! Why? What the hell happened here?

As Galan ran towards Grounded Coffee House, his body ached from the previous ordeal, but he pushed through the pain, his determination unwavering. However, as he closed in on the scene of devastation, his attention was drawn to a horrific sight in the middle of the street. There, lying motionless, was Hans.

Horror washed over him as he saw the extent of Hans' injuries. The once vibrant and jovial face was now marred by deep slashes, and his lifeblood pooled on the asphalt, creating a gruesome yet familiar scene to Galan.

"Hans?! Hans, what the hell happened?" Galan asked.

Hans trembled on the ground, trying to pull his intestines back inside his body as he attempted to speak, "I tried… To save … Miss Aria—"

"Save her from what? Hans?!" Galan cried out. "Save her from what?!" Galan repeated as he looked up, his eyes darting around, desperately searching for any signs of hope in the chaotic scene surrounding him.

Without hesitation, he ran towards the front of the burning building, the intense heat pressed against his skin, but his focus remained unwavering.

As he approached the fiery entrance, a wave of sorrow washed over him, seeing the flames dance ominously, seemingly mocking the tragedy that had unfolded. Amidst the chaos, he caught a glimpse of his beloved car, now a twisted wreckage embedded into a wall. His heart sank even further as he realized the extent of the devastation.

His breath caught in his throat as he noticed Alliyah trapped between the crushed car and the crumbling wall. Her once vibrant spirit now lay fragile and still, her upper body resting on the hood of the burning vehicle.

Galan's terror deepened as a chilling realization struck him like a bolt of lightning—Dana had the keys to his car. "No... No, no—" he exclaimed. In a desperate rush, Galan's feet pounded against the pavement, his heart beating in sync with the fierce intensity of the storm around him. Lightning streaked across the dark sky, briefly illuminating his panicked expression, while the subsequent clap of thunder muffled his cries for Dana. With adrenaline coursing through his veins, he took daring shortcuts through private properties. Scaling fences and hurdling obstacles, Galan navigated through the labyrinthine streets, his mind solely fixated on reaching the other side of town and his condo complex.

Galan's breaths were coming in ragged gasps when he finally reached the back of his building. Without hesitation, he took a leap of faith, scaling a wall with agile determination, feeling a brief sense of relief as his feet landed on solid ground behind the condo complex. But there was no time to rest.

Galan stopped dead in his tracks and fell to his knees, defeated. "Noooo...," he cried out. Looking through the glass elevator, he could see Dana sitting on the floor, a large knife in her stomach, and blood splattered everywhere on the walls. Galan forced himself to his feet. He walked to the elevator and placed his thumb on the scanner. The doors to the elevator opened, and Galan stepped inside. Kneeling before her, he took her in his arms. Galan began to shake, tears flowing from his eyes.

"Dana!!!!!!!!" Galan bawled.

"This isn't how I imagined you screaming my name," Dana said faintly with eyes closed.

"D... D, you're alive!" Galan cried out excitedly.

He lifted her in his arms. Dana groaned and tried to speak. "D, don't talk right now. I need to get you to a hospital. There is a chopper at your house; it will take us to a hospital. Just stay with me, ok?"

Galan: *I can't remove that knife; she would bleed out. Ironically, the knife is the only thing that's keeping her alive right now. There is nothing I can do except take her to that chopper. Hold on, kid, I've got you.*

Galan hurried through the rain to the helicopter. He walked briskly and saw that the helicopter had landed on the lookout point. "Stay with me, D, just a little further!" he claimed.

Aria ran out of her ruined house and into the street, holding her arm slashed and bleeding. Turning, she saw Galan holding Dana in his arms. "Get away from her!!!!" Aria screamed.

"She needs to get to a hospital, Aria!" Galan replied.

"I said, get away from her!" Aria repeated, picking up a big shard of broken glass.

"Aria, you're bleeding," Galan pointed out.

"Give me my sister! I need to get her out of this fucking town!" Aria shouted.

"Then, help me get her on the chopper," Galan suggested.

"No, you're staying here to deal with that psycho on the loose in Salt Pine Acres. She wants you. If I hand you over, my sister goes free," Aria retorted.

Galan stopped, "For once in your life, think about your sister before yourself!"

"I am always putting her first!" Aria snapped

"Your sister is dying; she lost a lot of blood. She could have minutes left, and all you care about is your hatred for me rather than her life. Help me get her on the chopper and to a hospital. We can finish this afterward," Galan stated.

"FUCK YOU! I will finish this right now and save my sister. You're the fucking monster, not me!" Aria yelled.

"Oh, I'm the monster? Are you for real?" Galan scoffed.

"What? Are you referring to what I said about us running away together and me pretending to love you? Are you fucking insane? You have known me for only a few days, yet you thought I would've really fallen in love with you in that time? You're nothing special; you're a nobody, Galan!" Aria fired back.

Galan's face relaxed. He looked down at Dana, unconscious in his arms, her blood dripping off his arms. "You think this is about what you did to me? I have been hurt so much that I'm numb to it. I have been used, lied to, cheated on, rejected, ghosted, you name it. I have never been good enough, and deep down, I knew that I wasn't worth anything on this earth. But you know what really broke me? The fact that every single one of them made me believe that there was a chance. That maybe, one day, it could be me. It was no surprise that you did that to me, but I clung to the hope that you might love me one day. That's why I trusted you despite a lifetime of experience that taught me not to.

"But I could care less about myself. My life means nothing to me. This is about Dana. Do whatever the hell you want to me, but I will not watch this kid be treated like this. And if you are going to stand in the way of me getting her to safety, I will go through you, too," Galan replied as he glared at her. Aria gasped and stepped back the instant he looked up at her with those piercing eyes.

Galan's senses heightened as he heard the approaching car, its engine revving fiercely. Before he could react or even turn around, a blur of motion raced past him. It was Aria's car, hurtling forward with astonishing speed. With a mix of shock and horror, Galan watched in disbelief as the car veered in front of him, directly toward Aria, who stood in front of her house.

The scene unfolded like a chaotic symphony of events. Aria's car hit her and crashed through the already battered fence surrounding her property.

Paige stepped out of the car. Aria was lying on the ground, bleeding and twitching helplessly. Holding a knife in her hand, Paige said, "You served your purpose. Good girl! Master always seems to find his way to you. So, what better bait to use to lure him out!?"

Paige grabbed her by her hair and looked her in the eyes, "Master would never hurt you; he never hurt any of them. But none of you have ever seen him in his darkest moments. You must have done a number on him for Master to go to these lengths; the pain he feels will not go unpunished. Because of people like you, he locked me in a cage for all these years."

Galan hurried on toward the helicopter, but the sound of something falling on the ground beside him made him stop dead in his tracks. Looking down, he saw a heart roll past his shoe, stopping just ahead of him. Paige stepped out from behind him, holding a blood-stained knife and wearing his white shirt, now covered in blood.

"Paige…," Galan exclaimed in horror.

"Yes, Sir," Paige answered as she walked toward him.

"Paige, she needs to get on that helicopter, or she will die," Galan stated.

"Master must choose. I have loved you through all of your feeble attempts at turning over a new leaf. But you always turned back to the first Paige of your book. Master needs to choose. No more waiting," Paige declared.

Dana looked at Galan and tried to speak. "Galan—" she whispered weakly as a tear rolled down her cheek. Galan's attention was focused on her in his arms in the rain.

"I have done nothing but love you. All this time, I obeyed, and I pleased Master. While everyone else hurt you, there has only been one person who loved you for you. No one could love you as broken as you are; only I could. Don't do to me what everyone else did to Master. Choose the right person," said Paige.

Galan laid Dana on the ground. He looked at her for a moment before he rose to his feet and walked to Paige. "I'm sorry for keeping you locked away for all those years. Truth is, I wouldn't be who I am without you," Galan responded.

"Do I have permission to touch Master?" asked Paige, biting her lips.

"Yes," Galan replied.

"You need to move on, starting with letting her die. She will only be a reminder of your love for Aria. Just let it all burn to the ground. Master belongs with me," Paige remarked with a smile as she placed her hand on his chest.

"Then let's disappear together tonight," Galan told her.

"Yes, we can go anywhere you want," answered Paige.

"Kiss me," Galan commanded.

Paige leaned in and closed her eyes. Galan reached into his jacket, pulled out the syringe, and drove it into Paige's neck. As he emptied the needle in her, he said, "You're wrong. You're not the only one who loved me when I was broken, but the right person would have waited." Galan let go of her, and she dropped to the ground.

With adrenaline coursing through his veins, Galan hurriedly lifted Dana from the floor, cradling her in his arms, and sprinted towards the waiting helicopter. The roaring winds and torrential rain attempted to hinder their path, but determination fueled Galan's every step. He knew they had no time to waste; Dana's life depended on their swift actions.

In a desperate frenzy, they reached the helicopter's open doors, and with the assistance of the paramedics on board, they carefully placed Dana onto the stretcher. Despite the storm's fury, Galan and Dana were now inside the relative safety of the aircraft, protected from the relentless elements as they took off from Salt Pine Acres.

Inside the helicopter, Galan's heart raced with fear and concern, his eyes never leaving Dana's pale face. The skilled medical team worked diligently to stabilize her, administering urgent care to address her injuries and monitor her condition. Each passing second felt like an eternity as they navigated through the turbulent skies.

As the helicopter battled through the violent weather, Galan stole a glance out of the window back towards Salt Pine Acres—his eyes fell on the ruins of Grounded Coffee House.

Chapter Forty-five

Dana made a full recovery, and after several cosmetic surgeries, even the scars weren't visible. She woke up in the hospital to her dad sitting at her bedside. She hadn't seen or heard from Galan in over two years. Dana launched Grounded Coffee House in different parts of the world. She had formed an empire so large she became the leading Coffee House anywhere in the world. She had graced the cover of magazines everywhere as the youngest self-made billionaire after a major player in the coffee industry bought out her franchise.

Malek's family received a note saying he would disappear from the public eye for the sake of his new relationship. She had said 'Yes,' and they were to be married. Attached to the envelope was a three-million-dollar cheque made out to Malek's mother.

Dana retired at twenty and just enjoyed her life that year, sailing on a yacht around the Caribbean. It was a nonstop party on the sea as she traipsed through the crowd with a drink in hand when someone bumped into her and made her spill her drink. "Dude, watch where the fuck you're going!" she said without looking up.

"Sorry," the guy replied.

Dana shook her head and mumbled, "Asshole." The water beaded off her top, so she was able to wipe it off easily.

"So, you just happen to walk around in a suit that is water resistant?" asked the guy standing beside her.

Hearing that voice, Dana broke out in a smile. She turned and jumped on him without even looking, wrapping her arms around him and holding him tight. She led him to her room on the yacht and threw him on the bed. Hopping on top of him, she wrapped her arms around him, still shocked that he was here with her.

"Where were you? You should have been back two years ago," Dana exclaimed.

"You don't watch the news, do you?" asked Galan.

"Why?" Dana replied.

Galan took out his phone, tapped away at the screen, and handed Dana a loaded video.

Dana played the video. It was a clip from the news dated two years ago. A news anchor on the screen began speaking, "A nightmarish scene was discovered in the mountains in the town of Salt Pine Acres. Emergency teams responded when a fire in the town could be seen from a city close to the base of the fifteen-thousand-foot elevated, highly exclusive town. What they found inside the gates was a scene unlike anything ever recorded in history. The streets were ladened with bodies, slashed beyond recognition. Plus, the entire town was burned to the ground, with body parts and organs at every turn.

"Due to the nature of the town, the names of the people involved were unavailable to the authorities or media. A small group of people survived the Salt Pine Acres Massacre thanks to a shuttle that transports employees to and from a housing unit further down the mountain. An entire town was wiped out in one night; its residents were among the world's most powerful and wealthiest families today.

"The witnesses of the horror scene all shared the same story. They claimed to have seen blood raining from the skies and flowing onto the streets and into their properties. Some residents of the lower level of this town claimed to have seen the waterfall adjacent to the town's lookout point run red for a brief moment. Eyewitnesses saw the start of the massacre when a house went up in flames, and soon after, several people ran into the street fighting. One survivor of a German family, who remains anonymous, said he had thrown the killer's knife back at the brave individuals attempting to stop the madman. This picture was taken by said person, showing the man responsible for the horror that occurred on that night."

A high-definition photo of Galan appeared with his face and hands covered in blood and his suit untainted by the blood on him. "Authorities are searching for this unknown man residents are now calling the 'Blood Rain Ripper.' Among them was a woman who claimed to have been locked away and chained in a room by the killer for years after she got romantically involved with him. This information linked the killer to a string of missing girls over the last eight years. This woman claimed the man never allowed her to call him by name. She was only to refer to him as 'Sir' or 'Master.' Anyone with information is encouraged to step forward. A manhunt for this man is ongoing, and authorities will not cease until he is brought to justice," the news anchor continued.

Dana watched until the end. She remained silent for a moment before she asked, "Galan, why are you here?"

Galan took a deep breath. He looked at Dana in her eyes and replied, "Paige made it out of Salt Pine Acres. Last night, someone tagged you on social media. They uploaded only one picture, a picture of this boat on the coast, captioned, 'Going to drown my problems at sea.' Their username was "new.leaf." Maybe I'm being paranoid, but what's another way of saying turning over a new leaf?"

"You mean—" Dana panicked.

"Paige is coming for you, and I need to get you off this boat, love," Galan responded.

Paige sat on a private jet, looking out the window to the sea below. Sitting across from her was a well-dressed gentleman with grey hair and a laptop on the table in front of him. The man was focused on the screen, flipping through files and videos on the laptop. The files moved across the screen: a picture of Garrick, Aria's car, Garrick's truck, Dana and Eder having sex in the storage room, a blacked-out video with audio of Galan and Aria having sex, a recording of conversations, and a GPS location of Dana's phone.

"Is that enough proof, Mister Scarlet?" asked Paige, twirling her hair and adjusting her glasses.

"How did you get all of this?" Mr. Scarlet inquired.

"His phone was on the body of one of his victims, a friend of Aria's. I was a prisoner of the Blood Rain Ripper. He captured me and kept me locked up. If anyone can help you find the man who killed your daughter, it's me. And I am afraid Dana is his next victim. We need to find him before he finds her. Chances are, he is on the boat with her right now," Paige replied.

Mr. Scarlet looked at the laptop and tapped the mouse, showing the picture of Galan in the rain during the Salt Pines Acres Massacre. "Tell me why I shouldn't send every single member of law enforcement after this man. I could have FBI, CIA, Homeland Security, everyone gunning for him!" Mr. Scarlet exclaimed.

"If you track this man down using them, Dana will be dead before they turn on their sirens. Nobody knows who this man is. He is a nobody. I know every trick in his book. There is one person who can get close enough to him to save Dana, and she is sitting right in front of you. I've studied him for the last twenty years. All I need is time and money. I know exactly how to make him come to me," Paige answered, smirking.

"And why should I trust you?" questioned Mr. Scarlet.

"It seems I am wasting my time then. If this isn't enough for you, then I hope you can protect your child. That sounds like a personal problem," Paige responded as she sipped champagne.

"Young lady, you should be very careful how you phrase the things you say to me. I will not tolerate cavaliere remarks about my child's safety," Mr. Scarlet snarled.

"Is that a threat, Sir?" asked Paige, smiling.

"You have been helpful until this point. Now I have no use for you," Mr. Scarlet claimed. Looking off to the seat behind Paige, he nodded his head, picked up a bottle of champagne, and sipped.

Paige's smile grew wider. Two men in suits drew guns from their holsters and stood beside Paige.

Paige began to giggle, biting her lips as she looked at Mr. Scarlet, "Do I have permission to say my last words, Sir?"

Mr. Scarlet raised his champagne glass to his lips and nodded 'Yes.'

Paige leaned on the table in front of her with her palms on her chin, "Pull up Eder Barlow's social media."

Mr. Scarlet looked at Paige before placing his glass back on the table. He reached into his pocket, pulled out his phone, and typed in 'Eder Barlow' on his social media. His eyes widened; all the files about his family were there and posted, with a timer at the top that read, 'To be officially posted.' Mr. Scarlet was granted early access to the post by design.

"What is this?" asked Mr. Scarlet in a serious tone.

"I know all about you, Mr. Scarlet. I spent the last four years piecing together bits of information. I know you have quite a reputation for being ruthless; that's cute. Now, if something happens to me, this goes out to the public if I am not there to disable the posts. Also, the last place I was seen was with you on your private jet. Just another scandal to add to the mix. Aria's death, a sex scandal for Dana, a serial killer love triangle, and the victim who went to confront the person she thought was the Blood Rain Ripper, disappearing after boarding his private jet. You aren't even capable of getting rid of little old me. How can you hope to catch the Ripper?" asked Paige with a smile. She looked over to the gun pointed at her by his security detail and tapped the gun's barrel. "Boop," Paige chuckled.

Mr. Scarlet grinned and nervously tapped the table. "You remind me a lot of Aria; she was as cold as you!" he remarked.

"This is just one of his tricks, and he has a lot more. If you go after him alone, you'll never see your daughter again," Paige replied.

"Alright, young lady. I'll stay out of your way. Tell me what you need to keep my daughter safe," Mr. Scarlet exclaimed.

"I had all the time in the world; all I need is resources to make it happen. The Ripper will come to me. No one can do that as well as I can," Paige claimed with a smile.

"What if you are right, and that monster is on the boat with my Dana right now?" Mr. Scarlet asked, shaken by the idea.

Paige smiled wide and chuckled, "I'm counting on that."

"You're what?" said Mr. Scarlet, sitting up in his seat.

Galan and Dana sat on the bed. Galan put Dana on his lap, her arms wrapped around his neck.

BROKEN TOYS

Paige: *"I have a little surprise if the Ripper shows up!"*

Footsteps approached the corridor outside of Dana's room on the Yacht.

Paige: *"I'm making sure he never leaves that boat the same. It took me some time, but I had four years to track down my little contingency plan!"*

Dana smiled, leaning in closer to meet Galan's lips.

A shadow peeked in under the door of Dana's room.

Paige: *"I sent someone to warn him I would be coming."*

Mr. Scarlet: *"Why would you warn him... He's only going to run now!"*

A knock on the door pulled away Dana and Galan's attention. They turned and faced the door. Galan placed Dana on the bed and walked to the door.

Paige: *"He won't run from this; I can guarantee that!"*

Galan neared the door when the knock repeated.

Mr. Scarlet looked at Paige. "What makes so sure he won't just take off again?"

Paige smiled.

Galan opened the door, and his body began to tremble at the sight before him. He stumbled back in shock.

Paige: *"Because I sent the only person who has a hold of him better than I do. They say you never forget your first love, after all."*

Mr. Scarlet: *"And who would that be?"*

Galan looked outside in disbelief; he gulped and mumbled, "Lillie—"
Paige: *"My baby sister—"*

END